Dear Reader,

I just wanted to tell you how delighted I am that my publisher has decided to reprint so many of my earlier books. Some of them have not been available for a while, and amongst them there are titles that have often been requested.

I can't remember a time when I haven't written, although it was not until my daughter was born that I felt confident enough to attempt to get anything published. With my husband's encouragement, my first book was accepted, and since then there have been over 130 more.

Not that the thrill of having a book published gets any less. I still feel the same excitement when a new manuscript is accepted. But it's you, my readers, to whom I owe so much. Your support—and particularly your letters—give me so much pleasure.

I hope you enjoy this collection of some of my favourite novels.

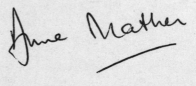

Back by Popular Demand

With a phenomenal one hundred and thirty books published by Mills & Boon, Anne Mather is one of the world's most popular romance authors. Mills & Boon are proud to bring back many of these highly sought-after novels in a special collector's edition.

ANNE MATHER: COLLECTOR'S EDITION

LOREN'S BABY

BY

ANNE MATHER

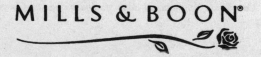

MILLS & BOON

*All the characters in this book have no existence outside the imagina-
tion of the author, and have no relation whatsoever to anyone bearing
the same name or names. They are not even distantly inspired by any
individual known or unknown to the author, and all the incidents are
pure invention.*

*First published in Great Britain 1978 by Mills & Boon Limited
This edition 1997
Harlequin Mills & Boon Limited,
Eton House, 18-24 Paradise Road, Richmond, Surrey TW9 1SR*

© Anne Mather 1978

ISBN 0 263 80557 3

*Set in Times Roman 11 on 11½ pt by
Rowland Phototypesetting Limited
Bury St Edmunds, Suffolk*

74-9712-48799

*Made and printed in Great Britain by
Caledonian International Book Manufacturing Ltd, Glasgow*

CHAPTER ONE

THE road widened at the top of the hill, as though inviting visitors to Port Edward to get out of their cars and take a look at the view before plunging down the narrow, precipitous lanes which eventually ran between the whitewashed cottages of the village. Telling herself it was because she wanted to see the village too, and not because it would provide a welcome delay to the culmination of her journey, Caryn thrust open the car door and climbed out.

Below, the sun-dappled roofs of Port Edward seemed too closely woven to allow for the passage of traffic, and beyond, the mud flats of the Levant estuary were exposed as the tide ebbed. An assortment of fishing vessels and pleasure craft were beached like so many gasping porpoises at their moorings, and children beachcombed in the shallow pools left stranded by the tide.

The road to the village said 'Port Edward only' and Caryn glanced about her thoughtfully. The address had said Port Edward too, but she remembered once Loren had told her that the house faced a creek where Tristan Ross kept his boat. If only she had paid more attention to those fleeting references to Druid's Fleet; but then she had never expected to have to come here. And didn't she also remember that there were trees?

A house standing among trees. . .

The cliffs that overlooked the estuary were not thickly wooded, but further upstream Caryn could see forests of pine and spruce clinging staunchly to the hillside. Obviously she had come too far towards the village. She would have to turn the car and go back to where the road from Carmarthen had forked across the river.

It was easier said than done, but the road at this hour of the evening was practically deserted, and she at last managed to manoeuvre herself back the way she had come. She felt tired, and half wished she had come by train, but it would have been awkward asking a taxi driver to bring her to the house and then expect him to wait while she saw Tristan Ross. Particularly when there was always the chance that he might not be at home. But Loren had said. . . Besides, if she was truly honest with herself she would admit that her tiredness had more to do with her mental than her physical state, and until she had this interview with Tristan Ross over, she was not likely to feel much better.

She sighed. Was she making a mistake? she wondered for the umpteenth time. Ought she to go through with this? *Could* she go through with it? And then she remembered Loren's face as she had last seen her, the cheekbones exposed and skeletal in her thin face, her eyes hollow and haunted. Her features had relaxed in death, but she would always remember her pain and despair. *Always*.

She came to the fork that led across a narrow suspension bridge shared by a disused railway line, and drove swiftly across it, glancing at her wristwatch as she did so. It was after six, but it had taken longer than she expected, and if Tristan Ross was put out by her late arrival, there was nothing she could do. Perhaps she should have driven into the village after all and asked for directions. But she was loath to draw attention to herself, particularly in the circumstances, and surely she was on the right track now.

The village was in sight again, but across the river now, and Caryn drove more slowly, watching for any sign which might indicate a dwelling of some kind. She saw a sign that said 'Water's Reach' and pulled a wry face. Why couldn't that have been Druid's Fleet? How much further did she have to go?

After reaching a point which at a lower level precisely matched the point she had reached on the opposite bank, she stood on her brakes and chewed viciously at her lower lip. She was getting nowhere, and not particularly fast. Where the devil was the house? She couldn't have missed it. There simply wasn't another house in sight.

Another three-point turn, and she was facing back the way she had come once more. Below her, in the estuary, the tide was beginning to turn, and ripples of water set the smaller craft stirring on their ropes. The sun was sinking steadily now, and a cool breeze drifted through the open window of the car. It would be dark soon, she thought crossly, and she was sitting here watching the tide come in as if she had all the time in the world.

Putting the engine into gear again, she drove

forward and with a feeling of inevitability brought the car to a halt at the stone posts supporting the sign 'Water's Reach'. There was nothing else for it; she would have to ask directions. Surely whoever owned Water's Reach would know where Druid's Fleet could be found.

Beyond the gateposts, the drive sloped away quickly between pine trees, and with a shrug she locked the car and with her handbag slung over one shoulder, descended the steep gradient. She could see the roof of a house between the branches of the trees, and as she got nearer she saw it was a split-level ranch-style building whose stonework blended smoothly into its backdrop of fir and silver spruce. A porch provided shelter as she rang the bell, and she stood back from the entrance as she waited, admiring the view away to the right where the dipping rays of the sun turned the sails of a yacht on the horizon to orange flames of colour. Only the wind was a little chilly now, striking through the fine wool of her violet jersey suit.

The door had opened without her being aware of it; and she turned to face cold grey eyes set beneath darkly-arched brows. Expertly streaked blonde hair was drawn smoothly into a chignon on the nape of the woman's neck, while the elegant navy overall she wore bore witness to the fact that she had been interrupted while she was baking.

'Oh, I beg your pardon.' Caryn hid her nervousness in a smile. 'I wonder if you can help me.' The woman, Caryn guessed she must be about thirty, said nothing, just continued to stare inquiringly at her, and she hurried on: 'I'm looking for a house called—Druid's Fleet. Do you—'

'Who is it, Marcia?'

The impatient male voice from somewhere inside the house was vaguely familiar, and the woman turned automatically towards the sound. Caryn, half afraid she was about to close the door in her face, exclaimed: 'I'm so sorry if I've come at an inconvenient moment, but—'

She broke off abruptly as a man appeared behind the woman. For a moment she was too shocked to do anything but stare at him, but perhaps he was used to the effect his appearance had on girls. And why not? Those harshly etched sardonic features, vaguely haggard in appearance, were apparently capable of mesmerising his viewers, and Loren had told her he got more mail than any other interviewer in his field. For all that, he was taller than she had expected, and his lean body showed no signs as yet of the dissipations he indulged in, and considering she knew he was at least forty, his corn-fair hair showed little sign of grey. Of course, he was deeply tanned from his last assignment in East Africa, the one Loren had kept all those cuttings about, and his hair was no doubt bleached by the sun, thus disguising any unwelcome signs of encroaching age, but in his dark mohair business suit, he didn't look a day over thirty-five.

Recovering herself, Caryn realised both he and the woman were looking at her now, and colouring hotly, she said: 'Mr Ross?' annoyed to find her voice trembled a little as she spoke.

'Yes?' He sounded impatient now, and she felt resentful that he should. After all, she had not expected to find him *here*. Come to think of it, what was he doing here?

'I—I've been looking for your house, Mr Ross,' she said carefully, unwilling to say too much in front of the woman, and his expression suddenly changed.

'Hey!' he exclaimed, his impatience disappearing as swiftly as it had come. 'You're not from the agency, are you? My God! I never thought they'd send anyone so promptly.' He looked at his watch. 'Hell, I've got to be at the studios in half an hour. Can you wait till I get back?'

Caryn opened her mouth to protest that she was not from any agency, and then closed it again. Why not, if it served the purpose? She could easily explain her subterfuge when they spoke privately together.

'Druid's Fleet?' she ventured, avoiding a direct reply, and he shook his head.

'This is Druid's Fleet,' he explained apologetically. 'I guess you saw the old sign on the gatepost. I keep that there to discourage unwelcome sightseers. That's who we thought you were.'

'Oh.'

Caryn was taken aback, and the woman, Marcia, gave Ross a curious look. Then Tristan Ross was inviting her in, and feeling only slightly guilty, Caryn stepped inside.

She found herself in a large open hall, with stairs leading both down and up. The floor was polished here, heavy wood blocks with a gleaming patina, that were an attractive foil for the skin rugs that enhanced its aura of age. There was an antique chest supporting a bowl of creamy yellow roses, and matching silk curtains billowed in the breeze beside the archway that led through to the dining room.

As Caryn followed Tristan Ross down the steps which led into the main body of the house, she was aware of Marcia coming behind her, and speculated on her relationship to the master of the house. His girl-friend, perhaps; or his mistress, she mused rather bitterly. He seemed to like to have a woman about the place. Loren had discovered that.

He led the way into a magnificent sitting room with long windows that looked out over the estuary. A padded window seat invited relaxation, or there were two squashy velvet couches, one either side of the stone fireplace, matching the heavy apricot velvet of the floor-length curtains. A coffee-coloured carpet fitted every corner, and the casual tables set around the room in no way encroached upon the feeling of space the room engendered.

Ross halted in the middle of the room and turned to face her. 'Have you eaten?'

Caryn shook her head, but hastened to add that she wasn't particularly hungry.

'Nonsense,' he exclaimed. 'Marcia will see you get something that appeals to you, and I'll be back in about two hours. I'm sorry about this, but I did warn the agency—'

'It's all right, really.' Caryn didn't want to get

involved in discussions about the agency right now. 'I—I don't mind waiting.'

'Very well.' He raised his eyes to Marcia who was standing in the doorway. 'Can I leave it to you to see that Miss—Miss—' He shook his head. 'I'm sorry, you didn't give me your name.'

Caryn thought quickly. 'Er—Mellor,' she got out jerkily. 'Susan Mellor.'

She thought his eyes narrowed for a moment, but then he was walking swiftly across the room again, past her to the door. 'Look after Miss Mellor, will you, Marcia?' she heard him say quietly, and then she heard him mount the steps again to the front door. It closed behind him a few moments later, and she was alone with her unwilling hostess.

The silence that followed his departure was broken only by Caryn smoothing moistened palms down her skirt. Then she faced Marcia with an apologetic smile.

'There's really no need to go to any trouble on my account. I—er—I honestly am not very hungry.'

Marcia considered her silently, and it was unnerving. What was wrong with the woman? Caryn thought impatiently. Why didn't she *say* anything?

'Have you lived here long?' she asked, and then realising how pointed that sounded, added: 'I mean—it's a very beautiful place to live, isn't it? I love Wales. I used to come here as a child. We used to camp on the Gower peninsula. . .'

Marcia inclined her head, as if in acknowledge-ment of Caryn's words, and then turned and walked away, across the lower hall and down two steps and through another door. Leading where? Caryn wondered. The kitchen, probably. What a taciturn creature she was! As if she couldn't have said something!

Left to herself, she relaxed somewhat. Well, she was here, and she was within reach of her goal. Or at least within sight of it. And she had been given two hours grace to augment her defences.

She walked across to the windows and admired the view. Then her eyes dropped to the terraced garden that fell away beneath her, and to the wooden flight of steps which led down to the boathouse. Loren had said there were thirty-seven steps, and she had had plenty of time to count them. Dangerous for a child perhaps, but that was not her problem.

Dropping her handbag on to the padded chocolate-brown cushions of the window seat, she half knelt beside it, feeling the familiar pang as she remembered what Loren had suffered. Why should he get away scot free?

She had been kneeling there for some time, hardly aware of the light fading until the switching on of a lamp brought her round with a start. Marcia had re-entered the room in that silent way of hers, and in her hands she carried a tray.

'Oh, you shouldn't have bothered!' Caryn exclaimed, sliding off the window seat, as Marcia set the tray down on one of the low tables nearby. But the smell of minestrone and fresh salmon was delectable, and she looked down on the meal the woman had prepared for her with undisguised gratitude.

Marcia spread her hands, and Caryn felt the guilt of false pretences colouring her cheeks once more. 'I say—won't you join me?'

Marcia shook her head. Her expression seldom altered, and Caryn was perplexed. Unless the woman *couldn't* speak, of course. But she must be able to hear. She had answered the doorbell, hadn't she? Yet how could she broach such a suggestion?

Marcia withdrew again, and with a shrug of defeat, Caryn seated herself on the couch beside the tray. She was hungry, she realised that now, and she remembered the old adage about fighting better on a full stomach.

But as she ate, she couldn't help wishing she had been able to ring Bob and Laura before coming here. It was going to be so late now before she got back to the hotel in Carmarthen, and she hoped they wouldn't worry. Still, he was in good hands, and that was the main thing.

Marcia reappeared with coffee as Caryn was finishing sampling the delights of a chocolate pudding. She had shed her overall to reveal a plain tailored grey dress, and looked more than ever like the lady of the house. Perhaps she was, thought Caryn doubtfully. Perhaps she should find out before Tristan Ross got back.

'That was absolutely delicious,' she said now, wiping her mouth on a napkin. 'Did you make the minestrone yourself? I've never tasted anything nicer.'

Marcia nodded, and retrieved the tray after setting down the coffee pot beside it. She was about to withdraw again, and on impulse Caryn got to her feet.

'Please,' she said. 'Don't rush away on my account.'

But Marcia's thin lips merely twitched slightly before she bowed her head and went away.

Caryn subsided on to the couch again. If Marcia wasn't dumb she was giving a damn good imitation of being so. She sighed, and reached for the coffee pot. Oh, well! If she didn't want to talk, she didn't want to talk. And maybe it was as well. She didn't want to get involved here—not more than necessary, anyway.

Her coffee finished, she looked about her restlessly. There was no television, which was unusual. She would have expected him to have one in every room. Was he on this evening? Was that why he had had to leave for the studios in Carmarthen? Or was it simply a pre-recording for something that was going out later?

Getting to her feet, she wandered round the large room. It was a man's room, she thought reluctantly. There were no ornaments to speak of, no china cabinet or collection of porcelain in sealed cases. There were bookshelves, but she couldn't believe anyone actually read such heavy, boring tomes, and she longed for the sight of a paperback or a magazine, anything to fill the time until Tristan Ross returned.

A silver trophy on the mantelshelf turned out to be an award from the Television Academy of Arts and Sciences for his contributions to the popular news programme *Action World*, and beside it was a bronze shield denoting Tristan Ross as Outstanding Television Correspondent for 1976.

Caryn pulled a face and put the awards down again, wondering in passing whether a silver trophy would smash if it fell into the stone hearth. It probably would, but she was not brave enough to find out. She could imagine her stammering apology: 'I—I'm s-sorry, Mr Ross. It—it just s-slipped out of m-my f-fingers. . .'

Outside darkness had fallen, and she went to take another look over the estuary. The lights of the village were comforting across the water, and here and there a mooring light winked on the rising tide. A person could get delusions of grandeur living here, she thought cynically. Remote from the problems of the world outside.

The sound of a car's engine broke the stillness, and although she hadn't heard him leave, Caryn guessed her host had returned. She glanced at her watch. Eight-thirty. She raised her dark eyebrows. He was prompt anyway; she should be thankful for small mercies.

A door slammed, and then surprisingly, a female voice called: 'Marcia! Marcia, I'm back! Whose car is that parked at our gate? I almost ran into the wretched thing!'

Caryn stiffened. Another visitor? Someone well-used to coming here anyway. Who else had a key to the door? Her lips tightened as she thought again of Loren's waxen features. Oh, Tristan Ross had such a rude awakening coming to him!

Light footsteps ran down the stairs, and a

moment later a girl appeared in the open doorway—tall, slim, almost as tall as Caryn, in fact,
who always considered her five feet eight inches
to be less than an advantage, with straight fair
hair and smooth pale skin. She was one of the
most attractive young women Caryn had seen for
some time, and her orange jump suit accentuated
the slender grace of her figure while exposing
more of the unblemished skin than was absolutely
necessary.

She stopped short when she saw the other girl,
and stared at her frowningly. Competition? wondered Caryn dryly, although she felt positively
gipsy-dark beside such Scandinavian fairness.
She tanned easily, and her skin was already
brown, its texture caring nothing for the burning
heat of the sun. She guessed this girl would have
to be careful, or she would burn all too easily.
And she probably was, Caryn conceded. She
looked as if she spent some time caring for her
appearance.

'Who are you?' she demanded now, and
relieved to find someone who was not averse to
speaking with her, Caryn answered:

'Susan—Mellor. I—I'm waiting to see
Mr Ross.'

The girl frowned and came into the
room. 'Why?'

It was a leading question, and Caryn hesitated.
She had no qualms about evading an answer, but
she was curious to know who the girl was, and
antagonising her was not going to help. In consequence she gave the answer Ross himself had
suggested:

'The—er—agency sent me.'

'The agency!'

The girl stared at her, and Caryn realised in dismay that if the next question was 'What agency?' she was stumped. What sort of agency might a man like Ross have contacted? Hysterical humour bubbled in her throat. She ought to be hoping it was as innocent as it sounded.

But the girl said: 'Do you mean the Llandath Agency?' and that was even worse.

Crossing her fingers behind her back, Caryn nodded. 'That's right,' she agreed manfully. 'The Llandath Agency.'

'You *liar*!'

It was worse than Caryn had imagined. The girl was staring at her unpleasantly, and what was worse, the woman Marcia had come to reinforce the opposition.

'Tris asked me to call at the agency,' the girl declared, glancing round at Marcia for her support. 'And I forgot! So what the hell do you think you're doing here? Are you a reporter or something? Or just one of those awful groupies?'

'I'm not a groupie!' exclaimed Caryn, fighting a ridiculous desire to laugh at the ludicrousness of the situation.

'What are you, then? Because I'm damn sure you're not a secretary!'

Caryn straightened her shoulders. 'As a matter of fact, you're wrong. I am a secretary,' she stated, more calmly than she felt. 'And—and Mr Ross—rang the agency.'

Half of it was true anyway, she consoled herself, but the girl wasn't finished yet. 'Tris wouldn't do that. Not when he'd asked me to call. Why should he? He knew I'd be in Carmarthen all afternoon.'

'Perhaps you'd better take that up with him,' remarked Caryn equably, and then started as a masculine voice said:

'Take what up with me? Angel, what's going on here? Why are you arguing with Miss Mellor?'

Tristan Ross came into the room. At some point on his journey home he had loosened his tie and unfastened the top button of his shirt, but he still managed to look calm and unruffled. Caryn noticed that contrary to tradition, the bottom button of his waistcoat was fastened, but his jacket was unfastened. Raking back the thick straight hair that was inclined to fall across his forehead, he regarded the two antagonists wryly, waiting for an explanation, and Caryn waited for 'Angel' to act entirely out of character.

'I didn't go to the agency, Tris!' she declared. 'I don't know what this woman's doing here, but she's not from Llandath.'

Caryn silently acknowledged the girl's attempt to classify her. Angel, if that really was her name, was younger than she was, but twenty-four didn't exactly put one in the middle-aged bracket.

Tristan Ross had listened expressionlessly to what Angel said, and now he turned to Caryn. 'Is that right? Are you not from the Llandath Agency?'

'I never said I was,' Caryn ventured slowly, and then when Angel began to protest, added: 'Not to you anyway. You—just—assumed that.'

His mouth turned down only slightly at the

corners. 'All right, I'll assume some more. You chose not to enlighten me because you wanted to get in here, is that right?'

'Oh, I'd have got in here, Mr Ross,' declared Caryn levelly, 'whether you assumed I was from the agency or not.'

'Is that so?'

She barely acknowledged the edge of steel that deepened his voice now. 'Yes, that is so.'

'I see.' He glanced frowningly at the two other women. Then: 'You sound very sure of yourself, Miss—Mellor, is it? Or is that assumed, too?'

To her annoyance, Caryn coloured again. 'Yes, as a matter of fact it is. My name is Stevens, Caryn Stevens. Loren Stevens' sister.'

She watched him carefully as she said her sister's name, but it aroused no great reaction. A flicker of his eyes was all the notice he gave it, and then he shrugged and said:

'Forgive me, but I'm afraid I don't see the connection. Why should the sister of a girl who left my employ more than six months ago want to see me? Or are you looking to take over your sister's position?'

Caryn gasped. 'How dare you!'

At last she aroused some reaction, and the thin lips tightened ominously. 'How dare I?' he demanded harshly. 'Come, Miss Stevens. I think this has gone far enough. Either tell me what in damnation you want or get out of here!'

Caryn gazed at the two women watching them so intently. 'I would rather say what I have to say in private,' she declared unevenly.

'Would you?' He made no attempt to dismiss their audience. 'Well, I wouldn't. Whatever it is, spit it out. Here! Where I have some witnesses.'

Caryn licked her lips. This was not what she had intended. She shrank from exposing her sister before two strangers. It was bad enough having to tell him. She could not bring herself to speak the words in front of anyone else.

'I—I can't,' she said at last. 'I—I won't.'

Tristan Ross's teeth ground together. 'Miss— Miss Stevens: I don't know why you've come here, but I should tell you that I have no secrets from either my daughter or my housekeeper.'

'Your—your daughter!' Caryn swallowed convulsively.

'Angel—Angela. Angela Ross. Didn't your sister tell you about her?'

'No.'

'Or about Marcia?'

'No.'

'You don't have to worry about her carrying tales, or isn't that what's troubling you?'

So the woman couldn't speak! Caryn felt a rush of sympathy, but then she gathered her small store of confidence about her. She straightened her spine, but even in her wedged heels he topped her by several inches, which was a disadvantage, she found. However, she had to go on:

'Mr Ross,' she said slowly, 'what I have to say concerns my sister, not me. Please—' She hated having to beg. 'Give me a few minutes of your time.'

Impatience hardened his lean features. 'Miss Stevens, I've just spent an uncomfortable half hour interviewing a man who refuses to admit that he's a bloody Communist, and I'm tired! I'm not in the mood for play-acting or over-dramatisation, and if this has something to do with Loren then I guess it's both—'

Caryn's hand jerked automatically towards his cheek, and he made no attempt to stop her. The sound of her palm rang in the still room, and only his daughter's protest was audible.

Tristan Ross just hooked his thumbs into the back waist-band of his trousers under his jacket and heaved a heavy sigh. 'Is that all?' he enquired flatly, but Angela burst out:

'Are you going to let her get away with that?' in shocked tones.

In truth, Caryn was as confused as the other girl. The blow administered, she was disarmed, and they all knew it.

With a sense of futility, she would have brushed past him and made for the door, but his hand closed round her arm, preventing her from leaving.

'Not so fast,' he said, and she noticed inconsequently how the red weals her fingers had left in no way detracted from the disturbing attraction of his dark features. Such unusually dark features with that light hair. The hair he had obviously bestowed on his daughter. *His daughter!* For heaven's sake, why hadn't Loren mentioned that he had a grown-up daughter? Did he have a wife, too? Was that why. . .

'Where do you think you're going?' he

demanded, and she held up her head.

'I—I'll write to you,' she said, saying the first thing that came into her head, and he stared at her frustratedly.

'Why? What have we to say to one another? If Loren has something to say why the hell didn't she come and say it herself?'

Caryn's jaw quivered. 'Loren is dead, Mr Ross. Didn't you know?'

At last she had succeeded in pricking his self-confidence. His hand fell from her arm as if it burned him, and feeling the blood beginning to circulate through that numbed muscle once more, Caryn felt a trembling sense of awareness. She was too close to him, she thought faintly. She could almost share his shock of cold disbelief, feel the wave of revulsion that swept over him.

'*Dead!*' he said incredulously. 'Loren—dead? My God, I'm sorry. I had no idea.'

'Why be sorry?' Angela spoke again. 'She was nothing but a nuisance all the time she was here—'

'*Angel!*'

His harsh interjection was ignored as Caryn added bitterly: 'Why pretend to be sorry, Mr Ross? You never answered any of her letters.'

'Her letters?' He shook his head. 'All right, Miss Stevens, you've won. We'll go into my study. We can talk privately there—'

'You're not going to talk to her, are you?' Angela's dismayed protest rang in their ears, but Tristan Ross just looked at his daughter before walking past her out of the room.

Caryn hesitated only a moment before following him. This was what she wanted, wasn't it? Why then did she feel so little enthusiasm for the task?

They went across the hall and down a passage that descended by means of single steps at intervals to an even lower level, and he thrust open a leather-studded door and stood back to allow her to precede him inside.

The room was only slightly smaller than the living room, with all the books Caryn could have wished for lining the walls. Paperbacks there were in plenty, as well as every issue of the *Geographical Magazine* for years past. A honey-brown carpet supported a leather-topped desk, a pair of revolving leather chairs, and several armchairs. A smaller desk in one corner held a typewriter and a pair of wire trays, with metal filing cabinets completing the furnishings. Here again, the windows overlooked the estuary, but it was dark and Ross drew the venetian blinds.

'Won't you sit down?' he suggested, indicating one of the armchairs, but Caryn preferred to stand. 'As you wish.' He took off his jacket and draped it over the back of one of the leather chairs. 'But if you'll excuse me. . .'

'Of course.'

He lounged into one of the revolving chairs, behind the desk, and in spite of his informal attire he was still the Tristan Ross she knew from so many current affairs programmes. Calm, polite, faintly sardonic; using his grammar school education to its fullest potential while still maintaining the common touch that encouraged the most unlikely people to confide in him.

'Right,' he said, and she thought rather hysterically that all that was missing were the television cameras. 'Suppose you tell me why you wanted to see me.'

Taking a deep breath, she decided to come straight to the point. 'You—knew about Loren, didn't you?'

'What did I know?'

He was annoyingly oblique, and she clenched her fists. 'She wrote and told you about—about the baby—'

'The baby!' His indolence disappeared. 'What baby?'

Caryn suddenly found she had to sit down after all, and backed until her knees came up against the soft velvety cushioning of an armchair. She sat down rather weakly on the edge of the seat.

'I said—*what* baby?' he repeated, getting to his feet to rest the palms of his hands on the desk in front of him, leaning slightly towards her. 'I warn you—if this is another of Loren's tricks—'

'I told you. Loren's dead!' she reminded him tersely, and his jaw clenched.

'So you did.'

'Why didn't you answer any of her letters?'

'For God's sake! I don't remember seeing any letters from her. And even if I had—'

He broke off abruptly and Caryn guessed what he had been going to say. 'You wouldn't have answered them?'

'Look,' he sighed, 'Mrs Forrest—that's the

name of the woman I employed on a temporary basis to take over after—after Loren left—she had orders to deal with—well, that sort of thing.'

'Fan mail?' demanded Caryn bitterly, and his eyes held hers coldly.

'Why not?' he challenged, and she wondered how she could have thought his eyes were dark. They were light, amber-coloured, the alert eyes of a prey-hunting animal at bay.

'She told you she was expecting *your* child and you ignor—'

'She did what?' He came round the desk towards her, the muscles of his face working tensely. 'Say that again!'

Caryn licked her dry lips. 'She—she was expecting your—'

'The bitch!'

Caryn came abruptly to her feet. 'Don't you dare to speak of my sister like that!'

'I'll speak of her how the hell I like!' he retorted savagely. 'God Almighty, what a bloody cock-and-bull story that is! And you came here to tell me that—'

'Not just for that,' she got out jerkily. 'Not just for that.'

He made an effort to calm himself, but he began to pace about the room and she was reminded of a predator once more. He moved so lithely, so naturally; with all the grace and none of the nobility of the beast, she thought fiercely.

'Of course,' he said coldly. 'You came to tell me she was dead. Well, perhaps it's just as well.' He stopped to stare into her working features.

'Perhaps it's just as well. I think if she'd still been alive, I'd have killed her!'

Caryn backed off again. 'And—and what about your son?' she got out chokingly. 'What about him? Do you want to kill him, too?'

CHAPTER TWO

SHE saw the colour leave his face as he looked at her. Even his tan took on a jaundiced appearance, and she realised what a tremendous shock this must have been for him.

'My—son?' he echoed faintly. 'You mean—there's a child?'

'Y—yes. A boy. He's—three months old.'

'Three months!'

Close to her like this, his eyes had a curious magnetic quality, the pupils dilated so that the tawny irises were almost extinguished. His lashes were thick and straight, gold-tipped she saw, like the sun-bleached texture of his hair. Impatience and confusion twisted the firm contours of his mouth, depriving it of its normally sensual curve. She wondered fleetingly if the child would be like him, and then squashed the thought as being unworthy of speculation.

The silence between them was beginning to get to her, and she shifted uncomfortably under his gaze, suddenly aware of the pulse jerking at his jawline, the strong column of his throat rising above the opened neck of his shirt. In the warm room, redolent with the salty tang of the estuary, a hangover from opened windows on the sun-filled afternoon, she could still smell the faint heat of his body mingling with less personal scents of soap and after-shave. It made her aware of her

own vulnerability, and she realised what a temptation he must have been to an impressionable girl
like Loren.

'Three months,' he said again at last. Sarcasm
curled his lips. 'Why wait so long?'

'Before coming here, you mean?' she asked
jerkily.

'That's exactly what I do mean.' His fingers
inserted themselves into the minute pockets of
his waistcoat. 'Or was I last on the list?'

'You—'

Her instinctive response was to hit him once
more, but he backed off mockingly, raising one
hand to defend himself. 'Oh, no,' he said, shaking
his head. 'Not again. We played that little scene
ten minutes ago. Melodrama was never my
strong point.'

'What is your strong point, Mr Ross?' she
demanded hotly. 'Seducing teenagers?'

The bones of his cheeks were clearly visible
as his breath was sucked in. Then, in cold denig-
rating tones, he said: 'Are you aware of the laws
governing slander? If you would care to repeat
those words in the presence of the other members
of this household, I think I can promise you you'll
find out.'

Caryn's lips trembled, but she had to go on.
'Do you deny seducing my sister, Mr Ross?'

He heaved a sigh. 'Would you believe me
if I did?'

'No.'

'Then that's rather a pointless question, don't
you think?'

Caryn sniffed. 'I might have known what

kind of man you'd turn out to be.'

'So why did you come here?'

'Because that child is yours, and he's your responsibility!'

'Ah, I see.' He gave a harsh laugh. 'It's money you want.'

'*No!*' Caryn was horrified. 'You—you don't think I've come here to—to blackmail you, do you?'

'You used that word, not me.'

'But you—implied it.' She made a grimace of distaste. 'Oh, you're twisting all my words. You're making it so—so sordid!'

'And isn't it?' he snapped. 'Coming here, telling me some crazy story about your sister dying and insinuating that it was my fault—'

'It was!'

'Oh, no.' He shook his head. 'If your sister's dead, it has nothing to do with me.'

Caryn forced herself to meet his eyes. 'How can you say that? You must have known there was a risk—'

'What risk?' he grated. 'For God's sake, I didn't know she was pregnant!'

Caryn tried to be calm. 'You must have known she might be,' she insisted. 'You left her to tell her family—'

'Her family!' He raised his eyes heavenward for a moment as if seeking patience. 'I didn't even know she had a family, until you came here purporting to be her sister.'

'I am her sister.'

'Very well. And I was her employer. Her *employer*! Do you understand? I seldom discuss personal matters with employees unless they impinge in some way upon the working capacity of the employee concerned. Is that clear enough for you?'

Caryn tried again: 'But your relationship with Loren was more than that of employer-employee.'

'Was it?'

'Well, wasn't it?'

'Did she tell you that it was?'

'I didn't need to be told,' Caryn declared tremulously. 'She was mad about you.'

'Really?' He was unmoved. 'And I was mad about her, too I suppose.'

'For a while. . .'

'For a while!' He brought his balled fist hard into the palm of his hand. 'My God, I can't believe anyone could be that—that—'

'Gullible?' she supplied coldly, but he snapped: 'No! *Stupid!*'

'Loren was not stupid,' she protested, and his lips sneered:

'Did I say Loren?' he taunted, and her fists clenched.

'You think you're so clever, don't you, Mr Ross?'

'No.' He shook his head irritably. 'Not clever at all. I was stupid. I knew what she was the minute I saw her. I should never have taken her on.'

Caryn couldn't permit this. 'Loren was a good secretary—'

'There are thousands of good secretaries.'

'She was loyal. She worked hard.'

'She made life impossible!' he muttered.

'You admit then that your relationship with her wasn't as platonic as you would have me think—'

'I admit nothing,' he declared, turning his back on her and walking back to his desk. 'Nothing!'

Caryn drew in a long breath and expelled it unsteadily. 'So you deny that the child is yours?'

There was silence for a moment and then he turned and rested back against the side of his desk, one hand on either side of him supporting his body. 'Tell me about the child,' he said. 'Tell me how she died.'

Caryn sought for words. 'I—she—when you fired her—' She waited for him to deny this, but when he didn't, she went on: 'When you fired her, she came back to London. To—to the flat.'

'Your parents' flat?' he inquired.

'No. Mine.' Caryn hesitated, then she went on: 'Our parents are dead. We were brought up in Maidstone by an elderly aunt, but when I was old enough, I left there to take a commercial course in London. Then when Loren was older, she did the same.'

'And you shared the flat?'

'Well, it was my flat really. Loren wasn't there all the time. She had. . .friends. . .'

'Friends?'

'Yes, friends.' Caryn saw no point in revealing that Loren had always preferred the company of men to women. 'Anyway, later on she got this job, down here—living in. I—I advised her not to take it.'

'Why not?' He was curious.

'Because of you. Because of your reputation,' declared Caryn firmly.

'What reputation?' he pursued tautly.

Caryn was discomfited. 'Does it matter?'

'Yes, I think it does.'

She sighed. 'You know what I mean as well as I do.'

'You shouldn't believe all you read in the papers, Miss Stevens,' he retorted.

'Obviously not,' she flared. 'They omitted to mention that you were married.'

'My wife died when Angela was three. Does that absolve me from that particular crime?'

Caryn flushed. 'It's nothing to do with me.'

'Is any of this?'

'Yes. I—I was with Loren when she died.'

He hunched his shoulders. 'Go on. When did she tell you she was pregnant?'

Caryn hesitated. 'Not for some time. She—she was so thin, you see. It—hardly showed.'

He frowned. 'Did she get another job?'

'No.' Caryn was reluctant to tell everything that happened those last few months, but perhaps she owed him that, at least. 'She—as you know, there are not that many jobs around. And—and she was—listless, without enthusiasm. She said she had written to you and asked you to take her back again.'

'She knew I was going to East Africa.'

'Yes. She collected all the cuttings.'

'My God!' He sounded disgusted.

'But she wrote to you after you got back. As I said before, you never replied.'

'I told Mrs Forrest to ignore those letters. I

knew what Loren was like. I knew she wouldn't give up that easily.'

'She depended on you. . .'

'She was a leech!'

'She was so happy here to begin with. She used to write such excited letters, telling me how you used to take her with you on certain assignments—'

'I took her once,' he declared heavily.

'Nevertheless, you took advantage of her.'

'I did what?'

'She told me how—how you used to—to pester her—'

'What?' He stared at her incredulously.

'—coming home drunk after parties. Forcing your attentions upon her—'

'Is that what she told you?'

'Of course.'

'And you believed it?'

'Why not? Loren didn't lie about things like that.'

'Didn't she?'

'I suppose you used to get her drunk, too,' Caryn accused him. 'Was that how you got into her bed?'

'Oh, my God!' His face twisted. 'Do you think I'd have to do that to sleep with her?' He shook his head.

'I don't believe you.'

He shrugged. 'Unlike your sister, I cannot arouse your sympathy or your trust.' He gave a bitter smile. 'But we're straying from the point, aren't we? You still haven't told me why you're here.'

'I should have thought that was obvious.'

'Well, I'm sorry. It's not.'

'I've told you. The child is your responsibility now.'

In what way?'

'You're his father. You should support his upbringing.'

'Financially? Or physically?'

'What do you mean?'

'Are you asking for money or aren't you, Miss Stevens?'

Caryn paused. 'Loren—Loren told me to come to you. To bring the child to you. She said—she said you would know what to do.'

He stared at her disbelievingly. 'And you accepted that?'

'Why shouldn't I?'

'After what she had told you about me?'

Caryn shook her head. 'That has nothing to do with it.'

'I disagree. It has everything to do with it. What does a man like me want with an innocent child? A man who goes around seducing teenagers? A man, moreover, who you have just accused of introducing your sister to drink!'

He's your son,' insisted Caryn doggedly, refusing to be alarmed.

'And your nephew. Or had you overlooked that?'

It's nothing to do with me,' Caryn exclaimed restlessly. 'It's not my child.'

His amber eyes narrowed. 'You sound very vehement about it. Don't you like children?'

'It killed my sister, Mr Ross. Do you think I can forget that?'

'Ah, I see.' He sounded sardonic. 'How convenient! Shift the blame—and the responsibility.'

'I have to work for my living, Mr Ross. I don't have time to take care of a baby.'

'It may have slipped your notice, Miss Stevens, but I work for my living, too.'

'That's different.'

'How different?'

'You—you have money. . .'

'I see. So it is money you want,' he mocked coldly.

'*No!*'

'Why should I believe you? How do I know you're not making the whole thing up? You're Loren's sister! Maybe you're in this together!'

Her white face seemed to sober him, and he muttered a rough apology: 'Okay, I'm sorry. I didn't mean that. You're nothing like her, thank God!'

Caryn's throat felt tight. 'Loren is dead.'

'Yes, yes, so you keep telling me.'

'It's true!'

'I believe it.' He expelled his breath on a long sigh. 'So: where is the kid?'

'In London. Spending the day with some friends who live in the adjoining flat to mine. Laura—that's the girl's name—she's expecting a baby herself in three months.'

'Really.' He sounded uninterested, and she wished she hadn't volunteered the information. She had only wanted to assure him that the child was in good hands. 'How soon can I see him?'

'You mean—you mean you'll have him?' Suddenly it all seemed totally unreal.

'You're prepared to give him away, aren't you? To a complete stranger?'

'You're his father,' she protested, but he shook his head.

'You can't prove that.'

'You can't prove you're not.'

'I wouldn't be too sure of that, if I were you.'

'Oh, please!' Caryn's cry was ragged. 'Will you or won't you take him?'

'Let's say I want to examine the goods first, hmm?' He paused. 'Does he have a name?'

'Yes.' Caryn was reluctant to admit it. 'Loren called him Tristan, but I——I——'

'You couldn't bring yourself to use it, is that it?' he questioned dryly.

'Maybe.'

He began to pace again, measuring the room with his lean, pantherlike strides. 'So—where do you live?'

'I can drive back and fetch him——'

'No.' He halted once more. 'No, don't do that. I'll come to London. You'd better give me your address.'

Caryn was loath to do so. 'I can easily bring him here.'

'I'm sure you can,' he agreed, 'but I prefer to do it my way.'

'You can't pay me off!' she burst out uncontrollably, and his lips curled.

'I don't intend to.'

A knock at the study door curtailed any response she might have made, and without waiting for his summons, Angela Ross appeared in the doorway. Her eyes flickered over Caryn without liking, and then she looked at her father.

'Tris, how much longer are you going to be? Marcia's made a pizza for your supper, and it's going to be ruined if you don't eat it soon.'

His features changed as he looked at his daughter. Watching him, Caryn felt a curious pang at the gentleness of his expression. Why couldn't he have looked at Loren like that? she thought resentfully. Why should this girl feel herself so secure when he owed just as much allegiance to the woman who had borne his child, and to his son. . .

'We're almost through,' he told Angela now. 'Miss—er—Stevens is leaving.'

Caryn squared her shoulders. 'If you'll give me a sheet of paper, I'll give you my address.'

She was aware of his daughter's raised eyebrows, but she didn't care. Angela would have to know sooner or later, and why should she protect her? It was up to her father to explain, if he could.

Angela hung around as Caryn wrote her address on the pad he handed to her, adding her telephone number in case it was needed. Tristan barely glanced at it as he tossed it on to his desk, and she was aware that he was waiting for her to go.

'I'll be in touch,' he assured her politely, his eyes glinting, with suppressed anger. She guessed he had not cared for her referring to some future association in front of his daughter, but that was just too bad, she thought half defensively.

Outside, the air had never smelt so sweet, and she walked up to where she had left the car on legs that threatened to give out on her. Well, she had done it, she thought defiantly, and wondered why she was suddenly so doubtful. . .

Caryn spent the night at the hotel in Carmarthen and travelled back to London the next morning. The journey seemed so much shorter going back, but perhaps that was because she had more enthusiasm towards her destination.

Her flat was on the second floor of a house in Bloomsbury. It was not the most fashionable area of London, but it was civilised, and the tall Victorian houses had an atmosphere that was missing from the stark concrete and glass sky-scrapers that had sprung up all around them. Mrs Theobald, who lived on the ground floor, had window boxes, and at this time of the year they were bright with geraniums, and gave a distinct individuality to Number II Faulkner Terrace. Caryn had rung her friends from the hotel that morning, and when she reached the second floor the door of the Westons' flat opened and Laura appeared with the baby in her arms.

'Hi,' she said, smiling, her freckled face showing sympathy for Caryn's aching legs. 'Come in and have a cuppa. Bob's already gone to the studio.'

Bob Weston was a commercial photographer, working for a small agency in Notting Hill. He photographed weddings and christenings, and occasionally did spreads for small magazines, but his ambition was to move into the more lucrative world of television.

'Thanks.' Caryn barely glanced at her nephew as she followed Laura into the flat, a facsimile of her own except that it was much tidier. She tried never to let herself feel any attachment for the child, knowing as she did that the authorities would not let her keep him much longer.

'He's been so good,' Laura exclaimed, closing the door before walking to a folding pram standing in the corner. 'He didn't even wake during the night.'

'No. He's very good.' Caryn sounded weary and indifferent, and Laura looked at her anxiously.

'Well?' she ventured. 'What happened? You were very vague on the phone this morning.'

Caryn flung herself into an armchair. 'I told you I saw—him.'

'Yes.' Laura padded through to the tiny kitchen to put on the kettle. 'But you didn't say what was going to happen.'

'He wants to see him.'

'Who?' Laura came to the door of the kitchen. 'Tristan Ross wants to see the baby?'

'Yes.'

Laura grimaced. 'So when are you taking him?'

'I'm not. He wants to come here.'

Laura ran a hand over the swelling mound of her stomach and subsided into a chair with evident relief. 'Heavens!'

Caryn forced a rueful smile. 'Yes. I'd better see about tidying my place up.'

'I didn't mean that. And besides, it isn't so bad.'

Caryn sighed. 'It isn't so good. But since Loren died. . .and having him. . .' She tipped her head towards the pram from which direction a low gurgling sound could be heard.

Laura shook her head uncomprehendingly. 'I don't know how you can consider giving him away,' she burst out unwillingly. 'He's adorable. And so sweet. . .'

'Oh, Laura!' Caryn shifted restlessly. 'How can I keep him? I don't earn enough to support him, for one thing. And who would look after him while I was at work? You can't much longer, and then. . .'

'But don't you love him?'

'There's not much point, is there?' murmured Caryn bitterly, getting up and walking across the room, coming to a halt reluctantly beside the folding pram. Of course he was sweet, she thought impatiently, as she saw the quiff of feathery fair hair, the plump little hands curling and uncurling, the softly pursed lips oozing dribbles down his chin. Laura was right—he was a good baby. But she had no time for babies.

The kettle whistled and Laura got up to make the tea, and returning to her seat Caryn reflected what good friends the Westons had been to her. Without their assistance, she could never have kept the baby this long, but she had been determined not to let the social services people take him. Not after what Loren had begged her to do.

And yet it hadn't been easy, making up her

mind to go and see Tristan Ross. For one thing, she had had to find out where he lived and whether he was there at the moment. He spent quite a lot of his time travelling, but fortunately Bob had had connections in the television industry, and he had supplied the information that when Ross returned from his present trip to Canada he was scheduled to do a series of programmes for a London television company.

Laura carried the tray of tea into the living room and set it down on a table near at hand. Caryn came to join her, and they each enjoyed the reviving flavour of the beverage.

Munching a biscuit, which she confessed she should not be eating, Laura asked when Tristan Ross intended to come to the flat.

'I don't know,' Caryn admitted with a sigh. 'But I gave him the phone number. I guess he'll ring first and make an appointment. He's used to doing that sort of thing.'

'What was he like?'

Laura was intrigued, but Caryn just poured herself more tea and gave an offhand shrug of her shoulders. 'You know what he's like,' she said. 'You've seen him on television plenty of times.'

'I know.' Laura gave an embarrassed laugh. 'But it's different meeting someone, isn't it?'

'I'm not a fan,' declared Caryn flatly, and her friend's freckled face coloured unbecomingly.

'I know that,' she murmured uncomfortably. 'I didn't mean to suggest you were.'

'Oh, I'm sorry, Laura.' Caryn felt contrite. 'Take no notice of me. I'm an ungrateful creature.

And after all you've done for me. . .' She made
an effort to be objective. 'He—well, he's taller
than you might imagine, and he's certainly—
well, sexy, I suppose.'

'You could understand why Loren was so
infatuated with him, then?' asked Laura
quietly.

'Oh, yes.' Caryn had to be honest, although it
went against the grain to find excuses for him. 'I
should think she found him fascinating. Any—
any impressionable woman would.'

'But not you?' suggested Laura dryly.

'Me!' Caryn looked affronted. 'You must be
joking!'

'Why? That's quite a solution to your problems, have you thought of that?'

'What do you mean?'

Laura looked uncomfortable now. 'Well, I—I
just meant—him being the baby's father, and you
its aunt—perhaps you might—'

'Get together, you mean?' Caryn was horrified.

Laura's colour came and went, but she stuck
to her guns. 'Well, why not? I mean, we all
know—that is, you know Loren was prone to—
exaggeration—'

'Laura, what are you saying?' Caryn stared at
her. 'Don't you believe Tristan Ross is his—'
she indicated the pram, '——his father?'

'Oh, yes.' Laura was quick to protest. 'I do, I
do. Only—well, maybe it wasn't as—maybe
she—wanted it, too.'

Caryn heaved a heavy sigh. 'I see.' She
moved her shoulders wearily. 'Okay, I'll accept
that perhaps Loren did—encourage him.' She

lifted her head. 'What girl wouldn't, for heaven's sake?'

'You said you wouldn't,' Laura reminded her, and Caryn looked down into her teacup.

'I know I did. And I meant it. But anyway, that still doesn't change things. I think he sacked her when he suspected she was pregnant. Nothing can alter that. And when she wrote and told him, he ignored her letters.'

Laura nodded slowly. 'I suppose you're right.' Then she looked at her friend. 'I just can't help thinking that you're going to regret this.'

'What?'

'Giving—him away. Caryn, he is your nephew!'

'He's Tristan Ross's son. He can do a lot more for him than I can.'

'I can't argue with that.' Laura straightened her spine, wincing at her aching back. 'I just wish that was our baby lying in the pram there. Without all the effort of having him.'

Caryn grinned, relaxing a little. 'You don't mean that. You're loving every minute of it. I've never seen Bob so attentive.'

Laura smiled too. 'No,' she agreed happily. 'He has been marvellous, hasn't he? Do you know he went out the other night at half past eleven to get me some fish and chips?'

'Fish and chips! At half past eleven!' Caryn grimaced. 'Oh, Laura, how could you?'

Laura giggled. 'I don't know. I was ravenous, that's all. I had to eat fruit and crackers all the following day before I dared go to the clinic. I have to watch my blood pressure, you see.'

'And having junior over there isn't helping things, is it?' remarked Caryn dryly. 'Let's hope his—*daddy* comes for him soon.'

Laura looked at her anxiously. 'Let's hope so,' she sighed, but she didn't sound convincing.

CHAPTER THREE

CARYN worked in Cricklewood, and every morning she delivered her nephew into Laura's capable hands, collecting him again when she came home at five o'clock. It was an arrangement that had worked very well, except that Caryn felt guilty about taking advantage of Laura's good nature. Still, she did pay for the service, and Laura insisted they could do with the extra money with the baby on the way.

However, the arrangement did not do a lot for Caryn's social life. She worked as secretary to the Dean of Lansworth College, and during the course of her duties she was brought into contact with a lot of young men. But perhaps fortunately none of them had appealed to her seriously, and her most lasting admirer was the Dean himself.

Laurence Mellor was a man in his early fifties, still virile and attractive, with a broad muscular frame and iron grey hair. His wife had run off with a fellow colleague in his first years as assistant at Lansworth, but he had weathered the storm of gossip which had followed and had eventually been made head of the art college. His intense interest in his work had probably been responsible for the break-up of his marriage, Caryn had surmised, but since he had become Dean the pressure was off, and he had more time to think about his personal life.

Caryn had been his secretary for four years. She had come to Lansworth from a position in a typing pool with a firm of solicitors, but like Mellor himself, she had been ambitious, and he had recognised her determination as soon as he saw her. They got along well together, and on those occasions when he needed a hostess he always called on Caryn.

He knew of the affair with Loren, of course, although not all the personal details. He knew she had been Tristan Ross's secretary for a while, but he had not connected that with her subsequent pregnancy. When she died, he was sympathetic, and he always prided himself on being open-minded about things like that. Consequently he had not connected her sister with Caryn's request for two days' leave of absence to visit a sick relative in South Wales.

Caryn returned to the college on Thursday, and to her relief Laurence was out of the office all morning attending a governor's meeting. By the time he returned she was immersed in her duties and able to answer his enquiries without obvious embarrassment. Even so, she was taken aback when he came to perch his ample frame on the corner of her desk and said without warning:

'Have you decided yet what you're going to do about Loren's baby? I don't think I approve of you working all day and all night as well.'

Caryn finished fitting the wedge of typing paper into the machine to give herself time to recover, and then said casually: 'I don't work all night, Laurence.'

'No.' He fingered his tie thoughtfully. 'But you

do look after him in the evenings, don't you? And there must be—nappies to wash. That sort of thing.'

He sounded as though such an occupation offended the fastidiousness of his nature, and she had to smile. 'There are nappies,' she agreed, 'but only wet ones. There are disposable pads on the market now, you know.'

'Nevertheless, you have very little free time these days,' he insisted. 'You can't go on like this, Caryn. It's not right. It's not as if the baby were yours.'

Caryn looked up into his broad expressive face. He was obviously concerned for her, but she couldn't help wondering if he had some occasion coming up when he would need her assistance, and was sounding her out about babysitters.

'As a matter of fact, I don't plan to keep him much longer,' she admitted slowly, and his face brightened considerably.

'No?'

'No.' She hesitated. 'There's someone—someone I know, who might—give him a home.'

'A relative?'

'Sort of.'

'I see.' Laurence looked much relieved. 'Well, I can't say I'm not delighted, because I am.' He slid off the desk to stand before her, taking his watch out of his fob pocket and examining it absently. 'As a matter of fact, something's come up, something I wanted to discuss with you. I was hoping you might be able to have dinner with me.'

Caryn hid the wry acknowledgement of her

suspicions, and frowned consideringly. 'I don't think I could make it tonight, Laurence,' she said apologetically. 'I've been away a couple of days, as you know, and I don't think I ought to ask Laura to babysit again tonight. Maybe tomorrow. . .'

'It can wait another day,' Laurence agreed at once. 'Tomorrow evening it shall be. Where shall we eat? In town—or out?'

'Wherever you like,' Caryn replied, quite looking forward to the break from routine, and Laurence went away saying he would think about it.

In fact they ate in town, at Beluccis in Soho, where Laurence was a valued customer. The restaurant was small, but not inexpensive, and a corner table was always found for him. The lighting was subdued and intimate, and Caryn had accompanied him there twice before.

He ordered Martinis, and then got straight to the point. 'I've been invited to the United States during the summer vacation,' he explained, and Caryn felt a twinge of interest. 'It's a tour of several university campuses, some lecturing, some studying. A kind of sabbatical, I suppose.' He paused as the waiter brought their drinks. 'But I don't want to go alone,' he went on, when they were alone again. 'I want you to come with me.'

'To the United States!' Caryn gasped. 'Laurence!'

'Well, why not? You're my secretary, aren't you?'

'Yes, but—'

'Ah, I see. You're worried about what people

will say. I don't blame you. Colleges are notorious places for gossip.'

'It's not just that, Laurence. I mean—the expense. . .'

He put his drink aside and reached across the table to take one of her hands in his. This was something he had done before, too. When he wanted something, he could be as persuasive as the next man. But this time Caryn was disturbed by the light in his eyes.

'Caryn,' he said softly, 'have you ever thought of getting married?'

'Married?' She shook her head. 'Not seriously, no.'

'Never?'

'No.' She tried to make a joke of it, not liking the serious turn the conversation had taken. 'No one's asked me.'

'I can't believe that.'

'Well, no one I would want to marry,' she conceded lightly.

'Marry me, Caryn. Marry me!'

She withdrew her hand at once, pressing it close into the other in her lap. 'Laurence!' she exclaimed, realising she had been afraid of this happening. 'You're not serious.'

'I am. I am.' He sighed. 'Is it my age? Is that the barrier?'

'I don't love you, Laurence. . .'

'Love!' He scoffed at the word. 'What is love? I loved Cecily and look where it got me!' He shook his head. 'You think I'm too old, don't you?'

'Laurence, if I loved someone, I wouldn't

care how old they were. Honestly.'

He refused to give up. 'You could learn to love me. I would teach you.'

'Why?' Caryn's brows ascended. 'Do you love me?'

He shifted restively. 'I've told you, I don't believe in that sort of emotional foolishness.' He pressed on: 'Caryn, we have so much in common. Our work, our liking for books and music. . .'

'It wouldn't work, Laurence. They're not good enough reasons for getting married!'

The waiter was hovering, waiting for their order, and somewhat impatiently Laurence suggested they chose what they planned to eat. But Caryn's appetite had been drastically reduced, and she insisted that an omelette with salad was all she wanted.

The waiter departed and Laurence returned to the attack. 'Very well,' he said levelly, 'if you won't marry me, at least come with me. I need you.'

'You need *someone*,' she corrected him quietly. 'And that's why I won't marry you, Laurence. Because I'm not just someone, I'm me! I don't want to spend my life as a cipher!'

He looked hurt. 'I think you're being unnecessarily harsh. If I've ever treated you that way, I'm sorry—'

'I'm not saying you have—yet. But if we were married. . . Oh, it's no use, Laurence. Let's forget it, shall we?'

'And the tour?'

'I don't know. I just don't know.'

He chewed at his lower lip. 'We could pretend

to be engaged. For the duration of the trip, I mean.'

Caryn laughed. 'You make it sound like the plot for a romantic novel! Honestly, I never believed people actually went in for that sort of thing.'

'What sort of thing?' he asked shortly.

'Pretending to be engaged!' She laughed again, feeling more lighthearted than she had done for days. 'Really, Laurence! If I wanted to come with you, do you think a little thing like gossip would stop me?'

He assumed an offended air. 'It's different for you,' he maintained. 'You're young—and very attractive. And you don't hold any position of authority in the college. I'm its principal. I can't afford to behave in a way that might prove detrimental to my office.'

Caryn relented. 'Oh, Laurence! All right. Don't look so mortified. I know what you mean, but—well, I'll think about it.'

'About what?' He was eager. 'Marrying me?'

'No.' She quickly disabused him. 'Going with you. As your "fiancée", if necessary.'

He leant towards her appealingly. 'Do give it careful thought, won't you?' he implored, but Caryn had the uneasy feeling that her association with Dean Mellor was being stretched to the limits.

It wasn't late when he took her home; no more than ten o'clock. Laurence seldom indulged in late nights. He always said he liked to go to bed and read for an hour before attempting to go to sleep, and consequently he retired earlier to compensate.

Caryn climbed the stairs to her flat rather thoughtfully. She wasn't sure what she ought to do about the trip to America. It was true, the idea of visiting that country was exciting, but as Laurence's fiancée? Real or imagined? She shook her head. Somehow she was loath to commit herself to something that might prove more difficult to get out of later than she could imagine.

There was a light showing under her door, she saw as she reached the top of the stairs, and she frowned. Generally, Laura kept the baby in their flat, finding it easier that way. She did occasionally babysit in Caryn's rooms, but that was usually when Bob was inviting some friends round to play cards, and she had not said anything about that tonight before Caryn went out. Still. . .

Caryn found her key and inserted it in the lock, and entered her living room. Then she stopped in astonishment. Laura was there, sitting nervously on the couch, but opposite her, his long length draped casually over one of Caryn's armchairs, was Tristan Ross.

He came to his feet as she entered, and she noticed half with impatience how incongruous his dark green velvet evening suit looked in the apartment. Before going out she had washed some of the baby's clothes and some nappies, and spread them over a clothes airer to dry. There were some blankets folded over the arm of one chair, and a half empty feeding bottle standing on the table, as well as a pair of her shoes and the tights she had worn for work that day strewn carelessly in one corner.

Laura stood up, too, and looked at her apologetically, making a helpless movement with her shoulders. 'Er—Mr Ross came just after you left, Caryn,' she explained awkwardly. 'He insisted on waiting.'

Caryn pressed her lips together for a moment, and then met Ross's eyes. 'I'm sorry.' She paused. 'You should have phoned.'

He acknowledged this silently, and then looked at Laura. Taking her cue, she moved clumsily towards the door. But Caryn stopped her: 'Don't go, Laura. . .'

'I think what we have to say needs to be said privately, don't you?' Tristan Ross suggested dryly, almost matching the words she had used at his house, and Laura nodded her head and made for the door.

'He—he's in the bedroom,' she murmured for Caryn's benefit, and Caryn smiled her thanks.

But when the door had closed behind her, Caryn had never felt more humiliated in her life. She despised herself for the slummy state of the room, for the obvious lack of organisation. And she despised him too for coming here and making her feel so small. Was he comparing this place to his beautiful home? How could he not do so? Still, she reflected cynically, perhaps it would persuade him that his child did not deserve to be brought up here.

Now she said curtly: 'Have you seen—him?'

'The boy?' He inclined his head. 'Yes, I've seen him.'

Caryn dropped her handbag on the floor. 'And?'

'He's a beautiful child. You should be proud of him.'

Caryn's lips parted. 'What do you mean?' she demanded.

Tristan Ross thrust his hands into his trousers' pockets, regarding her levelly. Strangely, he seemed unperturbed by his surroundings, and she decided he had no doubt seen worse in East Africa. He was probably prepared for any eventuality, schooled not to show emotion whatever the circumstances. It was his job, after all.

'I mean,' he said, 'that he's obviously been well looked after, whatever your mental aberrations.'

'What mental aberrations?'

He shrugged. 'Loren's death must have been quite a blow,' he reminded her. 'I can appreciate that.'

But she wondered if that was what he had truly meant. She wanted to ask him what his intentions were, now he had seen the baby. She wanted to ask him if he was prepared to admit that the child was his. But somehow she couldn't fashion the words.

Instead, she walked rather nervously round the room and said: 'Did Laura offer you a drink?'

'Tea, yes. I refused.'

Caryn hesitated. 'I have some sherry. . .'

'I don't want anything,' he replied, glancing significantly at the narrow platinum watch on his wrist. 'I have to leave in less than half an hour. I'm—meeting someone at eleven.'

'Eleven!' Caryn couldn't prevent the ejaculation, and then realised how gauche and provincial she must sound. To someone like him, eleven must seem quite early. But then he didn't have to be up to feed a baby at six-thirty a.m.

Ignoring her interjection, however, he went on: 'I've considered this matter carefully, and subject to certain conditions, I am prepared to support the child.'

'You are!' She stared at him tremblingly, hardly able to believe what he was saying.

'Yes.' He glanced behind him. 'May I sit down?'

'Oh! Oh, yes, of course. Please do.'

'Thank you.' He subsided into the armchair again, sitting with his legs apart, his hands hanging loosely between. He indicated the couch opposite where Laura had been sitting. 'Won't you join me?

Caryn shook her head. 'I—I'm all right,' she insisted, jerkily, and noticing her agitation, he pulled a wry face.

'I did say—subject to certain conditions,' he murmured. 'I think you ought to sit down while I tell you what those conditions are.'

Caryn came behind the couch, moulding the cushions under her palms. 'It's all right,' she said, ignoring a sudden twinge of apprehension. 'Go on.'

'Very well.' He looked up at her with those strange amber eyes of his. 'I'll take him to live with me providing you are prepared to come, too. He knows you. And I think he needs you.'

'*What!*' She was glad of the support of the

couch now, and she leant against it weakly. 'But I'm no nursemaid!'

'No, you're a secretary. You work for the Dean of Lansworth College, a man called Laurence Mellor. The man you've been dining with this evening, according to your friend Mrs Weston.'

'How do you—have you had me investigated?' She was aghast.

'I have a very efficient office. It's their job to find out about people. Particularly people I have to interview.'

'But I'm not one of your—your television interviewees!'

'No,' he conceded evenly. 'But I had to check your story, didn't I?'

'And—Loren. . .'

'And Loren,' he agreed.

Her lips curled. 'How cold-blooded can you get!'

'Practical,' he retorted calmly. 'Now, shall we discuss the details—'

'I wouldn't work for you!' She glared angrily at him. 'And you forget, I have a job!'

'I haven't forgotten anything. At least, I think not. The summer vacation starts in a matter of two weeks. By the time September comes round I'm sure Dean Mellor can find himself another secretary.'

'You're forgetting the fact that I wouldn't live in your house if you paid me in diamonds!' she stormed.

He shrugged. 'Then the deal's off.'

'What do you mean?'

'Exactly what I say.'

'But you've admitted—the child's yours—'

'I've admitted nothing!' he told her curtly. 'I said I was prepared to bring him up with certain conditions satisfied. If you're not prepared to satisfy those conditions, then I wash my hands of the whole affair.'

Caryn put a confused hand to her head, brushing back the moist hair at her temple. 'You can't do this. . .'

'Why not?'

She thought desperately. 'I—I'll go to the papers. . .'

'What will you say? How will you prove your allegations?'

'Loren was your secretary when she became pregnant.'

'So what? If every employer was blamed when their secretaries became pregnant. . .'

'You—you swine!'

'Why? Because I tell the truth. Who would believe you?'

'Mud sticks.'

'All right.' He rose to his feet. 'So you ruin me. What good does that do you?'

Caryn's lips trembled. 'I'll do it.'

'I can't stop you.' He walked towards the door. 'I'll bid you goodnight, then—'

'No!' Her cry was agonised. 'Mr Ross, please! How can you deny your own son?'

'How can you deny your nephew? He is your sister's flesh and blood, isn't he?'

Caryn faltered. 'What would I be expected to do?'

'Well, I'm not asking you to be his nursemaid.'

'But—you said—'

'I said he needed you. I think he does. But I'm prepared to employ a nanny to take care of his physical needs.'

Caryn looked blank. 'Then—what should I do?'

He paused by the door. 'I need a secretary. I have it on good authority that you're very efficient—' his eyes flickered sardonically round the room, '—in that direction.'

Caryn's face flamed. 'I intended to tidy up before you came,' she exclaimed defensively, and a faint smile lifted the corners of his mouth.

'I believe you. Well? Does this make a difference?' He looked at his watch again. 'I don't have much time.'

'But you can't expect me to decide a thing like this on the spur of the moment. . .'

'Why not?' He was unsympathetic. 'You know now what you really feel.'

Caryn glanced unwillingly towards the closed bedroom door. She had wanted *him* out of her life for good. Everything she had done for him she had done coolly and clinically, refusing to allow him to wind his way into her heart. She had known that sooner or later someone would come along and take him away from her, that she simply couldn't care for him alone. Now Tristan Ross was making her acknowledge him as an individual, as her nephew, asking her to witness his development, forging a bond of time between them that would inevitably become impossible to break.

She turned back to him, her face composed,

only her eyes revealing the torment she was suffering. 'Very well,' she said dully, 'I'll do it.'

'Good.' She had the feeling he had known all along that she would submit. But then he was used to dealing with people; he knew exactly the right line to take to achieve his own ends. 'When can you be ready to leave?'

Caryn caught her lower lip between her teeth. 'As—as you pointed out, the summer vacation begins in a couple of weeks. . .'

Belatedly, she remembered Laurence's trip to America. At least that was that particular problem solved. But what was she going to tell him?

'So you'll come as soon as the college closes,' Tristan Ross was saying, and reluctantly she nodded.

'I—I shall have to give notice.'

'To Mellor. I know.' Tristan frowned. 'What will you say?'

Caryn shook her head. 'I don't know. . .'

'I suggest you tell him you saw an advertisement for a secretary in South Wales, and when you applied I permitted you to bring the child along. Naturally, you didn't know it was me at the time of the application.'

'I did ask for time off to visit a sick relative in Wales,' she murmured, half to himself.

'There you are, then.' His expression was wry. 'You can tell him I remembered Loren, if you like.'

'But. . .' Caryn looked anxiously at him. 'Won't that look rather—odd?'

'Mellor doesn't move in the same circles I do.

Why should it look odd? It's a generous gesture, that's all.'

'Generous!' Caryn sounded bitter, and his brows quirked.

'It is, believe me,' he assured her. 'You'll find out, one of these days.'

He swung open the door, and suddenly she realised exactly what she was committing herself to. 'I—I don't know what a secretary of yours would do,' she exclaimed, and he gave her a humorous look.

'Take shorthand, answer letters, file papers; I presume you can do all those things.'

Caryn nodded stiffly. 'Of course.'

'Problem solved. I'll be in touch about the nursemaid.'

'You'll be in touch?' She didn't understand what he meant.

'I thought you might prefer to choose a nanny. I don't know much about these things.'

'Caryn was taken aback, but she had other things on her mind. 'Mr Ross...your daughter...'

'Leave Angel to me,' he retorted shortly, and with a brief salute, he left her.

CHAPTER FOUR

IT was early evening when the waters of the estuary came into view, and feeling the refreshing breeze that drifted off them, Caryn breathed a silent sigh of relief. It had been a long hot afternoon, and the humidity of the weather had contributed to the baby's discomfort. He had cried intermittently since leaving Gloucester, and she was inordinately glad she had Miss Trewen with her. Without the nanny's assistance, the journey would have seemed interminable, and she supposed she ought to feel grateful to Tristan Ross for suggesting they drove down together. Miss Trewen came from a famous nursing agency which prided itself on the competence of its members, and her previous employers had recommended her highly. That they had also held an aristocratic title meant less than the warmth in which they had held her, and Miss Trewen herself had confided that she had been with them for more than fifteen years. Caryn was rather bemused by the arrangement, never having had to deal with staff of any kind before, but as with everything else, Miss Trewen was more than up to handling the situation. Her age, like everything else about her, was indeterminate, but her gentleness and compassion were more than evident.

It seemed more than three weeks since she had last made this journey, Caryn reflected, but it wasn't. Yet so much had happened. So much had changed. And remembering her final interview with Laurence Mellor she was almost glad she was leaving London.

He had been shocked, of course, as she had known he would be. What she had not been prepared for was his jealous resentment.

'I thought I could trust you, Caryn,' he had said coldly, and when she protested that he could, he went on: 'You led me to believe you were as eager as I was for you to be free of the child. Now you say you're keeping him! Do the social services know about this?'

'Oh, Laurence!' Caryn sighed. 'Surely you could try and understand. Until now, there's been no question of me—well, keeping him. But if— if Mr Ross has no objections. . .'

'Tristan Ross!' Laurence sounded disgusted. 'I thought you said he fired Loren. What's he doing hiring you?'

Caryn flushed at this. 'Perhaps I'm better at my job.'

'And did you know whose secretary you were going to be when you went for this interview?'

'No. I've told you.' Caryn crossed her fingers. 'I—answered an advertisement.'

'And you lied to me,' he reminded her. 'A sick relative! Oh, Caryn, how could you?'

'I—thought a change might do us—both good.'

'And you knew this when I took you out for dinner? When I asked you to marry me? You let me go on hoping. . .'

'Laurence, I hadn't got the job then.'

'But you knew there was a possibility.'

'Oh—all right. Yes.' She sighed. 'Laurence, I could never have gone to the States with you. I know that.'

'Why?'

'Oh, because—because our relationship is getting too—too intense.'

'I don't agree with you. I think we work very well together. Now, after the holidays are over I shall have all the unpleasantness of educating a new girl into my ways.'

'Laurence!' She felt worse than ever. 'Please don't take it this way. I'd like us to—to remain friends.'

But he had maintained an aloofness towards her for the remainder of the college term, and only on her last afternoon did he relent sufficiently to shake her hand and wish her luck in rather gruff emotional tones. Caryn had been astonished. She had never realised what an emotional man he could be, and she wondered with a pang whether she ought not to have accepted his proposal after all. Maybe if he had been prepared to take the child as well. . .

It was too late now. That particular stage of her life was over, and her only regret was at leaving Laura and Bob. She knew Laura would miss the baby terribly, but in another ten weeks or so she would have a baby of her own, and then he would soon be forgotten. Because she had not known how long she was to stay in Wales, reluctantly she had had to let the flat go, too. But she couldn't afford to pay rent when she was not living there, and as yet she had no real idea of what financial arrangements Tristan Ross was going to make. He was already paying for the nanny. Would he expect her to support herself? Perhaps by working for him she would simply be allaying the expense.

'Is it much further, Miss Stevens?'

Miss Trewen was speaking to her from the back of the small saloon, and Caryn glanced over her shoulder. 'About half a mile,' she assured the older woman. 'I hope he's not been too much of a nuisance to you.'

'Heavens, no.' Miss Trewen sounded quite shocked. 'But we are wanting our supper.'

It took Caryn a moment to realise she meant that the baby was wanting his supper, and she hid a rueful smile. The royal 'we'. She would have to remember that.

The road crossed the suspension bridge and descended towards Druid's Fleet. The salty tang of the air was invigorating, and Caryn breathed deeply. There were going to be advantages to living here, there was no doubt about that. Whether they would compensate for the position Tristan Ross was putting her in remained to be seen.

She heard the sound of the music before they reached the gates of the drive. This time she turned between the gates, and let the small Renault coast the final few yards down to the house. It was a beautiful July evening and every window in the house seemed to be open emitting the deafening sound of beat music emanating from the kind of instruments Caryn had hitherto only heard in the Albert Hall. Miss Trewen tapped her shoulder, looking most concerned.

'What is that?'

Caryn was wondering the same thing herself. 'I don't know,' she admitted apologetically. Was Tristan Ross giving a party? she speculated anxiously. He knew they were expected this afternoon. Surely he realised this kind of atmosphere was not suitable for a baby—not, at least, until he was used to his new surroundings. And as for Miss Trewen. . . Caryn shook her head. The nanny was looking distinctly troubled.

It didn't help when the baby awoke at that moment and chose to add his own cacophony to the din. Bidding Miss Trewen to remain where she was for the moment, Caryn thrust open her door and got out. Wherever Tristan Ross was, she would find him, and when she did. . .

Slim and aggressive in her cream denims and cotton vest, she marched round to the door only to find it standing wide, like the windows.

'Mr Ross?'

Her words were drowned in the wave of sound that seemed to be coming from the back of the house. Gritting her teeth, she stepped into the upper hall and called again. Again there was no answer, and with a heavy sigh she descended the stairs to the lower level.

The noise was louder here, and she began to realise that what she could hear was actually instruments, not merely records, as she had surmised at first. Who on earth was it? And what was going on?

The sound led her across the hall to the door through which the housekeeper, Marcia, had passed the evening Caryn had first come to the house. She had thought it only led to the kitchens, but perhaps she was wrong.

With a definite feeling of trespass, she opened the door and went through. She could hear voices now, as well as the music, and laughter. Her fists balled. It was a party, then. What on earth did he think he was doing?

Beyond the door, the passage ran towards a huge glass-roofed loggia, and it was from here the noise was coming. As she made her way along the passage, Caryn began to glimpse young people moving among banks of greenery, their bodies undulating in time to the music. There was the smell of tobacco and alcohol, and the faint sweet aroma of joss sticks, and Caryn had no doubt now that it was a party. But whose? And for whom?

As she hesitated outside the loggia, a young man saw her and with admiring appraisal spreading over his face came towards her. 'Well, hello!' he greeted her warmly. 'Who are you? I don't remember seeing you at one of Angel's parties before.'

Angel! Caryn might have known. But where was Tristan Ross?

'I'm—not at the party,' she explained now, stepping into the loggia to put some space between them, and looking about her impatiently. There must have been about thirty people there, either talking or dancing or watching the group of musicians on a small dais at the far end of the verandah. None of them was paying any attention to the view which, like the sitting room above, overlooked the estuary, and nobody seemed to notice her either, dressed as she was in the kind of clothes they were all wearing. A table supporting an assortment of bottles was strewn with dirty glasses, and the air was getting quite thick with cigarette smoke.

'You're not at the party?' The young man was right behind her. 'It sure looks that way to me.'

Caryn sighed, and turned to him. 'Where is Mr Ross?'

'Mr Ross. Tristan Ross. Angel—Angela Ross's father.'

'Oh, Angel's daddy!' He nodded his head slowly, pulling out a pack of cigarettes and offering her one. Caryn refused, and he put one between his lips before continuing: 'He's not here.' He lit the cigarette and grinned. 'But you're here, and I'm here. So how about we get it together, hmm?'

Caryn gave him a crippling look. 'Just tell me where—Angela is,' she said coldly.

'Come on! Do you know who that is over there?'

'I don't particularly care—'

'That's Sweet Vibration, honey. Now don't tell me you haven't heard of them.'

Caryn blinked and looked again at the group on the dais. She had heard of Sweet Vibration, of course she had. Their last record had been Number One on the best-seller charts for five weeks, and in spite of her annoyance she was impressed. She supposed that was what came of having someone like Tristan Ross for a father. But that still didn't alter the fact that he had

known they were arriving this afternoon, and had
absented himself so his daughter could throw the
kind of party designed to unnerve the most patient
of nursemaids.

'Just tell me where Angela is,' Caryn repeated
now, and somewhat offended, the young man
indicated a group of people gathered near the dais.

'Right on,' he drawled, and wincing at his
Americanism, Caryn began to make her way
towards the other girl.

It wasn't easy. Several of the young men swung
her round, obviously imagining she was some late
arrival, and she was feeling the heat and lack of
air by the time she reached Angela Ross's circle.
It didn't help when Tristan's daughter regarded
her without evident recognition.

'Yes?' she said, and in that moment Caryn
knew Angela knew exactly who she was.

'I'm looking for your father,' Caryn told her,
refusing to be intimidated. 'Perhaps you could
tell me when he'll be back.'

Angel shrugged, and the group of boys and
girls around her exchanged amused glances.
'Why do you want him?' she asked.

Caryn was tempted to tell her, right there in
front of her friends. She wondered how Angela
would feel if she announced that she had brought
her father's illegitimate son to live with them.
How much did the girl know? How much had he
chosen to tell her?

'Just tell me when he'll be back,' she said,
impaling the younger girl with her green gaze,
and Angela unwillingly relented.

'I don't know,' she retorted shortly. 'I don't keep tabs on him.'

Caryn controlled her temper. 'Well, is there some way I can get in touch with him?'

Angela pouted. 'You can ring the studios, if you like. But he won't like it.'

'Thank you.'

Caryn was turning away when a hand descended on her shoulder, and she swung round aggressively to find a boy behind her whose face was curiously familiar. Then she realised. He was Dave O'Hara, the lead guitarist with Sweet Vibration. Her senses quivered pleasurably, and she was unable to summon the anger she had felt a moment before when she had thought the man who had met her was touching her.

'Is something wrong?'

Dave O'Hara's voice was definitely Liverpudlian in origin, overlaid with a veneer that combined a southern drawl with a transatlantic nasalism. But it was a friendly voice, and when Caryn looked at him, his eyes were friendly, too. He wasn't a lot taller than she was, and stockily built, with the short cut hair that was peculiar to their image.

'Nothing's wrong, Dave,' Angela said now, asserting herself. 'My father's new secretary's arrived, that's all. Inconveniently, as usual.'

Dave ignored Angela and continued to look at Caryn, his hand continuing to rest on her shoulder. 'Is that right?' he said. 'You're going to work for Tris?'

Caryn nodded. 'I was just looking for him.'

'Oh, hey, he'll be along in a minute,' Dave

assured her. 'He was called away rather unexpectedly, isn't that right, Angel?'

Now he looked at the other girl and she moved her shoulders in an indifferent gesture. In tight-fitting jeans and a flowing chiffon smock, Angela adopted a seductive air, but the young guitarist looked right through her.

'I know what I'm talking about,' he maintained, turning back to Caryn. 'Tris lets us rehearse here sometimes, and when we do Angel usually hauls in a gang of her cronies to join the party. When Tris was called away this afternoon, Angel called me. Enough said?'

It explained a lot, and Caryn was grateful. 'I'm sorry if I've spoiled the party,' she apologised.

'Are you?' Angela was still aggressive. 'I'll get Marcia to show you to your room.'

'Now is that any way to treat a guest?' Dave protested, at once, and she grimaced.

'Miss Stevens is not a guest!' she retorted, and then bit her lip when Dave's eyes narrowed at the use of Caryn's name.

'Miss Stevens!' he echoed. 'Say, that's a coincidence.'

'No, it's not,' declared Angela shortly. 'She's Loren's sister.'

'Is that so?' Dave looked at Caryn again. 'Well, what do you know?'

Caryn's brows drew together. 'You knew my sister?'

'Everyone knew your sister,' retorted Angela dryly. 'Didn't you know?'

Caryn coloured, but before she could make any retaliatory response, an angry masculine voice broke into the proceedings. It was a voice Caryn recognised only too well, and as if in sympathy the musicians still on the dais dissolved into discord and finally silence.

'I asked what the hell is going on here?' Tristan Ross stalked across the room towards them, and Caryn noticed that even Dave's hand fell from her shoulder. 'Angel! For heaven's sake, have you taken leave of your senses?'

Angela looked sulky. 'I don't know what all the panic's about—' she began, but her father interrupted her.

'I told you Miss Stevens and the child were arriving this afternoon!' he stated coldly. 'And what do I find? A red-faced nursemaid sitting indignantly in a car at the door trying to comfort a screaming child, while the most God-awful din is going on in here!' His gaze flickered almost malevolently over Caryn. 'What have you been doing? Succumbing to the Sweet Vibrations?'

'No!' Caryn was indignant, too.

'That's right.' Dave joined in. 'She came looking for you, Tris. And,' he added humorously, 'I don't dig being called a God-awful din!'

Tristan ignored that. 'I've installed Miss Trewen and her charge in the sitting room for the moment, but I want you lot out of here in five minutes, understand?' He faced his daughter. 'And the next time you do something like this, you'll join them.'

Angela pulled a face at him and turned away, as Tristan's hand came beneath Caryn's elbow. 'Come with me,' he said. 'I want to reassure Miss

Trewen you haven't been swallowed up in the mêlée.'

Caryn went with him almost gratefully. In spite of Dave O'Hara's kindness, the noise and confusion had been unnerving for someone who had just driven over two hundred miles, and now the silence was almost as deafening.

He released her as they reached the door into the passage and she went ahead of him towards the second door and through it into the lower hall. The door to the sitting room was closed, but when she would have crossed to it, he stopped her.

'Any problems?' he asked, and although Caryn shook herself free of his hand she paused to answer him.

He had obviously come straight from the studio, and was still wearing the formal attire of a mohair lounge suit and matching waistcoat. She could well imagine an impressionable girl like Loren comparing his cool sophistication with the wilder elements Caryn herself had just encountered and finding them lacking. . .

'No,' she said now, realising he was waiting for her reply. 'What problems could there be?'

'You approve of Miss Trewen, then?' he enquired, in a low tone, and she nodded half in embarrassment.

'How could I not? She's very efficient. You read her references too, didn't you?'

'References are not everything,' he stated flatly. 'I should know that.'

Caryn shrugged. 'You must know I've had no experience in dealing with—with employees, of any kind.'

'But you like her,' he insisted.

'Yes.'

'Good.' He frowned, gesturing behind him. 'I'm sorry about this—affair. Angel didn't take too kindly to the idea of having a baby in the house, and I guess she was just making her point.'

Caryn shifted uncomfortably. 'I can believe it.'

He sighed. 'I've told her the child is your nephew.'

'Is that all?' Caryn gasped.

His expression hardened. 'What else is there?'

She gulped. 'You ask me that!'

He looked impatient now. 'Look, this is neither the time nor the place to start those sort of arguments. I'm prepared to give you and the child a home. For the moment that should be enough.'

'Well, it's not,' she stormed angrily. 'What is—*she* going to think I am?'

'Who? Miss Trewen?' He shrugged. 'She knows—'

'Not Miss Trewen! Angela!'

'Did someone call me?' Angela herself floated into the hall at that moment followed by an assortment of young people and musicians, some carrying instruments, some not.

Tristan turned to her impatiently. 'I see you're moving out. Not a moment too soon.'

'See you!' called Dave O'Hara to Caryn as he went by, and Caryn couldn't suppress an answering smile.

Tristan intercepted their greeting and indicated the sitting room. 'I suggest we move before we're trampled underfoot,' he asserted shortly, and Caryn had perforce to go with him.

Miss Trewen was pacing the floor with the baby in her arms. She looked much relieved to see Caryn, and the girl felt a moment's sympathy for her. This must be much different from the circumstances she was used to. But Tristan Ross seemed in no way perturbed.

'I suppose you think this is a madhouse!' he declared, bestowing upon her the smile that had won him so many admirers. 'I have to apologise for the reception. Obviously I didn't make the position clear and my daughter chose this evening to invite her friends round.'

He could be charm itself when he chose, Caryn thought rather maliciously, wishing Miss Trewen would tell him exactly what she had thought of the fiasco. But the elderly nanny was easily placated.

'Our young man is hungry,' she explained, with a smile. 'And it's been a long drive. Do you think you could show me the nursery, and then I can attend to his needs?'

'Of course.' Tristan nodded at once, going to the door and shouting: 'Marcia, will you come here?'

It wasn't difficult to attract the housekeeper's attention now that the house was quite again. Marcia appeared, tall and attractive as usual, in a cerise overall this time. She looked questioningly towards Caryn and Miss Trewen, her face softening as her eyes rested on the child, and then turned politely to Tristan.

'I want you to show Miss Stevens and Miss Trewen to their rooms,' he said, and she nodded. Then he looked at the elderly nursemaid. 'Marcia is dumb,' he explained quietly. 'But if necessary, she can converse in sign language or on paper.'

Miss Trewen looked shocked but managed to silence any comment she might have been tempted to make, but Marcia surprised them all by going across to her and laying gentle fingers on the baby's head. Her face took on such an expression of gentleness that Caryn felt a lump come into her throat, and she looked at Tristan almost compulsively. He, of all of them, seemed the least surprised, and after a moment he said: 'Marcia!' again, in compelling tones, and with a faint smile she nodded her head and indicated that they should follow her.

'The cases. . .' murmured Caryn, as Miss Trewen followed the housekeeper, but Tristan shook his head.

'I'll fetch them,' he said. 'Where are your keys?'

'In the ignition,' Caryn admitted reluctantly. 'But I could get them.'

His smile was wry. 'Believe it or not, but I am capable of carrying a couple of suitcases.'

'There's more than a couple,' Caryn protested, remembering the roof-rack. 'And the pram, and the cot. . .'

'I'll get help, don't worry,' he assured her, and rather unwillingly she hurried after the others.

Marcia led the way up the stairs to the entrance hall, and from there, up a second flight of stairs to the upper floor. Caryn would not have liked to guess how many levels the house occupied. There were four she knew of, and even above them, a wooden ladder led to the loft.

But the upper floor was spacious, gracefully dividing into two wings with a central gallery that overlooked the lower halls. Arched doorways led into the individual wings of the house, with long corridors lined with white panelled doors. Miss Trewen was obviously impressed with the appointments of the building, and Caryn could hardly blame her.

A softly-piled cream carpet led them into the south wing, and Marcia traversed the full length of the corridor before halting outside a door at the end. She threw it wide, and they entered into a light sunny apartment, with windows on two sides, and walls decorated with characters from Winnie the Pooh and Peter Rabbit to Paddington Bear and the Wombles. The long windows which overlooked the cliffs and the estuary had been reinforced with safety bars along the lower panes, and as well as an assortment of toys which would have delighted any toddler, there was a pint-sized table and chairs, also decorated with transfers, and a rocker that Miss Trewen at once claimed for her own.

In one corner of the nursery there was a small electric hotplate, an electric kettle, and a sink, together with a cupboard which, when Marcia opened it, was shown to contain all the necessary equipment for feeding a baby. It was very comprehensive, and Caryn glanced rather apprehensively at the nurse.

While she was taking in the fact that someone had taken a great deal of trouble to make everything attractive, Marcia went ahead and opened the door into an adjoining room. Here a blue-

painted cot, and a pile of bed-linen sitting on a
cushion-topped ottoman, indicated that this was
where the child was intended to sleep, and Caryn
felt her face turning redder by the minute.

Miss Trewen, however, looked a little perturbed. 'Didn't Mr Ross know you were fetching
your own cot and feeding bottles?' she asked,
hushing the baby as he started to whimper again.

'Apparently not.' Caryn glanced awkwardly at
Marcia. 'Thank you.'

Marcia permitted herself a slight smile. It was
the first communication she had acknowledged
between them and Caryn felt a moment's relief
before feeling again the discomfort of the situation. How could she maintain the fiction of only
being an employee when Tristan Ross treated her
like this? Soon Miss Trewen was going to suspect
the child was hers—hers and Tristan Ross's!

Meanwhile, Marcia was continuing with the
tour. She was apparently enjoying herself, and
Caryn trailed behind them. Beyond the child's
bedroom was a room allotted to Miss Trewen,
with a bathroom between.

Caryn wondered where she was to sleep. Surely
not with Miss Trewen, although the nurse's room
did contain two beds. But before they went any
further, Tristan Ross appeared in the doorway to
the nursery, two suitcases in one hand and one
in the other. Behind him came an elderly man
carrying Miss Trewen's belongings, and the picnic hamper in which Caryn had packed all the
baby's feeding equipment.

'Well?' Tristan set down the cases outside the

door with some relief, and walked into the room. 'Is everything satisfactory?'

Caryn gave him an exasperated look. 'More than satisfactory,' she declared shortly, and his eyes flickered mockingly.

'Marcia had a free hand in equipping the place,' he remarked, his eyes resting on the child for a moment. Then he looked at Caryn. 'Don't you approve?'

Miss Trewen interposed then. 'Of course we do, Mr Ross,' she exclaimed, 'but it's most unusual for everything to be provided like this, down to the last detail.'

Tristan shrugged. 'Blame Marcia.'

'I don't blame anyone,' she protested, looking a trifle flustered herself now. 'I'm sure Miss—er—Stevens is quite—overcome.'

'Are you overcome, Miss Stevens?' he mocked, and Caryn had to bite her tongue to prevent the ready retort from bursting from her.

'Where am I to sleep?' she asked instead, deliberately keeping all expression out of her voice, and he raised his eyebrows at the housekeeper.

'Haven't you shown Miss Stevens her room?' he asked, and when Marcia shook her head, he added: 'Allow me!'

He was making fun of her, but short of being rude to him there was nothing she could say. He indicated to the elderly man to leave the nurse's cases in the nursery, and then invited Caryn to follow him. They went a few yards along the corridor before he opened a door and ushered her, protesting, into a large, comfortable bed-sitting room. That he also closed the door behind him

in no way relieved the tension she was feeling,
and ignoring the exquisite green and gold
appointments of the apartment she turned to him
angrily.

'Are you mad?' she demanded.

'Mad?' He lifted his shoulders indifferently.
'Perhaps. You obviously think so.'

Caryn seethed. 'You do realise what you've
done, don't you?'

He pretended to consider the matter. 'You think
I don't?'

'Stop anticipating me!' she exclaimed frustratedly. 'You are aware you've made Miss
Trewen suspicious, aren't you?'

'Suspicious?'

'Yes, suspicious!' Caryn sighed, trying not to
be disconcerted by the unexpected indulgence
of his regard. 'What employer would provide a
nursery like—like that, for the use of—of the
nephew of one of his employees—'

'Wait a minute,' he interrupted her. 'Didn't
you just complain that I wasn't making sufficient
provision for you downstairs?'

Caryn glared at him. 'That was different. . .'

'Oh?'

'I thought you ought to have told your daughter
the truth.'

'What makes you so sure I haven't?'

'You always answer with a question, don't
you?' she sniffed. 'The fact remains, Miss
Trewen thought it odd—'

'I don't give a damn what Miss Trewen thinks,'
he told her succinctly, flexing his shoulder
muscles, unconsciously drawing Caryn's atten-

tion to the dark skin of his chest shadowed beneath the cream silk of his shirt. 'Does that satisfy you?'

Caryn shifted uneasily. 'What do you mean?'

'I mean Miss Trewen is an employee, just as you are, and she'll take her orders from me or get out! Right?'

His ruthlessness was all the more disturbing after his earlier tolerance and Caryn realised anew that so far as she was concerned he was completely unpredictable.

'Yes, *sir*!' she responded now, and had the gratification of seeing her words hit the mark.

'There's no need to be insolent,' he said sharply, and she held up her head.

'If you'll just explain to me my position here, I won't say another word,' she retorted, and he pushed back the weight of his hair with an impatient hand.

'What now?'

'Miss Trewen thinks she's my employee,' Caryn related with scarcely-veiled sarcasm. 'Perhaps you could explain the position to her.'

The oath he stifled was unrepeatable, and Caryn's fingers sought the back hip pockets of her jeans as she shifted uncomfortably before him.

'Are you afraid she'll think the child's yours?' he demanded, and she gave an offhand shrug. 'Because if you are I'm afraid you're going to have to live with it. I see no reason to supply a nursemaid with the personal details of our life here.'

'And if she thinks the child's yours, too?'

Caryn suggested provokingly, and his lips twisted.

'That's her prerogative. Yours, too, as it happens.'

'He is your son!'

'I see you still persist in avoiding his name. I assume he has been registered.'

'Of course.'

'In my name?'

Caryn bent her head. 'No.'

'No?'

She looked up. 'The priest—the one who attended Loren at the end—he registered the child.'

'And?'

'He put it that the father was unknown.'

'My God!' He gave a low whistle. 'And the name?'

'I told you, Loren called him Tristan.'

'And he was registered as Tristan?'

'Yes.'

'So!' He frowned. 'Two Tristans. That won't do.'

'I don't see why not. I shall call you Mr Ross. So, I presume, will Miss Trewen.'

'And Tristan?' Caryn frowned her incomprehension, and he prompted: 'Junior! The baby! What will he call me?'

Caryn couldn't resist it: 'Daddy?' she suggested, and saw his sudden anger.

'He's not my son,' he declared shortly. 'I should have thought you'd have realised that by now.'

'Why? Why should I? Why should you have us here otherwise?'

'Christian charity?' he suggested dryly, and then shook his head. 'Oh, let's not start that particular argument again right now. It looks like we'll have to call him Tristan for the time being. Fortunately Angel calls me Tris, which does make a distinction.'

'Why doesn't she call you her father?' asked Caryn impulsively, and he regarded her sardonically.

'I suppose you're thinking I'm too vain to admit to having a daughter of nineteen, is that it?'

Caryn flushed, but she forced herself to go on: 'Are you?'

'Calling me Tris was Angel's idea. Around the studios it's easier, for one thing, and she prefers it. Does that answer your question?'

'It's nothing to do with me really.'

'I'd go along with that. However, I find it easier to put the record straight at the beginning.'

Caryn suddenly realised how long they had been standing here, in her bedroom, talking. If Miss Trewen had been suspicious before, what must she be thinking now?

'I think you ought to go,' she said abruptly, and saw his dawning indignation.

'You think what?' he demanded.

'Miss Trewen must be wondering what we're doing. You shouldn't have closed the door.'

'No? You'd have liked Marcia and the nanny to hear all our conversation?'

'No, but. . .' She sighed once more. 'I suppose

I should thank you. For—for what you've done. But—'

'—you find it hard?' His mouth turned down at the corners and he reached for the handle of the door. 'Don't fret about it. I can do without your gratitude. Dinner is at eight. Do you think you can find your way downstairs by then?'

'Oh, but—' Caryn broke off awkwardly. Then: 'Will Miss Trewen be eating downstairs?'

'I imagine Miss Trewen will take all her meals in the nursery,' he essayed, swinging open the door. 'But don't be alarmed. I shan't be joining you for the meal. I have a dinner engagement already—one I shouldn't care to miss.'

And with a mocking smile, he left her.

CHAPTER FIVE

IT was possible to reach the village across the mud-flats at low tide. Then the sandy bottom of the river was criss-crossed with the claw-marks of half a dozen different sea birds, all of whom came to feed on the seaweed and other debris left stranded by the tide. As it was holiday time, the birds had to take their chance with the children who scrambled down the cliffs to the beaches that lay beneath them, and the dozens of small craft that bobbed about like corks when the tide came in. Port Edward was not a holiday resort exactly, but its charm and beauty attracted a great number of visitors, whose cars jammed the narrow streets and made the locals grumble that they couldn't get about their daily business.

Druid's Fleet was remote from the hustle and bustle of the village. Caryn had soon learned that the steps which descended from the house to the waterline led not to the river, but a small creek which ran into it. Here, amid a thickly planted screen of trees, Tristan Ross had his boathouse, and although she had not been aboard the craft, she had glimpsed its sleek lines through the boathouse windows. She learned that Druid's Fleet was actually the name of the creek, fleet being a word of German origin meaning small stream or inlet, and that when Tristan bought this house it had indeed been called Water's Reach.

She learned this from Pepper, the gardener and general factotum, the elderly man who had helped Tristan carry up their cases that first day. Pepper had lived in Port Edward all his life, and he was steeped in the history of the place. He resembled its first early settlers, those exiles of Mediterranean origin, with short stocky bodies and dark features, whose curious megaliths rear their stone heads throughout the western area of Britain, but he had all the love of language of his Welsh ancestry. In those first days at Druid's Fleet he seemed Caryn's only friend, surrounded as she was by Marcia's silence, Angela's hostility, and Tristan Ross's enigmatism.

The child settled down well in his new surroundings, as well he might, thought Caryn rather uncharitably. A flat in London, constantly within sight and sound of people and traffic, could not compare with the peace and tranquillity of the Levant estuary, and with Miss Trewen's constant attention he thrived vigorously.

Miss Trewen herself adjusted, chameleon-like, to the change of scene. Somehow, she and Marcia managed to achieve a kind of communication, and their mutual affection for the young Tristan was a more than adequate reason for their liking for one another.

Angela, for her part, made no effort to adjust. Her obvious resentment that having a child in the house curtailed the amount of freedom she had for inviting people there was understandable, but Caryn, remembering her sister, could not help but think she was selfish. However, the younger girl departed with some friends for a holiday in

Barbados only a week after their arrival, which relieved the situation somewhat.

Working for Tristan Ross, Caryn found, was not like working for Laurence Mellor. To begin with, Tristan was seldom about when she was working, and seemed to prefer to leave all his instructions on the dictaphone for her to deal with while he was away. She had wondered how she would fill her time, used as she was to the régime of an office, but her fears of being idle proved groundless.

There was an amazing amount of correspondence to deal with, for one thing. Every letter, no matter how ingratiating or conversely how disgusting, had to be read, and replies had to be drafted. Caryn got into the habit of leaving those letters which required his personal attention to one side, and answered those that didn't herself. Every letter she wrote was left for his perusal, and very often she would go down to his study in the morning early to find him having already put in at least a couple of hours' work. Only occasionally did he work in the study when she did, and then it was mostly making telephone calls arranging interviews with people, or alternatively making apologetic refusals to some of the dozens of invitations he got to attend local functions. But his main work concerned his television appearances, and it was this which occupied most of Caryn's time. At the moment, he was contracted to make a series of programmes concerning the economy for a London television company, and in consequence he spent a lot of time visiting factories around the country, speaking to workers and management alike.

Surprisingly, Caryn enjoyed her work. Perhaps it was that in those early days she kept very much to herself, and what free time she had after the baby was in bed, she spent exploring her surroundings. She tried to spend at least an hour each evening in the nursery while Miss Trewen ate her supper in peace, and then, because it was less daunting, she ate her own meal in her room. She did offer to babysit, but the nurse refused the opportunity to go out.

'I'm not much of a one for going places,' she told Caryn ruefully. 'I never have been.'

'But you must have some time off,' Caryn protested, making a mental note to mention this to Tristan next time she saw him. 'What day would suit you best?'

Miss Trewen shook her head. 'I've already spoken to Mr Ross,' she explained, surprising the girl. 'I explained how it was when I worked for the Tranters. I preferred to save my days off until I could take a proper break.'

'I see.'

Caryn had no choice but to accept this. Even so, she thought resentfully that it was typical of Tristan Ross's attitude not to mention it to her.

Her opportunity to make her feelings felt came sooner than she expected. The following morning she found him waiting for her when she entered the study after breakfast, and judging from his appearance he was on the point of leaving.

'I've left a draft of the first programme on the tape,' he said at once, after bidding her a curt good morning. He was usually curt in the mornings, and Caryn had assumed he was one of those people who didn't like getting up. But for once she detained him when he would have departed.

'Mr Ross. . .'

'Yes?' He was clearly impatient, but she refused to be hustled.

'I understand Miss Trewen contacted you about her time off.'

He sighed, fastening the button of his leather jacket. 'That's right, she did,' he conceded, nodding. 'So? The woman wants to take a week, or maybe two weeks at a stretch. You have no objections, do you?'

Caryn caught her breath. 'It would be all the same if I had.'

His mouth turned down at the corners. 'What is it? I'm sure Marcia will be only too willing to share the nursing duties with you when it becomes necessary, if that's what—'

'That's not the point! You should have told me.'

'So—I forgot. No sweat!'

Caryn squared her shoulders. 'You persist in taking matters over my head—'

'Oh, come on!' He was losing the battle with his temper, and it was beginning to show. 'You've been here—how long? A week? How often have we conversed in that time?'

'You're seldom at home. . .'

'And when I am, you eat in your room.'

'That's not fair. We see each other in working hours.'

'Look, right now I'm involved in this economy

thing. When I talk to my secretary, I talk to my
secretary, not to young Tristan's aunt! Now, if
you have any complaints to make, you save them
for your time, not mine!'

Caryn gasped. She had forgotten how harsh his
tongue could be. 'Yes, Mr Ross,' she responded
tautly, her chin quivering, and with a stifled curse
he left her.

For the rest of that day, Caryn worked harder
than she had ever done before. She didn't know
whether his comments had been a criticism or
otherwise, but she determined he should have no
complaints to make about her work. By tea time
her eyes were aching, and when Marcia brought
her tray she looked concerned when she saw
Caryn's pale face. She usually brought her tea to
the study, but today after setting down the tray,
she pointed at the girl and then placed her fore-
fingers at the corners of her eyes and pushed the
skin of her cheekbones back expressively.

Caryn was moved by the sympathetic demon-
stration and nodded wearily. 'Yes, I'm tired,' she
admitted, pushing the typewriter to one side. She
pulled the tray towards her. 'Mmm, I'm going to
enjoy this.'

Marcia hesitated. Although her attitude to
Caryn had not altered, having a baby in the house
had definitely softened her nature. Pointing at the
typewriter, she moved her hands backwards and
forwards across each other, palms downward,
indicating clearly what she was suggesting.

Caryn glanced at her watch. 'It's only four
o'clock,' she said with a sigh, pouring her tea.
'I'd hate Mr Ross to come back and find I'd taken

a couple of hours off without permission.'

Marcia frowned, and then indicated the sunshine outside. It had been another lovely day, and Caryn had the windows wide to let in the scents and sounds of the estuary.

'I know,' she agreed now, realising it was not so difficult to communicate as she had thought. 'Maybe later.'

Marcia hesitated and then gave a resigned nod of her head. A raised hand indicated farewell, and she was gone, leaving Caryn feeling infinitely less isolated.

She worked until five-thirty, and then made her way up to the nursery. Miss Trewen had had Tristan out for a walk, and was presently engaged in preparing his tea. Walking across the rug where the nurse had laid him, Caryn knelt beside her nephew, allowing herself to enjoy his wriggling antics. In this hot weather he wore little but cotton pants and tops, and his plump arms were honey-gold and glinting with fine hairs. His skin was much fairer than Tristan's, she thought, and then shrugged away the teasing reflection. His hair, at least, resembled his father's, and on impulse she touched its silky softness. A lurking smile lifted his mouth and a pink tongue appeared, and Caryn felt an almost irresistible desire to pick him up and cuddle him. She had never felt this way about him before, and the realisation was nonetheless disturbing for that.

She rose to her feet and at once he began to whimper. Miss Trewen turned and then shook her finger at Caryn reprovingly.

'You've spoiled him now,' she said. 'Can

you entertain him until the kettle boils?'

Caryn hesitated, and then bent and lifted the child into her arms. Immediately his whimpering ceased, and he contented himself by poking his fingers into her mouth and tugging at the curling length of her hair. Seeing Caryn wince, Miss Trewen exclaimed:

'I hope you'll forgive me for asking, Miss Stevens, but is your hair naturally curly? I mean, it's so—attractive. I hardly like to suggest. . .'

'Unfortunately, yes,' Caryn replied without hesitation. 'It's always been like this. You can't imagine how I've longed for straight hair!'

'I can't imagine why,' retorted Miss Trewen, fingering her own mousey-grey locks. 'When I was a girl, curls were the thing, and I remember I spent pounds on perms! But all to no avail.'

Caryn smiled into Tristan's eyes. 'Is anyone ever satisfied with themselves?' she asked, stroking a long finger down his tiny nose, and started violently when a male voice answered: 'I'd be satisfied with you!'

Both women swung round, Miss Trewen rather disapprovingly, and Caryn's eyes widened when she saw Dave O'Hara standing in the half-open doorway.

'Am I intruding?' he asked innocently, and she sighed.

'What are you doing here? Angela's in Barbados.'

'Did I say I was looking for Angela?' he protested, and Miss Trewen's lips tightened as she turned back to the boiling kettle.

'I'll have Tristan's bottle ready in a moment,'

she said, and Caryn hastily asked:

'Who are you looking for then?'

'I came to see Tris, but Marcia explained that he's not here,' murmured Dave, coming further into the room and attracting the baby's attention. 'So this is Tristan junior, is it? Well, well!'

Caryn could not have felt more embarrassed. 'My nephew,' she declared shortly, and was much relieved when Miss Trewen came to take him from her. 'Shall we go downstairs?'

Dave shrugged, his brow furrowing for a moment as he looked at the child, but then he followed her out of the room.

On the first landing, Caryn faced him. 'I'll tell Tris—Mr Ross you called.'

'Do that,' he agreed softly. Then: 'Come out with me!'

'Out?' She moved uncomfortably. 'What do you mean?'

'For a meal. Dinner if you like.'

Caryn shook her head. Much as she liked Dave, that moment upstairs had made her realise the difficulties she might have if she became involved with anyone.

'I'm sorry. . .'

He frowned, running a hand round inside the neck of his denim shirt. 'Do you realise if I'd asked any other girl. . .'

Caryn saw the humour of the situation. 'Did I prick your ego?'

'No.' He was indignant. 'Hey—Caryn, isn't it? I asked Angel,' he added swiftly, when she looked surprised. 'Let's go for a walk then. Where's the harm in that? I want to talk to you.'

Caryn hesitated. 'I—I—'

'You can't think of an excuse! That's good. Come on! Where's the problem?'

'What do you want to talk about?' she asked suspiciously.

'You! Me! Us! Does it matter? I'll discuss the weather, if you'll come.'

'All right,' she agreed reluctantly. 'But I'd better let Marcia know where I'm going.'

Dave accompanied her down to the lower hall and through the door which led to the loggia. The kitchen opened off this hallway, and they found Marcia whipping up a jelly for a trifle.

'Hmm, something smells good,' Dave inserted, and Marcia cast him a reproving look. By means of mime, she managed to convey that the trifle was not for him, and he grinned goodnaturedly. 'Okay, okay,' he agreed without rancour. 'But if Tris invites me to dinner, how can I refuse?'

Caryn broke into their teasing display. 'We— I—Mr O'Hara has asked me to go for a walk with him,' she said, colouring in spite of herself, and Marcia nodded, tapping the watch on her wrist significantly, reminding her not to forget the time.

They left the house through the loggia where steep wooden steps led down to the terraced garden. Considering the gradient, Pepper had done a wonderful job of landscaping the hillside, and as well as flowers and shrubs, there were low walls and trellises, overhung with trailing vines and rambling roses.

'Shall we sit here a while?' Caryn suggested, but Dave shook his head.

'What's the matter? Can't an old lady like you stand going down to the river?' he teased, and she pulled a face at him before leading the way to the steps.

The doors of the boathouse were open, and Caryn walked along the wooden landing and peered inside. She could see the name of the yacht now. It was called *Betsy* and Caryn frowned, wondering why he had chosen that name.

'Have you heard of Betsy Ross?' asked Dave, answering her unspoken question, and she shook her head. 'She was reputed to be the woman who made the first flag depicting the Stars and Stripes,' he continued. 'And as Tris's mother is American, I guess he thought it was suitable.'

'I didn't know that.' Caryn was intrigued, and forgot for a moment her determination not to get involved in personal issues.

'Well, the story goes that before the Declaration of Independence—'

'No,' Caryn flushed, 'I don't mean that. I meant—I didn't know that—that Mr Ross's mother was an American,' she finished lamely.

'*Is.*' Dave corrected her dryly. 'She was alive and well and living in New York last time I heard of her.'

'Oh.' Caryn gave a small smile, and then emerged from the boathouse to accompany Dave along the towpath towards the estuary.

'His father was English,' he added wryly, glancing sideways at her. 'If you're interested.'

Caryn decided she had said enough about Tristan Ross and concentrated on protecting her eyes from the golden glare of the slowly sinking sun. The tide was just turning, and when they reached the confluence where the waters of the stream emptied themselves into the river, Dave suggested they took off their shoes and paddled.

Caryn looked doubtful for a moment, and then, with a shrug, she bent and turned up the cuffs of her cotton pants. Carrying her sandals, she followed Dave down the bank on to the sandy riverbed, her toes curling as the icy waters stole between them.

'Isn't this great?' he demanded, his own jeans turned up to his knees, a boyish grin making him look younger than his years.

'Great!' she conceded laughingly. 'Oooh, but it's cold!'

'You're soft,' he declared, splashing her deliberately. 'Have you ever swum in a river?'

Caryn shook her head, and he went on: 'We were playing a gig in Zurich one time, and we went swimming in the lake; Boy, was that cold! I was like an ice chip when I came out.'

Caryn grimaced. 'I've no doubt you soon found someone to warm you up again,' she mocked, and he didn't argue.

'There are always girls,' he allowed good-naturedly.

'All willing to make themselves available,' she teased, but his regard was suddenly unnerving.

'There's making and making,' he said, and she turned abruptly away, almost overbalancing in her haste to reach the bank. He caught her as she stretched out a hand to grasp a tussock of grass to haul herself up, and his hand on her arm was compelling. 'What's with you?' he asked, frowning. 'What did I say?'

'N-nothing.' Caryn tried to be offhand. 'I'm cold, that's all.'

'You don't feel cold.'

'Well, I am.'

He let her go, but his eyes continued to hold hers. 'I like you, Caryn,' he said softly. 'I like you very much.' He paused. 'Do you think I care whose that kid is up in the nursery?'

Caryn stared at him aghast for a moment, and then the whole realisation of what he was implying came through to her. Clenching her lips, she pushed him away before springing up the bank and running off along the towpath. She heard him call her name, but she paid no heed, wincing as her bare feet encountered stones on the path. She didn't stop to put on her sandals, and she was panting when she reached the top of the stairs. She leant there weakly against the rail, trying to get her breath back, and as she looked up she saw Tristan Ross watching her from the open door of the loggia. His cool businesslike appearance was in strict contrast to her own dishevelment, and with trembling fingers she rolled down the cuffs of her pants and put on her sandals before walking reluctantly up the steps and into the house.

She would have preferred to have passed him without speaking, but common decency made her mutter an unconvincing: 'Good afternoon.'

'Do you usually take the steps at a gallop?' he enquired with sardonic interest, and she knew she had to make some explanation.

'I—it was late. I was in a hurry,' she replied, but his eyes had gone past her, and glancing round she saw Dave had just reached the terrace.

'Funny,' he mused dryly. 'O'Hara must have felt the same.'

Caryn gave him a resentful look. 'All right, we were together.'

'And he made a pass at you?'

She hesitated. 'If you like.'

Tristan stepped in front of her. 'Did he or didn't he?'

Caryn looked up at him mutinously. 'If you must know, he implied that—that the baby was mine.'

CHAPTER SIX

THE following week Caryn met Tristan's editor, Mike Ramsey, and his cameraman, Phil Thornton. Because of his experience in television, on both sides of the camera, Tristan produced and directed his own films, but Mike was both his editor and his friend. A lot of the groundwork for the series of programmes had been accomplished now, but the format for presenting the information had still to be worked out. The introductory programme which dealt mainly with the economic climate of the rest of the Common Market countries was already 'in the can' as they termed it, but it was the other five which were going to present the most difficulties, subject as they were to the ever-changing economic patterns in the country.

Because they chose to work at Druid's Fleet, Caryn was made very conscious of her presence in Tristan's study, and although he protested she was not in the way, she insisted on moving her typewriter out to the loggia and working there. Their discussions were becoming a distraction to her anyway, and she did not want to feel any reluctant admiration for her employer's grasp of the situation or find herself agreeing with any of his ideas. She had no idea how long he intended to employ her, but she was prepared to stay indefinitely, if necessary, if it meant assuring the child of its rightful home, and the only way their association could continue was if the detachment between them could be maintained. After all, how could she expect an outsider to accept the situation if she couldn't accept it herself? All the same, there were occasions when she wondered exactly what she was doing here, and an awful feeling of depression swept over her. But fortunately those occasions were few and far between. Yet her position was nebulous, and she knew Miss Trewen, if not Marcia, considered her relationship with Tristan questionable.

About three weeks after her installation at Druid's Fleet, Tristan came into the loggia one morning while she was drinking her coffee. It was a misty morning, with the drifting dampness of rain spoiling the view from the windows and giving everything a cool, clammy feel.

Since he had been working at home, she had got used to seeing him in jeans and casual knitted shirts, but this morning he was wearing a brown vicuna lounge suit, whose closely-woven threads moulded the width of his shoulders and the narrow muscles of his thighs, and a curious pang, which she quickly suppressed, assailed her at the realisation he must be leaving again.

'How are you getting on?' he enquired, standing before her, the epitome of the successful male, and she lifted her eyes from their involuntary contemplation of his lean body.

'I've nearly finished this estimate—'

'No. I'm sorry. . .' It was unlike him to be so formal, and she waited half anxiously for him to explain what he meant: 'I was wondering whether you were enjoying the work, or whether you found it—repetitive.'

'Repetitive?' Caryn shook her head. 'No.' She paused: 'Why?'

He frowned. 'You've been typing re-drafts until you must practically know them off by heart.'

'I don't mind,' she said, somewhat stiffly, wondering what was coming next.

'Perhaps not.' He considered her thoughtfully. 'But it did occur to me that when we had that little—argument over Miss Trewen, I omitted to mention what free time and salary you should have.'

Caryn was amazed at the weak relief that filled her. 'I—I have free time. When you're away—'

'—you go on working,' he finished dryly. 'Sometimes into the evenings. Marcia doesn't miss much.'

'I haven't complained.'

'Did I say you had?' He gave her a look of resignation. 'I'm not here to criticise you, Miss Stevens, merely to assure myself that I'm not working you too hard.'

Caryn had no answer to this, and half impatiently he moved away from her to stand staring out at the misty morning. His hair had grown in the weeks since she had been here, and now overlapped his collar at the back, its straight smoothness in direct contrast to her own unruly curls. She found herself wondering how she would have felt if he had chosen to pay attention to her. Without Loren's previous experience to guide her, she realised with honesty she might well have become attracted to the man, but would she, like her sister, have given in to him? Would she have risked becoming pregnant on the off-chance that he might be prepared to do the decent thing and marry her? Of course, Loren could have had an abortion. She had no doubt that given the information a doctor might well have been prepared to terminate the life that was threatening to destroy hers. But curiously, or perhaps not so curiously, Loren hadn't wanted that, and then it was too late... Even so, neither of them had imagined that anything could go wrong at the birth in these enlightened times, and the unde-tected virus which had swept through the hospital was one of those chances in a million...

Tristan turned and found her gazing in his direction. With scarcely concealed embarrass-ment, she quickly switched her attention to the pile of letters still awaiting her attention, shuffling them almost nervously. What was he waiting for? Had he something else to say?

'We're leaving for London in a few minutes,' he said at last, and she permitted herself to look at him again.

'Yes?'

'Yes.' He came towards the desk again. 'I'll be filming there until Friday. As I've paid two months' salary into an account for you at the bank in Port Edward, I suggest you take a couple of days off while I'm away.' He paused. 'Take your nephew out. Have a picnic. I'm sure Miss Trewen would love it.'

'I'm not here to take—take the baby for picnics, Mr Ross,' she demurred firmly, and his lips tightened.

'Call him Tristan, for God's sake!' he snapped. 'That is his name. Or is it so distasteful to you?'

'All right. I'm not here to take *Tristan* for picnics.'

He sighed in exasperation. 'No. You're my employee. And I'll decide what you do.'

'I'm your secretary, Mr Ross, nothing else.'

'No?' He came to rest his hands on the table she was working on, pushing his face so close to hers that she had to force herself not to move her chair back to get away from him. 'You're forgetting the conditions.'

Caryn could see every pore in his face—the deep-set eyes, with their tawny streaks, narrow cheekbones, his thin upper lip and fuller, sensual lower one. His mouth fascinated her and his breath was warm against her temple. Her pulse fluttered nervously, and the eyes she raised to his held little of the angry determination she was trying to hold on to.

He stared at her grimly for several seconds, and then with an oath he straightened. 'Damn you, Caryn, why should I care if you work yourself to death?'

It was the first time he had used her Christian name, and it came strangely from his lips. It revealed that he did not think of her as 'Miss Stevens' at all, and the knowledge was disturbing.

Needing to do something, she pushed back her chair and got to her feet. 'I'm sorry if you think I'm ungrateful—' she began, only to have him harshly break in on her.

'Oh, I think that!' he declared. 'I also think it's time I stopped pussyfooting around and told you flatly that your sister was not the plaster saint you appear to think her. Angel told me I should tell you, but I was reluctant to do so. But now. . . What the hell!'

'I don't want to hear your biased opinions,' she exclaimed tremulously, but he ignored her.

'From the minute Loren came here, she began to cause problems, of one kind or another,' he incised. 'She was lazy and careless, and as for loving me. . .' He shook his head. 'She loved this way of life. She liked this house, and the people who came into it. She may even have regarded me as a meal-ticket, but that's all.'

'You were attracted to her. . .'

'She was eighteen, Caryn! Younger than my own daughter! I might have been fooled into feeling sympathy for her, but I was not sexually attracted to her!'

Caryn bent her head. 'Why are you telling me this? We've already aired our opinions, and we'll never agree.'

'Because I felt we knew each other better now,' he snapped coldly. 'Obviously I was wrong.'

'All you've told me is that Loren wasn't any good at her job. You should have fired her.'

'I did!' he declared angrily.

'When you thought she might be pregnant!'

'Oh, Lord!' He strode across the room towards the door. 'Forget it. Forget everything I said. I'll see you on Friday.'

Surprisingly, after he had gone all Caryn could remember was the look of anguish on his face as he left her. But what had he expected after all? Just because he had proved to be a considerate and intelligent employer did not change his moral image. He was used to wearing a mask before the cameras. How easy it must be for him to adopt the kind of pose he knew she would most want to see.

The weather changed again the following day, and on impulse Caryn decided to suggest a picnic to Miss Trewen. The nurse was most enthusiastic, and Marcia was prevailed upon to provide them with a hamper to take to the beach. Caryn asked the housekeeper to join them, but she demurred, and Caryn guessed that Marcia was shy of meeting other people.

They took the car and drove to Heron's Cove, a beauty spot near Caldy Sands, some ten miles distant. There were a number of cars already parked on the headland, and with each of them carrying a handle of the carrycot where Tristan lay gurgling, Caryn and Miss Trewen descended the stone steps to the cove.

Caryn was wearing her swimsuit, and after Miss Trewen and her charge were settled on the rug they had brought, she stripped off her denim skirt and cotton vest to reveal a dark blue bikini.

'Oh, my!' Miss Trewen looked up at her in surprise. 'Aren't you slim!'

'After having a baby, do you mean?' Caryn asked slyly, and Miss Trewen looked embarrassed.

'I—why—I never meant—'

'It's all right, Miss Trewen.' Caryn took pity on her. 'But Tristan's really not my child, you know. He was my sister Loren's son. She died only a few days after he was born.'

Miss Trewen shook her head. 'A tragedy!' she murmured. Then: 'But Mr Ross has been—very kind to you. Almost like—one of the family.'

Caryn decided the conversation had gone far enough. 'He has been a good friend,' she conceded lightly, and curtailed the discussion by running down the beach and into the chilly waters of Carmarthen Bay.

The next day was equally hot, and from her desk in Tristan's study, Caryn envied the holidaymakers she could see sunbathing on the decks of their sailing dinghies or swimming in the cool waters of the estuary. Even the village had a continental charm in the bright sunlight, and coloured blinds had appeared that gave it a curiously alien appearance.

Even wearing the minimum amount of clothing Caryn was sweating, and after lunching with Miss Trewen in the nursery, she suggested they went down to the beach again.

'Oh, not me. Not today,' declared the nurse, fanning herself. 'It's much too hot for the beach, and we had enough sun yesterday.'

Caryn glanced towards Tristan's cot and sighed. Miss Trewen was probably right. It was too hot for the beach, but she longed to submerge her body in cool water, and swimming in the estuary seemed too close to home somehow.

Telling Marcia she would be back by five, she put on her swimsuit, collected a towel and drove away. Taking the road she had traversed the day before, she drove past Heron's Cove and keeping the sea in view, turned on to a narrow peninsula that projected itself into the blue-green waters. There were no tarmac car-parks here, and she reached a spot which looked interesting and just left the Renault parked on the grassy cliffs.

As she scrambled down to the cove hidden beneath the curve of the rocky headland, she reflected that it was just as well Miss Trewen was not with her. The nurse could never have negotiated such a precarious path, even without the daunting presence of the carrycot. Still, she thought soberly, if Miss Trewen had been with her, she would in all probability have returned to Heron's Cove.

At the foot of the cliffs, seaweed-strewn rocks stretched out into foam-flecked water. Definitely not a swimming area, she decided ruefully, but she could wade into the waves and cool herself that way.

Her skirt and top came off, and she paddled at the water's edge. It was quite a novelty being entirely alone, although she did not dismiss the awareness of taking no unnecessary risks for that very reason.

After she had soaked herself thoroughly, and her hair was clinging wetly about her shoulders, she returned to the pebbly beach and finding a spot less lumpy than some others, she stretched her legs on the towel and reached for her skin lotion.

Apart from the occasional cries of the gulls that nested in the upper reaches of the cliffs, the only sounds were those of the sea on the rocks, and an occasional insect that was attracted by the scent of the seaweed. She half wished she had brought her transistor, and then inwardly chided herself for needing more than the natural sounds around her. She tried to imagine what it must be like to be marooned on a desert island, and decided it was not a prospect she would welcome.

Time passed, and the spot where she was lying became shadowed by the headland, providing a welcome respite from the direct glare of the sun. Caryn put a hand behind her head, and stared at the distant horizon, the blue of the ocean lost in a haze that melted into sky without any evident distinction. Tristan was a little like that, she reflected frowningly, shifting from one mood to another for no adequate reason.

But she didn't want to think about him, she decided impatiently. She didn't want to think that she was doing as he had suggested and taking time off while he was away, and she didn't want to find herself wondering what he was doing right now.

Even so, she couldn't help speculating upon who might be the woman in his life at the moment. Since she came to Druid's Fleet, he had entertained no one, to her knowledge, but his two television colleagues and Dave O'Hara.

She sighed. Of course, he hadn't been at the house all the time, and even when he was there, he often went out in the evenings. No doubt there was some woman in the background, someone he would consider suitable to become the second Mrs Ross, but as yet she had not heard of her. Since coming to Wales she had read few newspapers, however, and as most of her information about him had come from the gossip columns, she was probably out of touch.

The glare of sun on sea was very bright, and reluctantly her eyes closed. She felt very warm and comfortable, and even the uncertainty of her position at Druid's Fleet seemed far away and no longer so important. . .

It was much different when she opened her eyes again. It was cold for one thing, and the sun was no longer anything more than a shifting of shadows on the ocean. Impatiently she reached for her watch. She had taken it off when she went wading, putting it into the pocket of her skirt, and she stared disbelievingly at the square masculine face. It was after six. She had slept for two hours!

Scrambling to her feet, she tugged the striped cotton vest over her head and pulled on the denim skirt. Her bathing suit had dried on her, and gathering up her towel and bag, she turned to the cliff path.

It was more rugged going up than coming down, but when she looked back at the cove she thought how fortunate it was that the tide had not come right in and trapped her by the rocks. She had been rather foolhardy falling asleep, and she hoped Marcia had not worried about her. The roads were busy as she drove back to Port Edward. Dozens of holidaymakers had taken advantage of the good weather to go down to the beaches, and by the time she arrived back at Druid's Fleet it was almost half past seven. Her stomach was protesting at the long period without food, and she was looking forward to her supper with real enthusiasm.

A grey Mercedes was parked to one side of the door, and her senses sharpened. She knew it was Tristan's car, although it was unusual for him to leave it parked out in the front. A steep slope led down to a huge garage, and invariably he rolled the big car into that barn-like shelter.

'Damn!' she swore silently to herself, as she stopped the Renault and switched off the engine. He hadn't been expected back until tomorrow. Now he would know that she had been enjoying herself in his absence.

She thrust open her door and got out, collecting her belongings from the back seat and slamming the door behind her. The sound must have attracted attention because almost immediately the porch door opened and Marcia's anxious face appeared. She looked so relieved to see Caryn that the girl felt contrite, and she hastened towards her apologetically.

'I know, I know,' she said. 'I'm late. I'm sorry.'

Marcia shook her head expressively, and then gestured for Caryn to come inside, and as she did so Tristan came up the stairs from the lower landing. For once he looked less than controlled, his beige silk shirt unbuttoned down his chest, his navy trousers stained with mud and grass stains.

'*Caryn!*' he said incredulously, then more aggressively: 'Where the hell have you been?'

Caryn glanced round at Marcia closing the door behind her. 'I'm sorry,' she exclaimed. 'I fell asleep—'

'You did what!' Tristan had reached her now, and she could smell the sweating heat of his body which was also not normal for him.

'I—fell asleep. On the beach—'

'What beach?'

'What beach?' She looked up at him confusedly. 'I don't know what beach.'

'Then you bloody well ought to,' he swore violently, and she took an automatic step backward.

'I don't know what you're getting so annoyed about,' she protested. 'I'm late, I know, but—'

'Late?' He made an exasperated sound. 'You told Marcia you'd be back by five.'

'I know I did.' Caryn was beginning to feel annoyed herself. 'So what? I didn't know you were coming back today. If you have some work for me—'

'To hell with work!' he snapped savagely, and then turned away, raking a slightly unsteady hand through his hair. He seemed to be trying to calm himself, and when he turned back to her he had himself in control. 'All right,' he said heavily. 'All right. Perhaps I'm over-reacting.' He paused. 'I expect you're hungry.' His gaze flicked to Marcia. 'Prepare a tray for two, would you? And fetch it to the sitting room.'

Caryn realised her own palms were sweating, and they slipped unpleasantly along the strap of her bag. 'If you don't mind, I'll take a shower,' she said, aware that her voice sounded stiff. 'Then perhaps I could have my supper in my room. . .'

'You'll have your supper in the sitting room with me,' retorted Tristan harshly, and without waiting for her protest, he climbed the stairs to the upper landing, disappearing into the north wing.

After he had gone, Marcia spread her hands

helplessly, and, nodding, Caryn followed him up the stairs. But much more slowly.

Miss Trewen came to her room as Caryn was sitting before her dressing table applying a moisturiser to her face. The salt air had dried her skin in spite of the lotion she had spread so liberally, and it was good to feel the tautness relaxing under the lanolin. She was only wearing a thin cotton robe when the knock came at the door, and she called: 'Who is it?' in slightly uneasy tones.

'Only me,' ventured the nurse, tentatively opening the door, and Caryn beckoned her inside. 'I heard the commotion downstairs. Where have you been?'

Caryn sighed. 'I went to the beach. Not Heron's Cove,' she added quickly, 'just an inlet I found off the beaten track.'

'I see.' Miss Trewen threaded her fingers together. 'That would explain it, of course.'

'Explain what?'

Caryn frowned, and the older woman shook her head reprovingly. 'Why Mr Ross didn't find you,' she declared.

'He's been looking!' exclaimed Caryn disbelievingly, and when Miss Trewen nodded, went on: 'But why?'

'I believe you had told Marcia—'

'—that I'd be back by five,' Caryn finished impatiently. 'Yes, I know that. But honestly, I'm not a child—'

'Nevertheless, Mr Ross said there were some dangerous coves around here, and he was afraid you might get trapped by the incoming tide.'

'I see.' Caryn turned back to study her reflec-

tion without pleasure. It didn't fit her image of
Tristan Ross to think of him as a man who cared
about his employees' welfare, but remembering
his grass-stained trousers she wondered uneasily
if he had climbed down some cliff face looking
for her.

'He was very worried,' continued Miss
Trewen, adding to the feelings of guilt Caryn was
already experiencing. 'And when we heard that
news report. . .'

'What news report?' Caryn turned to stare
at her.

'About those two boys.' Miss Trewen frowned.
'I thought that's what Mr Ross was telling you
downstairs.'

'What two boys?' exclaimed Caryn, trying to
be patient, and Miss Trewen made a gesture of
regret.

'Two boys were drowned late this afternoon
in Carmarthen Bay. I believe their dinghy had
overturned and they'd tried to swim for the shore,
but. . .' she shook her head, 'they didn't make it.'

'Oh, lord!' Caryn swung round to rest her
elbows on the dressing table, cupping her chin in
her hands. 'If only I'd known. . .'

Miss Trewen nodded. 'Still, I don't suppose
you could have helped them,' she reassured her
absently, and Caryn had to hide the unwilling
smile that tugged at her lips. It was so easy for
Miss Trewen. She didn't get involved in personal
relationships, while she. . .

Caryn determinedly smoothed the cream into
her temples, and after assuring herself that the
girl had suffered no ill effects from her outing,

Miss Trewen left her, saying there was a television programme she wanted to see.

After brushing her hair into some semblance of order, Caryn opened the wardrobe and extracted a cream Dacron button-through dress that was loose and sleeveless, and displayed her gipsy darkness to advantage. Then, after sliding her bare feet into leather-thonged sandals, she went downstairs.

Tristan was already in the sitting room, helping himself to a Scotch from a tray of bottles and glasses on a table in the corner. He had changed, too, and his close-fitting velvet pants couldn't help but draw attention to the lean length of his legs. For once he wasn't wearing a jacket, and his black silk shirt threw his ash-fair hair into prominence. He, too, had had a shower, and droplets of water still glinted on the artificially darkened strands.

He looked round when she entered the room, and at once she was nervous. This was the first time their being together had been anything less than businesslike, and he must know the effect he had on women. It wasn't anything he did precisely, or even anything he said. He just had a certain *presence* that made her immediately aware of her own femininity. It made her stiffen towards him, and his casual offer of a drink was accepted through taut lips.

'Sherry, please,' she said, and although he raised his eyebrows, he made no demur. 'Dry, if you have it.'

He poured a schooner of the pale golden liquid and carried it across to her, his own half empty tumbler held casually in his other hand.

He wasn't wearing a tie this evening, and in the opened neck of his shirt she could see a narrow leather necklet. Something was suspended from it, but she couldn't see what, and realising she was staring, she quickly applied her attention to the sherry.

He studied her discomposure with narrowed eyes for a moment, and then he turned to the windows to stare out broodingly over the estuary. When he looked round again she had moved away from him and was hovering near the empty fireplace.

'Exactly where did you go this afternoon?' he enquired, before swallowing the remainder of the Scotch in his glass at a gulp, and she moved her shoulders uncomfortably.

'I'm not sure. I drove on to a peninsula. I just stopped the car and climbed down to some cove.' She paused, and then added swiftly: 'I'm sorry if I—alarmed you. I—didn't know about the two boys who were drowned.'

He frowned. 'You do now.'

'Miss Trewen told me. She said you'd gone looking for me.'

He walked slowly back to the table and poured himself another Scotch. With his back to her, he said dryly: 'And I suppose you didn't believe her.'

'No!' Caryn made a sound of protest. 'I mean—of course I believed her.'

'Did you?' He turned and surveyed her sardonically. 'And what did you think, I wonder? That I was just protecting my investment? That I wouldn't want to lose such a good secretary?'

Caryn didn't answer this, and somewhat restlessly, he paced back to the windows again. Watching him, she sensed his impatience, and wondered uneasily whether he was regretting employing her.

'I finished the drafts of the two scripts you left me, and the letters that came while you were away——' she offered, and he scowled.

'Tell me tomorrow,' he interrupted her abruptly, and she raised her glass to her lips with an unpleasant feeling of reproof.

It was with some relief she welcomed Marcia's appearance with the tray. She set it down on the low table near one of the velvet couches, and the succulent aroma of chicken casserole came to Caryn's nostrils. The housekeeper assured herself that they could help themselves and then mimed that she would bring the coffee later.

Caryn hesitated a moment after Marcia had gone, and then said awkwardly: 'Shall I?'

Tristan shrugged. 'Please do!' and with some misgivings she seated herself on the couch beside the tray.

There was some fresh salmon to start with, but Tristan didn't want any and she found her own appetite was depleted by his indifference. She turned instead to the casserole, and spooned flaky rice on to a plate before covering it with some of the milk-white chicken nestling in its creamy sauce. A sprig of parsley added colour to the dish, and to her consternation, when she held the plate out to Tristan, he came and seated himself on the couch beside her. But before eating, he picked up the bottle of wine that also occupied a corner of the tray and expertly removed the cork.

'Do you like Riesling?' he asked, as he poured some of the colourless liquid into a tall glass, and she managed a faint murmur of acquiescence.

His weight on the couch beside her was infinitely more disturbing than any amount of wine could have been, she reflected, forking a sliver of chicken into her mouth. She was supremely conscious of his thigh only inches from her own on the soft velvet cushion, and the fleeting penetration of the amber eyes which were occasionally cast in her direction.

'Is it good?' he asked once when she allowed her tongue to curl out and rescue a grain of rice from her upper lip, and she coloured in embarrassment.

'Very good,' she replied quickly, but his expression as he applied himself to his own meal was wry.

Caryn felt infinitely better with some food inside her. The fluttery sensation in the region of her solar plexus was no longer so evident, and she decided her nerves were primarily caused by hunger.

A delectable raspberry pudding awaited for dessert, but Tristan declined to try any of this and Caryn contented herself by taking a small helping for herself. Tristan refilled her wine glass even though only a small amount had been drunk out of it, and proceeded to finish the bottle. He lay back against the apricot upholstery, holding his glass up to the light and studying her through it.

Caryn soon ate the pudding, and wiped her mouth feeling replete. In spite of everything, she had enjoyed it, and when Marcia came to clear and fetch the coffee, she offered her compliments. The housekeeper allowed a small smile to lift her lips, and went away again, leaving Caryn to handle the coffee cups.

'How do you like it?' she asked, looking at Tristan, the coffee pot in her hand.

'How do I like what?' he countered lazily, and something in his expression made her look away from him. At once, he straightened away from the cushions and said: 'Black. With sugar!' as though regretting his momentary baiting.

Caryn filled his cup and spooned brown sugar into it. 'Is that all right?'

'Perfect,' he assured her, somewhat sardonically. Then: 'Tell me how long you worked for Laurence Mellor.'

His question was so unexpected that she stared at him. 'Don't you know? I thought you had a dossier on all your employees.'

He returned her stare steadily. 'I'm asking you.'

Immediately Caryn felt uneasy. 'Four years,' she replied shortly. 'Why do you want to know?'

He didn't answer this, but said instead: 'He wanted to marry you, didn't he?'

'How do you know that?'

Her involuntary exclamation was an admission, and he knew it. 'How about—he told me?'

'I don't believe that.'

His mouth twisted with wry humour. 'No. You wouldn't.'

Caryn put down her coffee cup and looked at him uncomfortably. 'Are you going to tell me?'

He set his glass down and sat with his legs
apart, his arms resting along his thighs. 'I
guessed,' he told her evenly. 'Do you
believe that?'

Caryn's brow furrowed. 'I don't know. . .'

He shrugged. 'Your previous employer was not
exactly unstinting in his praise of you. There had
to be one of two reasons. A—you were no good
at the job; or B—he was personally involved with
you. Obviously, it wasn't the former, so it had to
be the latter.'

Caryn's lips tightened. 'You're very clever!'
But it wasn't a commendation.

He sighed. 'No, I'm not. Just practical.'

'Calculating!'

'If you like. It pays to calculate the odds in
my job.'

Caryn examined her hands lying in her lap.
'Was that why you dismissed Loren?' she asked,
and heard his angry intake of breath.

'Will you never leave that alone?' he
exclaimed harshly. 'I've told you about Loren.
For God's sake, I'm supporting her child, aren't
I? What more do you want of me?'

Caryn quivered. 'An—an admission. . .'

'What of? Guilt? Remorse?' He turned towards
her angrily. 'What do I have to feel guilty about?
What remorse should I feel?'

'Only you know that,' she retorted shakily.

'You have such an opinion of me, haven't
you?' he pursued. 'What do I have to do to prove
to you that I'm not the monster you think I am?'

Caryn's mouth was dry, and her breath rasped
painfully in her throat. 'You don't have to prove

anything to me,' she got out raggedly, but clearly he didn't believe her.

'Do you know what I'm tempted to do?' he demanded, and suddenly his eyes were moving over her, lingering insinuatingly on the buttoned neckline of her dress, moving down over her swiftly rising breasts to where her hands plucked nervously at her skirt. He had never looked at her like this before, and she was made heatedly aware of the power he could exert when he chose to do so.

'I think it's time I went up to my room,' she declared, half rising to her feet, but his hand on her knee compelled her to remain where she was.

'Coward,' he said softly, mockery tinging his words. 'What do you think I'm going to do to you? What are you afraid of? You can always slap my face.'

'Mr Ross—'

'Yes, Miss Stevens?'

'Will you let go of my knee?'

'No.' He moved along the couch towards her, and her breathing almost stopped it, was so shallow. 'Why should I? You think the worst of me. Why shouldn't I prove it?'

'This is ridiculous! If you don't let me go—'

'Yes? What will you do? Call for help? Who will help you? Marcia? I don't think so. Miss Trewen? Hardly. Tristan? Unfortunately not.'

When she would have pushed him away, his hand imprisoned both of hers, and she was helpless before him, like a mouse caught in a trap.

'Mmm, this is nice,' he murmured, inhaling her perfume. 'Now what shall we do?'

Caryn clenched her teeth. 'Let me go!'

'And what will you do?' He waited for her reply. 'Scratch my eyes out?'

'It's nothing more than you deserve!' she panted, and as suddenly as he had taken hold of her she was free again.

But now weakness had taken hold of her lower limbs, and it seemed incredibly difficult to summon the energy to rise from the couch. Instead, he continued to look at her, the humour disappearing from his mouth as she returned his stare.

Needing something to hold on to, Caryn broke into words: 'Is—is your daughter enjoying her holiday?' she stammered foolishly, and he closed his eyes against the timidity of her expression.

'Oh, Caryn!' he groaned, opening his eyes again. He ran a hand round the back of his neck, tipping his head back flexingly, and then got up from the couch. 'Yes, she's enjoying her holiday,' he said flatly. 'Do you want another drink?'

'What? Oh, no.' Caryn shook her head, and with a shrug he went to pour himself another Scotch.

When he turned, she had risen to her feet, the burgeoning peaks of her breasts clearly outlined against the fine material of her dress.

'You're leaving,' he remarked, without expression. 'Yes. Run away, little girl!'

Caryn caught her breath. 'I don't like your insinuation, Mr Ross. If this is how you make your conquests, I'm sorry I've been wasting your time!'

His eyes narrowed, the thick lashes hiding the tawny irises. 'Is that what you think, Miss Stevens?' he drawled. 'Should I disillusion you?'

'You disillusioned me a long time ago,' she retorted, and reluctant admiration touched his lips.

'*Touché*!' He put down his glass. 'But I don't think you know the meaning of the word.'

'I know——' she was declaring vehemently, when she realised he had moved so that he was between her and the door.

'What do you know, I wonder?' he taunted. 'I don't believe you've ever slept with a man.'

Caryn's face burned. 'And——and is that your criterion?' she demanded unsteadily. 'I'll have you know——' She broke off briefly as he came towards her, his hands closing round her upper arms, firm and unyielding, but she forced herself to go on: '——there are more important things in life than going to bed with——with some arrogant male——'

Her words were punctuated by gulps as he bent his head towards her, his lips barely stroking the warm curve of her neck, the sun-tanned skin of her shoulder revealed by the sleeveless dress. She wanted to struggle, but it didn't seem an adult thing to do, and she continued talking in a determined effort to show him he really was wasting his time with her.

'——you can't understand that, of course. You——you show a——a fine contempt for my sex, taking—taking them without respect or—or love—'

His tongue probed the hollow of her ear, and a quiver of emotion ran through her. His alcohol-scented breath was not unpleasant, and as he drew her closer she could feel the powerful muscles of his thighs pressing against hers. His lips trailed along the curve of her jawline, but when they touched the corner of her mouth she realised that, adult or not, she had to get away from him.

She opened her mouth to speak again, and then gasped as his mouth covered hers, the dark sweetness of his kiss invading and intimate. The hardness of his chest was crushing her breasts, but it was a pleasurable sensation, and his hands were cupping the back of her head, his thumbs probing the sensitive hollows behind her ears. Her clenched fists pressed determinedly to her sides jerked resistingly, but when his kiss hardened into passion, they reached towards him, spreading over his chest to the nape of his neck. Her unconscious yielding made him almost lose his balance, and he parted his legs to support them both, drawing her even closer between.

The shrilling of the telephone was both harsh and unwelcome, and sobering. Caryn opened her eyes to find Tristan closing his, and with a groan of protest he put her from him and went to answer it. Only then did she become aware that several buttons on her dress were unfastened, and her pulses throbbed as she saw the marks of his fingers visible on her body.

His back was to her as he picked up the receiver, and she looked longingly towards the

door. Apart from anything else, she didn't want
to eavesdrop on his conversation, she told herself,
not wanting to acknowledge the awful sense of
self-disgust that was sweeping over her. After
everything she knew about him, she thought
with dismay. That she should have let him touch
her. . .

He turned, as if sensing her withdrawal, and his
eyes revealed the cynical twist of his expression.
'Yes,' he was saying, to whoever it was on the
phone, 'I know. Yes. Well, it's been pretty hectic.
I know that, but—'

Caryn looked away from him, and walked jerkily towards the windows, and as if impatient to
get away, she heard him making some excuse
about not being able to come over because he
was tied up at the moment. Who was asking? she
wondered bitterly. Another woman!

She heard the receiver being replaced, and half
afraid he would come across to her and try to
take up where he left off, she swung round.

'I'm sorry about that,' he remarked, fingering
the leather cord around his neck, and she
glimpsed the copper amulet that was attached
to it. 'I'm afraid I've been neglecting people
lately.'

Caryn had no intention of entering into a
conversation with him. 'I'm rather tired,'
she said coldly. 'Is it all right if I go to bed
now?'

Hunching his shoulders, he pushed his hands
into the pockets of his pants. 'Of course,' he
agreed, inclining his head, and feeling curiously
let down, Caryn made for the door. But before

she opened it, he said: 'I suppose I've damned myself beyond all redemption!' and she looked back at him half uncertainly.

Then she gathered her composure. 'You simply proved the kind of man you are.'

His expression grew mocking. 'How convenient! Would it do any good to tell you that I had no intention of making love to you?'

'It's a little late—'

'No.' He shook his head. 'You mistake my meaning. I meant I didn't mean to—go to bed with you.'

Caryn gasped indignantly. 'I do not go to bed with men!'

'You will,' he assured her laconically, and then, as if bored by the conversation, he went to rescue the drink he had poured earlier.

Caryn hesitated. Whichever way she turned, he seemed to get the better of her. And in spite of everything that had gone before, she was suddenly loath to leave him thinking he had had the last word

'You—you believe I'd have gone to bed with you, don't you?' she persisted woodenly, and he turned to her, swallowing some of the whisky from his glass as he did so.

He wiped his mouth on the back of his hand, and then he said quietly: 'I wouldn't presume to anticipate such a thing. Why should you think I would?'

Caryn shifted from one foot to the other. 'But you said—'

'If you choose to interpret my words that way. . .' he shrugged, 'I can't stop you.'

'Why—why, you—'

He smiled rather sardonically. 'Go on, say it. It's been said before.'

'I bet it has!'

'But not by a woman,' he added mockingly, and without another word, she pulled open the door and left him.

CHAPTER SEVEN

DURING the following two weeks, Caryn saw nothing of her employer, and she told herself she was glad. The morning after the evening she had spent in his company, she had awakened with a definite feeling of apprehension, and it had not dispersed until she had discovered that Tristan had left for London again as abruptly as he had appeared. Exactly why he had come to Wales, she had no way of knowing, and she eventually assumed he had been assuring himself that she had plenty to do in his absence. Obviously after she had retired he had done some work, because in the morning she found several tapes awaiting her attention. At least his departure gave her a respite, and she supposed she ought to thank him for that.

Dave O'Hara turned up one afternoon towards the end of the second week and came strolling into the sitting room where Caryn was engaged in checking a report Tristan had left her to type. She wasn't enthusiastic at seeing him, but his whimsical smile begged forgiveness and she laid the report aside resignedly.

'How are you?' he asked, halting in the middle of the floor, his hands tucked carelessly into the pockets of a nylon jerkin he was wearing.

'I'm fine,' she replied, crossing her slim legs, realising as she did so that living by the sea was making her skin more gipsy-like than ever. 'What are you doing here?'

'Looking for you,' he declared honestly. 'I've got the bike outside. Come for a ride with me!'

'On a bike!' she exclaimed disbelievingly, and he laughed.

'A motor-bike! You know—put-put!'

Caryn had to smile at this, but she shook her head. 'I'm sorry, I can't.'

'Why not? You're not so busy. Tris hasn't been home for a couple of weeks.'

'How do you know that?'

'He told me.'

She stiffened. 'When?'

'At his pad. Last Sunday.'

'You were at Tri—Mr Ross's apartment last Sunday?'

'Sure,' Dave nodded, then pulled a reflective face. 'That was some party he gave.'

'He gave a party?'

Caryn felt singularly stupid repeating everything he said, but somehow she had not associated Tristan's absence with parties. And yet why shouldn't he entertain? Why *wouldn't* he? He was invited to plenty of functions, and he did know a lot of people.

She was annoyed now that she had let Dave see how his news had affected her, and his casual: 'Didn't you know?' left her in no doubt that he already knew the answer.

'It's nothing to do with me,' she demurred, picking up her typing again and shuffling the pages together. 'Now, if you'll excuse me. . .'

'Aw, come on!' Dave stepped in front of her

as she rose to pass him. 'Tris will be here at the weekend and then you'll tell me you have even less time.'

Caryn's fingers stilled. 'Er—Mr Ross is—coming here? At the weekend?'

Dave nodded impatiently. 'Yeah. He's bringing Melanie down for the weekend.'

Caryn's lips formed the word: 'Melanie?'

'Melanie Forbes! Surely you've heard of her.'

'*That Melanie!*' Caryn swallowed convulsively. Of course she had heard of Melanie Forbes. Who hadn't? She was a singer who had recently made her name as an actress as well, and because she was beautiful as well as talented her picture was always appearing in the papers. The fact that her father was Sir George Forbes had nothing to do with it, they said, even if he did run one of the larger television companies and spent a good deal of his time and money financing charity performances.

'Yes, that Melanie!' agreed Dave now, scuffing his boot against the soft carpet. 'So you're really determined not to come out with me?'

Caryn hesitated. Dave's news about Tristan bringing this girl down here for the weekend was disturbing, and she told herself it was because she was thinking of her nephew. Nevertheless, her taste for industry had waned somewhat, and she wasn't looking forward at all to the next few days.

Sensing her indecision, Dave pressed his advantage: 'You'd enjoy a ride, Caryn. It's stuffy in here. You'd be out in the open air—feeling the wind against your skin! You can always work at the weekend,' he added slyly.

Caryn looked at him uncertainly. 'I don't have a helmet.'

'Tris does. Borrow his.'

'I don't know where it is.'

'I'd guess it's in the garage,' Dave asserted dryly. 'Well? Are you coming?'

'All right.' Caryn gave in, but she looked down rather regretfully at her cotton sundress. 'I'll have to change.'

'Jeans and a shirt,' declared Dave firmly. 'That's all you need. I can supply the rest.' He grinned. 'And you can make what you like of that!'

Marcia looked disapproving when Caryn told her where she was going. For once she got her little notebook off the dresser in the kitchen and wrote: *TELL HIM NOT TO DRIVE TOO FAST!* in capital letters.

'I will,' said Caryn, touched by the woman's concern, and wondered not for the first time how Marcia, with her looks, came to be anyone's housekeeper.

Dave had recovered the helmet, and Caryn tried it on. It was a little big for her, but the strap tightened it under her chin. She felt ridiculous, and said so, but Dave just turned his thumbs up and grinned his approval.

Certainly, she decided later that afternoon, a motor-bike could weave its way through busy traffic more easily than a car. On roads jammed with holidaymakers, they passed them all, and reached the village of St Gifford in the late afternoon.

'Where are we going?' she asked, leaning over Dave's shoulder to voice the question, and he grinned.

'We're going to a party,' he averred, and saw her look of dismay before he added swiftly: 'Calm down! I'll have you home before dark.'

'But Marcia—'

'I told Marcia where we were going. The group are all here, and their girl-friends, and some other friends. We're going to have a barbecue on the beach.'

Caryn felt angry. 'You should have told me.'

'Why? Would you have come if you'd known?'

'No.'

'That's why I didn't tell you.'

'Oh, Dave!'

'No, that's not how you say it,' he teased. 'You say—oooh, Dave!' and he made it sound rather seductive, but Caryn was not in the mood for his humour.

St Gifford was smaller than Port Edward, just a collection of bungalows and cottages over-looking a narrow headland. Its main industry was fishing, and because of its size it didn't attract a lot of tourists.

Dave drove down on to the narrow quay, and then turned up a gravelled slope to where a rambling bungalow over-looked a narrow stretch of sand cut off from the small harbour by the sea wall. The sound of beat music drifted from the back of the house, and Caryn turned to Dave as he climbed off the bike.

'Whose bungalow is this?'

'Greg's,' he answered, mentioning the name

of one of the other members of Sweet Vibration.
'Does it matter who owns it? We all live here.'

'You do?'

'Well, sometimes,' he conceded good-
naturedly. 'Come on. I could sure use a beer!'

Caryn followed him reluctantly. She should
have stuck to her original intention and not gone
out with him, she thought ruefully. She had
allowed her feelings about Tristan to catapult her
into a situation she would dearly like to change.

They entered the bungalow through a wide
porch, and thence along a passage which ran from
front to back. They came out on a wide patio,
and were immediately greeted like long-lost
cousins. At least a dozen young people were
spread about on li-los and padded loungers, and
the music, louder here, came from the electronic
equipment wired from a room inside. Refriger-
ated trolleys clinked with cans of beer, and the
sickly scent of joss sticks was even evident
outdoors.

'Hi, there!' The strongly American-flavoured
drawl came from Allan Felix, the only transatlantic member of the group. He came to meet them
with a slim blonde girl clinging to his shoulder,
who cast slightly malicious looks at Caryn's vivid
darkness.

'You know Al, don't you?' Dave asked, putting
an arm round Caryn's shoulders and drawing her
forward, but she shook him off and nodded at the
American without enthusiasm.

'Say, you need a drink, I can see that,' Allan
exclaimed, his drooping moustache giving
character to his otherwise immature features.

'What'll it be? Beer? Lager? Coke?'

'Coke would be fine,' said Caryn, not really wanting anything and wanting his girl-friend's ire even less.

'That's Lindy,' Dave volunteered, as the blonde girl pouted after Allan, and Caryn gave him an indifferent stare.

Room was made for them on the loungers scattered about the paved area, and Caryn had to admire the sculptured stone tracery that bounded the patio, and the tumbling glory of honeysuckle and clematis that climbed about the lattice-work. The members of the group she knew by sight, of course, and one by one the others introduced themselves, most of the girls much less aggressive than Lindy. The uniform of the day seemed to be jeans and shirts, although one or two of the girls wore bikini bras underneath and had taken off their shirts.

Caryn guessed that most of the girls were younger than she was. The members of the group she was less sure about. Dave, she guessed, was in his late twenties, but Allan Felix and Greg Simons, and the drummer, Gene David, looked younger.

Allan returned with her Coke and as Dave was leaning over to talk to someone else, the American squatted down beside her.

'Don't I know you?' he asked, frowning, and she gave him an old-fashioned look.

'Techniques don't change, do they?' she countered. 'Why don't you try—*do you come here often*?'

Allan grinned. 'Point taken. But I meant it.

You do remind me of somebody. I don't know why—something about the eyes, I guess.'

A thought suddenly struck her, and she felt contrite. 'You might have known my sister,' she ventured reluctantly. 'Loren?'

'Loren Stevens! Of course.' He knew who she meant at once. 'That's your sister? Hey—how is she?'

Caryn licked her lips. 'She's dead.'

'Dead?' He stared at her aghast. 'God, I'm sorry.' Lindy came to hang over his shoulder, and he glanced round at her impatiently. When she didn't take the hint, he elbowed her away, saying: 'Push off!' She went with a heightening of colour, and Caryn felt dreadful.

Feeling she had to say something, she asked: 'Er—did you know Loren well?' but he shook his head.

'Not very. She was always around the house, you know. I guess Dave knew her better than we did.'

'I see.' Caryn's eyes flickered reflectively over the other boy. Of course, Dave being a friend of Tristan's, he was bound to have seen more of her than any of the others.

'So. . .' Allan clearly wanted to change the subject. 'You're working for Tris now. How do you get on with Angel?'

Caryn was non-committal. 'I hardly know her. She's been away for the last month.'

'Cool!' he grinned. 'But keep away from Dave when she's around. She doesn't like competition.'

'Dave?' Caryn was surprised, and hearing his name mentioned he turned back to her.

'You called?' he asked teasingly, but she just coloured and shook her head and applied herself to her Coke.

In spite of the fact that there was a ready supply of food and drink, and lively company, Caryn soon got bored. She wasn't too, interested in drinking except when she was thirsty, and the scent of the joss sticks was not one she enjoyed. Everyone else drank pretty steadily throughout the afternoon and early evening, and by the time they began to set up the barbecue on the beach, they were all, with the possible exception of Lindy, slightly drunk. Caryn was not a prude, but she deplored their behaviour, and the idea of riding back to Port Edward on the back of Dave's bike filled her with misgivings. He ought not to be driving anywhere, and she wished she had suggested coming in her car. But then she had not known their destination, or that they were staying all evening.

She went into the bungalow once to use the bathroom, and wondered if there was a telephone. Perhaps if she rang Druid's Fleet and asked Marcia to come and get her? The housekeeper knew how to drive, and there was a Mini that she used to go shopping in Carmarthen. Maybe if she just told her what was going on she would feel better.

She met Lindy in the hall as she came out of the bathroom, and on impulse, she asked her if there was a telephone.

'Why d'you wanna know?' she demanded sulkily, and Caryn sighed.

'I want to ring home—that is, to the place where I live.'

'Why?'

'I'd like to leave,' declared Caryn, taking the chance that as Lindy had no love for her she might be glad to see the back of her.

'You wanna leave?' Lindy looked suspicious. 'You and who else?'

'Only me,' exclaimed Caryn, in a low tone, aware that any minute one of the others could come upon them. 'Please. Is there a phone?'

'Sure. There's one in there,' replied Lindy, gesturing with her thumb towards a door to one side of the front porch, and thanking her, Caryn hurried towards it.

The room she entered was a living room, and judging from the smell of tobacco smoke it was seldom aired. But sure enough, there was a telephone by the couch, and she closed the door and went eagerly towards it.

It took her a few seconds to find the code for Port Edward, but she knew Tristan's number by heart, and she dialled the figures with trembling fingers. It seemed to ring for an age before anyone answered it, and when the receiver was lifted, the voice that gave the number was masculine.

She was silent for a moment, and he repeated the number, and with bated breath, she said: '*Tristan!* Tristan, is that you?'

'Caryn?' He sounded surprised. Then, more sharply: 'Is something wrong?'

Caryn's brain worked furiously. Why was Tristan there? Was he alone? Or was Melanie Forbes with him?

'I—why—no,' she answered him now, before adding quickly: 'Could I speak to Marcia, please?'

'Marcia?' His voice had cooled perceptibly. 'Caryn, where are you?'

'Oh, please, I don't have much time. . .'

Caryn could hear voices in the hall outside, and she was terrified someone would come in and ask her what the hell she thought she was doing.

'*Caryn!*' Her name grated now. 'Where are you? I want to know.'

'Didn't Marcia explain?'

'Marcia wrote a note that told me only that Dave was taking you out for a meal, and then to the pictures in Carmarthen.'

'Oh, lord!'

Her troubled words were audible to him, and she heard his baffled oath. 'If you don't tell me where you are, I warn you, when you get back here—'

'I'm at a place called St Gifford,' she confessed hastily.

'St Gifford!' She sensed his anger now. 'At Greg Simons' place?'

'Yes. . .'

'God Almighty! What are you doing there?'

'I—I didn't know where we were going,' she began, but he cut her off.

'I'll be there in a little under an hour!' he snapped harshly, and the phone went dead.

She was emerging from the living room when she saw Dave coming looking for her. 'What have you been doing?' he exclaimed, his eyes moving past her to the living room door, and she made an awkward gesture.

'I've just been looking around,' she replied offhandedly, and although he looked suspicious for a moment, he had other things on his mind.

'Well, come on,' he urged. 'We've got the barbecue going, and Greg wants to know how you like your steak.'

Caryn accompanied him across the patio and down the rocky steps to the beach. It was gritty sand, and scratched her toes, but she kept her discomfort to herself, and sat on one end of a wooden seat, knees drawn up, wondering in an agony of apprehension what Tristan would do. The others had set a transistor going and were making hilarious attempts at dancing on the sand, but when Dave tried to persuade her to join them, she shook her head, pretending she was watching Greg cook the steaks.

Lindy sidled across to her, and quirked an eyebrow. 'Well?' she demanded. 'Did you find it?'

Caryn frowned at her, wishing she would keep her voice down, but Allan overhearing them asked: 'Find it? Find what?'

'The loo, stupid!' replied Lindy shortly, and Caryn breathed more freely.

The charcoal got too hot and the first lot of steaks blackened unappetisingly. Another batch were rescued from the kitchen and Caryn glanced surreptitiously at her watch. It was after eight o'clock. How much longer was Tristan going to be? She found she was waiting for his arrival with almost desperate anticipation.

Dave came back to her, tailed by a redhead

who had shed her shirt and jeans to reveal a black bikini. 'Come on,' he said, raising the can of beer he carried to his lips. 'You ain't havin' any fun!'

Caryn ignored him, and suddenly his hand shot out and caught a handful of her hair. 'Don't you turn your back on me!' he told her angrily, and she winced as her scalp tingled from the fierceness of his hold on her hair.

'Leave her be!' The redhead gazed up at him impatiently. 'Come'n, dance with me.'

Dave released Caryn's hair, but his mouth was aggressive. 'What is it with you?' he demanded. 'Loren used not to be so standoffish.'

Caryn stared at him contemptuously, and as she did so, she heard Allan give a low whistle. 'Look who's here! The boss man himself.'

Both Dave and Caryn turned to see Tristan coming down the steps, lean and disturbingly familiar in dark blue corded pants and a matching shirt. But he was not alone. A slender reed of a girl was with him, her honey-brown hair secured back from her face with an orange velvet band. Her dress was orange too, long and silky, and obviously unsuitable for a barbecue on the beach. Caryn knew who she was at once. Melanie Forbes, in the flesh.

Dave cast a curious look in Caryn's direction as he went to greet the newcomers. 'You're just in time,' he declared expansively, gesturing towards the barbecue. 'Steaks for everyone!'

'Not for me, darling!' Melanie obviously knew the group. 'Steaks are much too fattening!'

Tristan's eyes had sought and found Caryn's, but she didn't move. She couldn't help it, but she resented the fact that he had brought his girl-friend with him. Why couldn't he have come alone? Wasn't it embarrassing enough?

'So what gives?' asked Greg, going to join them, but before Tristan could explain, Melanie exclaimed:

'Where's Tris's secretary? That's why we're here. Apparently she wants to go home!'

Caryn's face went first scarlet, then white, as they all turned to look at her. She had never felt so small in her life, and she stared down miserably at her toes.

'It's my fault.' She heard Tristan's voice through the mists of agonised embarrassment. 'I told Caryn I was taking her back,' he stated calmly, although as she ventured to look at him she saw different emotions smouldering in the depths of the tawny eyes. 'She rang Marcia to tell her she'd be late, and I'm afraid I blew my top.'

Only Dave appeared to doubt this. 'Caryn rang Marcia?' he echoed. 'She didn't tell me.'

'Is there any reason why she should?' enquired Tristan evenly, and suddenly another note had entered the proceedings.

'Oh, come on, darling!' Melanie tugged at Tristan's arm. 'For goodness' sake, where is she? Then we can go. You promised we'd go to the Donnellys' later.'

Caryn got up off the bench and came towards them. 'I'm here,' she said clearly, and saw the disparaging look Melanie cast in her direction. She guessed she did deserve it at that. She hadn't combed her hair since riding the motorbike, and it tangled curls framed her face like a dark halo.

Her make-up was non-existent, but the dusky tan of her skin needed little in the way of cosmetics, if she had but known it.

Tristan indicated that she should precede them up the steps, and with an apologetic farewell to the others, Caryn went ahead. She went through the house and out through the porch, stopping beside the grey Mercedes almost reluctantly.

Tristan passed Melanie and swung open the rear passenger door. He looked at Caryn and her lids lowered mutinously as she obediently got into the back of the car. He slammed the door behind her, and then smiled his apology at Melanie for keeping her waiting.

'I didn't introduce you,' he said, as he levered himself behind the wheel, beside the other girl. 'Caryn, this is Melanie; Melanie—Caryn.'

Melanie barely glanced round at the third passenger, but pulled a face at Tristan. 'Honestly, darling,' she said, as they pulled away, 'was it necessary to speak to Dave like that? In front of all his friends?'

Tristan made no answer, and she tried again: 'Don't you think this whole thing is rather silly? I mean, it's obvious Miss—Miss—'

'Stevens,' supplied Caryn stiffly, and was rewarded by a slight smile.

'—Stevens, then; it's obvious Miss Stevens is perfectly old enough to take care of herself!'

'Just mind your own business, will you, Melanie?' he suggested, showing none of the charm which Caryn knew he could exert when he chose, and the girl beside him turned to stare sulkily out of the window.

But by the time they reached Druid's Fleet she had come round again, and was talking quite animatedly about some friends called Beth and Peter, whose party she wanted them to attend later.

Tristan turned between the gates of the drive and let the Mercedes coast down to the door. At once Caryn thrust open her door and got out, but by the time she had circled the car to the porch, he was beside her.

'I want to talk to you,' he said quietly, and she glanced back at Melanie, still in the car.

'Not now,' she protested pointedly, but he nodded his head.

'Right now.'

'But Melanie—'

'Leave Melanie to me,' he stated grimly, and thrust open the door into the hall.

Caryn preceded him inside and stood looking at him uncertainly. It was worse than suffering Laurence's disapproval, she thought, and she resented his attitude. She hadn't asked him to come and fetch her. He had taken that decision. And yet he seemed to be blaming her for what happened.

'I'm sorry,' she said, deciding to take the bull by the horns. 'I've spoiled your evening.'

'You have a habit of doing that,' he retorted, pushing the door to behind them, but not securing it. 'Whatever possessed you to go off with O'Hara?'

'I didn't go off with O'Hara! I've told you, I thought we were just going for a ride.'

He gave her a narrow look. 'Yet Marcia maintains that he told her he was taking you to the cinema.'

'I can't help that.'

'You deny you knew you were going to the cinema?'

'I? Deny it?' She stared indignantly at him. 'Why should I deny it? I'm not a liar.'

'Aren't you?'

Caryn stared at him in silence for a few moments, her mouth working impotently, and then without another word she turned and ran up the stairs and along the corridor to her room.

She leant back against the closed door, trying to still the racing of her heart, and then gasped when it was suddenly propelled inward. Tristan stood just inside the door, and when she would have evaded him, he caught her shoulder and pressed the door closed again with her against it.

'Wh-what do you think you're doing?' she blurted. 'This is my room!' but her words made no difference to the metallic hardness of his eyes.

'I said I wanted to talk to you, and if we have to do it here, that's okay by me,' he stated, one hand on either side of her now, imprisoning her against the glossy panels of the door. 'Do you realise this is the second time in as many weeks that you've disrupted my life?'

'I've told you I'm sorry. What more can I say?'

'What exactly did Dave say to you?'

'Does it matter?'

'I think so.'

She sighed, shifting restively. 'He said——how would I like to go for a ride!'

'And you went——just like that?'

'No.' Caryn denied it, and then qualified the negation by adding: 'Why shouldn't I, anyway?'

'You're asking me that? After tonight's little fiasco?'

She bent her head. 'They didn't do anything. . .'

'I see.' His voice was incisive. 'So you'd have stayed there if I hadn't come to fetch you?'

'I didn't have much choice, did I?'

He straightened, his arms falling to his sides. 'I can see I'm wasting my time in talking to you. I foolishly imagined your phone call was a cry for help!'

He moved away from her, and at once she felt a heel. Her motive for ringing Marcia had been one of distress, and he had not been mistaken in recognising that note of panic in her voice.

'I'd better go,' he said, running an exploring hand over the buttons of his shirt, checking that they were all in place. One had come unloosened in his exchange with Caryn, and his fingers moved to fasten it while she watched feeling miserable. But when the button stubbornly refused to go into its hole, she stepped forward and said jerkily: 'Let me!'

Her nails brushed his chest as she went to fasten the button, scraping against the fine covering of sun-bleached hair that curled upon itself. It made what she was doing that much more intimate somehow, and her gaze darted up to his almost apologetically.

'You should have told me to mind my own business,' he said as she secured the button, and much against her will her fingers lingered against the silken feel of his shirt, wanting to stay his departure.

'You—you were right,' she confessed in a low voice. 'I did want to get away from there. They—they were drinking too much, and—and I was afraid that Dave might—might—'

'—get the wrong idea?' he finished softly, and she nodded.

'I really didn't know where he was taking me, and when I found out. . .'

'You panicked?'

'Something like that.'

'Oh, Caryn!' The urgency in his voice caused her to look up at him, but he put her away from him and went towards the door. 'I'll have Marcia bring you up a tray,' he added more gently, and she realised he was feeling sorry for her now.

Perversely, this knowledge did not please her. She didn't want his sympathy, she thought with a return of anger. She didn't want him going back to Melanie and telling her what a fool Dave had made of her. Melanie would like that, she decided maliciously, without possessing a shred of proof to justify her belief.

'Don't bother,' she retorted now as he reached for the handle. 'I'll speak to Marcia myself. You look after Melanie. I'm sure she'll reward you more than adequately for anything you do for her.'

Tristan stiffened. 'What do you mean by that?'

'Nothing.' Caryn moved her shoulders off-handedly. 'You'd better hurry. I don't suppose she likes being kept waiting any more than you do.'

'You little bitch!' He stared at her furiously. 'You know damn all about it!'

Caryn shrugged. 'Dave told me who her daddy was.'

'Oh, did he?' Tristan took a step towards her. 'When was this? Before or after the joyride?'

Caryn scuffed her toe. 'Does it matter?'

'It might. If I thought you were jealous—and that was why you chose to go out with O'Hara!'

'*Jealous!*' Caryn's laugh was cracked. 'You must be joking!'

'Must I?' He didn't look convinced.

'Oh, go to hell!' she declared shortly, and turned her back on him.

She heard his angry ejaculation, and then hard hands gripped her arms, jerking her back against him. For several seconds he just held her there, imprisoned against him, and then, when she started to struggle, he twisted her round and covered her mouth with his own.

His lips bruised hers, but when she tried to speak against him her parting lips only made his kiss that much more intimate. Gradually weakness took the place of aggression. In a short time she was kissing him back, which was all the more degrading when she knew his strongest emotion at that moment was anger.

He was wanting to hurt her but, in spite of himself, she felt the moment when her closeness began to arouse him against his will. The throbbing pressure that surged between them was something she had never felt before, and a low groan escaped him as he realised what was happening.

'*God!*' he muttered thickly, staring down at her, his hands on her shoulders inside the unbuttoned neckline of her shirt, and then, with an obvious effort, he dragged himself away from her and made it to the door.

'Tris. . .' she whispered huskily, gazing after him, but the door slammed hollowly behind him.

CHAPTER EIGHT

SHE had gone into the bathroom to rinse her hot face in cold water when someone knocked at her bedroom door. Guessing it might be Miss Trewen, Caryn hastily fastened her shirt across her breasts as she walked back into the bedroom. But before she had time to call: 'Who is it?' her door opened and Melanie appeared.

Caryn was so astounded to see the other girl, her first reaction was one of guilt, and she could feel the revealing colour staining her cheeks.

'Did you want something?' she asked, trying to behave normally, and Melanie regarded her without liking.

'Is Tristan here?' she asked, looking about her, and Caryn pushed her hands into her hip pockets to hide their trembling.

'Tris—Mr Ross?' she asked unevenly. 'Why, no!'

'But he was with you a few minutes ago, wasn't he?' exclaimed Melanie impatiently. 'I heard you arguing downstairs when I was waiting in the car.'

Caryn absorbed this, and then shook her head. 'I'm afraid I don't know where he is now.' That at least was true!

'Huh!' Melanie took another look around the bedroom. Then she leaned on the door-knob and said: 'This is a nice room, isn't it? Much nicer than mine, actually.' As Caryn didn't know what to say to that, she remained silent, and Melanie continued: 'How long have you been here? I can't remember when it was Tristan said he employed you.'

Her meaning was obvious. She wanted to make their respective positions clear right from the outset, and Caryn wondered why she wanted to argue with her. It was unlikely that their paths would cross very often—unless Tristan married her.

But that eventuality she forced aside, along with her own attraction towards him, and the disturbing realisation that if she stayed here, sooner or later she might find herself as helpless in his hands as Loren had been.

All the same, she wondered where he had gone when he left her, and the possible solution brought another wave of colour into her cheeks.

'I—I've been here nearly six weeks,' she said now, suddenly becoming aware that Melanie was getting impatient, and the other girl frowned.

'That long? Don't you find it rather lonely here, with only Marcia for company?'

'You're forgetting the child and his nurse, Melanie,' Tristan remarked behind her, and she swung round to gaze at him in teasing disapproval.

'So there you are!' she exclaimed, and hearing the faint edge to her voice, Caryn decided her irritation was not all pretence. 'Where have you been?'

Tristan came into view, changed now into cream suede slacks and a matching fine wool jerkin. 'I was—hot,' he explained, his eyes flick-

ering coldly over Caryn before melting into
Melanie's. 'I took a quick shower. Forgive me.'

Melanie's fingers slid between his and gripped
his palm. 'Can we go to the Donnellys' now?'
she asked, moving so that her small breasts
brushed his arm, and Caryn looked away.

'I don't see why not,' he agreed mildly, and
with a fleeting glance in Caryn's direction, he
drew Melanie outside and closed the door.

Caryn slept badly. She blamed it on the salmon
Marcia had prepared for supper, but in all honesty
she knew her problems were mental rather than
physical. After Tristan and Melanie had left, she
too had taken a shower, but instead of cooling
her blood it had quickened it, and she lay there
in the moonlit shadows wondering how much
longer it would be before Tristan and his girl-
friend returned from their party. At three o'clock
she fell into an uneasy slumber from which she
was awakened some time later by the sound of a
closing door. Guessing her employer was home,
she expelled her breath on a long sigh, but
although she waited until the dawn light was
colouring the eastern sky, she heard no sound of
a second door closing.

In consequence she overslept, and it was after
nine before the brightness of her room alerted her
to the fact that it was Friday and her employer
might well be waiting for her to take dictation.

She forwent her shower and washed and
dressed quickly in a navy blue shirtwaister, with
elbow-length sleeves. She seldom wore tights
these days, but today she put some on, and a

pair of heeled shoes instead of her sandals.

She was hurrying down the split-level hall to the study when she encountered Marcia coming from the opposite direction. They both stopped, and Caryn quickly asked if Tristan was waiting for her, but Marcia merely shook her head. Smiling, she put her palms together and placed them against her bent cheek, signifying as clearly as any words that their employer was still in bed.

Caryn's shoulders sagged. 'I thought he might be waiting for me.' She gave a rueful smile. 'I overslept, too.'

Marcia shook her head, and taking the girl's arm, drew her back along the hall and through the door that led to the kitchen. Miming raising a cup to her lips, Marcia raised her eyebrows, and Caryn nodded.

'Yes,' she said, 'I would like some coffee. And some toast, too, if it's not too much trouble.'

Miss Trewen came in as Caryn was finishing her breakfast, carrying the baby. At almost five months, he could hold his head quite erect, and responded with a gurgling smile to anyone's attention.

Immediately Caryn got up to take him from the nurse, and Miss Trewen surrendered him gladly.

'He's been awake half the night,' she exclaimed, lifting the lid of the coffee pot anticipatorily. 'Is there another cup, do you think?'

Caryn pushed Tristan's fingers out of her mouth, and giggled as he tangled them in her hair. 'Have you been a naughty boy?' she exclaimed, finding an escape from her own problems in playing with him, and he blew bubbles in her face.

'Mr Ross has a guest staying, did you know?' the nurse asked, after Marcia had provided her with a fresh pot of coffee, and Caryn nodded, glad of the distraction of the child to hide her real feelings.

'I—met her last night,' she answered, pushing her face close to Tristan's, and as she did so she was struck by a fleeting glimpse of familiarity. It was gone in a second, but the impression lingered, teasing her memory by its lack of definition. She frowned into the baby's eyes, seeking to redis-cover that trace of identity, and turned to the door almost apprehensively when it unexpectedly opened.

It was Tristan who came in, looking much the worse for his late night. His deep-set eyes were pouched and lacklustre, and deep lines were etched beside his mouth. He was wearing a navy towelling robe over white silk pyjama trousers, and it was the first time Caryn had seen him without his day clothes. In consequence, her eyes lingered on him longer than was necessary and eventually encountered the chilling depths of his. Then he switched his attention to the baby in her arms, and she felt desperately vulnerable at that moment. After all, the child's future depended on her maintaining a working relationship with this man, and last night she had done much to destroy it.

He seemed surprised to find the three women of his household all together, and Miss Trewen immediately began to make excuses for being there.

'Tristan's beginning to cut a tooth, Mr Ross,'

she exclaimed apologetically, 'and I've had quite a wakeful night.'

The smile he gave her was wry. 'I've had one of those myself, Miss Trewen,' he assured her, his words cutting through Caryn's defences without effort. 'Don't hurry away on my account. Marcia, do we have any magnesia?' Marcia gave him a look of disapproval, and his response was good-natured. 'I know, I know—I drink too much. But do we have any?'

Caryn felt Miss Trewen beside her and would have surrendered the baby to her, only Tristan chose that moment to come across himself and speak to the child. It necessitated him coming close to Caryn, and the wide bottoms of his pyjama trousers actually brushed her ankles. He allowed his namesake to grasp one of his fingers, and judging from the way the baby responded to him it was not the first time he had spoken to him. Then, under cover of the baby's gurgling, Tristan's eyes moved to Caryn, and he said cynically:

'And you said babies didn't interest you!'

'This baby does,' she murmured huskily, and his lips curled.

'I wonder. Perhaps I should be flattered at the attention you pay—*my* son!'

Caryn glanced at Miss Trewen in an agonised way, but fortunately she was looking the other way and Tristan's words had been so low as to be scarcely audible even to her. Nevertheless, she moved away from him, taking the baby out of reach of his fingers and arousing a cry of protest because of that. But at least it brought Miss

Trewen's attention back to her charge, and she lifted him out of Caryn's arms with a murmur of reproval.

'Come along,' she said. 'It's time for our nap, isn't it?'

Marcia set a bottle of magnesia down on the table with a force that made the coffee cups rattle, and Miss Trewen disappeared as Marcia began to remonstrate with her employer by means of hand signals.

Tristan glanced round at Caryn, and his expression was mocking. 'You should enjoy this,' he drawled. 'Marcia is telling me what a fool I am.'

Caryn coloured. 'I'll go along to the study, Mr Ross,' she stated, moving towards the door, and he shrugged his acquiescence. 'Will you be working this morning?'

Tristan swallowed some of the magnesia from a spoon, and grimaced expressively. Then he wiped his mouth with the back of his hand, and regarded her sourly.

'You can have the next few days off,' he declared at last. 'Melanie's father will be joining us here for the weekend, and although some of our talk will be business, you don't need to be involved.'

'I see.' Caryn felt suddenly flat. 'But I don't mind working.'

Tristan's nostrils flared. 'I've told you—take some time off.' He paused. 'Go to London, why don't you? See that friend of yours in Bloomsbury.'

'Laura?' Caryn caught her lower lip between

her teeth, feeling suddenly guilty. Apart from a letter after they had arrived in Port Edward she had not corresponded with Laura, and she realised with a pang that her time for having the baby must be getting very near.

'What's the matter?' Seemingly he could ignore Marcia's unobtrusive presence. 'I thought you'd welcome the chance to get away from here for a few days.'

Caryn caught her breath. 'Per-perhaps I would.' She smoothed her moist palms down the skirt of her dress. 'When do you want me to leave?'

'When do I—' He broke off abruptly, his face contorted with sudden anger, and his hands sought the corded tie of his bathrobe. 'I think I'd better get dressed. I'll speak to you in the study in fifteen minutes, Miss Stevens!'

Alone with Marcia, she shifted awkwardly, but the housekeeper just pulled a sympathetic face and Caryn felt a surge of affection for the other woman. Without Tristan's disruptive presence, Druid's Fleet had become a real home to her, and it was that much more painful to feel she was being excluded from it.

In the study, she tidied her desk, filed away the copies of the report she had been typing the day before, and checked that all the dictaphone tapes were stacked in their box. Then she moved to Tristan's desk, gathering up his pens and slotting them back into their holder. She had seated herself in his chair to put some files back in a lower drawer when the door opened and he came in. Immediately, her instinct was to spring to her feet and return to her own desk, but something, some rebellious spirit kept her where she was.

He had had a shower, and the thick smoothness of his hair lay like wet silk against his head. His brown velvet jerkin matched the colour of his denims, and their narrowness accentuated the lean strength of his hips and the powerful muscles between.

He closed the door and leaned back against it for a moment before straightening and walking towards her. He halted before the desk, folding his arms, feet apart, and said: 'How does it feel?'

Caryn's palms moulded the leather seat. 'Very—comfortable.'

'You think so?' There was no trace of humour in his face, and she felt uncomfortable.

'Why did you want to speak to me?' she prompted, but he continued to look down at her with such a brooding expression that she was forced to take action. Pushing back the chair, she got to her feet and came round the desk, only to find he had stepped into her path.

'Did you sleep well?' he demanded unexpectedly, and she gulped.

'Did I sleep well?' she echoed. 'What's that to you?'

'I'd like to know whether you were able to lay your head on the pillow and coax the mists of Morpheus after what you did to me!' he declared savagely. 'I like to know what I'm dealing with! I Whether the *lady* has a conscience!'

Caryn trembled. 'Mr Ross,' she began unsteadily, 'I'd like to apologise for—for what I said last ni—'

'Like hell you would!' His hands descended on her shoulders, cruelly penetrating. 'What's caused this sudden change of heart, I wonder?' He frowned. 'Why should you apologise to me? It's not in character. Unless. . .' His eyes narrowed. 'Unless you're afraid I'll turn you— and junior—out!'

'All right!' She almost shouted the words at him. 'All right. That's the truth!' You hold us both in the palm of your hand, don't you? Well, there's nothing I can do about that, not right now, and if I have to grovel—well, I guess I'll do that too!' She paused only long enough to take a breath. 'But don't think you can make me feel guilt for the way you feel this morning, because you can't! I didn't do anything to you that a couple of hours spent with Melanie Forbes wouldn't put right, and you spent more than a couple of hours with her, didn't you? In fact, I wouldn't be surprised if you spent the whole night with her! It's such a saving on bed-linen, isn't it?' she flung at him.

There was an awful silence after that, only broken by the steady ticking of the clock on the mantelshelf, and the tortured sound of her breathing. Caryn's spirits plummeted. Oh God! she thought. She had really done it now! How on earth could she justify an accusation like that?

His hands fell from her shoulders and he looked down at them as if they might have been contaminated. 'That's what you think, is it?' he asked expressionlessly, and her nerves jangled discordantly. 'Would you have thought better of me if I had slept with you?'

Caryn's throat contracted. 'No—'

'But you knew what you'd done,' he persisted. 'Why shouldn't I have—relieved my frustrations with someone else?'

Caryn's breath caught and held. 'Is that your excuse?' she choked, and his lips twisted.

'According to your opinion of me, I don't need an excuse. What are you afraid of, Caryn? That I might make Melanie pregnant, too? And marry her?'

Caryn couldn't take any more of this. 'If you want me out of the house for the weekend, then I'll go,' she stated tightly, and saw the contempt in his eyes.

'Oh, yes,' he said bitterly, 'I want you out of the house for the weekend. But not for the reasons you think. Now, get the hell out of here before I do something to cripple that sordid little mind of yours!'

She was reaching for the door handle when Melanie's face appeared coyly round the corner of the panelling. Her expression changed sharply when she saw Caryn, and then dimpled once more when she glimpsed Tristan by the desk.

'Oh, you are here, darling!' she exclaimed, widening the aperture to reveal a pink flowered cotton wrapper that moulded her small pointed breasts. 'I thought that was what Marcia was trying to tell me. Honestly, darling, I don't know how you stand having her about the place—not being able to take any messages, or answer the phone.'

'Marcia suits me,' he stated grimly, and Caryn

recognised the note of thinly-veiled anger in his voice if Melanie didn't.

'I know you feel responsible for her, darling,' she went on, unwittingly provoking, 'but it wasn't your fault that her husband and her baby were slaughtered by those crazy African tribesmen—'

'Leave it, Melanie!'

As in the car the evening before, he silenced her with a curt rejoinder, and Melanie's cheeks bloomed with unbecoming colour. Caryn decided it was time she was gone, and with a muffled word of apology, she brushed past the other girl and walked quickly up the corridor.

But in her room her shoulders sagged weakly. Considering it was barely ten o'clock, it had been a gruelling day so far. But at least Melanie's careless words had revealed a little of Marcia's background, and imagining the horrifying scenes she must have witnessed, Caryn felt an over-whelming sense of pity for her. How she came to be working for Tristan, she could only guess, but reluctantly she had to concede that giving the woman a home and a purpose in life was the kind of thing he would do.

After packing her case, she went along to the nursery to tell Miss Trewen she was going away for the weekend. The nurse was busy tidying the room after putting Tristan down for his morning sleep, but she smiled when Caryn came in.

'I wanted to have a private word with you, Miss Stevens,' she said, and Caryn's already taut nerves stretched.

'You did?'

'Yes.' Miss Trewen rummaged in her capacious handbag and came out with a letter. 'This came this morning. It's from an old college friend of mine. I wrote to her soon after we came here. She lives in Aberystwyth, you see, and I hoped she might suggest a meeting.'

Caryn tensed as she guessed what was coming. 'And she has?'

'She wants me to spend a day with her, actually,' admitted Miss Trewen eagerly. 'Do you think Sunday would be all right?'

'Sunday?' Caryn swallowed with difficulty. 'Well. . .'

'I'm sure Mr Ross won't mind. I mean, it has been six weeks. . .'

'Oh, yes, indeed.' Caryn forced a faint smile. 'You're—entitled to it, naturally.' She bit her lip. 'I—yes, Sunday would be fine.'

'Oh, good. I thought I would ring her this afternoon, if it was all right.'

Caryn nodded. 'As a matter of fact, I—er—I'm going away myself today.'

'You are?' Miss Trewen looked surprised. 'Well, well. Two minds with but a single thought.'

'Yes.' Caryn made a casual movement of her shoulders. 'I'd better be going.'

'You'll be back tonight?'

'Er—no. Tomorrow.'

'Tomorrow! I see. Mr Ross doesn't need you.'

'It was his idea, actually,' Caryn confessed reluctantly, and the nurse looked concerned.

'Oh, dear! Am I spoiling your weekend?'

'Heavens, no!' Caryn wondered why the idea

of coming back a day earlier than expected filled
her with relief. One day less for Tristan to decide
he could do without her, she pondered uneasily,
and walked towards the door. 'See you tomorrow
evening, then.'

Miss Trewen nodded. 'Have a good time,' she
urged, and Caryn swallowed back the impulse to
admit that she didn't really want to go at all.

CHAPTER NINE

SHE felt guilty about her lack of enthusiasm when she met Laura. The other girl was obviously so delighted to see her, and exclaimed at once how well Caryn was looking.

'How lucky you are, living by the sea!' she said enviously, and studying Laura's heated face and swollen ankles, Caryn wondered how she could ever have thought that London was a suitable place to bring up a family.

'There are advantages,' she admitted now, coming into Laura's flat which, in spite of its size, was always so beautifully clean. 'Where's Bob?'

'Where do you think?' Laura pulled a face. 'Working.' She sighed. 'If only he could get a job out of the city, so we could buy a house in the country! But on his salary. . .'

She trudged into the kitchen to put on the kettle, and Caryn wandered to the window. Outside the chimneypots of London were no substitute for the wide reaches of the estuary, and the traffic that hooted two floors below was an assault to ears attuned to the gentler sounds of the river.

Laura came back into the room and flopped down into a chair. 'Three more weeks of this!' she declared, fanning herself with a newspaper. 'I don't know if I can stand it.'

Caryn looked at her sympathetically. 'How do you manage the stairs?'

162

'I don't. Except when I have to attend the clinic. Bob does all the shopping for us, and I'm stuck up here from dawn till dusk waiting for him to come home.'

'But what about your mother?' exclaimed Caryn, remembering the rather sour-faced woman who had been an occasional visitor at the flat, but Laura shook her head.

'She never got on with Bob, you know that. And—well, after you left there was an awful row one evening about me being here alone all the time, with no one to turn to if the baby should come early.'

'But what about the other flat?'

'It hasn't been let yet. I've heard that the land-lady's daughter is going to take it when she gets married, in October. But I don't know if that's true or not.'

'Oh, Laura!' Caryn felt really worried about her friend now. 'Your mother's right, you know. You should have someone you could call on.'

'Who do you suggest? Mr Sugden? Or that awful Miss Peel?'

Caryn frowned. 'Well, Mr Sugden is at work all day himself,' she said reflectively, understanding Laura's reluctance to speak to him. Word had it that he was a divorcee, but privately they both thought he was rather a peculiar fellow, in more ways than one. Miss Peel was another matter. Only about ten years older than Caryn, she had the first floor front, and although she had no obvious means of support, she never seemed short of gentlemen callers. Neither of them were what Caryn would have termed 'approachable' and her concern for her friend increased.

'Well,' she said now, seeing how depressed Laura was beginning to look, 'if you've got somewhere I can sleep, I can stay until tomorrow, and I insist on doing the weekend's shopping as I'm here.'

'Oh, Caryn!'

To her consternation, she saw a tear trickling down Laura's cheek, but with a determination she was far from feeling, she ignored it, and marching into the kitchen made the tea. By the time she came back, Laura had herself in control again, and Caryn managed to divert her by telling her how baby Tristan was developing, and describing in ludicrous detail her own experiences at the hands of Sweet Vibration. She omitted all references to Tristan Ross, however, and the small voice inside her that monitored her true feelings chided her for being a coward.

The two days went remarkably quickly. Going to the stores for Laura, Caryn realised how out of touch with the prices of things she had become, and how soon she had adapted to her new way of life. It was dangerous, she reflected, climbing the stairs to the flat again. Sooner or later, the position with Tristan was going to become untenable, and she would find it doubly hard to take up her old life if she let all the threads of it escape her. She tried not to think what she would do if he did decide to fire her. Or indeed how baby Tristan would fare without his father's patronage. . .

Laura's husband, Bob, was grateful for her visit.

'Laura gets few visitors these days,' he told her, when his wife was out of the room. 'I worry about her, but what can I do? Someone has to earn the bread.'

'I wish there was something I could do,' confessed Caryn with a sigh. 'I feel a heel for abandoning her right at the time the baby's due.'

Bob nodded, then glancing surreptitiously behind him, he whispered: 'Look, don't say anything to her, will you, but I'm going for an interview next week, with Area-South Television. If I get the job, we may just be able to afford a house, out near the studios at Willesden.'

'Oh, Bob!' Caryn's face flushed with pleasure. 'That would be marvellous!'

'I know.' He hunched his shoulders. 'The only thing is, as I've had no experience in television, my chances are practically nil!'

Caryn's excitement evaporated. 'And is it compulsory? Having experience, I mean?'

'No. But if a guy goes along who has experience—well, I guess I'm out of the running.'

Caryn frowned, thinking hard. Area-South Television. Wasn't that the company Melanie's father controlled? Her brain ran on. Maybe it wasn't entirely ethical to think the way she was doing, but Bob and Laura deserved a break. If the other applicants were already working in television, the chances were they were already earning twice as much as Bob, and therefore not half so desperate. But, and this was the crunch, how could she expect Melanie to help her? The girl didn't even like her, and although the feeling was mutual, Melanie had had the added insult of

Tristan setting her down twice in Caryn's presence.

Tristan!

Of course. He was the logical person to ask. But how could she ask him for anything after the way she had behaved?

Bob, who had been watching the play of emotions across her expressive face, now leaned towards her. 'Caryn,' he said, and she looked at him questioningly. 'Look, I don't like putting this to you, but—well, I happen to know Tristan Ross has shares in Area-South. You couldn't see your way clear to—putting in a word for me, could you?'

Caryn stared at him. 'Oh, Bob—'

'I know, it's a bloody cheek. But I'm desperate, Caryn. And there's no one else can help us but you.'

Hearing it put like that, Caryn was in an impossible position. 'But I don't know Mr Ross that well,' she protested.

'You live in his house, don't you? You work for him. I know you're good at your job. Surely as a favour to his secretary—to his almost sister-in-law—'

'Bob, Tristan Ross still denies that the child is his.'

Bob sighed. 'Okay, okay.' He rose abruptly to his feet. 'Sorry I asked.'

'Don't be.' Caryn felt terrible. 'Look, I'll see what I can do.'

Parting from Laura was upsetting. The other girl wept, and Caryn left the flat feeling utterly miserable. But it wasn't her fault! she told herself impatiently. The trouble was, she felt guilty on several counts.

It was quite late in the evening when she arrived back at Druid's Fleet, and Marcia met her with the news that Mr Ross had taken his guests out for the evening.

'Did he know you were coming back?' she scribbled on her pad, and Caryn frowned.

'Didn't Miss Trewen explain?' she asked, and when Marcia looked blank, added: 'She's going to Aberystwyth tomorrow, to spend the day with some college friend of hers. She asked me if I would look after Tristan.'

Marcia acknowledged this with a frown. Then she nodded, and wrote again: 'I don't think Sir George is aware there's a baby in the house, but I know Melanie resents what she thinks is the unfair favouritism shown to Loren's child.'

Caryn sighed. 'Then maybe I'd better make myself scarce as well. I shouldn't like to cause any more trouble.'

Marcia gave her a wry look, and she coloured shamefacedly. 'Well! I didn't ask to come here!'

Marcia wrote again: 'Have you ever considered that it might not be Mr Ross's child?' and Caryn looked at her disappointedly.

'Don't you believe me?' she exclaimed, and Marcia bent her head to the pad.

'I think Loren needed love—a man's love—very badly. When Mr Ross wouldn't give it to her, she went elsewhere.'

Caryn gasped. 'I thought you were my friend!' she cried. She turned blindly for the door. 'Why else would a man take on the financial responsibilities for a child?' she demanded hotly, but Tristan's words: '*Christian charity!*' echoed hollowly in her head.

Miss Trewen woke her on Sunday morning, coming into her room at half past seven and arousing her from the pre-dawn slumber she had only just managed to achieve.

'Sorry to disturb you,' the nurse whispered, with a teasing smile, as Caryn scrambled up, dragging the sheets around her chin. 'But my taxi's coming at half past eight, and I thought I ought to brief you before I left.'

Caryn blinked. 'Of course.' She shook her head, trying to think coherently. 'What do you want me to do?'

'I should say get dressed first,' murmured Miss Trewen, obviously in high spirits, and Caryn nodded and slid her legs over the edge of the mattress.

A cold shower did wonders for her concentration, and by the time she appeared in the nursery, casually attired in jeans and sweater, Miss Trewen had Tristan washed and dressed, and propped upon some pillows on the floor.

'He's waiting for his breakfast,' the nurse exclaimed, a faint look of disapproval crossing her face at Caryn's lack of formality. 'If you'd like to come over here, I'll show you his menus for the day.'

Caryn had fed the baby his lightly boiled egg and cereal, and was assisting him to drink from his cup when Marcia came into the nursery. Half afraid their interchange the night before might have soured their relationship, Caryn was relieved to see the housekeeper smile warmly in her direction, although she reflected dryly that her affection was probably directed towards the child. But the tray she carried was not for Miss Trewen, who had already had her breakfast, and Caryn smiled her thanks as Marcia gestured that a car was downstairs.

'It's the taxi,' exclaimed the nurse eagerly, and when Marcia nodded, she looked pleased. Then she turned to Caryn: 'Now, you can manage, can't you? I haven't forgotten anything?'

'I did cope quite adequately until he was three months old,' Caryn pointed out patiently. 'But no, you haven't forgotten anything.'

The two women went out together, and Caryn grimaced at her nephew. 'Well,' she said encouragingly, 'it's just you and me, brother! Think we'll get along?'

Tristan laughed, showing a revolting mixture of milk and cereal rolling round on his pink tongue, but Caryn realised with a pang that she wasn't at all revolted.

After finishing his breakfast, Tristan lay on the rug and played for a while, while Caryn had hers. He lay there, reaching for his woolly duck and his rattle, shrieking his irritation when they persistently eluded his inexpert grasp. Then it was time for his nap, and rather than risk meeting either Melanie or her father downstairs, Caryn put him into his cot instead of taking him for the walk she would have preferred.

Still, the weather was definitely cooler today, and several spots of rain on the windows heralded a downpour. Caryn tidied up the nursery, put the rug and pillows and toys away, and then carried her tray downstairs to the kitchen.

Marcia was slicing runner beans into a saucepan, and smiled as she came in. Caryn put her dishes in the sink, waved away the housekeeper's protest, and washed them up herself. Then she turned rather awkwardly to her.

'Marcia. . .about last night. . .'

Marcia shook her head, and there was an air of finality about the gesture. 'Forget it!' she mouthed silently, and Caryn decided she might as well.

She was on her way back upstairs when the front door opened and Tristan came in, brushing the droplets of rain from his zipped black windcheater. She had automatically paused when the door opened, but when she saw who it was, she quickened her step.

'Caryn!' His use of her name in the circumstances revealed his surprise at seeing her, and he came to the foot of the stairs, gazing up at her frowningly. 'I thought you were in London.'

She was in a quandary. After their last encounter, how could she behave towards him in a friendly fashion? It simply wasn't in character. And yet, remembering what she owed Bob and Laura—their sympathy and gentleness when Loren died, their friendship and companionship, their willingness to help with the baby—how could she turn her back on them when they needed her most? But what a position to be in, guessing the contempt he would display when he discovered what she wanted!

Now, she came down a stair and said stiffly:

'Miss Trewen wanted to spend the day with—
with a friend. I offered to look after Tristan.'

His mouth thinned. 'There was no need for
that. If you had told me, I would have arranged
for Marcia to take over for one day. You didn't
have to spoil your weekend.'

'Marcia has enough to do as it is. With—with
your guests.'

His nostrils flared. 'We could have eaten out.
That's no problem. I could have hired more staff.'

'It wasn't necessary,' she exclaimed, realising
nervously that if she wasn't careful their conversation would degenerate into an argument. 'I
didn't mind—honestly.'

'But you don't like looking after babies—you
told me.'

Caryn drew an unsteady breath. 'Maybe I've
changed my mind.'

'Why should you do that?'

'Oh, for heaven's sake, does it matter?'
Caryn's fingers tightened round the baluster rail
as she tried to control her impetuous tongue. 'I'm
here now, and that's all that matters.'

'I should have been told.'

'I thought Miss Trewen had told you.'

'Obviously she didn't.' He regarded her broodingly. 'Well, as you are here, you can join us for
dinner this evening.'

'I—don't think I can.'

'Why not?'

She hesitated, wishing desperately that he had
entered the house just a few moments later. 'I—
Tristan needs attention. . .'

His eyes rested disturbingly on her mouth. 'Don't we all?'

'Mr Ross. . .'

'Dinner,' he retorted harshly. 'At eight, Miss Stevens.'

During the afternoon, Caryn alternately sought to find reasons not to attend the dinner party or tried to justify her motives for going. If she did not join Tristan and his guests she knew she would anger him and while she knew he could not force her to go down, what better chance would she have of putting Bob's case to him? And yet wasn't that a foolhardy hope at best? Melanie was not likely to allow her escort out of her sight long enough to have a private conversation with him, and if the morning's encounter was anything to go on, he was not likely to listen to her anyway.

Baby Tristan had his tea at four o'clock, and then a bottle after his bath at six-thirty. He was just beginning to appreciate the benefits of being in water and Caryn was glad she had put on Miss Trewen's waterproof pinafore before tackling that particular task. Even so, she was hot and the floor was swimming with water before she managed to haul him out.

Dried and powdered and in his nightshirt, he smelled delicious, with that warm satisfying smell peculiar to babies. Curled on her knee, he took his bottle like an angel, and only began to protest when Caryn put him down to sleep.

'You mustn't be naughty tonight,' she told him severely, learning over the tall side of the cot. 'Your Aunt Caryn has to go and put on her best dress and make polite conversation at a dinner party. Be thankful you're not expected to attend!'

Tristan settled down eventually, but not before making her later than she could have wished, and she had to forgo her bath and take a shower instead. Fortunately, she had chosen the dress she was going to wear during the afternoon, and it took very little time after her shower to put on her shreds of underwear and slide the clinging folds of the red silk jersey over her head.

It was a beautiful dress, she reflected, considering her mirror image, but perhaps a little bright for a simple dinner party. Still, she had no time now to change, and if Tristan didn't like it, he had only himself to blame.

She came down the stairs at a quarter to eight, and found Tristan and his guests having drinks in the sitting room. All eyes were turned in her direction as she came into the room, and just for a moment she allowed herself the satisfaction of knowing that her appearance compared favourably with Melanie's crystal blue chiffon. Then a burly, grey-haired man made his way towards her, and although he wasn't a lot like his daughter, she guessed this had to be Sir George Forbes.

'Caryn, isn't it?' he said, before Tristan could introduce them. 'Good of you to even the numbers. Pity you weren't here last night. Could have done with a bit of luck on my side.'

Conscious of Tristan's eyes upon her, Caryn allowed the older man to shake her hand, but she withdrew it firmly when he would have held on.

'Were you unlucky last night, Sir George?' she parried, keeping her smile in place, and he explained that they had attended a private gambling party.

'Do you like gambling, Miss Stevens?' Melanie asked silkily, but this time Tristan interposed,

'Caryn's an expert when it comes to games of chance, aren't you?' he asked, his eyes faintly hostile, and Caryn was glad when Sir George spoke again and she could evade a direct reply.

'Tris tells me your sister used to work for him,' he remarked, remaining uncomfortably close to her, and she nodded.

'Sherry?' suggested Tristan, attracting her attention, and awkwardly she nodded again: 'Thank you.'

'Tris fired her,' put in Melanie spitefully. 'Miss Stevens' sister, I mean.' She flicked a malicious glance at Caryn. 'She became—how shall I put it?—an embarrassment to him.'

'As you are now?' snapped Caryn impulsively, and saw the other girl's look of fury.

'Well said!' Sir George had obviously been imbibing quite freely already, and although Caryn's words had been unbearably rude, he took no offence at them. But Melanie did.

She turned to Tristan. 'Are you going to stand there and let that—that creature insult me?' she demanded, and his mouth thinned into an uncompromising line.

'As what she said was true, I don't see what I can do,' he retorted evenly. 'However,' his gaze flicked over Caryn contemptuously, 'I think she regrets saying it as much as you regret hearing it.'

Caryn's lips worked impotently for a moment,

and she toyed with the idea of telling him exactly what she did think. But then common sense and discretion won the day, and she contented herself with a hard little look in Tristan's direction.

Dinner was served in the dining room. It was the first time Caryn had eaten in the impressive room that overlooked the drive at the front of the house. After the splendid views at the back, the front was something of an anti-climax, in spite of its boxwood hedges and flowering shrubs.

The meal Marcia served was delectable as usual. Prawns in aspic were followed by veal cutlets served with a sherry sauce, and there was a featherlight lemon soufflé to finish. Even Caryn, conscious as she was of Melanie's overt hostility and Tristan's brooding melancholy, could not resist trying everything, and the wine that accompanied the food relaxed a little of the tension she was feeling.

Marcia had brought in the cheese board when a car turned between the drive gates and cruised down to the door. Although it wasn't yet dark, it was impossible to see who it was from Caryn's position at the far side of the table, and Tristan's curt ejaculation made her think sinkingly of Dave O'Hara. But she was wrong.

'It's Angel!' he declared, thrusting back his chair and getting to his feet. 'Now why the hell couldn't she have let me know she was coming back today?'

'Angel?' Melanie's lips curved upwards. 'Oh, good!'

'Your daughter, Ross?' Sir George asked as Tristan strode towards the door. 'Good show!'

Only Caryn was unenthusiastic about the new arrival, and she thought cynically that if only Angela had arrived sooner she would have been spared the discomfort of this dinner party.

The front door was open and Tristan was helping the taxi driver to bring in his daughter's cases when Angela herself appeared, sleek and tanned after a month in the sun.

'Melly!' She and the other girl greeted one another eagerly, and Sir George had left his seat to go and join them.

'Sir George!' Angela exclaimed, leaving her friend to hug the older man, and Caryn could see the way Melanie's father's lips curled in anticipation. And why not? she thought dryly. In denim dungarees that accentuated the slender lines of her body, her silky blonde hair loose about her shoulders, Angela was the epitome of well-fed sophistication and unlike Caryn was more than willing to suffer his lustful glances. Her skin gleamed with the glow of good health, and only when she saw Caryn still seated at the dining table did her laughing good humour give way to sardonic irritation.

'Am I interrupting something?' she enquired of her father, who appeared at the door at that moment, having disposed of the taxi driver. 'I didn't know your secretary joined you for dinner, Tris. Or is this a special occasion?'

Caryn rose to her feet. She had had just about enough baiting for one evening. 'Your father invited me to make the numbers even, Miss Ross,' she declared stiffly. 'As they're odd again now,

I'll solve the problem and leave you to drink my share of the coffee!'

'Now wait a minute—'

Angela's automatic retort was drowned by her father saying grimly: 'Sit down, Caryn!' but she ignored both of them.

'I'd really rather not,' she was beginning, and as if on cue, the baby's cry suddenly broke upon the awkward silence that had fallen. 'You see,' she got out huskily, 'duty calls!'

She had lifted her nephew out of his cot and was rocking him gently on her shoulder when she became aware of a shadow falling across them from the doorway. It had to be Tristan, and without turning, she said rather chokily: 'Please, go away! I can manage.'

'Oh, well, if that's how you feel. . .'

Miss Trewen's voice was affronted, and Caryn swung round guiltily, staring in bewilderment at the nurse. 'Miss Trewen, I. . .' She moved her shoulders helplessly. 'I'm sorry, I didn't know you were back. Oh, heavens, I didn't mean you!'

'My friend drove me back,' declared Miss Trewen, only slightly placated. 'I thought you must have heard me come upstairs.'

'No.' Caryn shook her head, unable to explain that she had been too depressed by the events of the evening to hear anything but her own erratically beating heart.

'Well, if that's the case. . .' Miss Trewen held out her arms. 'Let me take him. I think Mr Ross is looking for you.'

Caryn was tempted to hold on to the baby, but if it came to a choice between offending Miss

Trewen and hiding her own misery, Miss Trewen would win every time. She passed the baby over to the nurse, and walked back into the nursery as Miss Trewen closed the bedroom door behind her.

The light in the nursery was harsh after the shadowy bedroom, and Caryn was blinking away a certain moistness when she realised she was no longer alone.

'Is he all right?'

Tristan straightened from his lounging position in the doorway, and came into the room. Watching him, Caryn wondered why it was that she should feel this overwhelming attraction for the man she had come here to hate!

'Miss Trewen's with him,' she replied tersely. 'Don't let us detain you. I'll wait and speak to her when she's settled him down.'

Tristan came to stand in front of her, looking down at her intently. 'Are you all right?'

'Why shouldn't I be all right?' she protested, smudging her hand across her cheeks. 'Oh, please, don't feel sorry for me!'

'Why not? What makes you so unique?' He hesitated, then he said huskily: 'It suited you, you know.'

'Wh-what suited me?'

'Having the baby in your arms,' he said surprisingly, and her head jerked up.

'You—saw—me?'

'From the doorway,' he conceded softly, and she knew she had not been mistaken in sensing his nearness. 'Then the good Miss Trewen appeared, and I got out of the way.'

Caryn's breathing quickened at his words, and

her heart palpitated alarmingly. Close to him like this, his eyes were no longer harsh and cold, but warm and golden, like the sun, with all its heat.

'Caryn,' he said, and rather than look at him, she quickly turned away, knocking one of the baby's rattles from the table as she did so. She bent automatically to pick it up as he did the same, but instead of rescuing the rattle, his hands cupped her face, and then, with an urgent exclamation, his mouth was covering hers with all the warm emotion of which she knew he was capable. She straightened, her legs like jelly, and the kiss hardened and lengthened, parting her lips and drawing on the moist sweetness within. Her hands by her sides touched his hips, and their involuntary withdrawal was overridden by an almost compulsive need to feel him close to her. Her hands slid over him, and he shuddered as he gathered her closer, letting her feel the whole weight of his desire.

'*Tristan!*'

Melanie's voice drifted along the corridor from the upper landing, and with an abrupt movement Caryn was free, and Tristan was striding out of the nursery. Even as she stood there feeling that her whole world was caving in about her, she heard Melanie's light laugh, and with a crippled cry she ran to the door and slammed it behind him. So much for helping Bob and Laura, she thought bitterly. She couldn't even help herself.

In the morning, she felt no better. Instead, an intense awareness of impending disaster had descended upon her, and with cold reason she acknowledged that if she stayed here it was no longer just a possibility that she might become involved with Tristan. It was already too late for possibilities. Insidiously perhaps, against her will definitely, she was involved with him, and how could she betray her sister's memory by becoming the mistress of the man who had been the indirect cause of Loren's death?

She was in the nursery with Miss Trewen, having breakfast, when they had unexpected visitors. After the most perfunctory of raps at the door, Melanie and her father came in, and Caryn's sense of impending disaster magnified a hundred times. Why had they come here? Of what possible interest could baby Tristan be to them?

Miss Trewen, on the other hand, was flattered. She rose to greet them in something of a fluster, and Caryn's nails dug painfully into the palms of her hands.

'I hope you don't mind this intrusion, dear lady.' Sir George was at his most gallant, but his eyes flickered speculatively over Caryn's bent head. 'We're leaving this morning, and I felt we shouldn't go without introducing ourselves to the youngest member of the household.'

Miss Trewen glanced awkwardly towards Caryn then. 'Well, of course you're not intruding, Sir George. We've just had our breakfast, and we're having a little play on our rug before we have our nap.'

For once Miss Trewen's mannerisms failed to make Caryn smile. Glancing round, she encountered Melanie's vaguely mocking expression, and the other girl's lips curled contemptuously when she met Caryn's regard.

Sir George was accompanying Miss Trewen across to where the baby was lying kicking on his rug, and after another malicious look at Caryn, Melanie went after them. They stood looking down at the plump little legs kicking excitedly into the air, and Caryn suddenly wanted to rush across and snatch up the baby and hide him from their ungentle curiosity.

But it was too late. Sir George bent down towards Tristan, chucking him under the chin, and as the baby's face crumpled into a noisy objection, the man uttered a sound of surprise.

'Hey there!' he exclaimed, and Caryn waited apprehensively for him to notice the baby's resemblance to Tristan. For she had no doubt that the other girl had brought her father here for just this reason, although why Melanie should want to advertise the fact she couldn't imagine; 'Melly, doesn't he remind you of someone?'

Miss Trewen and Caryn exchanged a glance, and suddenly Caryn could sit still no longer. She slid off her chair, and as she did so Melanie gave a startled gasp.

'Yes!' she cried, and Caryn took an involuntary step towards her. 'Good lord! Dave O'Hara to the life!'

Caryn had never been so near fainting in her life. Her face lost every scrap of colour, and she stared at the others with lips turning faintly blue.

Melanie straightened, and looked at her mockingly. 'Oh, dear,' she exclaimed spitefully. 'Didn't you see it? Tristan noticed it the first time he saw him.'

Caryn couldn't believe it. With a return of

strength to limbs that had been temporarily para-
lysed, she rushed across the room, pushing Sir
George aside with little ceremony, staring down
at her nephew as if she'd never seen him before.

It was true! she thought sickly. And so many
things fell into place. The feeling when she saw
Dave that she had met him before, the fleeting
resemblance she kept seeing in the baby that she
had thought was Tristan. But she had seen Tristan
in him because that was what she had wanted
to see. . .

'I can see we've shocked Miss Stevens,'
remarked Melanie lightly, but her father looked
less self-satisfied.

'Look here, Caryn,' he said, half apologetically, 'I thought you knew. Melanie—well, I was
led to believe that—oh, God! What a situation!'

Miss Trewen shifted uncomfortably, and
belatedly Caryn realised that all this must be
double-talk to her. Pushing back the weight of
her hair with an unsteady hand, she tried to pull
herself together, and taking pity on her, Sir
George ushered his daughter towards the door.

'We'll—er—we'll be going,' he said, bluster-
ing himself a little now. 'Caryn, we'll no doubt
see you again. Miss Trewen.'

He raised a hand in farewell, and the door
closed behind them, leaving Caryn to make what
explanations she could. But she wasn't ready for
explanations. She needed time to think, not least
about what this meant in terms of her own
situation.

'I'm sorry, Miss Stevens,' Miss Trewen spoke
uncomfortably, and Caryn quickly reassured her.

'Don't be. I guess it had to happen sooner or later.'

'But what's happened?' exclaimed the older woman anxiously. 'Who is this Dave O'Hara? Your sister's husband?'

'Oh, no. No!' Caryn put a hand to her throat, feeling sick. 'He's just—Dave O'Hara. Lead guitarist with Sweet Vibration.'

'What is Sweet Vibration?'

'A group. A pop group. You know—top ten, and all that.'

'And he's—Tristan's father?'

Caryn bent her head. 'Apparently.'

'You didn't know?' Clearly Miss Trewen was shocked now.

'No, I didn't know.'

'But—'

'I can't explain now,' muttered Caryn huskily. 'I can't. You'll have to give me time to absorb this. Then —then we'll talk.'

Miss Trewen sighed. 'Does this mean we'll be leaving here, Miss Stevens? I would like to know that.'

'What? Oh. . .' Caryn swallowed convulsively. That was something else she had to consider. 'I— I don't know. I just don't know. . .'

And with that Miss Trewen had to be content, but as she stumbled along to her own room, Caryn wondered how Loren could ever have lied to her as she had. . .

CHAPTER TEN

IT was Monday morning, and no doubt Tristan was waiting to issue her instructions for the week, but Caryn lingered in her room, pacing the floor, hands pressed to her burning cheeks, unable to summon the courage to face him.

What did it mean? she asked herself again and again, and could come up with no satisfactory answer. Oh, it was simple enough to guess what had happened. She had only to remember Tristan's anger when he found she was with Dave to realise he was afraid of what might happen, but why hadn't he told her? And more importantly, why hadn't he told *Dave*?

And yet, thinking of the pop star and his life style, Caryn shuddered. Dave was a boy still, totally incapable of understanding the needs of a baby. Was that why Loren had lied to her?

There was pain in that realisation. Whatever happened, whatever motive there had been behind this, Loren had lied to her. And if she had lied about one thing, had she lied about another?

But no! Loren had cared about Tristan Ross—Caryn was sure of that. She had talked of no one else all the time she was pregnant, and thinking of this another awful thought struck her. Could Loren have slept with both men? Could the child have belonged to either? Had she hoped it would be Tristan's? Was that why she had sent Caryn to him when she knew she was dying?

The whole situation was appalling, and Caryn wrapped her arms about herself closely, as if to protect herself from the dreadful repercussions of the Forbes' revelations.

Ultimately she knew she would have to speak to Tristan. By remaining in her room she was only putting off the evil day, and goodness knows, she had plenty to do. If the child wasn't his, then somehow she would have to take it away, but whether she could find another post where a child was welcome was doubtful. Of course, she could always apply to be someone's housekeeper. She had seen advertisements for such where 'one child' was not objected to. But what would the authorities have to say about that? She had only just managed to persuade them to let her keep Tristan, but the circumstances here were vastly different from the average housekeeping post. She pressed her lips tightly together. Laurence Mellor would say she had brought the whole thing upon herself, and it seemed so unfair that just when she was beginning to let herself believe that she was not going to be separated from the child, that unspeakable thing might happen. Unless Tristan wanted her to remain. . .

She thrust this unworthy thought aside. How could she let him go on supporting a child that was not his? How could she accept his—*charity*, for that was what it was?

He had known—she was convinced of that. So why had he done it? Pity? Guilt? *Christian charity!* There had to be more to it than that. He had had no love for Loren, he had shown that many times, so why had he taken it upon himself to give her son—and Dave O'Hara's—a home?

It was after nine-thirty by the time she summoned up the courage to speak to her employer, but when she reached the study she found only taped instructions waiting for her. Beside them was a note stating that he was driving Melanie and her father back to London, and nothing else.

She stared down at the note, blinking back the tears of pain and frustration that filled her eyes, and then sank down into the chair at her desk and buried her face in her hands. Oh, God, she thought miserably, she didn't want to leave Druid's Fleet. Not because of her job—or baby Tristan's welfare; but because she loved Tristan Ross, against all reason. . .

'Where's my father?'

Angela's voice broke carelessly into her misery, and she raised her head dazedly to find Tristan's daughter standing squarely before her desk.

'Your father. . .' she said, somewhat stupidly, and Angela's arrogant features grew irritated.

'Yes. My father. Your employer, Tristan Ross. Where is he?'

Caryn pushed her fingers across her cheeks and held up her head. 'He—er—he's left for London.'

'He's what?'

'He's left for London,' said Caryn again, forcing her own troubles aside. 'He's driven Miss Forbes and her father back to town.'

'Damn!' Angela's mouth tightened. 'Damn, damn, damn! Now why the hell has he done that?'

Caryn couldn't answer her, so she remained silent, but Angela wasn't satisfied yet.

'I understood from Melanie that they expected to stay for a few days.'

Caryn hesitated. 'They—came on Thursday,' she said. 'They've been here four days already.'

Angela regarded her coldly. 'And you know nothing about it, of course.'

'What could I know?'

Angela looked as though she might say something, and then moved restively across to the windows. 'Tell me,' she said, with her back to Caryn, 'how much longer do you think you can stay here? How much longer is it going to take for you to realise that my father is only satisfying some ridiculous guilt he feels about getting rid of your sister?'

Caryn stiffened. 'What do you mean?'

Angela swung round, resting against the sill. 'Don't pretend you don't know what happened as well as I do.'

Caryn rose to her feet. 'If you'll excuse me—'

'No, I won't excuse you. And what's more, I think you ought to stop pretending you believe in this myth about Loren.'

Against her will, Caryn's attention was caught. 'What—what myth?'

'This myth of her being in love with my father. Loren wasn't in love with anybody, except perhaps herself.'

'You have no grounds—'

'I have every ground!' snapped Angela coldly. 'My God, do you think I couldn't see what game she was playing? Do you think I didn't know what was going on?'

'I think you were jealous!' declared Caryn tremulously, and as soon as the words were uttered, she realised how true that could be. Allan Felix had hinted that Angela considered Dave O'Hara her property. How galling it must have been for her to learn that he and Loren. . .

'*Jealous!*' Angela's face was contorted with anger now. 'Jealous! Of that little—' She used an epithet which made Caryn's colour pale. 'How dare you suggest such a thing? I had no need to be jealous of her. Tris wouldn't look at her. Not in a thousand years! Whatever sordid little details you have read about him, my father is a decent man, and no one can say otherwise. That's why your being here is so—so ludicrous—'

'I didn't mean your father!' declared Caryn unsteadily, prepared to defend Loren, whatever her faults. 'I meant Dave O'Hara!'

Angela uttered a shrill laugh. 'What?' she exclaimed disbelievingly. 'You think I'm jealous of you and Dave! My dear girl, if he's been friendly to you while I've been away, then believe me, that's only because I've not been around!'

'I don't mean me,' Caryn persisted, reflecting that either Angela was a very good actress or Allan had been totally wrong about her.

'Who, then?' Her eyes widened. 'Oh—you mean Loren!' Her lips curled. 'My God, we are scraping the barrel, aren't we? You don't honestly believe Dave cared about your sister, do you?'

Caryn stared at her, then she shuddered uncontrollably. 'You believe it was only—promiscuity, then?' She shook her head. 'I think you believe in myths too, Miss Ross.'

'What are you talking about?' Angela straightened away from the window. 'What do you know about anything?'

'I know—I know it takes two to to—well, anyway, Loren's baby is alive and real—and no one, not even you, can deny that!'

'Why should I want to deny it? Just because your sister got herself pregnant and died having the child it doesn't make her some kind of saint, you know. Oh, I admit you fooled my father into thinking so, but you can't fool me! Just who was the child's father, by the way? I would like to know.'

Caryn stared at her through hollowed eyes. 'You mean—you mean—' Her throat worked convulsively, and Angela, alarmed by her pallor, came towards her.

'What is it?' she exclaimed. 'What's wrong? Oh, for the lord's sake, I'm sorry if I've upset you, but you must know, deep down, that Loren was not the little innocent you like to think her.'

Caryn shook her head, looking down helplessly at the desk, and Angela actually placed a hand on her shoulder. 'Miss Stevens—Caryn! Heavens, calm down! Calm down! All I asked was—'

'I know—what you asked,' said Caryn chokingly, and suddenly comprehension dawned on Tristan's daughter.

'That's it, isn't it? she exclaimed, staring at Caryn. 'The child's father! You do know who it is, don't you?' She became impatient again.

'Well, come on—who is it? You'll have to tell me. I mean to know.'

Caryn sank down into her seat. 'I thought you knew. . .'

Angela's eyes narrowed, and now her hand fell to her side as she lost colour. 'You don't mean— I don't believe you!' She stared at Caryn, trying to get her to deny it. 'Dave? *Dave?* He—wouldn't do such a thing!'

Caryn made a helpless gesture towards the door, and with an ejaculation, Angela stalked out of the room and her footsteps could be heard as she ran along the corridor.

She was back in less than five minutes, and now her face was ashen. She looked at Caryn, and then with a moan, she dragged herself into her father's chair and burst into tears.

Caryn could find it in her heart to feel sorry for her. All her previous arrogance had disappeared, and now she was just a teenage girl whose boy-friend had been unfaithful to her. Realising there was nothing she could say to salve the pain she must be feeling, Caryn left the room, closing the door silently behind her.

In her own room, she stood blindly at the windows. No wonder Tristan had said Loren had been nothing but trouble from the moment she came here! No wonder he had dismissed her when he learned what was going on. Why had he done it? To protect Loren—too late as it turned out— or Angela, whom he obviously cared for deeply? Whatever his reasons, the pieces of the puzzle were falling into place now, and all that was left was his reasons for accepting Loren's baby into his home.

It might well be as Angela said. That he felt guilty for what happened. But nothing could alter the fact that Loren had used her working relationship with him for her own ends. She had known if she had come home to Caryn and told her that she was pregnant with the child of some pop idol, her sister would have felt little pity for her. Maybe she had even told Dave she was pregnant, and he had denied all knowledge of it. Maybe she had hung on in the hope that she might be able to persuade him to marry her, and when all else failed it was too late to get rid of it. There were so many maybes, so many possibilities, but what was becoming blatantly obvious was that Tristan's initial hostility towards her had been well warranted.

So now what could she do? She couldn't stay here. She couldn't accept Tristan's charity any longer. But she had no intention of going to the baby's real father and asking anything of him. So where did that leave her? Back with the possibility of a housekeeping post a long way away from Druid's Fleet. . .

Caryn arrived back in London in the late afternoon.

It had been surprisingly easy getting away. She had told Marcia that as Mr Ross was away she was going to drive up to town again to see a friend who was ill, and that she would ring as soon as she knew when she would be back. Miss Trewen, after her successful day out, saw nothing unusual in Caryn's departure, and as Angela was not around, Caryn left without difficulty. It wasn't entirely untrue, she consoled herself as she neared the suburbs of the city. Laura was not well, and she would find time to see her in between visiting employment agencies.

But she had no intention of taking advantage of Bob and Laura's hospitality, and the first thing she did on reaching London was to find a small hotel and book in for the night. Her room was small, and she had to share a bathroom, but at least it was clean and reasonably central.

It was too late then to start making the rounds of the agencies, so she visited a newsagent near the hotel and carried a copy of *The Times* back to her room. There was always the chance that she might find employment independently, and she had read these columns on other occasions with a wry smile.

First of all, she turned to the ordinary Situations Vacant columns. There were plenty of those, but most were professional vacancies, many of them overseas. It crossed her mind that she might enjoy working abroad, but taking a baby to a foreign country was always tricky.

She smiled as she saw the columns of secretarial posts. She wondered what those prospective employers would say if she turned up with a baby in her arms. No, secretarial jobs were out. At least, for the present.

But then one particular advertisement caught her eye. *Wanted*, it said, *personal, private secretary. Excellent position for qualified person.*

Apply: Dean Mellor, Lansworth College, Cricklewood.

Laurence! she thought, in astonishment. Of course, his trip to the States must be over, and now he was advertising for a secretary before the new college term began.

It was strange how the thought of Laurence was comforting somehow. Perhaps because he was a link with her old life, the life she had once shared with Loren. She stared at the advertisement until the light in her room began to fade, and the unwelcome pangs of hunger overcame the misery she was feeling inside her.

Sleep, as was becoming usual these days, eluded her until the early hours, and then she slept only shallowly, wakening when the wagons in a nearby railway siding began being shunted about by their handlers.

Over toast and coffee in the hotel dining room, she read the personal columns of the newspaper she had overlooked the night before. But there was nothing that appealed to her, and she left the hotel soon after nine, intent on covering as much ground as she could in the day. She left her overnight bag at the hotel, and was given the option of keeping her room for another night.

By five o'clock, her feet were aching, and the pounding in her head responded little to aspirins. She had visited no fewer than ten agencies, and although she had two possible interviews for tomorrow, neither of them particularly fitted the bill. One was as nursemaid to an Iranian oil executive's children, but the idea of living in such a place filled her with alarm. The other was less

frightening: housekeeper to a widower in
Coventry. But the agency thought he might well
object to such a young child, and said that if
Tristan had been three or four years older it would
have been better.

She ordered a sandwich at the hotel and spent
the evening in her room, resting her aching body.
She knew she ought to ring Druid's Fleet, if only
to ascertain that the baby was all right, but she
was simply too weary.

In the morning, she tried to look on the bright
side. Life in Iran might be fun, or alternatively
the Coventry widower might like babies. She
determinedly swallowed two slices of toast,
because she was hungry, having had no dinner
the night before, and after several cups of black
coffee, set out again.

She was interviewed for the Iranian post at an
hotel in Bond Street. When she arrived, however,
there were at least twenty other girls waiting to
be interviewed, and by the time she stepped
across the thickly carpeted threshold of the suite
the Iranians were occupying, she knew she had
no chance of succeeding.

Her other interview was at the agency itself.
A dour businessman spoke to her in a private
office, and when Caryn told him she had the care
of a five-month-old baby, he became quite angry.

'You did say you didn't object to a child,' she
pointed out, with sinking heart, but he just opened
the door.

'I said a child, not a baby!' he declared
brusquely. 'Do you think I can do with sleepless
nights and nappies about the place? No, I'm sorry,

Miss Stevens, we were both misinformed.'

It was barely lunchtime when Caryn returned to the hotel. She had the addresses of several more agencies to try, but right now she hadn't the heart for it. Instead, she bought another copy of *The Times* and ate some lunch with it propped in front of her.

Laurence's advertisement was still there, like a baited hook to torment her. She wondered how many applicants he had had, and decided he would not be short of contenders. She sighed. If only Loren had never begged her to take her baby to Tristan Ross! She would, in all probability, still be working for Laurence, and the baby would have been adopted by some childless couple who would have given him a really good start in life. Instead, she had accused an innocent man of being its father, insinuated herself into his home, allowed the baby to wrap himself around her heart, and fallen in love with the one man who, because she was Loren's sister, thought she was easy game. . .

In the afternoon, she wondered what she should do. The idea of visiting Laura was attractive, but if Bob was there, how could she face him? She had promised to do what she could to help them, and had succeeded in helping nobody, not even herself.

Almost unthinkingly, she found herself getting on the bus to Cricklewood, but when she got off before the college she knew it had been her destination all along. She didn't know what she intended to do, but if Laurence was there she would speak to him, and maybe he would advise her as he had done in the past.

The college was strangely deserted. The students had not yet returned after the summer break, and only the maintenance staff and an occasional tutor walked the cloistered corridors.

Laurence's office was on the first floor, and Caryn was not stopped as she made her way up the wide marble staircase, and along the echoing hall. His secretary's office—her office, for four years—was empty, and she stood in the doorway staring at her desk. She had been happy here, she thought, although now she knew that there was another kind of happiness.

She was standing there, trying to summon up the courage to go and knock at Laurence's door, when she heard the sound of footsteps behind her, and glancing round, she saw her erstwhile employer traversing the corridor towards her, his black cloak billowing out behind him.

'Caryn!' Laurence exclaimed disbelievingly. 'Lord, it is you! Taylor said it was, but I didn't believe him!'

Taylor was one of the janitors, and although Caryn hadn't seen him on her way up, he was usually to be found about the place.

'Hello, Laurence,' she said, forcing a smile to her lips, but when she would have shaken hands with him, he brushed her outstretched arm aside and gathered her into an unexpected embrace.

'Caryn,' he said huskily. 'Dear Caryn! How lovely it is to see you!'

Caryn drew back, half in embarrassment, and he went past her to open the door of his office. 'Come in,' he invited. 'I'm not busy at the moment, although I shall be later. I've got half a dozen applicants coming to interview for your job.'

'I see.' Caryn licked her lips and followed him into his office, closing the door behind her. 'You're looking well, Laurence. Did you have a good trip?'

He moved his shoulders in a dismissing gesture. 'So-so,' he said, without emphasis. 'It's not a trip I would care to take again. Not alone, at least.' He paused. 'But you—how are you? I must say you're looking rather—tired.'

'I am tired,' Caryn admitted, sinking down into the chair opposite his desk. 'I've been trailing round London for the past two days, and I'm worn out.'

'Trailing round London?' Laurence Mellor frowned. 'Why?'

Caryn had taken the decision to tell him as soon as she got off the bus, and now she said quietly: 'I'm leaving—Mr Ross. It—well, it hasn't worked out as I planned. I'm looking for another post.'

Laurence gasped. 'Then look no further. Come back to me!' he said at once; as she had known he would.

Caryn bent her head. 'I couldn't do that, Laurence.'

'Why not?'

She looked up. 'You don't understand. I—I've been looking after Tristan—the baby, that is— for five months now. And I want to go on doing so.' She paused. 'It's as simple as that.'

Laurence looked disturbed. 'But I don't understand. How does that stop you from resuming your old job?'

Caryn sighed. 'Oh, Laurence! Do I have to spell it out for you? I need someone to look after the baby as well as somewhere to live if I come back to you. And quite frankly, I—I couldn't afford to employ anyone.'

Laurence absorbed this. 'So what is your intention? What kind of post are you looking for?'

Caryn tried to sound objective. 'Well—a housekeeping post, perhaps, or nursemaid to someone's children. Some post where a baby isn't objected to.'

Laurence looked horrified. 'But you're not a nursemaid, Caryn, or a housekeeper. You're a secretary—and a damn good one!'

'Thank you.' Caryn managed a smile. 'You're very good for my ego. But unfortunately, secretaries aren't usually accompanied by dependants.'

'And have you had any luck?'

She shook her head. 'I had two interviews today—one with an Iranian oilman, who said he would let me know, and one with a widower from Coventry, who almost blew his top when he found out how old Tristan was.'

'I see.' Laurence doodled absently on the pad on his desk. 'And—er—have you had any further thoughts about what I asked you?'

Caryn frowned now. 'What you asked me? About going to America, do you mean? But you've already been—'

'No, no! Not that.' Laurence sounded impatient. 'The other thing I asked you. To marry me.'

Caryn caught her breath. 'But you weren't serious, Laurence,' she exclaimed. 'I mean, that was only an expedient for the trip. . .'

He looked squarely at her. 'No, it wasn't. I might have let you think so, I might even have thought so myself for a while, but since you left, Caryn, I've realised I did mean it.'

CHAPTER ELEVEN

'OH, Laurence!' Caryn stared at him unhappily. 'We've had all this out before. You know I don't love you—'

'No. But I love you,' he said, shocking her into silence. 'I thought I'd never care for anyone else when Cecily left me, but it's not true. I do care for you, Caryn. I care for you a lot.'

Caryn got to her feet. She didn't know what she had expected coming here. Laurence's sympathy, perhaps, his understanding. Well, she had his sympathy, but anything else was out of the question. Maybe she had hoped he would offer to employ her and increase her salary, or alternatively offer her a job as *his* housekeeper. But telling her he loved her—she had not expected that.

'I'm sorry, Laurence,' she said. 'I—I don't know what to say.'

Laurence was on his feet and regarding her across the width of his desk. 'You should think about it, Caryn,' he said. 'Is it such a terrible thing to ask? Wouldn't it solve your problems, once and for all?'

'Wh-what problems?'

'Why, Loren's baby, of course. If you married me, he would at least have a decent start in life.'

Caryn pressed an uneasy hand to her throat. 'But I couldn't marry you for that!'

'Why not? People do marry for the oddest reasons, you know.'

Caryn shook her head helplessly. 'I'm flattered, of course.'

She sought for reasons. 'Laurence, you don't even like children!'

'I've never had any. Perhaps if I had, my feelings would change.'

'You mean—you mean—*we* might have children?'

'Why not? I'm not too old, you know.' He sounded affronted, and she made an apologetic gesture.

'I know, I know. It's just that—oh, Laurence! You've rocked me on my heels!'

'Then think about it,' he said magnanimously, consulting his watch. 'But now, I'm afraid, my dear, I have to ask you to go. Whatever you decide, I still have these interviews to conduct.'

Caryn groped her way to the door.

'Of course,' he added, 'if you do—change your mind, that is—accept my offer, you'd be welcome to your old job back, if you wanted it.'

'And—and Tristan?'

'We could employ a nanny. I'm sure there are some excellent women around.'

Miss Trewen, thought Caryn dazedly. Miss Trewen could keep her job.

'Look,' said Laurence, 'you run along now. Where are you staying, by the way? I ought to have the address.'

'The White Feather. In Kensington,' replied Caryn, still in that dazed voice, and before she knew it, he had ushered her out into the corridor, and was telling her he would ring her there that evening.

But as she rode back to Kensington in the bus, Caryn's brain cleared. How could she contemplate marrying Laurence whatever the circumstances? He was too set in his ways, for one thing, and his words about having children had made her see that he would expect a real marriage, in every sense. It would solve her problems, of course it would, but did the end justify the means? She rather thought not. What did disturb her was that she had even considered it. Before going to live at Druid's Fleet, she would never have left him in any doubt, whereas now, with two unsuccessful interviews behind her, she had actually weighed the pros and cons. Might Laurence even be able to persuade her if she saw him again? Might not desperation drive her to accept his offer?

She wished now she had not given him the address of her hotel. She should have told him she would ring him. That way, she was not committed. Not to anything.

On impulse, she checked out of the hotel when she got back, and left a message should a certain Mr Mellor call to tell him she would be in touch. Then she put her case into the boot of her car, and drove across town to Bloomsbury.

Parking in the narrow street was difficult, but eventually she managed to wedge the Renault between a hand-painted Mini and a grocer's van. Then she left her case in the boot, and ascended the two flights of stairs to Laura and Bob's flat.

Laura opened the door to her knock, but this

was a vastly different girl from the one she had said goodbye to only five days ago. Now Laura's face was bright and cheerful, and although it sobered for a moment when she saw Caryn, the smile that lurked about her lips would not long be denied.

'Caryn!' she exclaimed, stepping towards her friend and hugging her tightly for a moment. 'Oh, Caryn, where have you been?'

'Where have I—Caryn was beginning, when Bob's face appeared over his wife's shoulder, and with a sinking feeling she wondered if they imagined she was the bearer of good tidings.

'What an uproar you've caused!' Bob added to what his wife had already said, and then he came forward and shook her hand warmly. 'Caryn, I don't know how to thank you.'

This was all double-talk to Caryn, and she shook her head helplessly. 'I'm afraid I don't know what you mean. . .' she began, but they both drew her into the flat and the door was closed behind her before Laura tried to explain:

'Tristan Ross has been here,' she said, wrinkling her nose reprovingly. 'He's very worried about you. Have you seen him?'

Caryn's legs gave out on her and she sank down rather weakly on to the nearest chair. 'Tristan?' she breathed. Then more formally: 'Mr Ross!'

'Yes.' Bob took up the story. 'Apparently you just walked out on him for no reason.'

'No reason!' echoed Caryn disbelievingly. Then, realising explaining that remark entailed too many personal details, she added: 'What did he say?'

'What did he say?' Laura glanced sideways at her husband. 'Well, he said he was—extremely worried about you, and that if we saw you, we had to let him know immediately.'

Caryn's shoulders sagged. 'Is that all? Did he mention the baby? Is he all right?'

'Tristan junior is fine,' Laura assured her. 'Bob, go and put the kettle on, there's a love. I want to have a few private words with Caryn.'

'Okay.'

Bob grinned and marched into the kitchen, discreetly closing the door behind him, and the minute he had gone, Laura sat down opposite her friend and grasped Caryn's hand in hers.

'Now,' she said, 'let me thank you for—for speaking out for Bob. You don't know what this means to us, Bob getting a better job. It's like a dream. And I know—I just know he wouldn't have got it if it hadn't been for you. He told me what he'd said to you—'

Laura's words began by going over Caryn's head, but gradually the gist of them began to make sense. That job Bob was being interviewed for, he must have got it. And they thought it was all true.

'Oh, really, Laura. . .' she was beginning, when the other girl shook her head.

'Don't say anything,' she commanded. 'I know you're going to say it was nothing to do with you, but—well, we won't believe you, so forget it. But I just wanted you to know. . .'

If anything, Caryn felt worse. How could she

stay here now accepting their hospitality on false pretences? Hadn't she had enough of that already?

'So. . .' Laura was speaking again, and Caryn came back to the present to hear her saying: '. . .so what did you walk out for? Mr Ross said he couldn't understand it.' She paused. 'And he was so cut up. . .'

Caryn's pale cheeks took on a rather hectic colour. 'It's a long story, Laura. The crux of it all is—Tristan Ross was not the father of Loren's baby.'

Laura's sandy lashes flapped incredulously. 'He's not!'

'No.' Caryn sighed. 'So you see, I can't stay there any longer.'

'But what will you do?'

'I don't know.' Caryn looked up as Bob came back into the room. 'Hmm, tea,' she smiled, glad of the respite. 'I could do with a cup.'

Laura looked by no means satisfied with Caryn's explanation, but the tea silenced them all for a while, and presently Bob took up the question of his new job.

'There were half a dozen of us,' he said, speaking for Caryn's benefit, and making her feel so guilty. 'But all along, when I was being interviewed, I just had the feeling I was going to get it.'

'I'm so glad.' Caryn could at least be honest about that and she had raised her cup to her lips again when there was a thunderous rapping at the door.

Laura started and looked at Bob, and he got

frowningly to his feet. 'Who can that be?' he asked, looking at his wife, and in that instant Caryn knew. She put her cup down and rose to her feet, more nervous than she had ever been in her life before, and said clearly:

'It's Tristan!'

'Tristan!' Laura exchanged a glance with her husband, and then Bob had reached the door and was pulling it open.

'Mr Ross!' Caryn heard him saying, confirming her worst fears, and then Tristan had brushed past him into the room saying angrily:

'Where's Caryn? I know she's here. I saw her car outside.'

Caryn stilled her trembling lips by pressing them together and stepped forward. 'Here I am, Mr Ross,' she said stiffly, and then gasped when he came towards her and pulled her unresistingly into his arms.

'Where have you been?' she heard him say chokingly, burying his face in the hollow of her nape, and then he drew back to look at her as the sound of the kitchen door closing again signified that Bob and Laura had left them alone.

Caryn stared up at him uncomprehendingly, and thought inconsequently how haggard he was looking. But before she had time to formulate her thoughts, he spoke again.

'I've been out of my mind!' he muttered, his thumb probing between her lips. 'And if I hadn't had the idea of visiting Laurence Mellor this afternoon, I should never have thought of coming back here again.'

'You—you've seen Laurence. . .' she whis-

pered faintly, and he nodded. 'But he didn't know
I was coming here.'

'No, I know. He gave me the address of your
hotel. But when I found that you'd checked out,
I had the brainwave of trying here again, just
in case you came to see Laura before leaving
town.'

'I—I see.'

Caryn considered this tremulously while he
continued to look at her, and then, very quietly,
he said: 'Why in God's name did you run
away?'

'I—didn't run away.'

'What would you call it?'

She trembled. 'After—after what happened,
you must see I couldn't stay.'

There was silence for a moment, and then he
said evenly: 'Why? What's changed? I knew
Tristan was O'Hara's child from the beginning.'

'Then you should have told me!'

'Why? What good would that have done?' A
moment's pause. 'Would you have believed me?'

Caryn drew herself away from him, unable to
think with the hard muscles of his body touching
hers. 'You—you may have a point there, but—'

'But nothing!' His expression hardened. 'I
wanted you in my home, isn't that enough?'

'But why?' She stared at him.

'Why do you think?'

She didn't dare to think. 'I think this has gone
quite far enough—'

'No,' he retorted, and now his voice was harsh
and low. 'No, Caryn, it hasn't gone far enough!'
and with hard determination he jerked her

towards him again, and his mouth found the trembling weakness of hers.

He was not gentle with her. She could sense his impatience and his need to make her aware of him as he was aware of her, and despite all her efforts to evade him, eventually the probing pressure of his mouth forced hers apart, and then she was lost.

He kissed her long and expertly, caring little for their whereabouts, only making her want him as he undoubtedly wanted her. The fine material of his suit was no barrier to the thrusting urgency of his body, and she knew when she opened her eyes and looked into his that for once he was making no attempt to control the situation.

But at last he put her away from him, and raking his hand through his hair, he said: 'Do you have a coat or anything? We're leaving.'

'Tristan. . .' Caryn's hand fluttered to her temple. 'I—I—'

'We're leaving,' he repeated doggedly, and as if on cue, the kitchen door opened and Bob and Laura came slowly back into the room.

'Caryn. . .' Laura glanced awkwardly at her friend and then at Tristan. 'Are—are you going back to—to Wales?'

'No—'

'Yes!' Tristan's affirmation overrode Caryn's denial, and with a futile shake of her head, Caryn preceded him out of the flat.

Downstairs, she would have gone towards her car, but Tristan shook his head. 'I'll have that picked up later,' he declared tautly, and led her to the grey Mercedes, double-parked with a distinct disregard for any other road user. He opened the passenger side door, thrust her inside, and then walked round to get in beside her, and although she knew she ought to protest she remained silent.

They did not take the road west, however. Much to her astonishment, Tristan drove into the heart of the city, and his concentration on other traffic curtailed any conversation they might have had. He drove through the park and turned into Park Lane, and finally brought the car into an underpass which turned out to be the underground garage for a huge block of luxury apartments. Of course, she thought nervously, Tristan had an apartment in town. Was that where he was taking her?

'Out,' he said unceremoniously, opening the door for her, and now she voiced her protest.

'I'm not going up to your apartment!'

'Aren't you?' His voice harshened. 'Do you want me to carry you?'

'Tristan——'

'Save it. The lift's over here.'

She went with him, telling herself they couldn't talk down here, but really only making excuses for her own traitorous behaviour. And yet it wasn't traitorous to feel as she did for Tristan, she thought miserably. Only stupid. Wasn't Loren's experience enough for her?

The lift swam up to the fourteenth floor with a smoothness that belied the effort. They emerged into a glass-roofed corridor, and she realised this was the penthouse suite. A panelled door had ROSS written in small gold letters, and then he had inserted his key and was pushing her before him into a wide green-carpeted hallway. Beyond was the huge living area of the apartment, but its plate glass and angled modernity was softened by warm colours and antique furniture. There was even a fireplace, surely only ornamental, that helped to create the illusion of age that was amazingly not out of place in these contemporary surroundings. Book-shelves, a writing bureau, a gate-legged table with claw feet; and lots of soft armchairs and cushions invited relaxation.

Caryn walked into the middle of the floor, having registered all these things at a glance, and stood there waiting for Tristan to speak to her, feeling rather like one of the Christians in the arena at Rome. Tristan himself seemed in no hurry now he had her there, and closed the living room door with a definite click, before strolling slowly towards her.

'Now,' he said huskily, 'shall we take up where we left off?'

Caryn backed away from him. 'It's no use,' she declared unevenly. 'I know you've—you've been very kind to me—to the baby—but it's over.'

'You're wrong,' he stated, but he made no effort to go after her. 'It's only just beginning.'

Then he sighed and indicated one of the comfortable chairs. 'Won't you sit down? I'm afraid I can't offer you tea, my housekeeper here only comes in when I need her, and she didn't know I would be needing her today. But there's—sherry, if you like. Or something stronger?' He raised his eyebrows.

Caryn shook her head, and when she still continued to hover by the fireplace, Tristan turned away and walked across to the windows.

'Suppose you tell me what happened,' he said. 'How did you find out about—about the child being O'Hara's?'

Caryn gasped. 'You know!'

'I know?' He turned to face her, hands behind his back. 'I assure you I don't. Unless. . .' He paused. 'The resemblance is beginning to appear, I admit. . .'

'No!' Caryn shook her head. 'Your—your—Melanie pointed it out.'

'Melanie!' Now she really had his attention, and judging from the way his nostrils flared, she did not envy Melanie's next interview with her—her—her what? Caryn hesitated. Her fiancé, perhaps? She inwardly winced. He was too old to be called her *boy*-friend.

'What did Melanie say exactly?' His voice was cold now, but she had to go on.

'She—she and her father—they came to the nursery.'

'When?'

'The—the morning they were leaving.'

'What!' He stared at her. 'You mean—they actually told you in front of Miss Trewen?'

'They didn't so much tell me as—as recognise the likeness.'

Tristan's lips tightened. 'Melanie knew whose child he was. I told her.'

Caryn said nothing, and he took a deep breath. 'And that was why you left?'

Caryn frowned. 'How did you know I knew if Melanie didn't tell you?'

'Angela told me.'

'Oh! Angela.'

'I gather you had quite a *tête-à-tête* with her.'

'I wouldn't call it that exactly. I'm sorry, I didn't know she didn't know——Oh, that sounds awful. What I mean is——'

'I know what you mean. I was going to tell her myself when she got back. After——after that business with O'Hara——'

'What business with O'Hara?'

'Him taking you to St Gifford. I warned him to stay away from you.'

'You did——what?' The words came out very faintly.

'I warned him to stay away from you. I had some people in for drinks one Sunday, and I used it as a pretext to get him there and tell him.'

'I see.' Caryn caught her lower lip between her teeth. That must have been the so-called party Dave had mentioned. Was that when he had had the idea to come back to Port Edward and date her? Because Tristan had warned him off? But then if it hadn't been for what he had said about Melanie, she would probably never have gone with him.

'Anyway,' Tristan went on, 'I decided I'd put up with his ways long enough.' He sighed. 'Angel was mad about him, you see, and I guess I tried to find excuses for him because of that. I guessed something was going on between him and Loren, and that was part of the reason why I fired her. I didn't know it was already too late.'

Caryn digested this with difficulty. 'And——and you knew——'

'—right from the start,' he agreed heavily.

'But—but why let me stay?'

'I told you at the Westons' apartment.'

Caryn's cheeks flamed. 'I—I'm not like Loren. Whatever you may think, I—I'm not like her. . .'

'What are you talking about?' He came towards her, and she knew this was where she had to stand and fight. 'What has Loren to do with us?'

'I—I won't—that is, I know you can make me, but I won't stay with you—'

His hand over her mouth silenced her with a gulp. His eyes were darker now, darker and strangely angry. 'What in hell do you think I'm saying?'

She made a muffled sound, and impatiently he released his hand. 'I—I don't sleep with men,' she got out jerkily, and a faint smile touched his lips.

'You said that once before,' he said, taking her by the shoulders and drawing her resisting body towards him. 'And I said you would. Don't you think husbands and wives should share the same bed? Or is that another of your funny little quirks?'

'Hu—husbands and wives?' she stammered. 'What do you—'

'What do you think I mean?' Impatience coloured his tone again. 'For God's sake, Caryn, I'm asking you to marry me! There! Is that clear enough for you?'

Caryn reached up and touched his face. 'You—mean it!'

He turned his mouth into her palm. 'Let's say

I can't go on taking cold showers,' he murmured huskily, and her arms slid completely round his neck.

Their hunger for one another could not be assuaged with mere kisses, and eventually Tristan pulled her down on to his knees on one of the low armchairs, saying half grimly: 'There are still things that have to be said.' He hesitated. 'About Loren. . .'

Caryn buried her face in his shoulder. 'Angela told me a little about her, and I believe her, but I don't think she was as black as she's been painted.'

Tristan sighed, his lips against her temple. 'No,' he agreed, speaking against her skin, 'but she did—disrupt my household. She and O'Hara both.'

'And you?' Caryn murmured softly.

Tristan's fingers absently caressed her throat. 'Yes, me,' he said flatly. 'I've asked myself what my part in it all was, and I honestly can come up with no satisfactory answer. I know she saw working for me as a sort of glamorous occupation, and I guess the presence of groups like Sweet Vibration added to her delusions. But I don't honestly think she saw me as anything but an employer until after that affair with O'Hara. Then, when it became obvious that there was no chance that he'd marry her, she turned her attention to me. I guess that was when I knew she'd have to go.'

'When she came back to London, she talked of no one but you.'

'A defence, I suppose. Or maybe she intended

coming back and—well, asking me for money.'

'Blackmailing you, you mean?'

Tristan shook his head. 'Nothing so serious. Loren was not really bad, only irresponsible.'

Caryn pressed herself closer. 'Thank you for saying that.'

Tristan bent his mouth to hers and then, when their lips clung, he drew back again. 'So—then you came to me, threatening all manner of things, and what happened? I suddenly found myself wanting to help you—to make up to you for what happened to Loren. I didn't realise until later exactly how small a part Loren played in my feelings for you.'

'But you never said,' Caryn protested, and his hand slid along her thigh.

'Would you really have listened to me? Wouldn't you just have thought I had some ulterior motive? I wanted you to get to know me, to like me, before I showed you how I felt.' He shook his head 'That day you were late back from the beach—God, I could have killed you then! Falling asleep in some cove where the tide could have come in. . . And I was searching every cove I knew trying to find you!'

'Oh, Tristan!'

'You may well say "Oh, Tristan". You've given me some pretty hairy moments.'

'Like the night I rang you from St Gifford?'

'Like the night you rang from St Gifford,' he agreed.

'But you came back early both times. You weren't expected.'

'I couldn't keep away from the place,' he muttered, burying his face in her hair. 'Or you! Don't you know right now I should be at the studios recording tomorrow evening's programme?'

'But, Tristan—'

She would have sat up, but he pressed her back, his mouth curving sensually. 'Stay where you are. This is far more important than any television programme.' His lips parted. 'So—will you marry me? And soon? I don't think I can wait much longer.'

Caryn lifted her shoulders. 'But Melanie. . .'

'What about Melanie?'

'I thought—that is—she calls you darling.'

'Melanie calls everybody darling.' He smiled. 'Did she make you jealous? That was the idea.'

'Tristan!' She sat up to stare down at him. 'It wasn't!'

'It was. Melanie's really a friend of Angel's. Didn't you guess?'

Caryn shook her head. 'Then why did she reveal whose baby it really was?'

He gave a mocking smile. 'Well, I'm not saying that perhaps Melanie didn't have ideas of her own,' he teased, and Caryn dug her elbow into his ribs.

'I can hardly believe this,' she said tremulously. Then, with feeling, she said: 'I'm so glad things have worked out for Bob and Laura, too.' She smiled reminiscently. 'He's going to work for Area-South television as well.'

'I know.'

Tristan's reply was laconic and she looked sharply at him. 'How do you know? Oh—they told you.'

'No.'

Tristan shook his head, and mystified, Caryn frowned.

'Then how did you—' An idea dawned. 'Did you know he was having an interview?'

Tristan nodded. 'Warmer,' he agreed. 'I recognised the name, and the address.'

'But did you. . .' She hesitated. 'That is. . . Bob asked me. . .'

'. . .to intercede for him?'

'With you. Yes.'

'I thought he might. That was one of the reasons why I suggested you came to London last weekend. Besides, you needed the break.'

'But why did you want Bob to speak to me?'

He shrugged. 'I wanted you to have to come to me and ask me for something. I guess I wanted to show you I wasn't the brute you imagined me to be.'

'I didn't really imagine that,' confessed Caryn honestly. 'From the very beginning, I had to fight against being—attracted to you.'

'That sounds more interesting,' he murmured huskily, and there was silence in the apartment again.

'Miss Trewen will be pleased,' murmured Caryn drowsily at last.

'Mellor won't,' remarked Tristan, not without some satisfaction. 'When I saw him this afternoon, I told him I loved you and that I was going to marry you. He said you were considering his proposal.'

'Poor Laurence!' Caryn kicked off her shoes

and curled her legs about Tristan's. 'I shouldn't have gone to see him.'

'Well, I'm glad you did,' retorted Tristan. 'What on earth have you been doing anyway?'

'Trying to find another job. One where they would take a baby.'

'Oh, Caryn. . .' Tristan's fingers unbuttoned her shirt and his mouth sought the rosy peaks exposed to his gaze. Then, with a sound that was half groan, he lifted her into his arms and deposited her in the armchair he had just vacated.

'I can't go on holding you without—' He broke off abruptly. 'I think we'd better go out for something to eat. Unless you want to drive back to Wales tonight.'

'Is Angela expecting you to return?'

'Angel hopes we return together. After what I told her, she knows if we don't, her life won't be worth living.'

'Poor Angel!'

'Angel will survive, she's that kind of person. Myself, I'm not so sure. . .'

Caryn frowned. 'Will you tell Dave about—about the baby?'

'Some day, perhaps,' Tristan replied thoughtfully. 'I don't know. Maybe we can give him a better home than O'Hara ever could. And at least he'll have brothers and sisters. . .'

'I wonder what Marcia will think.'

'Marcia will be pleased. She likes you, you know that. And having the baby about the place has made a tremendous difference to her.'

Caryn nodded. 'It must have been a dreadful experience for her, losing her own family like that. Do you think she will ever speak again?'

Tristan's face looked grim for a moment. 'When I met her she was in the local hospital, recovering from the attack. They cut her tongue out, you know. That's why she doesn't speak.'

'Oh, Tristan!' Caryn was appalled. 'How ghastly!'

'It was—at the time. It still is, I suppose. Except that now she's adapting to her new life. It's two years since her husband was killed. Life has to go on.'

'Yes.'

Caryn absorbed this silently, then, noticing his rather strained expression, she uncurled herself from the chair.

'Do you want to go out?' she asked, and Tristan's tawny eyes grew dark.

'No,' he admitted softly. 'I want to love you. I want to show you what making love really means. But I've no intention of shocking that prudish little mind of yours any more than it's already been shocked, so we'll go out.'

Caryn came towards him and wound her arms round his neck. 'What if I told you I was suspending my rule about sleeping with men?' she murmured.

'Well, so long as the suspension only applies to me, I'd go along with that,' he agreed huskily, and gathered her fully into his arms.

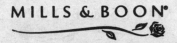

MILLS & BOON®

Back by Popular Demand

COLLECTOR'S EDITION

A collector's edition of favourite titles from one of Mills & Boon's best-loved romance authors.

Don't miss this wonderful collection of sought-after titles, now reissued in beautifully matching volumes and presented as one cherished collection.

Look out next month for:

Title #9	**Living with Adam**
Title #10	**Sandstorm**

Available wherever Mills & Boon books are sold

MILLS & BOON®

Anne Mather

COLLECTOR'S EDITION

If you have missed any of the previously published titles in the Anne Mather Collector's Edition, you may order them by sending a cheque or postal order (please do not send cash) made payable to Harlequin Mills & Boon Ltd. for £2.99 per book plus 50p per book postage and packing. Please send your order to: Anne Mather Collector's Edition, P.O. Box 236, Croydon, Surrey, CR9 3RU (EIRE: Anne Mather Collector's Edition, P.O. Box 4546, Dublin 24).

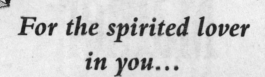

Lynne Graham was born in Northern Ireland and has been a keen romance reader since her teens. She is very happily married, to an understanding husband who has learned to cook since she started to write! Her five children keep her on her toes. She has a very large dog who knocks everything over, a very small terrier who barks a lot, and two cats. When time allows, Lynne is a keen gardener.

Also by Lynne Graham

His Queen by Desert Decree
The Greek's Blackmailed Mistress
The Italian's Inherited Mistress

Billionaires at the Altar miniseries

The Greek Claims His Shock Heir
The Italian Demands His Heirs
The Sheikh Crowns His Virgin

Vows for Billionaires miniseries

The Secret Valtinos Baby
Castiglione's Pregnant Princess
Da Rocha's Convenient Heir

Discover more at millsandboon.co.uk.

THE SHEIKH CROWNS HIS VIRGIN

LYNNE GRAHAM

MILLS & BOON

First Published in Great Britain 2019
by Mills & Boon, an imprint of HarperCollins*Publishers*
1 London Bridge Street, London, SE1 9GF

© 2019 Lynne Graham

ISBN: 978-0-263-27063-1

MIX
Paper from
responsible sources
FSC® C007454

This book is produced from independently certified FSC™ paper
to ensure responsible forest management.
For more information visit www.harpercollins.co.uk/green.

Printed and bound in Spain
by CPI, Barcelona

CHAPTER ONE

ZOE DESCENDED THE steps of her grandfather's private jet and as the sunlight of Maraban enveloped her she smiled happily. It was spring and the heat was bearable but, best of all, she was taking the very first brave step into her new life.

On her own, on her own *at last*, free of the restrictions that her sisters would have attached to her but, most importantly of all, free of the *low* expectations they had of her. Winnie and Vivi had been amazed when Zoe had agreed to move to a foreign country for a few months without freaking out at the prospect. They had been equally amazed when she'd agreed to marry a much older man to fulfil her part of their agreement with their grandfather, Stamboulas Fotakis. Why not? It wasn't as though it was going to be a *real* marriage, merely a pretend marriage in which her future husband made political use of the fact that she was the grand-daughter of a former princess of a country called Bania, which no longer existed.

Long before Zoe was even born the two tiny realms of Bania and Mara had joined to become Maraban and apparently her late grandmother, the Princess Azra, had been hugely popular in both countries. Prince Hakem wanted to marry Zoe literally for her ancestry and she would become an Arabian princess and live in the royal palace for several months. There she would enjoy glorious solitude with nobody bothering her, nobody asking how she felt or worriedly enquiring if she thought she should have more therapy to help her cope with ordinary life. Even though she hadn't had a panic attack in months, her siblings had always been on edge around her, awaiting another one.

Zoe adored her older sisters but their constant care and concern had held her back from the independence she needed to rebuild her self-esteem and forge her own path. And taking part in this silly pretend marriage was all she had to do to finally obtain that freedom.

All three sisters had agreed to marry men of their grandfather's choosing to gain his financial help for their foster parents, John and Liz Brooke. Winnie and Vivi had already fulfilled that bargain. But in Zoe's case, no pressure whatsoever had been placed on her and, indeed, John and Liz's mortgage arrears had been paid off shortly after her sister Vivi's marriage had taken place. Yes, she thought wryly, even her extremely ruthless grandfather had shrunk from taking the risk of putting pressure on his youngest granddaughter, having taken on board her siblings' conviction that she was hopelessly fragile and emotionally vulnerable. Nobody had faith in her ability to be strong, Zoe reflected ruefully, which was why it was so very important that she proved for her own benefit that she *could* be strong.

Like her sisters, Zoe had grown up in foster care, and a terrifying incident when she was twelve years old had traumatised her. But she had buried all that hurt and fear, seemingly flourishing in John and Liz's happy home, only for those frightening insecurities to come back and engulf her while she was studying botany at university. Having to freely mix with men, having to deal with friends asking why she didn't want a boyfriend, had put her under severe strain. Her panic attacks had grown worse and worse and, although she had contrived to hide her extreme anxiety from her sisters, she had, ultimately, been unable to deal with her problems alone. Weeks before she sat her final degree exams, she had suffered a nervous breakdown, which had meant that she had had to take time out from her course to recover.

Although she had subsequently completed her degree and worked through the therapy required to put her back on an even track where crippling anxiety no longer ruled her every thought and action, her sisters had continued to treat her as if she could shatter again at any moment. While she understood that their protectiveness came from love, she also saw that their attitude had made her weaker than she need have been and that she badly needed the chance to stand on her own feet. With her sisters now married, one living in Greece and the other in Italy, coming to Maraban was Zoe's opportunity to prove that she had overcome her unhappy past.

Zoe stepped into the limousine awaiting her, grateful for the reality that her arrival in Maraban was completely low-key. Prince Hakem had insisted that no public appearances or indeed anything of that nature would be required from her. He might be the brother of the current King but he had no official standing in Maraban. Zoe's grandfather should have been travelling with her but a pressing business matter had led to him asking if she could manage alone if he put off his arrival until the following day. Of course, she could manage, she thought cheerfully, gazing out with lively interest at the busy streets of the capital city, Tasit, which was an intriguing mix of old and new. She saw old buildings and elaborate mosques with quaint colourful turrets nudging shoulders with redeveloped areas boasting soaring skyscrapers and office blocks. Maraban was evidently right in the middle of the process of modernisation.

Oil and gas wealth had transformed the country. Zoe had read everything she could find on Maraban and had rolled her eyes at the discovery that nobody appeared to know why her grandmother, Princess Azra, had failed to marry the current King, Tahir, as she had been expected to do. The bald truth was that Azra had run off with Stamboulas Fotakis sooner than marry a man who'd already had three wives. Presumably that story had been suppressed to conserve the monarch's dignity. Luckily, Stam had told her everything she needed to know about his late wife's background.

Darkness was falling fast when the limo driver turned off the road and steered between imposingly large gates guarded by soldiers. Zoe strained to see the enormous property that lay ahead but the limo travelled slowly right on past it, threading a path through a vast complex of buildings and finally drawing up beside one. She was ushered out and indoors before she could even catch her breath and was a little disappointed to find herself standing in a contemporary house. A very *large* contemporary house, she conceded wryly, with aggressively gilded fancy furniture and nothing whatsoever historic about it. A female servant in a long kaftan bowed to her and showed her up a brilliantly lit staircase into an entire suite of rooms.

Her disappointment that she wasn't going to be living in the ancient royal palace slowly ebbed as she scanned her comfortable and well-furnished surroundings. It wasn't ideal that none of the staff spoke her language and that she didn't speak theirs but miming could accomplish a lot, she told herself bracingly as her companion mimicked eating to let her know that a meal was being brought. And long before she went home again, she should have picked up at least a few useful phrases to enable her to communicate more effectively, she told herself soothingly.

A maid had already arrived to unpack her suitcases when a knock sounded on the door. Zoe made it to the door first.

A slimly built young man and a uniformed nurse hovered outside. 'I am Dr Wazd,' the man told her stiffly. 'I have been instructed to give you a vaccination shot. The nurse will assist.'

Zoe winced because she hated needles and she was surprised because she had had all the required shots for Maraban. But then what she did know that a medical doctor would not know better? She rolled up her sleeve and then frowned as she saw the doctor's hand on the syringe was shaking. Glancing up at him in surprise, noting the perspiration beading his brow, she wondered if he was a very newly qualified doctor to be so nervous and she was relieved when the nurse silently filched the syringe from him and gave her the injection without further ado. It stung and she gritted her teeth.

No sooner was that done than a tray of food arrived and she sat down at the table to eat, noting that she was feeling dizzy and woolly-headed and surmising that she was already suffering the effects of jet lag. But while she was eating, she began feeling as though the world around her were slowing down and her body felt as heavy as lead. Feeling dizzy even seated, she rose to go to the bathroom and had to grip the back of a chair to balance. As she wobbled on her heels, blinking rapidly, a suffocating blackness folded in and she dropped down into it with a gasp of dismay...

His Royal Highness, Prince Faraj al-Basara, was in a very high-powered meeting in London dealing with his country's oil and gas production when his private mobile thrummed a warning in his pocket. Few people had that number and it only ever rang if it was very, *very* important. Excusing himself immediately, Raj stepped outside, his brain awash with sudden apprehension. Had his father taken ill? Or had some other calamity occurred back home in Maraban?

Maraban was a tiny Gulf state but it was also one of the richest countries in the world. A terrorist incident, however, would bring the home of his birth to a screeching halt because the security forces were equally tiny and these days Maraban relied on wealth and diplomacy to stay safe. When Raj thought nostalgically of home, it was always of a place of stark black and white contrasts where four-wheel-drive vehicles and helicopters startled livestock in the desert and where a conservative Middle Eastern ethos struggled to cope with the very different mores and the sheer speed of change in the modern world.

It was eight years, however, since Raj had last visited his home because his father, the King, had removed him from his position as Crown Prince and sent him into exile for refusing to go into the army and for refusing even more vehemently to marry the bride his parent had chosen for him. No, he had not been a dutiful or obedient son, Raj acknowledged with grim self-honesty, he had been a stubborn, rebellious one and, unfortunately for him, there was no greater sin in his culture.

That said, however, Raj had, since, moved on from that less than stellar beginning to carve his own path in the business world and there his shrewd brain, intuition and ability to spot trends had ensured meteoric success in that sphere. He had also learned how to steer Maraban into the future from beyond its borders, making allies, attracting foreign businesses and investment while constantly encouraging growth in the public infrastructure required to keep his country up to speed with the latest technology. And his reward for that tireless focus and resolve? Maraban, the home that he loved, was positively booming.

He was pleasantly surprised when he answered his phone and recognised his cousin, Omar's voice. Omar had pretty much been his best friend since the dark days of the military school they had both been forced to attend as adolescents, an unforgettable era of relentless bullying and abuse that Raj still winced to recall. As Crown Prince he had had a target painted on his back and his father had told the staff to turn a blind eye, believing that it would be beneficial for his only child to be toughened up in such a severe environment.

'Omar…what can I do for you?' he asked almost cheerfully, relieved of the anxiety that his elderly father had taken ill because Omar would not have been chosen as messenger for that development. *That* call would only have come from a member of his father's staff. After all, his mother had died while he was still a boy. The memory made him tense for his mother had died in a manner that he would never forget: she had taken her own life. It had taken a very long time for Raj to accept that her unhappiness had surpassed her love for her nine-year-old son and he had never forgotten his sense of abandonment because, once she was gone, everything soft and loving and caring had vanished from his childish world.

'I'm in a real fix, Raj, and I think you are the only person with sufficient knowledge to approach with this,' Omar declared, his habitually upbeat voice unusually flat in tone. 'I've been dragged into something I don't want to be involved in and it's serious. You know I'm a royalist and very loyal to my country but there are some things I *can't*—'

'Cut to the chase,' Raj sliced in with a bemused frown. 'What have you been dragged into?'

'Early this morning I received a call from someone at the palace who asked if I would look after a "package" and keep it safe until further notice. And that's the problem, Raj… I didn't get delivered a package, I got a woman.'

'A *woman*?' Raj repeated in disbelief. 'Are you joking me?'

'I wish I was. All the women in the tribe are outraged and I've been thrown out of my tent to accommodate her,' Omar lamented. 'My wife thinks I'm getting involved in sex trafficking.'

'It could *not* be that,' Raj pronounced with assurance because the penalty for such a crime was death and his father was most assiduous in ensuring that neither drugs nor prostitution gained ground in Maraban.

'No, of course it couldn't be,' Omar agreed. 'But even though the order came from the very highest level of the palace I should not be asked by *anyone* to imprison a woman against her will.'

'How do you know the order came from the very highest level?' Raj demanded.

His cousin mentioned a name and Raj gritted his teeth. Bahadur Abdi was the most trusted military adviser in his father's inner circle and could only be acting at the King's command. That shocking truth shed an entirely different light on the kidnapping because it meant that Raj's father was personally involved. 'Who the hell *is* this woman?'

'You're not going to like the suspicion I'm developing any more than I do,' his cousin warned him heavily. 'But I contacted the palace as soon as I appreciated I was being asked to deal with a *live* package and I was told that she was the last descendant of the al-Mishaal family, which was a shock. Thought they were all dead and buried long ago! Were you even aware that *my* father divorced my mother two months ago?'

Raj was shocked enough by both those revelations

to listen keenly as Omar described his mother's refusal to discuss the divorce and the oddity of her continuing calm over the termination of a marriage that had lasted almost fifty years and had spawned four children and at least a dozen grandchildren. Prince Hakem, Raj's uncle and Omar's father, however, was an embittered and ambitious man, who ever since Raj's exile had been striving to become the recognised heir to the throne in Raj's place. Ironically, Raj didn't even really feel that he could blame his uncle for his ambition because, as the King's younger brother, Hakem had spent his whole life close to the throne but virtually ignored and powerless, his royal brother refusing to grant him any form of responsibility in the kingdom. Furthermore, only the King could name his heir and Hakem had long desired a role of power and the rise in status it would accord him.

'So, what's the connection with this woman?'

Omar shared his suspicions and Raj paled and experienced a spontaneous surge of rage at such a manipulative plot being played out in virtual secret behind the palace walls. 'Surely that is *not* possible?'

'It may not be. I must admit that the woman doesn't look remotely as if she carries Marabanian blood. She's got white-blonde hair...looks like something out of that fairy tale... *The Sleeping Beauty*,' Omar revealed heavily.

Raj parted compressed lips. 'Princess Azra of Bania was the daughter of a Danish explorer, who was blond,' he murmured flatly. 'I don't know much about Azra's elopement with her Greek tycoon, who was working in Maraban when the two countries joined, but I do know her flight with another man created a *huge* scandal.

She was supposed to become my father's fourth wife and instead, she ran off with Fotakis and married him.'

'Didn't know that…but then it's not really my slice of history in the same way as it's yours.' Omar sighed heavily. 'Just give me some diplomatic advice about what to do next because I'm at a standstill. This woman has *obviously* been kidnapped. Our doctor says she's been drugged, so she's unconscious and she arrived with no means of identification. But even if she *is* one of the al-Mishaal family's next generation from that marriage all those years ago I still can't believe that any *young* woman would agree to marry a man as old as my father—'

'It would shock you what some Western women would be willing to do to become an Arabian princess with unlimited wealth at their disposal. Suggest that a crown could also be on offer and there would be many takers of that particular bargain,' Raj breathed with cynical derision, his lean, darkly handsome features clenching hard as he reflected on his own experiences and the shattering betrayal he had endured…and worst of all, only *after* he had destroyed his standing with his father for ever. Even years after that youthful disillusionment, he was grimly aware of the pulling power of his status and wealth in the West. In his radius even seemingly intelligent women frothed and gushed like champagne, desperate to attract and bed him. Sadly for them, he didn't find being chased, flattered or potentially seduced remotely attractive because he preferred to do his own hunting in that field. And, almost inevitably, that shattering act of infidelity following on from

his mother's suicide had underlined his growing conviction that women were not to be trusted.

'Possibly not…shocked,' Omar clarified as tactfully
as he knew how because he too was probably thinking
about that old and demeaning history that still scarred
Raj's pride. 'But I *can* tell you that if that is my father's
game, very few of our people would like or accept such
a marriage. My father is unpopular: he's as old school as
your father. I don't know anyone who would be willing
to accept him as the heir in place of you, *no*, not even
if he *has* somehow contrived to bring back the ghost of
the al-Mishaal royal family as a potential bride!'

Raj had been away from palace politics for a very
long time but he had not forgotten the scheming games
of one-upmanship involved. In the role of Hakem's
bride, Princess Azra's granddaughter would be a price-
less figurehead, Raj acknowledged grimly. Half the
population of Maraban came from Banian roots and
all had been seriously dissatisfied forty-odd years ago
when the joining of the two states was not matched as
had been promised by a marital alliance between Bania's only Princess and Mara's King. All those people
had felt cheated by the absence of Banian blood in the
royal family tree of Maraban. It would be a triumph for
his uncle to marry Azra's descendant and it definitely
would increase his popularity, which was precisely why
Raj's father would never have allowed such a marriage
to take place: King Tahir did not tolerate competition
or, for that matter, a little brother he deemed to be getting too big for his boots. After such a publicity-grab-
bing stunt, Hakem could only have been hoping to be

named the King's heir and step into Raj's former position as Crown Prince in his nephew's stead.

Omar broke into Raj's racing thoughts. 'Tell me, what am I to do with her?' he demanded, infuriated that an innocent woman had been kidnapped to prevent a marriage he believed to be wholly inappropriate. 'How do I safely *and* decently rid myself of this appalling responsibility? '

And Raj told him with a succinctness that shook both of them before he powered back into his meeting to apologise and explain that a family crisis demanded his immediate attention. He contacted an investigation firm, who had done excellent work for him in the past, to request an immediate file on his uncle's putative bride. He needed information and he needed it fast yet he was aware that he was struggling to concentrate.

Why?

For the first time in eight years, Raj would be returning to the country of his birth and, although anger was driving him at the prospect of being forced to deal with another unscrupulous and mercenary woman, on another much more basic level he was quietly exhilarated at the prospect of seeing his homeland again...

Zoe surfaced from an uneasy, woozy dream to find someone helping her to lift a glass of water to her lips. Her eyes refused to focus and her body felt limp but she knew she needed the bathroom and said so. Someone helped her rise and supported her—more than one someone, she registered dimly, because her limbs were too weak to carry her. She tried to scan her surroundings but the walls being weirdly bendy spooked her and momentarily she shut her eyes as she was helped back to bed. She had been drugged, taken somewhere, she registered fearfully, fighting without success to stay conscious and focus. She had to protect herself, *had* to protect herself! That self-saving litany rang through her brain like a wake-up call...but even that panic couldn't prevent her from sliding down into oblivion again.

When Raj received the info on Zoe Mardas, he was forced to rapidly rearrange his expectations. Why on earth would such a woman be willing to marry a man almost as old as her grandfather? Clearly, financial greed would be a most unlikely motive for a woman with the billionaire Stamboulas Fotakis at her back. Fotakis was her grandfather and, by all accounts, an extremely protective relative. Other more stressful concerns then started dawning on Raj. The Greek tycoon would scarcely take the kidnapping of his granddaughter lying down. He would not allow it to be hushed up either. Yet, even more strangely, it did look as though Fotakis had been the prime mover and shaker behind the proposed marriage between Hakem and Zoe. What was Stam Fotakis getting out of it? Some lucrative business deal? Or a title for his granddaughter? Raj pondered those unknowns and decided to contact Fotakis direct...

Someone was brushing Zoe's hair when she next woke up, someone murmuring softly in a foreign language. She opened her eyes and saw an older woman, who smiled down at her from her kneeling stance by her side while she brushed Zoe's long mane of pale blonde hair with admiring care. She did not seem hostile or threat-

ening in any way and Zoe forced a smile, her innate
survival instincts kicking in. Until she knew what was
happening she would be a good little prisoner, playing
along until such time as her grandfather came to rescue her; because one thing she *did* know: Stamboulas
Fotakis would not be long in putting in an appearance.
He would create a huge fuss the instant he realised that
Zoe had gone missing and no rock would be left un-
turned in his search for her, she reflected with a strong
sense of relief.

Gently detaching her hair from the woman's light
hold, she sat up and the woman stood up and helpfully
showed her straight to the bathroom. Even by that stage,
Zoe was recognising that she had not been disorientated
the night before when she had thought the walls surrounding her looked rather odd. Evidently, she was no
longer at the villa in the palace complex, she was in a
tent, a very large and very luxurious tent decorated with
rich hangings and opulent seating but, when all was said
and done, it was *still* a tent! And the connecting bathroom was also under canvas. Zoe felt hot and sweaty
and looked longingly at the shower, but she didn't want
to risk the vulnerability of getting naked. She freshened
up with cold water, dried her face and frowned down at
the unfamiliar long white fine cotton shift she now wore
in place of the skirt and top she had travelled in. That
creepy nervous doctor and his sidekick, she thought in
disgust. She would never trust a doctor again!

Why had she been taken from Prince Hakem's villa?
Although no one had ever told her that it was *his* villa,
she had simply assumed it was. Presumably somebody
didn't want this marriage of his to take place, she rea-

soned reflectively. No problem, she thought ruefully, there had been no need to assault her with a syringe, send her to sleep and ship her out to a tent because she would quite happily go home again without any argument. Furthermore, she rather thought that would be her grandfather's reaction as well because he had demanded very strong assurances from her bridegroom-to-be that she would be safe and secure in Maraban and he would be appalled at what had happened to her. Surely her becoming a princess to follow in the footsteps of her formerly royal grandmother, Princess Azra, would not still be so important to Stam Fotakis that he would expect his granddaughter to risk life and limb in the process?

Two women were setting out a meal when she returned to the main tent and she roamed as casually as she could in the direction of the doorway that had been left uncovered. What she glimpsed froze her in her tracks in instant denial. She saw a circle of tents and beyond them sand dunes that ran off into the horizon. She was in the desert, so escaping would be more of a challenge than she felt equal to because she would need transport and a map at the very least for such a venture. The discovery that she had been plunged into such an alien environment sent her nervous tension climbing higher and she swallowed hard. Where else had she expected a tent to be pitched but in the desert? she asked herself irritably.

Above one of the tents she espied the rotor blades of a helicopter. Was that how she had arrived? Had she been flown in? She shuddered as another far more frightening thought suddenly occurred to her.

Why was she assuming that she had been kidnapped to prevent the wedding taking place in forty-eight hours? Her grandfather was an extremely rich man. It was equally possible that she had been taken so that a ransom demand could be made for her release. That scenario meant that someone laying violent hands on her was a much more likely development, she decided sickly, her tummy hollowing out. As one of the women carefully threaded her stiff arms into a concealing wrap and even tied it for her, Zoe could feel all the hallmarks of an impending panic attack assailing her and she was already zoning out as her thoughts raged out of her control.

She saw a mental image of herself beaten up in a photo for her grandfather's benefit. Her heart raced and she turned rapidly away from the view of the encampment, incapable of even noticing that the two women with her were hastily bowing and backing out of the tent again or that a male figure now stood silhouetted in the doorway. Her throat was tight, making it hard for her to catch her breath. She was shivering in spite of the heat, cold, then hot, dizziness making her sway as panic threatened.

I'm fine, I'm strong, I can cope, she chanted inwardly. But the mantra that usually worked to steady her failed because for several unbearable seconds she was simply overpowered by fear.

A male voice sounded directly behind her and a hand brushed her shoulder. Startled, terrified, Zoe reacted automatically with the self-defence tactics she had spent months learning so that she had the skills she needed to ensure her personal safety.

She spun at speed, her elbow travelling up for a chest

blow and her clenched fist heading for a throat strike while her knee lifted to aim at the groin. Raj was so disconcerted by a woman the size of a child attacking him that he almost fell over in sheer shock and then his own training kicked in and, light as dancer on his feet, he twisted and blocked her before bringing her down on the rug beneath their feet with careful hands.

'Let go of me, you bastard!' she railed at him, clawing, biting and scratching and in the act contriving to dislodge the white *keffiyeh* that covered his head.

Still reeling with disconcertion, Raj backed off several steps because he couldn't subdue her without hurting her and he refused to take that risk. She squirmed frantically away and the sheer terror in her face savaged his view of himself. Her eyes were glassy, her face white as snow.

'You are quite safe here. Nobody is going to hurt you.' Raj crouched down to her level while she wriggled back against a carved wooden chest like a trapped animal and hugged her knees, rocking back and forth. She was tiny and his every instinct was to protect her. 'On my honour, I *swear* that you are safe...' he intoned with as much conviction as he could get into the assurance, because she wasn't listening to him and she wasn't looking at him.

He was annoyed that his cousin had not sent his English-speaking wife, Farida, in to Zoe immediately to explain that there was no threat of any kind against her. But most of all, he cursed his father and the omnipotence he wielded in Maraban, for Raj was convinced that his wily father had ordered the kidnapping of Hakem's youthful bride-to-be. Would his father have counted the cost to the woman involved? Would he even have foreseen that he was unleashing the kind of explosively damaging scandal that no self-respecting country could withstand? No, his father, Tahir, would not have looked at that bigger picture of cause and effect. He would simply have set out to ensure that his ambitious brother's plot to raise his status was foiled while steadfastly refusing to acknowledge the likelihood of unexpected consequences.

In a fierce temper at that frustrating knowledge, Raj sank down beside Zoe Mardas on his knees and began to coax her into attempting a breathing exercise, aimed at calming her down. Extraordinary green eyes, clear as emeralds, skimmed over him and she blinked, long feathery lashes dipping. For a split second he was frozen in place by her ice-cool Scandinavian beauty. He coached her in breathing in, holding her breath and then very slowly breathing out again. She did so and then shot him an exasperated look, *not* the kind of look Raj was accustomed to receiving from young women.

'Yes, I do know how to do that for myself!' Zoe told him sharply as soon as she was breathing normally again. 'Why do you know how?'

'For a while in my teens, I suffered similar episodes,' Raj admitted, startling himself with that candour as much as he startled her; for the severe bullying he had endured at military school had for years afterwards left him damaged. He could only think his candour had been unwisely drawn from him by his glimpse of her at her most vulnerable and a natural need to put her at her ease.

In receipt of that surprising admission, Zoe stared

back at him in wonderment because in her experience men were much less willing to admit to suffering such a condition. But before she could question him further to satisfy her curiosity, he vaulted gracefully upright again. She watched him smooth down his rumpled white buttoned tunic and snatch up the white head cloth she had dislodged in their tussle. And then, strikingly, for the first time in her life Zoe looked at a man with interest because there was no denying it: whoever he was, he was without question the most beautiful creature she had ever seen. Dense silky blue-black curls covered his well-shaped skull while high cheekbones and hollows fed into a truly spectacular bone structure sheathed in olive skin. Dark-as-the-devil eyes glittered below straight ebony brows. A faint shadow of stubble surrounded his wide sensual mouth, his full soft lower lip tensing as he noticed her lingering scrutiny.

Turning pink, Zoe hurriedly glanced away while scolding herself for staring but, really, with looks of that quality, he had to be accustomed to being stared at by women, she reasoned defensively, uneasy with her speeded-up heartbeat and the sudden tightening of her nipples.

She wasn't *that* sort of woman, she reminded herself resolutely. Sex didn't interest her. Basically, men didn't interest her. She had been thrown off the path of normal development at the age of twelve when an attempted rape had devastated her. Ever since then she had held herself apart, avoiding mixed company unless it was family-orientated. She was perfectly happy around her brothers-in-law, Eros and Raffaele, and she hadn't been nervous either when dealing with the male parents at the childcare nursery where she had worked for months immediately after her recovery from her breakdown. Back then a full-time job in her own field of botany had seemed too challenging as a first step back into the real world.

'Who are you?' she asked baldly.

'You may call me Raj. I am no one of importance here,' he intoned in smooth dismissal, for he intended to fly back out of Maraban within the hour because he could not risk discovery and possible arrest. 'But this nomadic base camp is where my cousin, Sheikh Omar, lives at this time of year.'

Zoe bridled as she scrambled upright, wishing for about the thousandth time that she was even a few inches taller, for being only four feet eleven inches tall was not an advantage when it came to persuading people to take her seriously. Unsurprisingly, Raj towered over her but he wasn't quite as tall as her brothers-in-law, both of whom put her in mind of giants when she was around them. 'Is he the man responsible for bringing me here...*against my will*?' she stressed acidly.

'No, he is not,' Raj told her emphatically. 'Nor would he harm a hair on your head but he has kept his distance because he does not speak English.'

'Then who *is* responsible for bringing me here?' Zoe demanded, standing her ground, tensing her spine to keep her back and shoulders straight and her head high. Her favourite self-help book urged that even if you didn't *feel* confident, it was still possible to fake confidence and by so doing actually acquire it.

'I'm afraid I can't tell you that,' Raj countered flatly.

Zoe's green eyes flared as if he had slapped her. *'Why not?'* she demanded.

'It would serve no useful purpose.'

Zoe breathed in very deeply to contain the temper she hadn't known she had until that moment. He was so incredibly patronising, so superior and his attitude affected her like a chalk scraping down a blackboard, setting her teeth on edge. 'That's my decision to make, *not* yours,' she said succinctly.

Engaged in replacing his *keffiyeh*, Raj looked heavenward, involuntarily amused by that argument. She was like a doll with that tiny stature of hers and her phenomenally long blonde hair and she barely reached his chest.

'You're not taking me seriously,' she condemned.

'I'm afraid not,' Raj conceded grudgingly. 'I arrived here to sort this unfortunate mess out and that is what I intend to do.'

'Is it indeed?' Zoe snapped, incredulous that he had simply admitted his inability to treat her like an intelligent individual because, in her experience, most people lied on that score, denying that her diminutive size coloured their attitude towards her.

Raj paced several steps away from her, having discovered that proximity was unwise. His attention kept on dropping to that soft full pink mouth, that shimmering fall of pale hair, the barely noticeable little feminine curves hinting at her physical shape beneath the robe. He shifted, a kick of lust at his groin exasperating him for it was inappropriate and Raj was *always* very appropriate in his reactions to women. He controlled his responses, he did not allow them to control him and he had never understood the intoxicating lust that he had heard other men talk about, because only one woman had ever tested his control and, even then, it had not overwhelmed him.

'I intend to have you conveyed home as soon as it is possible...unless you are unwilling to give up the possibility of marrying my uncle, Prince Hakem, and becoming a princess,' Raj murmured bluntly. 'I suspect my aunt, his wife of many years, whom he recently divorced, would be relieved to have the ingrate back by default, little though he deserves her forgiveness and understanding...'

CHAPTER TWO

'ARE YOU TELLING me that Prince Hakem was already married at the time he agreed to marry me?' Zoe gasped in astonished disbelief, her triangular face tightening and losing colour at that horrendous concept.

'Of course, you were *already* aware of that reality,' Raj informed her with considerable scorn in his tone. 'After all, he has been married for many years. He has four children and a very large number of grandchildren… However, I assume that your grandfather was unwilling to accept a polygamous marriage, so my uncle *had* to divorce his wife before he could be allowed to marry you…'

Zoe was stunned by what she was learning. She wondered if her grandfather had been aware of those same unpleasant facts and then she told herself off for shying away from the unlovely truth that Stam Fotakis had wanted his granddaughter to become a princess regardless of what it would take to achieve that end. Prince Hakem had *had* to divorce his wife to take Princess Azra's granddaughter as a bride! Zoe was appalled and mortified and guilt-stricken, feeling that she should've done her homework better and shouldn't be in the position of finding out such a crucial fact when it was too late to change anything. Hakem's poor wife! Raj was definitely correct in his conviction that her grandfather would never have accepted a polygamous marriage and would only ever have settled for his grandchild becoming the Prince's sole wife.

'I didn't know… I *swear* I didn't know that he was a married man!' Zoe protested vehemently, a guilty flush driving off her previous pallor. 'In spite of what you seem to think, I would never have agreed if I had known that he was getting rid of his real wife just to marry me for a few months.'

Raj had no idea why she was bothering to defend her behaviour by pleading ignorance of the reality that his uncle had been a perfectly happy married man before her availability had ignited his ambition. Zoe Mardas might look convincingly like a storybook princess or a heavenly angel, but Raj had an innate distrust of that level of physical beauty and a cynical view of humanity. Beautiful on the outside but what less than presentable motives were she striving to conceal from him? He had discovered for himself that beautiful on the outside too often meant ugly on the inside.

In any case, Zoe could not possibly be as naïve as she was pretending to be. She *had* to know her own worth in Marabanian terms. Thousands of delighted Banians would flood the streets to celebrate an alliance between a royal Prince and Princess Azra's grandchild. His uncle had come very close to pulling off a spectacular coup in the popularity stakes.

'I assume you are willing to go home now?' Raj queried, marvelling at his own restraint in asking her that question because, frankly, he was determined to get her out of Maraban by any means within his power.

'Of course, I'm willing to go home!' Zoe shot back at him in reproach. 'Good grief, I'm not wanting to marry a man I've never even met, who divorced his wife just to become my bridegroom! Do I look that desperate?'

'I don't know you. I have no idea what your motivations are or, indeed, *were*,' Raj parried with the intrinsic hauteur that came as naturally to him as breathing, his exotically high cheekbones taut, his arrogant nose lifted, his hard jaw clenched.

Zoe's colour heightened, her eyes brightening with anger, for in a couple of sentences, he had cut her down to size, enforcing the distance between them while also underlining his indifference to her feelings about anything. He looked different with that headdress covering his riot of coal-black curls. While the *keffiyeh* framed and accentuated his superb bone structure and those dark deep-set eyes set below slashing ebony brows, it also made him look older and off-puttingly sombre.

'I confess that I am surprised, however, that you have not even met Prince Hakem. While such traditional matches still occasionally occur in Maraban, they are no longer the norm and I would not have thought a woman from your background would have been prepared to accept a husband sight unseen,' he admitted smoothly, dark eyes glittering back at her in cool challenge.

A wild surge of temper rocked Zoe where she stood, thoroughly disconcerting her, and her small hands coiled into tight fists by her side. The derision lacing his intonation and his appraisal was like a slap in the face. He might say that he didn't know her but she could see that, regardless of that reality, he had still made unsavoury assumptions about her character.

'Who the hell do you think you are to talk to me like this?' Zoe suddenly hissed at him, out of all patience and restraint because the way he was looking at her, as though she were some sort of lesser being, infuriated her. 'I came to this wretched country in good faith and my trust has been betrayed. I was drugged, *kidnapped* and subjected to a terrifying experience! Now you start judging me even though you don't know the facts.'

'I agree that I don't know the facts, nor do I need to know them,' Raj countered, disconcerted by the passion etched in her heart-shaped face as she answered him back. He wasn't used to that—he wasn't used to that kind of treatment at all.

He had been reserved from childhood, discouraged from letting his guard down with anyone, continually reminded about *who* he was and *what* he was and exactly what his rank demanded. After his mother's tragic death, he had had to learn to conceal his feelings and his insecurities, had had to accept that such personal responses were out of step with his status. An accident of birth had imprisoned him in a separate category, denying him the relaxation of true friends or freedom. When he had finally broken out of that prison, he had discovered to his consternation that that often icy reserve of his, which kept people at a distance, was as much a natural part of him as his face.

'Well, you're going to hear the facts, whether you want to or not!' Zoe snapped back at him curtly. 'Prince Hakem approached my grandfather to suggest the marriage, *not* the other way round. I didn't meet him beforehand because there was no need for me to meet him when it was never intended to be a normal marriage. I was to go through the ceremony and live quietly afterwards in the Prince's home. He swore that he would treat me like a daughter and that no demands would be made of me. Then after several months I was to go home and get a divorce…'

Raj's spectacular eyes gleamed as darkly bright as polar stars while he absorbed that surprising information. He understood now why his aunt had agreed to the divorce without making a fuss. Hakem must have promised to remarry her once he was free again and, in support of her husband's royal ambitions, Raj's aunt had been willing to make that sacrifice. 'But what was in this peculiar arrangement for you?' Raj persisted with a frown of bewilderment. 'It cannot surely have been enriching yourself when your grandfather is such a wealthy man…'

'Status!' Zoe almost spat out the word as if it physically hurt her and, indeed, it did. 'I would've become a princess and, while that doesn't matter much to me, it means a great deal to my grandfather and I wanted to please him. He's done a lot for me and my sisters.'

'Being a princess wouldn't have been much of a consolation while you were living in Hakem's home,' Raj informed her very drily. 'Hakem's wife and children are well known and well liked and everyone who knew them would have been ready to loathe you on sight.'

'Well, the marriage is not going to take place now, is it?' Zoe cut in thinly, turning away from him to wander across to the far side of the tent. 'After all that's happened, *nothing* short of handcuffs and chains would persuade me to stay in Maraban!'

Raj was disconcerted to find his brain sketching an erotic mental image of her chained to a bed, all flyaway blonde hair, passionate green eyes and little heaving pale pink curves for his private delectation. He stiffened and shifted restlessly while he fought to kill that untimely vision stone dead. But, sadly for him, there was nothing politically correct about his body and within seconds he was filled with desire.

'You know, I don't want to be rude or melodramatic,' Zoe began shakily.

'You may not want to be but you can't help behaving that way?' Raj incised hoarsely, knocked off balance now by his libido, that intimate imagery of her strengthening rather than fading and exercising the most extraordinary power over him.

Zoe spun. 'You're the one being rude!' she condemned, challenged to catch her breath when she clashed involuntarily with his intense gaze. 'Acting like being kidnapped is normal and refusing to tell me who orchestrated this whole stupid charade!'

'I am withholding that information because there is *no* possibility of the man involved being punished,' Raj admitted hoarsely.

What was it about that jet-dark gaze that made goose bumps rise on her exposed skin and sent little shivers running down her taut spine? Why did she suddenly feel so ridiculously overheated? Why did her tummy feel as though butterflies were fluttering through it? Instinctively she pressed her thighs together on the ache low in her core and she blinked in bewilderment and growing self-consciousness, her colour heightening as the explanation for her reaction dawned on her and shot through her like a lightning bolt. It was attraction, simple sexual attraction, and she was experiencing it for the first time *ever*. It made her feel all jumpy and twitchy, like a cat trying to walk across hot burning coals. Sheer shock crashed through her slender frame as she endeavoured to rise above her inner turmoil and focus on the conversation.

'And why is there no possibility of punishment?' Zoe demanded boldly.

'I will not discuss that with you. Please get dressed and we will leave.'

'To go where?' Zoe demanded in surprise.

'We are flying first to Dubai and then on to London, where you will be reunited with your grandfather,' Raj explained. 'As that arrangement is acceptable to him, I assume it is equally acceptable to you.'

'Acceptable?' Zoe echoed and she moved forward with a frown, her astonishment unhidden. 'Are you telling me that you have actually *spoken* to Grandad?'

'Of course.' Raj's intonation was clipped and businesslike. 'He was very angry about your disappearance and I had to reassure him that you were safe and that I would personally ensure that you are restored to his protection as soon as possible.'

But Zoe was still struggling to come to terms with the startling reality that he had already discussed the entire episode with her grandfather because that he should have boldly taken that step was utterly unexpected. Most people avoided Stam Fotakis in a temper and tried to wriggle out of accepting responsibility for anything that annoyed the older man. In fact, the only person she knew who ever stood toe to toe with her grandfather when he was in a bad mood was her sister, Vivi, whose temper matched his. Whoever Raj was, he was fearless, she decided enviously, for when her grandfather started roaring like an angry bull, Zoe simply wanted to keep her head down and take cover.

'I'm in a hurry. We will leave as soon as you are ready. My time here is limited,' Raj admitted flatly, tension tightening his smooth bronzed features. 'I would be obliged if you would be quick.'

'Well, I would need my clothes back to be quick, and I don't know where they are,' Zoe told him thinly, lifting her chin.

With an exclamation, he strode to the doorway and, a moment later, a little woman in tribal dress came running to do his bidding. Zoe's garments were located and laid in her arms, freshly laundered and fragrant. She stalked into the bathroom to look longingly at the shower and then she thought defiantly, What the hell? I'm not putting on clean clothes unless I'm clean as well!

As Zoe stepped beneath the flowing water with a deep sigh of relief, Raj strode out of the main tent, the old rules of polite conduct kicking in even though it felt like a lifetime since he had had to pay attention to such outdated beliefs. She was a single woman and he was a single man and he was in a very old-fashioned place where only his rank had granted him the right to speak to her alone. Even so, he had noted that the females in Omar's family were hovering nearby to ensure that the proprieties were observed. He was relieved that her attack on him had gone unnoticed for that would have very much shocked the tribe, none of whom would have recognised the need for a woman to learn the skills to protect herself. Male relatives were supposed to protect the women in the family.

Evidently, however, Zoe Mardas had not been protected, Raj reckoned thoughtfully, wondering what had happened to her, wondering why she had been so terrified and acknowledging that he would never know. He didn't get into deep conversations of that nature with women. His relationships, if they could be called that, were superficial and consisted of lots of sex and not much else. He doubted that he would ever want anything more from a woman. Why would he? Love had once made him stupid. He had given up everything for love and had ended up with nothing but the crushing awareness that he had made a serious mistake.

'Raj!' Omar gasped as he surged up to him, red-faced from the effort and winded, a small, rather tubby man, who rarely hurried at anything he did. 'You need to leave. One of the camel traders phoned to tell me…a bunch of military helicopters are flying in.'

'Soldiers love to rehearse disasters. It'll be some war game or something,' Raj forecast, refusing to panic. 'I told Zoe to hurry as politely as I could but you know what women are…'

'Raj, if you're caught on Marabanian soil, you could be arrested, *imprisoned*!' Omar emphasised in frustration. 'Grab that stupid woman and get in that helicopter and go!'

The racket of rotor blades approaching made both men throw their heads back and peer into the sky.

'Do you see those colours? That is the royal fleet, which means your father is on board!' Omar groaned in horror.

'It's too late to run. I'll have to tough it out.'

'No, *run*!' Omar urged abruptly. 'Right now...leave the woman here. I think this was a trap. I think she was dumped with me because they knew I was sure to ask you for your help. In the name of Allah, Raj, I will never forgive myself if you come to harm because of my thoughtlessness!'

A trap? Raj pondered the idea and as quickly discarded it. Why would his father, who had considered him a disappointment practically from the day of his birth, seek to trap him in Maraban? Sending Raj into exile, finally freeing himself from a son and heir who enraged him, had been the best solution for both of them, Raj reasoned ruefully.

'My father always warned me that Tahir was very devious, *very* calculating,' Omar breathed worriedly.

'He is,' Raj agreed. 'But he has no reason to *want* to find his son breaking the terms of his exile. Why would he? That would only embarrass him. I'll stay out of sight. Ten to one, he's taken one of his notions to call a tribal meeting and hash over boundaries and camel disputes. He revels in that kind of stuff...it takes him back to his youth.'

'The army craft are encircling the camp to land in advance,' Omar informed him.

'Standard security with the monarch on board,' Raj dismissed.

'No, I'm telling you,' Omar declared in growing frustration at his friend's lack of concern. 'This was a trap and I don't know how you're going to get out of it...'

CHAPTER THREE

THE RACKET OF the helicopters nearby unnerved Zoe and she dressed in haste, flinching from the cling of her clothes to her still-damp skin. When a woman entered the bathroom to fetch her, she was grateful she had hurried and she walked out through the main tent, glad to be embarking on her journey home.

It was a surprise, however, when she was not escorted to the stationary helicopter she had espied earlier and was instead led into another tent, where a group of women were seated round a campfire.

'The King is visiting,' the woman opposite her explained to her in perfect English. 'My husband, Omar, can only receive the King in his tent, which is, unfortunately, the one you have been using, which means that you will have to wait here with us.'

'Your husband?' Zoe studied the attractive brunette, who wore more gold jewellery than she had ever seen on one woman at the same time.

'Sheikh Omar. The King is his uncle. I am called Farida…and you?'

'Zoe,' Zoe proffered, accepting the tiny cup of black

coffee and the plate of sliced fruit she was given with a grateful smile. 'Thank you.'

Hopefully she would be on her way home within the hour, she reasoned, munching on a slice of apple with appetite. 'Where's Raj?' she asked curiously. 'I thought he was in a hurry to leave.'

'Prince Faraj is greeting his father,' Farida framed with slightly raised brows.

Zoe coloured, wondering if her familiar use of Raj's name had offended. 'I didn't know he was a prince,' she said ruefully. 'He said he was nobody of any importance.'

Farida startled her by loosing a spontaneous giggle and turned, clearly translating Zoe's statement for the benefit of their companions. Much laughter ensued.

'The Prince was teasing you. He is the son of our King.'

Zoe's eyes widened to their fullest extent and she gulped. '*He's* the bad-boy Prince?' she exclaimed before she could think better of utilising that label.

'The bad boy?' Farida winced at that definition. 'No, I don't think so. He is my husband's best friend and he took a dangerous risk coming here to see us. '

'Oh…' Zoe noticed that Farida didn't risk translating her comment about Raj being a bad boy and resolved to be much more careful about what she said. According to Raj these people had had nothing to do with her kidnapping and they had looked after her well while she was unable to look after herself. She didn't want to slight them.

After all, she knew next to nothing about Raj, had

merely read that tag for him on a website she had visited, which had contained the information that he had been sent into exile years ago for displeasing his father, the King.

'Risk?' she found herself pressing, taut with curiosity. 'What did he risk?'

'That is for his telling—*if* he has the opportunity,' Farida said evasively. 'But do not forget that the Prince is the King's *only* son, his only child in fact. He was born to the King's third wife when he had almost given up hope of having an heir.'

Zoe nodded circumspectly, unwilling to invite another polite snub and swallowing back questions that she was certain no one, least of all Farida, would wish to answer. Stupid man, she thought in exasperation. Why on earth hadn't he told her who he really was? It was not as though she could have guessed that he was of royal blood. She felt wrong-footed, however, and, recalling how she had assaulted him, gritted her teeth. It was his own fault though: he shouldn't have crept up on her like that.

An adorable toddler nudged her elbow in pursuit of a piece of apple and Zoe handed it over, waving her hand soothingly at Farida, who rebuked the little girl.

'No, my daughter must learn good manners,' Farida asserted.

'What's her name?' Zoe asked as the toddler planted herself in her lap and looked up at her with eyes like milk-chocolate buttons, set beneath a wealth of wavy black hair.

Farida relaxed a little then, and talked about her three children.

* * *

Accompanied by Omar, Raj strode into his cousin's tent where his father awaited him, seated by the fire.

'I thought I would find you here,' his father informed him with a look of considerable satisfaction. 'You are grown tall, my son. You have become a man while you have been away. Omar, you may leave. We will talk later.'

Raj's appraisal of the older man was slower and filled with concern because he could see that Tahir had aged. It was eight years since he had seen his father in the flesh. His parent had been in his fifties when Raj was born twenty-eight years earlier and the agility that had distinguished Tahir then had melted away. From a distance, Raj had watched his father's slow, painful passage to the tent, recognising that the rheumatoid arthritis, which had struck his parent in his sixties, now gripped him hard in spite of the many medical interventions that had been staged. He was still spry but very thin and stiff, the lines on his bearded face more deeply indented, but his dark eyes remained as bright and full of snapping intelligence as ever.

'Sit down, Raj,' the King instructed. 'We have much to discuss but little time in which to do it.'

Raj folded lithely down opposite and waited patiently while the server ritually prepared the coffee from a graceful metal pot with a very long spout. He took the tiny cup in his right hand, his long brown fingers rigid as he waited for one of his father's characteristic tirades to break over his head. Tahir was an authoritarian parent and had become even more abrasive and critical after the death of his third wife, Raj's mother. Sadly, that had been the period when Raj had been most in need of comfort and understanding and, instead of receiving that support, Raj had been sent to a military school where he was unmercifully bullied and beaten up. From the instant Raj had left school, he and his father had had a difficult relationship.

'I knew that Omar would run to you for help. He never had a thought in his head that you didn't put there first,' Tahir remarked fondly. 'We will not discuss the past, Raj. That would lead us back to dissension.'

'I'm sorry, but this woman...' Raj began even though he knew the interruption was rude, because he was so keen to find out why his father had acted as he had and had risked an enormous scandal simply to take his brother down a peg or two.

'You never did have a patient bone in your body.' Tahir sighed. 'Have sufficient respect to listen first. I want you home, Raj, back where you belong, as my heir.'

Raj was stunned. For a split second he actually gaped at the older man, his brilliant dark eyes shimmering with astonishment and consternation.

His father moved a hand in a commanding gesture to demand his continuing silence. 'I will admit no regrets. I will make no apologies. But had I not sent you away, my foolish brother would never have plotted to take your place,' he pointed out grimly. 'For eight years I have watched you from afar, working for Maraban, loyally doing your best to advance our country's best interests. Your heart is still with our people, which is as it should be.'

Raj compressed his lips and gazed down into his

coffee, dumbfounded by the very first accolade he had ever received from his strict and demanding parent.

'Do you want to come home? Do you wish to stand as the Crown Prince of Maraban again?'

A great wash of longing surged through Raj and his shoulders went stiff with the force of having to hold back those seething emotions. He swallowed hard. 'I do,' he breathed hoarsely.

'Of course, my generosity must come at a price,' the King assured him stiffly.

Unsurprised by that stricture, Raj breathed in deep and slow. 'I don't care who I marry now,' he declared in a driven undertone, hoping that that was the price his father planned to offer him. 'That element of my life is no longer of such overriding importance to me.'

'So, no longer a romantic,' his father remarked with visible relief. 'That is good. A romantic king would be too soft for the throne. And it is too late to turn you into a soldier. But your marriage... On that score I cannot compromise.'

'I understand,' Raj conceded flatly, shaking his hand to indicate that he did not want another cup of coffee, for any appetite for it had vanished. Sight unseen, some bride of good birth would be chosen for him and he and his bride would have to make a practical marriage. It would be a compromise, a challenge. Well, he was used to challenges even if he wasn't very good at compromises, he acknowledged grimly. But he would have to learn, and fast, because it was unlikely he would have much in common with the bride chosen for him.

'I should thank Hakem for bringing the Fotakis girl to my attention because I didn't even know she existed,' the King mused with unconcealed satisfaction. 'I was outraged when I realised what my brother was planning to do. I was even more outraged when I realised that I had no choice but to approach Fotakis himself... the man who stole the beautiful Azra from me. But he has given his permission.'

Only then registering what the older man was proposing, Raj threw his head back in shock. 'You're expecting me to marry *Zoe*?'

'And to do it right now, today. I brought the palace *imam* with me,' his father told him bluntly. 'This marriage would be your sign of good faith, your pledge to me that from now on you will act as a sensible son. Marry her and I promise you that nothing will stand in your path.'

'Zoe wants to go home!' Raj pointed out incredulously. 'She will not want to marry me.'

'Her grandfather has given his permission,' the King pointed out with a frown of bewilderment. 'A prince for a prince and a bridegroom less than half Hakem's age, you make an acceptable substitute in Fotakis's eyes. You have no choice in this, Raj. The girl is too great a prize to surrender, a huge gift to our people. No more popular bride than Azra's granddaughter could be found for you. We will have a big state wedding to follow. I believe she is as beautiful as her grandmother. You should be pleased.'

Raj compressed his lips on the reality that his father was insane. He talked as though women still dutifully and happily married the husbands picked by their most senior male relative. But even in Maraban those days were long gone. It was now only men of his father's venerable age who still expected the right to tell their offspring who they should marry.

'Zoe wants to go home,' he repeated steadily.

'You have two hours to persuade her otherwise. I have already prepared an announcement to be made from the palace,' the King told him solemnly. 'Their Prince has come home and done his duty at last.'

'Zoe was expecting to divorce Hakem within a few months,' Raj reminded his parent tautly.

'Yes, you can let her go once the fuss has died down. You can choose your own second wife,' Tahir informed him with the lofty air of a man bestowing a gift on the undeserving. 'I won't interfere, although there is one exception to that rule. That whore, Nabila...you cannot bring her into the family under any circumstances.'

At the mention of that name accompanied by that offensive term, Raj lost every scrap of colour, his eyes lowering, his expression cloaked by his spiky black lashes, for he had just learned that his father *knew* what had happened eight years earlier between his son and his first love. Discomfiture filled him to overflowing but the meeting, Raj recognised by that final warning, was over. He vaulted upright with something less than his usual grace. 'There is no risk of that development. I've not seen her in many years,' he revealed stiffly.

'Go and get ready for your wedding,' his father urged, clearly not accepting the possibility that Zoe might refuse to marry him. 'And send Omar in!'

Having had her breakfast, Zoe was ushered into another tent and left there alone. She checked her watch, shifted her feet, frustrated that she didn't know what the cause of the hold-up was. When Raj entered, she spun fully round to face him and then she froze, remembering uneasily that he was a prince and that she had not treated him as she should've done. But then that was *his* fault, she reminded herself, lifting her chin again. He looked tense, the smooth chiselled bones of his face taut beneath his bronzed skin, his dark deep-set eyes curiously intent on her.

'I thought you were in a hurry to leave,' she reminded him, wondering why even that scrutiny could heat her up inside her skin as if she were being slowly roasted. He made her feel hot and bothered and uncomfortable and if that was sexual attraction, well, then she wanted no part of it. Those physical reactions were affecting her ability to behave like a rational being.

'My father spoke to me *and*...our situation has changed,' Raj admitted, half turning towards the open doorway, avoiding a more direct look at her, lest he lose his concentration.

Any man would've looked though, he assured himself. Her beautiful hair was restrained in a long braid but he still remembered that silken veil unbound. Her shapely legs were exposed by a short skirt. The matching top in soft pastels moulded to her rounded breasts, and on her feet were the most ridiculously impractical heels he had ever seen a woman wear in the desert. Of course, she hadn't known that she would be waking up in the desert, but those towering heels, which still only contrived to lift her a couple of inches in height, were downright dangerous. At the same time, there was something absurdly feminine and cute about those tiny glittery sandals with their plethora of straps. He dragged in a deep breath, gritted his white even teeth. *Cute?* What was he thinking?

That it was safer to look at her feet than her breasts or her legs when his body was behaving as though it belonged to a sex-starved teenager. Since when had he been unable to control his libido? He could not recall ever having that problem before.

Zoe was very stiff, picking up on the undertones in the atmosphere while reading the physical tension he was putting out in waves. '*Our* situation?' she queried, surprised by that designation.

'*Ours,*' Raj emphasised. 'I don't know how much you know about me.'

'Well, you told me that you were nobody of any importance but Farida told me the truth—that you are the King's son,' Zoe countered in a tone of reproof. 'I also know that you were sent into exile.'

'Eight years ago,' Raj clarified sombrely. 'I refused to marry the woman my father chose for me because I was in love with someone else. There were other factors but essentially that is what caused my long estrangement from my father. You may not be aware of it but in my world a son is expected to be obedient and, to be fair to my father, I was a rebel from day one.'

More than a little disconcerted by that very personal explanation of his troubled relationship with his parent, Zoe coloured, her green eyes clinging to his brooding dark features and the fluctuating emotions he was striving to hide; only those expressive eyes of his continually gave him away, glimmering and glittering, alive with all the passion he struggled to contain. Unwilling fascination gripped her and she gave way to her curiosity. 'What happened with the woman you loved? Did you marry her?'

'No, she cheated on me,' Raj admitted flatly.

'I'm sorry,' she muttered automatically, wishing she hadn't asked.

'You don't need to apologise. It happened a long time ago when I was still young, trusting and naïve. I am not the same man now,' Raj parried wryly.

Because that woman had broken his heart, Zoe registered, recalling her sister, Winnie's heartbreak when she had had to leave the man she loved, after discovering that he was married. Zoe had never experienced anything that intense and she wasn't sure she wanted to either. But then she had never had a boyfriend. After the attempted rape she had fortunately escaped, she had feared and avoided men. She had had one or two male friends at university who had stayed close to her for a while to test her boundaries, hoping she would warm up to them but it hadn't happened. She had stayed apart and untouched and was much inclined to think that that was the best way to live. Without risk, without hurt, without disappointed hopes and unrealistic dreams of some fantasy happy future.

'You said "our" situation,' she reminded him, keen to steer the conversation out of deep waters. 'What did you mean by that?'

'My father has offered me a most unexpected suggestion,' Raj framed with care, brilliant dark eyes locked to her heart-shaped face and the eyes bright as emeralds against her porcelain pale skin. The contrast was breathtaking. 'He has asked me to come home and take my place as his heir again.'

'My goodness, that's wonderful news! I mean...' Zoe hesitated '...if *that* is what you want?'

'I want to come home with my whole heart. This is the first time I have been home in eight years,' Raj admitted harshly, his sincerity bitingly obvious. 'But unfortunately, the King's proposition came with a key stipulation attached. My father has asked me to take Hakem's place as your bridegroom and marry you.'

Zoe blinked several times and continued to stare at him, her heart thumping rapidly enough that it seemed to thunder in her ears. 'But...but why? That's a crazy suggestion!'

'Not if you consider who you are,' Raj pointed out with a wry twist of his wide sensual mouth. 'Half our population are originally from your grandmother's country and they were most resentful when my father and their Banian Princess failed to marry at the same time as the two states allied to become one. As a result, the royal family does not reflect the origins of both countries. If the King's son were to marry Princess Azra's granddaughter, it would be very popular with our people. Principally, *that* is why my father wants us to marry.'

'But I never even met Azra. She died before I was born,' Zoe argued. 'It's just an accident of birth.'

'No, it is your heritage and a vital and proud heritage to those who remember the Princess and a country that now only exists as part of Maraban,' Raj contradicted. 'I should also mention that your grandfather and my father have been in touch—I should imagine only through an intermediary—and this suggestion that you remain here to marry me instead has been discussed by them.'

'Good heavens… Grandad *knows* about all this?' Zoe gasped, already shaken by Raj's serious respect for her ancestry, which was, she realised finally, far more valued in Maraban than it would ever be anywhere else.

'Your grandfather is agreeable to the exchange of bridegrooms,' Raj delivered.

Zoe turned slowly pale with anger. 'But what about me? What about what *I* want?' she demanded starkly.

'That is why I am here…*asking*,' Raj stressed sardonically. 'Your grandfather and my father are quite happy to believe that only their consent is required. I am not that foolish.'

Her anger drained away again. 'Thank goodness, someone here has some sense,' she mumbled.

'You were willing to marry Hakem sight unseen,' Raj reminded her.

Zoe's knees felt weak and she flopped down on a cushioned seat as if her breath had been stolen from her. She was at a crossroads. 'That's different, that was before all this happened and I realised Hakem had abandoned his wife for me and stuff like that,' she argued uncomfortably. 'It was a mistake to agree. Now I just want to forget all this nonsense and go home again.'

'But I am asking you to stay here and marry me,' Raj stated with precision. 'And it is an entirely selfish request.'

Taken aback at that confession, Zoe tilted her head back to look up at him. 'Is it?'

'Yes. It would mean the end of my exile and my estrangement from my father,' Raj pointed out grittily. 'And not only that, my marriage to Azra's granddaughter would delight my people as well. What is in it for you other than the acquisition of an entirely use-less title, I don't know, but it would at least be as much as you would have received from my uncle. I can also promise to treat you as well as he would have. He is a decent man, regrettably poisoned by his pointless need to compete with my father.'

What is in it for you? Zoe appreciated his honesty with regard to the advantages to him should he marry her. Even so, her understanding of his position did nothing to stop her brain from whirling with wild indecision. She had been ready to go home and give up on her quest for greater independence but now Raj was offering her another option. Yet somehow marrying him struck her as a far more intimidating prospect than marrying a much older man, who had sworn he would treat her like a daughter. Raj was so much younger, more aggressive, more virile... Her brain ran out of descriptive words as she glanced warily at him.

He was so poised in his long white buttoned tunic, a black cloak folded back over his broad shoulders, his lean, darkly handsome face grave and cool while he awaited her answer, those glorious dark-as-the-devil eyes gleaming with an impatience he was too polite and intelligent to voice. A positive reply would mean a lot to him. She understood that, she really did. She also still yearned for the opportunity to live an independent life, unfettered by the expectations of her family. But most of all, she wanted to prove herself to herself and she wanted to be strong without leaning on anyone else for support. Even less did she want to run home with her tail between her legs and disappoint her grandfather as well.

'What would it take to win your agreement?' Raj pressed, the skilled negotiator that he was breaking cover.

Zoe coloured as if he had turned a spotlight on her and dropped her head. 'Well, I don't know what your expectations would be but I can assure you now that I wouldn't want sex. I'm not into sex. It's something I can live without, but *you*?'

That he couldn't even look at her without thinking about sex was a truth Raj decided he needed to keep to himself. Overpowering curiosity assailed him at the same time. What had put her off sex? One bad experience? An assault? Those were not questions he could ask and he suppressed the urge to probe deeper even as he winced inwardly from the upfront immediate rejection she was handing him. She didn't want sex with *him*. He had never met with that kind of rejection before and he pushed away that awareness, deeming it arrogant and ultimately unimportant in the greater scheme of events.

'I can offer you the exact same marital agreement that persuaded you that you could marry my uncle,' Raj broke in to insist with measured cool.

Zoe tossed her head back in surprise. Little tendrils of white-blonde hair were beginning to cling to her damp brow because she was feeling too warm even in the shade of the tent. Probably because even talking about sex set her cheeks on fire with self-consciousness, but she knew that she had to be frank with him. There was no other way and no room for any misunderstandings if she was candid from the outset. It shook her to acknowledge that she was seriously considering the marriage he was suggesting, for it was unlike her to take a risk. And Raj, her sixth sense warned, would be a risk.

'Unfortunately, you're not old enough to treat me like a daughter!' she told him ruefully.

'But I am old enough not to put pressure on a woman, who doesn't want me, for sex,' Raj retorted without hesitation. 'I appreciate that you would have to take that guarantee on trust but it *is* the truth. I have never had to put that kind of pressure on a woman and I never will.'

'OK,' Zoe mumbled, feeling that they had done the topic of sex and not having it to death. 'I admit that I would like to stay in Maraban and explore a little of my heritage.'

'I could make that possible,' Raj told her.

'Where would we live?'

'In the palace, which is, I must admit, a little dated,' Raj acknowledged, choosing to understate the case because he himself considered his surroundings immaterial as long as the basics were in place.

His father, unhappily, had a great reverence for history and it had proved a major battle to persuade Tahir to allow even modern bathrooms and cooking facilities to be constructed in the ancient building. Guests were lodged in one of the very contemporary villas built within the palace compound to provide convenient accommodation for visitors while preserving his father's privacy.

'I could live with dated,' Zoe muttered uneasily. 'I'm really not very fussy. My sisters and I lived in some real dives before we met our grandfather a couple of years ago and he invited us to move into a property that he owns in London.'

'The palace is not a dive,' Raj murmured with reluctant amusement. 'To sum up, you are prepared to consider my proposal?'

'Thinking about it, wondering if I can trust you.' That admission slid off the end of Zoe's tongue before she could snatch it back and her face flamed with guilt.

'I keep my word...*always*,' Raj proclaimed with pride, dark eyes aglow with conviction. 'You have nothing to fear from me. You would be doing me a very great favour. The last thing I would do is harm you. In fact, if you do this for me, I will protect you from anything and anyone who would seek to harm you.'

He was gorgeous, she thought helplessly, standing there so straight and tall and emotional, *so* very *emotional*. She had never met a man who teemed with so much emotion that he couldn't hide it. She had never met a man she could read so clearly. Reluctant hope, growing excitement and the first seeds of satisfaction brimmed in his volatile gaze. She couldn't take her eyes off his, could still hear the faint echo of his fervent promise to protect her from all threats.

'We would still be able to get a divorce after a few months?' Zoe checked anxiously.

'Of course. We would not want to find ourselves stuck with each other for ever!' Raj quipped with sudden amusement.

And for the very first time in a man's presence, Zoe felt slighted by honesty. She scolded herself for being oversensitive. Naturally, he wouldn't want to stay married for good to a woman he didn't love and neither would she wish to stay with him, would she? He was simply voicing the facts of their agreement.

'Then...' Zoe rose to her feet, suddenly pale with the stress of the occasion and the big decision she was making for herself without consulting her sisters, who probably would've voiced very loud objections '... I will agree to marry you and I can only hope that it brings you the advantages that you believe it will.'

Raj took a sudden step forward and raised his arms and then let them fall again as he stepped back. 'Forgive me, I almost touched you but I am sure you prefer not to be touched.'

'I do.' But Zoe was lying. He had been about to sweep her up in his arms and hug her and she was disappointed that he had recalled her rules and gone back into retreat. He was passionate, a little impulsive, she suspected, the sort of guy who occasionally in the grip of strong feeling would act first, think later. She would have liked the hug, the physical non-sexual contact, the very warmth and reassurance of it, but it was better that he respected her boundaries, she told herself urgently. 'So when will this marriage take place?'

'Today.'

'*Today?*' she exclaimed in soaring disbelief.

'My father does not trust me enough to allow me to return to the palace without immediate proof that I have changed my ways,' Raj told her grimly. 'This marriage will provide that proof. He brought the palace *imam* here with him.'

'We're getting married here...*now*?' she prompted incredulously. 'What on earth am I going to wear?'

'My father leaves nothing to chance. I would suspect that his wife has brought appropriate clothing for you.'

'Which wife?' she prompted curiously.

'He only has one wife still living. My mother died when I was nine and her predecessor died about ten years ago. The Queen, his first wife, is called Ayshah,' Raj proffered. 'She is pleasant enough.'

Zoe breathed in deep and slow. She was going to marry Raj and make a go of her life all on her own. She would stay in Maraban for several months and there would be no more panic attacks. She would pick up some of the language, learn the history and find out about her grandmother's culture. It would be an adventure, a glorious adventure, she told herself firmly while watching Raj stand by the doorway, quite unconscious of her appraisal. He smiled with sudden brilliance. And gorgeous wasn't quite a strong enough word for him at that moment...

CHAPTER FOUR

'MY FATHER TELLS me that the King is arranging a state wedding to take place in two weeks' time and for that you can wear a Western wedding gown,' Farida informed Zoe in a discreet whisper. 'The King wants to make the most of your entry into the family.'

Apprehensive enough about the wedding about to take place, Zoe could have done without the news that there was to be a second, which would be a public spectacle. Such an event lay so far outside her comfort zone that even thinking about it made her feel dizzy. But she squashed that sensation. Baby steps, she told herself soothingly. She would cope by dealing with one thing at a time, and fretting about the future would only wind her up. Right at that moment it was sufficient to accept that she was about to legally marry a man she had only met for the first time that day.

Marrying Raj's uncle, however, she would have been doing the same, she reminded herself wryly, and at least Raj came without previous attachments such as wives, children and grandchildren. Yes, she had definitely dodged a bullet in not marrying Hakem. Raj was single and refreshingly honest. He had admitted that he had once suffered panic attacks too. He had even admitted to defying his father over the woman he loved and subsequently discovering that she had cheated on him, which must have been a huge disillusionment. Most men that Zoe came across would have concealed such unhappy and revealing facts. That Raj had been so frank had impressed her.

Surrounded by fussing tribeswomen presided over by the elderly Queen Ayshah, who sat in the corner, entirely dressed in black, barking out instructions, Zoe studied her reflection in the tall mirror. She was so heavily clothed in layers and jewellery that she was amazed she could move. A beaten gold headdress covered her brow, a veil covering most of her hair, weighty gold earrings dangling from her ears, hung there by thread. She had very narrowly sidestepped having her ear lobes pierced there and then and she had Farida to thank for tactfully suggesting thread be used to attach the earrings instead. More primitive gold necklaces clanked and shifted round her neck with every movement while rich and elaborate henna swirls adorned her hands and her feet. What remained of her was enveloped in a white kaftan covered in richly beaded and colourful embroidery. Below that were several gossamer-fine silk layers, all of which rejoiced in buttons running down the back. Getting undressed again promised to be a challenge, she thought ruefully.

She had insisted on doing her own make-up though, having run her eyes over her companions, already festooned in their glad rags and best jewellery for the wedding, their faces over-rouged, their eyelids bright blue. Only Farida had gone for the subtle approach. Zoe had used more cosmetics than she normally did and had gone heavy on the eye liner when urged to do so but at least there was nothing theatrical about the end result.

'My wedding celebrations lasted a week,' Farida told her.

'A *week*?' Zoe gasped.

'But yours will only last the afternoon. The King does not wish to spend the night here. The state wedding celebration parties will go on longer, I expect,' Omar's wife chattered. 'Everyone loves these events because they get to see family and friends, but this has been arranged so quickly that it is a very small and quiet wedding—but the jewellery Raj has given you is magnificent.'

'What jewellery?' Zoe whispered.

'Everything you're wearing comes from the royal house. Traditionally, the jewellery is your wedding gift.'

'The King must've brought that with him as well,' Zoe muttered.

'Yes, you were getting married today whether you wanted to or not!' Farida laughed. 'But who could say no to Raj?'

Zoe could feel her face heat and was grateful when the sound of music outside the tent sent all the women to the doorway. She followed them and glanced out to see some sort of ceremonial dance being performed with much waving of swords and cracking of whips. Men leapt over the campfire, competing in feats of daring that made her flinch and at one point close her eyes. A moment later, she was ushered out in an excited procession into another larger tent filled with people. She was led up to the front where a venerable older man appeared to bestow some sort of blessing on her and gave a long speech before handing her a ring. Farida showed her which finger to put it on. In the middle of the speech, she finally glimpsed Raj, resplendent in a sapphire-blue silk tunic, tied with a sash, his lean, darkly handsome features very serious. She tried and failed to catch his eye.

Another, even older man spoke more briefly and then moved forward to flourish a pen over a long piece of parchment, which he duly signed. In fact, several people signed the parchment and then she in turn was urged forward to sign as well, before being led away again without a word or a look exchanged with Raj.

'And now we party!' Farida whispered teasingly in her ear.

'You mean…that's it *done*? We're married now?' Zoe exclaimed in wonderment.

'As soon as you signed the marriage contract, it was done. I would've translated for you but I didn't want to risk offending the King by speaking during the ceremony,' the lithe brunette confided. 'You are now the Crown Princess of Maraban.'

'And I don't feel the slightest bit different!' Zoe confided with amusement, reckoning that her grandfather would be sorry to have missed the ceremony but she assumed he would be attending the state wedding, which was to follow. Her sisters would have to come as well and she smiled at the prospect as Farida guided her into yet another tent full of chattering women where music was starting up in the background.

Introduction after introduction was made and plate after plate of food was brought. There were no men present. Farida explained that the reception after the state wedding would not be segregated but that rural weddings were of a more conservative ilk. Zoe sipped mint tea and watched the festivities as the dancing began. Married, she kept on thinking; she couldn't believe it. But she wasn't really married, she reminded herself wryly, not truly married because she and Raj were not going to live together as a married couple. She wondered how he was feeling. Was he wishing she were his ex-love, who had let him down? Or did the significance of the actual marriage escape him because he was not in love with his bride? Or, more likely, was he simply happy that he was back in Maraban and accepted by his father again?

At one point, Zoe drifted off in spite of the noise and liveliness surrounding her and wakened only when Farida discreetly pressed her hand. She blinked in bemusement, for an instant not even knowing where she was. Darkness had fallen beyond the tent and it was quieter now, only a couple of women dancing, the rest gathered in chattering groups. Slowly her brain fell back into step and she suppressed a sigh, murmuring an apology to Farida for her drowsiness.

'Your body is probably still working on ridding you of the sleeping drug you were given at the palace. Our doctor said it would be a couple of days before you fully recovered from that. I am so sorry that that happened to you,' the other woman said sincerely.

'You were involved in it against your will...not your responsibility,' Zoe pointed out gently.

'And sadly, the instigator will only be celebrating

the reality that he has regained his son,' Farida murmured ruefully.

The last piece of the puzzle fell into place for Zoe and her eyebrows shot up in surprise as she finally appreciated that only Raj's father could have had her kidnapped and remained safe from punishment of any kind. That was why Raj had remained silent about the identity of the perpetrator; that was why he had seemed to feel partially responsible for her ordeal. Clearly the King had been determined to prevent his brother, Hakem, from marrying her.

'It is time for you to retire,' Farida told her, reacting to a signal from Queen Ayshah, who raised her hand and gave her a meaningful look.

That the old lady was still going strong while she felt weary embarrassed Zoe. She lumbered upright, feeling like an elephant in her cumbersome layers of clothing, hoping it was cooler outside than it was inside. But that was a false hope, she recognised when the humid air beyond the tent closed in around her and she was forced to trek across the sand in her wildly unsuitable shoes that dug in at every step. A camel was led in front of her and made to lie down. Farida instructed her to climb into the saddle, which, weighted down as she was by fabric and jewellery, was no easy task, but at last the deed was accomplished and the animal scrambled up again and swayed across the sands in the moonlight, accompanied by whoops from the women crowded round her and with the aid of the herdsman with his very modern torch.

'It is symbolic,' Farida explained. 'Queen Ayshah stands in your mother's place and she is sending you to your bridegroom.'

Zoe rather thought it was more as if she were a parcel to be delivered, although thank heaven, she reflected with a choked giggle, Raj wouldn't be expecting to *unwrap* the parcel. She slid more than she dismounted from the camel and picked herself up off the sand, thinking fondly that she was having an even more exciting wedding day than either of her sisters had enjoyed while wondering when her mobile phone would be returned to her so that she could bring her siblings up to date with events.

She almost staggered into the tent lit by lanterns that awaited her and there she froze in consternation. A large bed confronted her and it dawned on her at last that this was her wedding night, which she was expected to spend in close proximity to her new husband. She wasn't going to get her own tent this time or even her own bed because she was supposed to *share* the bed. In silence she pulled a face because she hadn't anticipated that, although she knew that she should've done.

After all, her agreement with Raj that their marriage would be platonic was a private matter that neither of them was likely to discuss with anyone beyond their immediate family. Grateful when the women retreated again she sank down on the bottom of the low divan and breathed in deep while she waited for Raj to arrive. My goodness, she was getting so hot. She straightened and walked into the primitive bathroom that had been erected alongside and clearly in haste for their comfort. A mirror sat propped up on a chest and piece by piece she removed the heavy gold jewellery and set it on the chest along with the veil.

At that point she heard shouts and catcalls outside and she scrambled up to return to the main tent just in time to see Raj striding in and covering the door again with obvious relief. 'Everyone gets overexcited at weddings,' he said wryly, studying her with fixed intensity.

Colour mantled her cheeks, self-consciousness reclaiming her as she hovered. 'Perhaps they're also celebrating the fact that their Prince is home again,' she suggested.

'It is possible,' Raj fielded with quiet assurance.

He wore confidence like invisible armour and she envied him that gift, wondering how he could ever have suffered the ignominy of panic attacks. He had the innate calm of a man comfortable in his own skin yet, from what little she had already learned, his past was littered with drama and disappointment. Yet he had overcome those realities and moved on, much as she wished to do.

'Do you know where my clothes are? Are they still back at the house I was taken from?' she asked uncomfortably.

'I will enquire for you in the morning,' Raj murmured smoothly.

'I don't even have a toothbrush!' Zoe protested, falling back on trivialities rather than dealing with her insecurities over the situation she was in.

'I will give you one,' Raj informed her in a tone of finality.

Zoe swallowed hard on a burst of angry exasperation. Was she supposed to go to bed naked with all her make-up on? It wasn't his fault that she had been separated from her luggage, she told herself urgently, and she shouldn't take her ire out on him. Deal with it, she instructed herself, and she went back into the bathroom and removed the ornate kaftan before beginning to undo the buttons of the layers beneath. Arms aching, perspiration dampening her face, she stalked back uneasily into the bedroom. Raj was on his phone, black eyes skimming to her instantly. He cast the phone down and studied her enquiringly.

'I'm afraid I need your help with all these buttons,' she framed in considerable embarrassment. 'I don't want to tear anything...'

'No, that would indeed be embarrassing,' Raj conceded. 'It would look as though I ripped the shifts off you.'

Breathing fast, Zoe spun round, presenting him with her slender back. 'I just don't get why it has all those buttons in an absolutely inaccessible place!'

'Because you are not supposed to take it off by yourself,' Raj informed her softly, a faint tremor racking her as she felt the gentle pressure of his fingers against her back as he undid the buttons, because a man had never got quite that close to her before and that he should be undressing her, even though it was at her request, was still a challenge. 'Your bridegroom is supposed to remove the three shifts slowly and seductively. It is a cultural tradition.'

'Oh...' Zoe gasped and then as the ramifications set in, *'Oh,'* she said again.

'You will have Ayshah to thank for the shifts because I don't think most brides bother with this particular tradition these days,' Raj told her huskily, skimming the first shift down her arms and letting it drop to the rug beneath her bare feet before embarking on the next set of buttons. 'That is a shame.'

'Is it? A bridal version of the dance of the seven veils...or whatever?' Zoe heard herself wittering on nervously, cringing even as the words escaped her.

Raj rolled his eyes and gritted his even white teeth because peeling her out of the silk shifts was testing his self-control. Her skin glimmered through the gossamer-fine tissue like the most lustrous of pearls and that close the sweet scent of her, of roses and almonds, was unbelievably feminine and alluring. Raj tugged down the second shift and let it fall before stepping away, carefully not looking at what would now be an enhanced view of her body because he did not require that encouragement.

Bemused, Zoe spun round, registering that he had stopped and walked away. 'I don't want to sleep in this one,' she muttered uncomfortably. 'These shifts are precious to your stepmother. They were put on me with a care that implied they were made of solid gold.'

'She is not my stepmother,' Raj incised curtly. 'She is my father's first wife.'

'Right... OK,' Zoe framed, registering that she had hit a tender spot with that designation, but very much out of her depth when it came to labelling or understanding the doubtless complex relations created in a family consisting of more than one wife. 'But what am I to sleep in?'

Raj was forced to look at her and the image locked him in place. She was so clueless he swallowed hard on impatient words. She might as well have been standing there naked for the thin material hid very little.

The pert little swells of her small breasts were obvious, not to mention the intriguing tea-rose colour of her prominent nipples and the pale curls at the apex of her thighs. Raj sucked in a sustaining breath, hot and hard as hell. 'I will get you something of mine,' he asserted, rather hoarse in tone, his dark deep voice roughening the vowel sounds.

'I'm sorry I'm being such a pain,' Zoe mumbled uneasily as Raj dragged out a leather holdall and opened it to rummage through it.

'I didn't bring much because I didn't think I'd be staying long,' Raj sighed, finally extracting a T-shirt and a pair of boxers for her use.

Zoe grabbed the garments with alacrity and spun round beside him. 'Just undo the last ones, please, and I'll be out of your hair,' she promised.

Raj suppressed a groan, his attention locking on the sweet curvaceous swell of her bottom. Presented with the delights of her in reality his imagination could take flight with ease and he ached with arousal. He grappled with the buttons, no longer deft, indeed all fingers and thumbs as he thought of laying her down on the bed and teaching her the consequences of teasing a man. But even as he thought of such a thing, he was grimly amused by it because he knew she was quite unaware of the effect she was having on him and that he would never touch a woman who had stated so clearly that she did not want to be touched. In fact, he had never been with a woman less aware of her seductive power over a man and, while at first he had found that absence of flirtation and flattery refreshing, now, suddenly, he was finding that innocence of hers a huge challenge.

'Now you can go and take it off and get changed,' Raj informed her thickly.

Zoe turned back to him, catching the harsh edge to his voice and looking up at him to see the dark glow of his eyes accentuated by the flare of colour over his high cheekbones. 'Raj…what's wrong?' she questioned helplessly.

'How honest can I be?' Raj asked.

'I want you to feel that you can always be honest with me. In fact, that's very important to me.'

'Even if it embarrasses you?' Raj prompted.

'Even if it embarrasses me,' Zoe confirmed without hesitation.

'You are half naked and very beautiful,' Raj breathed huskily. 'I have sworn not to touch you but I am still a man and you tempt me. You can still trust me to keep my word but I would be grateful if you…' He fell silent because Zoe had already backed into the bathroom, her face as startled and as red as fire.

Only ten feet from him, separated only by tent walls, Zoe looked at herself in the last shift and she burned all over with mortification. She'd had no idea quite how sheer the shifts were because at no stage had she seen her reflection in them in the mirror. Half naked seemed like an understatement when she was showing everything she had got! Shame and chagrin enveloped her. He had said she tempted him. Dear heaven, did he think her display had been deliberate? No, surely not. She peeled off the last shift, laid it carefully to one side and stepped into the shower, hoping it would cool her off. She didn't want to go back into the bedroom and look him in the eye again.

Cold water drenched her and she stood there as long as she could bear it, before, shivering, she got out and grabbed a towel off the pile. He had been frank with her and she was glad of that, she reflected ruefully. If they were to live in close proximity, she would have to be more careful, more *aware* in a way she had never had to be before. His T-shirt fell past her knees and she put on the boxers, although they struck her as overkill.

'Zoe?' Raj murmured quietly.

She peered into the bedroom and he handed her a toiletries bag.

When even her teeth were clean, she *had* to return to the bedroom but she looked nowhere near him as she crossed to the bed and climbed in straight away.

Raj went for a long cooling shower and tried to re-member when he had last had sex. It had been weeks and weeks. He should make more effort in that depart-ment, he told himself firmly. Had he formed the habit of regular sex, he was convinced he wouldn't have been so tempted by Zoe. But then, it had been years since he had enjoyed regular sex, he acknowledged ruefully. These days he had occasional one-night stands and he never spent the night because he had discovered that spending too long with the same woman only encour-aged the kind of entanglements and expectations that made him feel trapped. 'One and done', he called his routine. He didn't do relationships, he didn't do girl-friends, he didn't do dates. Nabila had sent him flying off such a conventional path.

But Zoe, the wife he could not touch, he was learn-ing to his cost, was a whole new ball game…

Zoe peered out from under the sheet as Raj strode

across the tent, his long, lean, powerful body clad only in boxers. Her eyes widened, drawn by the flex of steel-hard muscle across his bronzed torso. He was a work of art, she thought numbly, barely able to accept that such a thought could be hers and that for the first time ever she was admiring the male body, which had until that moment inspired her only with fear. But then Raj was something else, Raj somehow fell into a totally different category and she didn't understand how that was or even why. Yet he was one of the most masculine men she had ever met. Everything about Raj from his innate poise to the rough stubble now darkening his jaw line and the well-honed strength of his physique screamed male. She closed her eyes tight, blanked her mind and slowly, inexorably fell asleep.

The nightmare that assailed her was an old familiar one. She was sprawled on the floor of an old hut, sneering thugs surrounding her while another cut off her clothes with a terrifyingly sharp knife. She was trapped. Shouting or screaming only earned her another punch and she was already in a great deal of pain because one arm and a leg were broken and, she believed, several ribs. She could barely see out of her swollen eyes but there was nothing wrong with her ears and she could hear every one of the filthy, perverted things they were threatening to do to her. She was petrified, lapsing in and out of consciousness, fighting the sickening effects of concussion…and outside a thunderstorm was crashing and banging like extra evidence that she had been plunged into a living hell.

'It's OK…it's OK,' a vaguely familiar voice was assuring her and she clung to that voice like a drowning swimmer, letting it pull her fully out of the bad dream.

'No,' she croaked in a shaken whisper. 'I'll never be OK again.'

Outside the thunder crashed deafeningly loud and she flinched and gasped, registering that there really was a storm outside, just as there had been the night she had almost been gang-raped. 'I don't like storms,' she muttered, clutching at his warm, solid body for support.

'You were having a nightmare, moaning, shouting for help. I tried to wake you up,' Raj admitted. 'But it took a long time to bring you out of it.'

'The storm confused me, probably woke me in the end… There was a storm in the nightmare too…except it wasn't really a nightmare, it was something that happened to me…but it's been years since I dreamt about it,' Zoe framed shakily. 'I'm sorry.'

'You don't need to apologise. We can't police our dreams,' Raj dismissed, leaning away from her to light the lantern by the bed.

Her anxious eyes widened at the sight of him because being in bed with a half-naked man felt so very alien to her. And Raj was all male as he stretched, that fantasy V-shape flexing across his lower rock-hard abdomen as he shifted to reach for a glass of water and handed it to her.

Colour rising, Zoe gulped down water as if she were suffering from dehydration. She didn't like the way her brain was spewing random sexual thoughts at her. It was scary being that close to Raj and wanting to touch him. *Touch* him? What insanity was attacking her? Since when had she wanted to touch a man? Yet all of a sudden she could imagine *touching* Raj, smoothing a hand over that satin-smooth golden skin laid down over muscle. She sat up and put the glass down just before another deafening crash of thunder boomed and it sent her careening into the shelter and security he offered like a homing pigeon.

Raj had never before found it a problem to have an armful of fragrant woman in his arms. But when the woman was Zoe, it was a major problem. He had heard her shouting for help and saying, 'No, *please...*' over and over again and a kind of unholy rage had gripped him that someone so small and defenceless had been driven to begging, her fear and desperation palpable. Only it became complicated when she got too close to him and his body reacted against his will. He was so hard he dared not leave the bed for fear that she would notice and get scared that he couldn't be trusted. But he was not made of stone.

He closed his arms round her, murmuring soothing things in his own language, doing his best to resist urges that he felt should shame him. 'Were you raped?' he asked in a roughened undertone.

Zoe flinched, her slender body trembling in his hold, and she looked up at him. 'No. I was lucky. I was beaten up but I was rescued before it got that far.'

Raj's level black brows lifted. *'Lucky?'* he derided, not only stunned by what she had told him, but also feeling honoured that she had trustingly bestowed such a terrifying secret on him.

And Zoe laughed and spontaneously smiled. 'Yes, very lucky. I'm a survivor.'

That glorious, utterly unexpected smile was more

than Raj could withstand. Zoe looked up into eyes as bright as liquid starlight and marvelled at the beauty of them. He lowered his head and claimed her soft pink mouth with his.

The thunder boomed beyond the tent. Lightning strafed the ground, lighting up the walls, but Zoe didn't hear or notice any of that because there was a kind of magic in Raj's kiss and it was like no kiss she had ever had before. And yes, she had had kisses before, had tried several times at university to get into the spirit without succumbing to the terror of getting out of her depth with some guy who might then get angry and refuse to listen to her protests. When Raj slid his tongue between her parted lips, an insistent heat she had never felt before flared between her thighs. His hands stroked through her hair and she felt her breasts swell and her nipples tighten and tingle. The warmth of his skin and the weight of him against her led to the discovery that her body liked those masculine aspects of him. Even more did she appreciate the aromatic smell of him, an insanely attractive combination of musky male and designer cologne, which tugged at something very basic inside her. His tongue brushed hers and withdrew, leaving her aching for more, every nerve ending on fire.

And then he set her back from him and dragged in a shuddering breath while still looking at her as though she were the only woman in the universe, a gift of his that yanked at her heart strings. 'I'm sorry,' he breathed in a raw undertone. 'I broke my promise not to touch you.'

'Do you see me running or screaming?' Zoe demanded, shaken by his sudden withdrawal while her body was still humming and pulsing like an unfamiliar entity.

Raj's slightly swollen and very sensual mouth compressed, dark eyes glittering with angry regret. 'I will not make excuses for myself but I assure you that *this* will not happen again. Go to sleep, Zoe. You are safe.'

Since she didn't have much choice, Zoe turned away and snaked back to her own side of the bed, defensively turning her back to him. She had only herself to blame for the way she felt, she thought unhappily. She had told him she wasn't interested in sex, had shown him her fear and, in return, he had sworn not to touch her. Naturally he was angry that he had broken that pledge. Sixth sense told her that Raj didn't usually break promises and probably didn't think much of those who did. But he had warned her earlier that he found her attractive and their current circumstances of false intimacy and mutual dependence only made resistance more difficult.

But for the first time in her life, Zoe had *wanted* a man and she knew that she wasn't likely to forget the crazy buzz of excitement that he had unleashed inside her. She, she reflected in mortification, had been more tempted than he was because he had quickly called a halt.

And what had she wanted to do?

To her eternal shame, she had wanted to snatch him back and *make* him keep on kissing her and, not only that, in the back of her mind she had been well aware that she craved more than that. Somehow, and she really didn't know how or when it had happened, she was finally ready to *try* sex, to experiment, but there was no room for sex in their agreement, particularly in a marriage destined to last only a few months.

When she wakened in the morning, Raj was gone, but one of her suitcases sat in a prominent position near the bed. With a smile of relief, she got up and went to open it before going to freshen up. Clad in light cotton trousers and a pink top, teamed with glittery sandals, she found breakfast awaiting her on her return. She was really hungry and tucked in with appetite, although she was no fan of the yogurt drink included, reckoning it was probably one of those healthy options that she rarely enjoyed.

She walked out of the tent and an explosion of utterly unexpected colour greeted her. A field of flowers stretched before her and she walked in amongst the colourful blooms in wonderment at such a floral display in so seemingly inhospitable a landscape.

'Zoe…stay where you are!' Raj shouted at her, incensed to see her outside and unprotected and wandering with a toddler's absence of caution.

'What on earth—?' she began, glancing up from the pink, purple and mauve blooms she was studying as she crouched.

But Raj, black curls shining, was sheathed in jeans and a T-shirt and already striding towards her, careless of the flowers he crushed beneath his feet, clearly untouched by the beauty of the scene. He scooped her up bodily in his arms, exclaiming in Arabic. 'And what the hell are you wearing on your feet?' he then demanded incredulously.

'Sandals!' she snapped. 'You stood on the flowers

of an *asphodelus fistulosus* and it was the only *one* in this mass of bugloss.'

'There are scorpions and snakes, lying in the shade below the flowers!' Raj bit out, startling her. 'Here you wear only proper footwear that protects you.'

'Oh… OK.' Zoe nodded, recognising concern and superior knowledge when she saw it. 'I didn't know… but the flowers were so beautiful.'

Raj carried her back to the tent, thinking that he would never forget that first glimpse of her in that sea of flowers, white-blonde hair falling to her waist and glittering like highly polished platinum in the sunlight, and those huge green eyes blinking dazedly up at him as he lifted her, full of shock and incomprehension of the risk she had taken. He had trod on pretty flowers and it had bothered her. She was sensitive, also possibly a little ditzy to walk out thoughtlessly into what could be a very hostile environment. But it was his duty to take care of her, watch over her, his job to protect. And the enormity of such a responsibility sat heavy on his shoulders for an instant because he had never been responsible for another human being before.

Nor did he want to be responsible, he told himself staunchly. He would take care of her to the best of his ability without ever forgetting that she was not *truly* his wife and he refused to think of her as such. Zoe was a short-term prospect, not a keeper. He would be ice, he would remain impervious to her charms. He was not about to complicate things by getting too involved with her. He had hard limits and he would observe them, retaining softer feelings, if he could even experience such emotions again, for his future *real* wife. There would be none to waste on Zoe, even if she looked adorable posed amidst flowers. What an asinine thought that was! He surely had more sense than that, enough intelligence to keep his distance, he instructed himself bitterly; he had learned his lesson with Nabila.

Innocent didn't mean she was a virgin. He would never believe a woman's word on that score again! Cute didn't mean trustworthy. Nabila had lied like a trooper and he had not recognised her deceit. Adorable definitely didn't mean loveable. Cute and adorable were words that should never feature in his vocabulary because caring about the wrong woman hurt like hell and he wasn't revisiting that mistake for anybody!

CHAPTER FIVE

WITHIN AN HOUR a brief flight in the helicopter returned them to the palace.

Zoe walked through an ancient porticoed entrance and instantly felt as though she had been transported into another world and another time. An awe-inspiring giant hallway full of pillars and elaborately tiled walls greeted her as well as a wealth of fawning servants, some of whom were in actual tears welcoming Raj back to his home. Brushing off their blandishments with palpable embarrassment, Raj hurried her on into the building while a cohort of attentive staff fell in behind them.

'My father has placed us in the oldest part of the palace, which is...unfortunate,' he told her in a clipped undertone. 'It is, however, where the Crown Prince always has his apartments, so I cannot fault him for following tradition.'

'Why's it unfortunate, then?' she queried uneasily, even while her eyes fled continually to her surroundings. She was enthralled by the exotic quality of the internal courtyard gardens she espied from the stairs and the fabulous views out over the desert, not to mention the stonework, the domed roofs and the stern palace guards, dressed as though they had stepped out of a medieval painting, armed with swords and great curved knives. The palace was everything she had dreamt of when first coming to Maraban but far more grand and mysterious than she had naïvely expected.

'Only one bedroom has been prepared for us,' Raj breathed curtly, his strong jaw line clenching. 'It will be difficult to give you privacy.'

'We'll manage,' Zoe told him with an insouciance she could not have contemplated before meeting him in the flesh. She knew in her very bones that she could trust Raj, believed that he would never try to force her into anything, but when she pondered that conviction, she was challenged to understand why she had such faith in him. He'd shown her empathy, tenderness, kindness the night before, she reminded herself ruefully.

'That is very generous of you but not strictly within our agreement,' Raj pointed out, refusing to be soothed.

'Can't be helped,' Zoe murmured, breathless from trying to keep up with his long stride as he traversed long corridors at speed and mounted flights of stone stairs with lithe ease. 'This is a very large building.'

'But *not* modernised,' Raj retorted grimly, throwing wide a door before a hovering servant could reach for it and guiding her into a simply vast room in which a bed hunched apologetically in one corner.

'Plenty of space though!' Zoe carolled like Job's comforter.

The remainder of her cases were already parked along with the one that had travelled out to the desert

encampment. A maid glided up and tilted one sugges-
tively, looking eager to unpack, while Raj stalked across
the huge Persian rug, like a jungle predator at bay looking for something else to complain about.

A connecting room, she quickly learned, contained
cavernous wardrobes.

'This suite was last occupied by my father fifty-odd
years ago,' Raj informed her grimly. 'You can tell.'

'You didn't use these rooms when you were
younger?'

'No. Before my marriage I was expected to live in
my father's household.'

Zoe passed on into a ridiculously gigantic bathroom with a great domed roof studded with star tiles.
The bathroom fittings huddled somewhat pathetically
against the walls. 'It just needs more furniture,' she told
Raj with determined cheer. 'We could have one of those
fainting couches in the middle and I could lie there like
Cleopatra eating grapes.'

His starlit eyes focused on her without warning, an
intensity within that look that made something quiver
and burn low in her pelvis. *'Naked?'*

'Whatever turns you on,' Zoe mumbled, face burning, outclassed in her attempt to be light-hearted and
dropping her head even while she pictured herself lying
there naked for Raj's enjoyment. A ridiculous fantasy,
she scolded herself, for there would be nothing particularly sexy or seductive about her very small curves
on display.

'I have staff to introduce you to now,' Raj announced,
biting back the comment that seeing her naked in any
circumstances would work a treat for him. There would

be no flirtation between them, he instructed himself harshly, no foolishness.

'*Staff?*' she exclaimed in dismay.

'Principally my PR team, but you will have your own PA to keep you well informed of events. My father has made certain requests. He would like you to give an interview to our leading newspaper.'

Zoe had frozen. 'An...*interview*?' she yelped in dismay.

'Saying how you feel about arriving in your grandmother's country and being on the brink of a state wedding. My team will advise you and remain with you during it. There is also a fashion stylist, who will recommend a suitable wedding dress and new clothes.'

'I brought a wedding dress and an entire wardrobe with me,' she informed him helpfully.

'It would be distasteful to me were you to wear the dress you purchased for the marriage you planned to make to my uncle,' Raj delivered succinctly. 'You will wear nothing bought for that purpose.'

Zoe just couldn't see why it should matter what she wore. 'Don't you think you're being too particular?'

Raj settled hard black eyes on her, startling her. 'No. I know what I like. I know what I *don't* like. The concept of you wearing anything chosen with another man in mind offends me.'

Zoe sucked in a sustaining breath, deciding that he was more sensitive to her past history than she had appreciated. She returned to supervising the maid hanging her clothes because it seemed safer to keep her head down.

'You will be kept very busy over the next few days

choosing wedding apparel,' Raj informed her from the doorway.

'Can I use your phone for a few minutes?' Zoe asked abruptly. 'Mine needs charging and I want to catch up with my sisters and my grandfather.'

'Of course.' Raj dug out his phone, cleared the password and handed it to her. 'I will see you later.'

And then, just like that, he was gone and she was staring at the space where he had been, all black silky curls with his dark, devastatingly beautiful face taut and uninformative. She had wanted him to stay with her, had wanted *more*. For a charged moment, she couldn't cope with seeing that large gap between reasonable expectation and sheer idiocy for, naturally, Raj wasn't planning to hover over her like a protective and loving spouse because he wasn't really her husband in the truest sense of the word. No, he was genuinely offering her what she had told herself she needed and craved: an independent life in which they would live separate in mind and body. So why did that sensible arrangement now seem much less inviting? Why did his attitude currently feel like something of a rejection? She shook off that strange notion and told herself to stop overthinking everything before she drove herself mad.

Her grandfather was delighted to hear from her and eager to be assured that Raj was treating her properly, while adding that he would be arriving for the wedding, the fierce pride in his voice as he mentioned 'state' wedding so strong that it made her roll her eyes and swallow back a sigh. Winnie and Vivi were far less accepting of the change of bridegroom.

'He's a lot younger than the oldie,' Vivi warned her

worriedly. 'Make sure he doesn't try to get too friendly because he may have a different agenda.'

And when Zoe protested about how kind and considerate Raj had been so far, Winnie snorted. 'He's a prince, a future king—obviously he'll be full of himself. And I looked him up online…he's incredibly good-looking. Watch out for him trying to change the terms of your agreement.'

But when Zoe went to bed that night there was no sign of Raj being full of himself or looking to change the terms of anything. He had joined her earlier for dinner out in their private courtyard, a space shaded by towering and somewhat neglected trees and shrubs, and he had then excused himself to work. She had been measured up for a new wardrobe, had looked at length at designer dresses on a screen and had stated her preferences. By the end of the day she was too exhausted to stay awake, wondering where Raj was.

Raj worked late into the night before bedding down on the sofa in his office. It was the safe option. A vision of Zoe naked troubled his rest and at four in the morning he was on his phone trying to find out what a fainting couch was; for some reason he was determined to buy one regardless of cost. He groaned out loud at the conflict tearing at him. He didn't want to get involved. He didn't want to have sex with her…except when his resistance was at a low ebb. Why the hell would he buy a fainting couch for her to pose on? He found a purple velvet one hung with tassels and pictured her with a driven exhalation of breath before he thumped the cushion beneath his head. No couch, no flirtation, no sex, no intimacy whatsoever, he reminded himself grimly.

* * *

'Well, I couldn't say much for the accommodation,' Vivi remarked with a decided sniff.

Zoe bit back a tart response because her sister had been making critical comments ever since she had arrived the night before and it was starting to annoy her. 'It's very comfortable and Raj says I can take furniture from any of the unused rooms in the palace or buy new stuff, but contemporary wouldn't really work in surroundings like these. I haven't had time yet to change anything with all this wedding craziness going on.'

'That monster bathroom is just ridiculous,' Vivi opined snarkily.

'Raj's father wouldn't agree to any structural alterations when the bathrooms first went in. As far as he can, the King wants to preserve the palace as it was when he took the throne and I can understand that. It's a very old and historic building and he feels more like the custodian for future generations than the owner who has a free hand,' Zoe pointed out.

'You've got more confident...that's clear and I definitely approve of that,' her eldest sister, Winnie, said warmly. 'Here you are giving interviews and the like. I never thought I'd see the day.'

'Oh, the interview was easy,' Zoe carolled. 'Raj's PR team headed off any too personal questions for me and advised me on what to wear and all the rest of it.'

'But you picked your own wedding gown,' Winnie said knowingly, scrutinising the tiny glittering figure of her youngest sister. The dress was an elegant sleeved sheath with a modest neckline. Elaborate embroidery sewn with crystals and pearls adorned the lightweight tulle and it was the perfect fit for her petite frame. 'It's very chic.'

'Oh, stop changing the subject, Winnie,' Vivi cut in curtly, keen to cut through the chit-chat to what she believed was truly important, which was *protecting* Zoe. 'You know that you're as worried as I am. We *talked* about it last night.'

'And we're not going to talk about it any more,' Winnie declared, throwing her fiery sibling a pleading look. 'It was Zoe's decision to do this and the deed is done. They're already married.'

'With *one* bedroom in a palace the size of a small city!' Vivi interrupted worriedly, seriously suspicious of that development. 'How's she going to fight off a guy twice her size?'

Zoe paled at the tenor of the conversation. 'I won't have to fight him off. Raj sleeps elsewhere. We haven't had to share a bed since that first night I told you about, and that was kind of unavoidable and he apologised for it.'

'Raj is smooth, sophisticated, *predatory*,' Vivi outlined in condemnation, finally speaking her mind, for she had taken one look at Raj in all his good-looking, silkily soft-spoken glory and seen him as a major threat to the terrifyingly innocent and fragile little sister she loved. How could such a very handsome and wealthy man *not* be predatory? Zoe's near rape had almost destroyed her and Vivi didn't want her sister plunged into any situation that could threaten her peace of mind. 'I would imagine he is never stuck for the right word in a difficult situation.'

'He's not predatory,' Zoe argued with distaste. 'He's been kind. He's courteous and considerate and that's all we need right now.'

'Leave it, Vivi,' Winnie said ruefully. 'All you're doing is putting more pressure on her.'

Zoe's hand shook a little as she reapplied her lipstick. She was furious that Vivi had called Raj predatory after only meeting him for an hour over the formal dinner that had been staged the night before. Stam Fotakis, her grandfather, had been grudgingly impressed by Raj, pointing out to her with satisfaction that, unlike her sisters' husbands, Raj had never been tagged a womaniser.

Diamonds flashed with every movement of her body. Raj had sent her jewel cases containing a tiara, a necklace and earrings. She didn't know whether they were family heirlooms or bought specially for her use and she hadn't had the chance to ask him because she had barely seen Raj since their move to the palace two weeks earlier. He joined her for dinner every evening but his manner was formal and distant and she didn't know how to break through that façade.

And although she had tried to penetrate that barrier to establish a friendlier vibe, Raj remained resolutely detached and very, *very* polite. His attitude frustrated the hell out of her. She didn't know what the matter with him was or what was travelling through his brain. The warmer, milder, more approachable side of Raj had vanished as though it had never been.

Although she could have had no suspicion of the fact, Raj's attitude was frustrating his royal parent even more.

'Any normal man would want to *keep* her!' King Tahir was proclaiming to his stony-faced son.

'I have no intention of keeping Zoe as a wife,' Raj asserted quietly. 'You knew that going into this.'

'She's a beautiful, gentle girl. Everyone who has met her has talked highly of her. She could be a tremendous asset to you with her personality and ancestry,' his father fumed. '*Why* are you sleeping in your office with a beautiful wife in your bed? Have you forgotten how to woo a woman?'

The obstinacy that ran through Raj like a steel backbone flared and he gritted his teeth. 'She agreed to a fake marriage and I will abide by that agreement as I will abide by the one I made with you.'

The King paced the floor and silence fell. It was the silence of unresolved differences and residual bitterness that most often distinguished meetings between father and son. It took effort for the older man to persist. 'I loved your mother. I *know* she was unhappy as my wife but I loved her very much and the mode of her death devastated me,' he bit out harshly. 'I have to live with my regrets and my mistakes but I still remain grateful for the time I had with her.'

Raj swallowed hard, unable even to look at his father and utterly taken aback by that confession. He had never realised that his father actually loved his mother but he did recall that, after her passing, the older man had lived like a hermit for over a year. Not guilt so much as grief, Raj adjusted now, his view of the past softening the trauma of loss just a little.

Ironically, even appreciating that could not lift his gloom because there was nothing to celebrate when marrying a very beautiful woman who appealed to him on every level but who would ultimately leave him. His mother had left him by taking her own life, Nabila had left him through betrayal of all that he held dear. But then, hadn't he *agreed* that Zoe would ultimately leave him? Hard cheekbones colouring at that timely recollection, he reminded himself that he was in control of events and walking the path he had chosen. By the time Zoe walked out of his life again, he would surely be glad to reclaim his freedom.

The state wedding was so official and serious that Zoe's face ached with her set and determined smile. Being the cynosure of all eyes was taxing for her, but she wouldn't let herself dwell on that reality because she was well aware that all brides were subject to close scrutiny. Instead she reminded herself that she was lucky enough to have her grandfather, her sisters and their husbands with her for support. Sadly, the formality of the event had persuaded her sisters that their young children were better left at home and she suppressed a sigh. Winnie's son, Teddy, was a very lively little boy and her toddler daughter was full of mischief while as for Vivi's twin boys, sitting still for any length of time was a massive challenge for them, but Zoe was still disappointed not to have had some time with her nephews and niece because she had always adored children and had grieved over the truth that she was unlikely to have any of her own.

Yet her recognition of her attraction to Raj and her enjoyment of that amazing kiss had made her think that just maybe there was hope for her in the future. Maybe some day, after all, she would be able to have a relationship with a man like any normal woman, and if that happened then she just might have children of her own to love and care for eventually. More than anything else, what she had learned about herself since arriving in Maraban had convinced her that staying in her grandmother's country was the very best thing she could do to steer herself back into the land of the living. There was a whole world out there waiting to be discovered and for the first time in years she was filled with hope and optimism.

In the short term, however, she acknowledged wryly, there was the marrying, the constant smiling and the solemn bridegroom to contend with at their reception. If a smile had cracked Raj's face once she must not have been around to see it. A half-smile would play about the corner of his full sensual lips in the most infuriatingly tantalising way and she would watch and watch those lean, darkly beautiful features of his, but the real thing never quite made it, even for the authorised wedding photographs, which had proved to be an exercise in rigid formality.

Yet everywhere in Raj's radius, a virtual party was in swing, his return to being Crown Prince clearly a development that was celebrated by the many important guests attending, who ranged from visiting royal connections to business tycoons, top diplomats and local VIPs. His popularity was undeniable, although he was quick to dampen comments that tactlessly suggested that some day he would take Maraban forward in a different way from his father. Zoe sat through a lot of business talk before escaping back in the direction of her sisters.

She had already done her stint with Queen Ayshah, who had employed Farida as a translator and had embarrassed the other young woman greatly by insisting on passing on her convictions of what it took to be a good royal wife. A feminist would have had a field day with those rules, Zoe reflected with strong amusement, but then the elderly Queen had grown up in a different world where a woman's happiness and even her life could be utterly dependent on retaining her husband's favour. Thankfully, Raj would have no such power over her, Zoe thought fondly as she took a detour towards the cloakroom before approaching Winnie and Vivi.

In the big anteroom surrounding the cloakroom, a tall, slender woman rose from a chair and addressed her. 'Your Royal Highness?' she murmured with modestly evasive eyes. 'May I have a word?'

Zoe looked up into one of the most beautiful faces she had ever seen: a flawless oval graced by almond-shaped brown eyes with remarkable lashes, a classic slim nose and a pouty full mouth. The woman wore a sophisticated silk suit, tailored with precision to show off her well-formed figure and falling to her ankles while still toeing the line of local mores on modest dress. The pale golden hue of the outfit set off her glowing olive colouring and her wealth of tumbling black wavy hair to perfection.

'I am Nabila Sulaman,' she revealed in a very quiet voice. 'I was Raj's first girlfriend and, as I'm sure you're aware, it ended badly between us.'

Thoroughly disconcerted by that introduction, Zoe merely gave an uncertain nod while her mind raced to understand why the wretched woman would want to approach her.

'I run one of your grandfather's construction firms and he brought me here with his party of business people. I would definitely not have received an invite on my own behalf,' Nabila admitted, startling Zoe even more with that freely offered information. 'I'm very much a career woman and I don't want past mistakes to taint my future now that I've returned to Maraban to work. My parents suffered a great deal over my short-lived relationship with Raj. My father is a diplomat but he has been continually passed over for promotion since I blotted my copybook with the royal family. I am speaking to you now because a lot of time has passed since then and I was *hoping* that you could persuade Raj to bury the hatchet.'

Zoe winced at that bold suggestion. 'I'm sorry but I don't think I'm the right person to intercede for you. I don't interfere with Raj's life and he doesn't interfere with mine.'

'How very modern he must have become,' Nabila remarked with a dismissive toss of her beautiful head and an amused smile. 'Well, I think you should know that I'm in charge of the Josias project as CEO of Major Holdings, and that Raj and I will be working together in the near future. Please make him aware of that. I'm leaving now.'

'But Raj is here. You could speak to him yourself,' Zoe pointed out.

'No. I don't want to put him in an awkward position and surprise him in front of an audience,' Nabila declared with assurance. 'We haven't seen each other since we broke up.'

'Oh...' Bemused, Zoe watched the poised brunette walk away again and she entered the cloakroom with a lot on her mind. Nabila was gorgeous, clever and successful and had once been the woman Raj loved and wanted to marry, Zoe reflected ruefully. Loved and wanted to marry *a long time ago*. Eight years back, she reminded herself, practically pre-history in date. But even though that was her mindset she still headed straight for her grandfather to check out his opinion of the brunette.

'Nabila Sulaman? She's one tough cookie, a real go-getter,' Stam opined. 'Had to be to get so far in the construction field. She's Raj's ex?' Her grandfather grimaced. 'I wouldn't have included her in my party if I'd been aware of that.'

'Oh, it doesn't bother me,' Zoe hastened to proclaim just as her sisters joined them and then, of course, the entirety of her short conversation with Nabila had to be recounted.

'She's got some brass neck!' Vivi declared. 'I wish I'd been with you. Didn't you learn anything from us growing up?'

Zoe blinked and studied her sibling's exasperated expression. 'What do you mean?'

'You don't tangle with an ex. You certainly don't give her any information... I mean, what you were thinking of, telling her that you and Raj don't interfere in each other's lives?' Vivi demanded ruefully. 'How normal does that sound? You *want* the ex to think you're the love match of the century.'

'Put a sock in it, Vivi,' Winnie cut in. 'Zoe doesn't have to pretend if she doesn't want to. It's a marriage of convenience and both of them know and accept that. It's not personal for them the way it was for you and me.'

Zoe had lost colour. No, it was *not* personal, she repeated staunchly to herself, because, unlike her sisters and their husbands, Zoe had had no prior relationship with Raj before their marriage. Yet even in acknowledging that truth she was taken aback by the revelation that she would have liked to have scratched Nabila's beautiful eyes out because Nabila had *hurt* Raj. A long time ago, she reminded herself afresh, and he was perfectly capable of looking out for himself.

When the festivities were almost at an end, Zoe went to change into more comfortable clothing for their journey. They were to be out of the public eye for two weeks and she couldn't wait to reclaim some privacy. Apparently, the royal family owned a very comfortable villa by the Gulf on the Banian side of Maraban, and Raj had already promised to show her the beauties of her grandmother's birthplace, which was greener and less arid in landscape. She pulled on a light skirt and T-shirt, teaming them with a pair of glitzy high sandals, one of the many, many pairs she harboured in her wardrobe but had never previously worn. She had a serious shoe fetish and knew it.

'We're fortunate to be making so early an escape,' Raj remarked, sliding into the limo beside her, a lean, lithe figure in jeans and a shirt, his black curls tousled as though he had changed out of his wedding finery in as much of a hurry as her. 'If my father wasn't so eager to pack us off on a honeymoon, the celebrations would have lasted all week.'

'Farida mentioned that weddings usually last for days here, but then it was our *second* time round the block,' she pointed out before pressing on, doing what her conscience told her she had to do, which was to warn Raj that he would be working with his ex on some project that she didn't recall the name of. 'I met your ex-girlfriend, Nabila, at the reception.'

Raj's arrogant head turned, a frown building, his lean, darkly handsome face forbidding. 'That is not possible. She would not have been invited. Nabila is a common name in Maraban.'

'Apparently she came in my grandfather's party of guests,' Zoe persisted. 'She's the CEO of some company called Major Holdings and she asked me to warn you that you would be working with her on some project.'

'The Josias hospital project.' Raj's intense dark eyes shimmered almost silver in the fading light. 'But I need no warning. I am not so sensitive,' he breathed with roughened emphasis.

And then he didn't say another word for what remained of the fairly lengthy journey that took them to the airport and a flight and, finally, a bumpy trip in a SUV. And, unfortunately that brooding silence told Zoe everything she didn't want to know or surmise about the exact level of Raj's sensitivity. He was like a pot of oil simmering on a fire but all emotion and reaction was rigidly suppressed by very strong self-control that acted like a lid. But knowing that, accepting that she hadn't a clue what he was thinking, didn't make Zoe feel any happier. For the first time with Raj, she felt very alone and isolated...

CHAPTER SIX

WITH DIFFICULTY, RAJ emerged from circuitous thoughts laced with outrage at the prospect of being exposed to Nabila's deceitful charm again and stepped out of the SUV. He expected to see the sprawling nineteen-twenties villa that his family had used as a holiday home since his childhood. He blinked in disbelief at the very much smaller new property that now stood in its place and signalled the army major in charge of their security to seek clarification of the mystery. A couple of minutes later he returned to Zoe's side.

'Apparently, my father had the old villa demolished several years ago because it was falling into disrepair and he thought it was too large to renovate,' Raj explained. 'It was built by your great-grandparents at a time when the Banian royal family had half a dozen daughters. My family used it rarely after your mother's father died. My father likes the sea but the Queen does not.'

Relieved that Raj was talking again, Zoe murmured, 'Did you come here much as a boy?'

'Often when I was very young with my parents. My mother loved it here.' His lean strong face tightened, his perfect bone structure pulling taut beneath his bronzed skin. 'I remember her skipping through the surf and laughing. No worries about etiquette or protocol or who might be watching and criticising her behaviour. She could be an ordinary woman here again and she loved it.'

'An *ordinary* woman?' Zoe queried, puzzled by that label.

Momentarily, Raj turned away to evade the question because he disliked talking about past traumas. In his experience a trouble shared was not a trouble halved and he preferred to gloss over such issues. Without skipping a beat, he deftly changed the subject. 'My father should have told me that there was a smaller property here now,' Raj breathed. 'As he only comes here alone, there may only be one bedroom.'

'Oh, let's not get into *that* debate again!' Zoe carolled with a comically exaggerated shudder that locked his eyes to her animated face. 'We're adults, we'll get by, even if you make me sleep on the floor!'

Her green eyes could dance like emeralds tumbling in sunlight, Raj noted abstractedly, settling a hand to her spine to guide her down the path because it was dark and she could hardly move in her high heels without stumbling on the stony surface beneath their feet. He had watched her throughout the day, had been forced to watch her teeter and sway and steady herself on furniture every time she lost her balance. She might continually wear high heels but had evidently not yet learned how to comfortably walk in them. The idea of her falling and hurting herself made him want to go into her wardrobe and *burn* every one of those preposterous shoes. It was an odd thought to have and he tagged it as such and frowned in bemusement.

'You know, I wouldn't do that.'

'You're not sleeping on the floor either!' Zoe warned him as they approached the well-lit front door. A lovely wrap-around veranda fronted the building and their protection team surged ahead of them to check that the house was safe. 'Where have you been spending the night since we got married?'

'My office.'

'Is there a bed there?'

Raj shrugged a broad shoulder. 'A sofa,' he admitted grudgingly.

Zoe gritted her teeth in annoyance. 'Are you *that* scared of me?'

Dark colour scored the hard, slanted lines of Raj's spectacular cheekbones and his stunning eyes flashed gold with angry disbelief. At that optimum moment the protection team reappeared to usher them inside. It didn't take long to explore the interior of the beach house. There was a surprisingly large contemporary ground-floor living area and a winding staircase led upstairs to a spacious bedroom and bathroom.

'There's no kitchen!' Zoe exclaimed abruptly, glancing out at the walled swimming pool beyond the patio doors. 'How are we supposed to eat here?'

'The staff stay in a new accommodation block built behind the hill and cater to our needs from there,' Raj told her. 'Meals will be delivered. It's not a very practical arrangement but my father enjoys his solitude.'

'I'm starving,' Zoe admitted.

'I will order a meal.'

'I'll go for a shower and change into something more comfortable,' Zoe said cheerfully.

She was halfway up the stairs when Raj spoke again. 'I am not scared of you, nor was I implying that you would choose to tempt me into breaking my promise,' he assured her levelly. 'But it annoys me that my father is making it so difficult for me to offer you the privacy I swore to give you.'

'And why *is* he doing that?' Zoe prompted, tipping her head to gaze down at him, her cheeks warm from his misapprehensions about her. No, she wouldn't ever set out to deliberately tempt him but she was painfully conscious that she wanted him to make some kind of move on her because she was keen to explore the way he made her feel. It was just sex, she told herself guiltily, sexual urges tugging at her hormones, and there was nothing more normal than that, she told herself in urgent addition, nothing to be ashamed of in such fantasies. It was simply her bad luck that she was married to an honourable male who believed in keeping his promises and not taking advantage. Luckily for her, she could not even imagine a scenario where she would tell him honestly how she felt and, for that reason, the humiliation of making a total fool of herself over him was unlikely.

In the meantime, all she could freely do was glory in the sheer physical beauty of Raj, his wonderful broad-shouldered, lean-hipped and long-legged physique that magnetically glued her attention to him, the dark deep-set eyes that were silver starlight when he stared up at her, his perfect golden features taut. Heaven knew, he was gorgeous and it was little wonder she was obsessed, she conceded ruefully. He had broken through her barriers, made her experience feelings she had never known she could feel, but he hadn't intended to do that and now she was stuck with the rules according to Raj, which had about as much give in them as steel bars.

'My father believes you could be my perfect *for ever* wife. He's hoping for more than a pretend marriage from us and obviously he's doomed to disappointment,' Raj extended drily.

'Oh…' Deprived of speech by that piece of bluntness and stung by the assurance that she was safe for ever from being asked to entertain the idea of something *other* than a pretend marriage, Zoe sped on into the bedroom.

There was so much she didn't know about Raj, she reflected. All she had were the bare bones of his background and the fact that his first love had cheated on him. At least, she was assuming that Nabila had been his first love but, really, what did she know? Little more than was available on the Marabanian website about the royal family. And ignorance was *not* bliss. Raj had frozen and backed off the instant she'd asked about his mother. Nabila wasn't the only no-go zone; his mother clearly was as well. Zoe heaved a sigh as she showered, wondering what had made Raj quite so complex and reserved.

Raj glanced up from his laptop as Zoe reappeared downstairs, clad in some kind of pastel floaty dress that bared most of her shoulders and a slender length of shapely leg. Not even the most severe critic could have deemed the outfit provocative, but her pert little breasts shifted as she completed the last step and he went instantly hard, cursing his libido and the fierce desire he was holding back that was becoming harder and harder to contain. Most probably he would need her covered from head to toe not to be affected, he conceded wryly, and what good would that do when he had already seen her virtually naked and could summon up that mental image even faster? He clenched his teeth together, hating the sense of weakness she inflicted. It was weak to want what he knew he shouldn't have. He prided himself on being stronger and more intelligent than that.

Nabila had been enough of a mistake to scar a man for life, a warning that his judgement wasn't infallible, that people lied and cheated to get what they wanted or merely to make a good impression and cover up the less presentable parts of their character. But, at least, he no longer carried resentment where Nabila was concerned, he reflected absently. Time had healed his bitterness and maturity had taught him more about human nature. Even so, the very prospect of having to deal with Nabila in any form, most particularly in a professional capacity in the company of others, was deeply distasteful to him. It was even more offensive to him that Nabila had dared to approach his wife and introduce herself. That had been brazen and, although he knew that Nabila could be utterly brazen and calculating, he could not begin to understand why she had made such an inappropriate move.

'Wow...look at the food!' Zoe whispered in wonderment as she glimpsed the array of dishes spread across the low table in front of him. 'You should've started without me.'

'I do have *some* manners,' Raj told her huskily, amusement glimmering in his shrewd gaze.

'I never said you didn't,' she muttered in some embarrassment, lifting a plate to serve herself and watching him follow suit. 'But I did take ages in the shower.'

Raj could have done without that visual of her tiny, delicately curved body streaming with water. 'I had a shower before we left the palace.'

'I didn't have time and it was so warm in that car even with the air conditioning.' She sighed. 'So, I'm about to ask you to be straight with me on certain issues because if you aren't I could slip up and say something embarrassing to the wrong person,' she pointed out, trotting out the excuse she had come up with in the shower to make Raj talk about what he didn't want to talk about. 'Who was your mother?'

Raj tensed and swallowed hard. 'She was a nobody in the eyes of most. Ayshah and my father's second wife, Fairoz, were both royal princesses from neighbouring kingdoms and my father married them to make political alliances when he was in his early twenties. Since *he* did *his* duty in the marital line you can understand why he expected me to be willing to do the same eight years ago.'

'Yes, but he grew up during a very unsettled period of Maraban's history when there was constant war and strife. It was different for you because you didn't live through any of those wars or periods of deprivation,' Zoe told him calmly, her retentive memory of what she had read about Maraban's history ensuring that she had a clear picture of past events. 'Now tell me about your mother and why she was nobody in the eyes of others.'

'She was a commoner, a nurse. My father had heart surgery in his fifties and she looked after him in hospital.'

Zoe smiled in approval. 'So, it was a romance?'

'Well, no, for most of my life I assumed he simply took my mother as a third wife in the last-ditch hope that a much younger woman could give him a child,' Raj confided with a twist of his full sensual mouth. 'That was the perceived reality. It never occurred to me that he had fallen in love with her until he admitted that to me only a few days ago. Now I am shamed by my prejudice but, in my own defence, my mother was a very unhappy wife and I remember that too well.'

'Why was she unhappy?' Zoe pressed.

'Picture the situation, Zoe,' Raj urged with rueful emphasis. 'Two childless older wives of many years were suddenly challenged by a much younger new arrival and they didn't like it. They didn't think my mother was fit to breathe the same air as their husband and when she quickly fell pregnant, as they had failed to do, their resentment and jealousy turned to loathing. They bullied her cruelly and treated her like dirt. My father likes a quiet life in his household and he did not interfere between his wives. He ignored the problems.'

'I'm *so* sorry,' she murmured, registering that Raj must have been old enough to understand how his mother was being abused and that his troubled relationship with his father and Ayshah probably dated from that period.

'By the time I was nine years old, she was so depressed that she took her own life with an overdose. It happened here in the old original house. Perhaps that is also why my father had it demolished,' he admitted in a driven undertone. 'There, now you know the whole unhappy story of my childhood.'

Zoe reached for him, her small fingers spreading to grip his much larger hand in a natural gesture of sympathy, finger pads smoothing over the sleek brown skin. 'Thank you for telling me,' she whispered. 'I wouldn't have pushed so hard if I'd known it was a tragedy.'

'She was a wonderful, loving mother but it was many years before I could forgive her for leaving me,' Raj confessed in a rueful undertone.

'I have no memory of either of my parents. I was only a baby when they died in a car crash,' Zoe told him with regret. 'Cherish the memories you have, try and build a bridge with your father. Everybody needs family, Raj.'

'I prefer not to need *anyone*. Independence, in so far as it is possible, is safer. Do you want something sweet to finish?' Raj enquired in casual addition. 'There is a fridge hidden in that cupboard over there. The maid filled it with desserts.'

Listening to him, Zoe had lost much of her appetite, but she scrambled upright and fetched the desserts to serve, knowing that Raj would welcome that distraction. It seemed that she always, *always* put her foot in it with him. She should have been more patient, should have waited until he was willing to talk, instead of forcing the issue. Beating herself up for her nosiness soon led to her faking a yawn and saying she was going up to bed.

Raj worked on his laptop for an hour, giving Zoe time to fall asleep. He mounted the stairs as quietly as he knew how and then he saw her, lying on the bed in something diaphanous, the pool of light surrounding her veiling her entire body in soft gold. She looked up from her book, green eyes wide, little shoulders tensing, petite breasts pushing against the finest cotton to define the pointed tips and that was the moment that Raj finally lost the battle. Hunger surged through him with such power it virtually wiped out conscious thought. She was there, she was where he wanted her to be and, in that moment, she *was* irresistible.

Zoe was fiercely disconcerted when Raj simply stalked like a prowling jungle cat across the room and bent down to snatch her up into his arms. 'Raj?' she exclaimed uncertainly, all the breath from her body stolen by that action.

'I want you… I *burn* for you,' he breathed rawly. 'Tell me to put you down and I will walk away. I will not try to railroad you into anything you don't want.'

Zoe stared up into his silvered eyes and her entire body clenched while her heart pounded in her ears. 'I want you too,' she admitted breathlessly, barely able to credit that she had the nerve to admit that and yet if he could admit it, why shouldn't she?

As he cradled her in his arms, a faint shudder of relief racked his lean, powerful frame and he claimed her parted lips with so much passion he took her by storm. Head swimming, mouth swollen, she plunged her fingers into his silky black hair, revelling in the crisp luxuriance of his curls and holding him to her. There was no sense of fear, no sense of threat and she rejoiced in that freedom, pushing up into the heat of him as he brought her down on the bed. She yanked at his shirt as he reached for her nightdress, their combined movements ending up in a tangle.

'We're behaving like teenagers!' Raj rasped in disbelief, gazing down, nonetheless, at her flushed and lovely face with ferocious satisfaction. He had never craved anything as much as he craved her hands on his body and he leant back from her to pull his shirt up over his head and discard it.

Zoe looked up at him, secretly thinking that she was behaving like a teenager because her experience of men was probably about that level. She truly was a case of arrested development, cut off from normality at the age of twelve when everything to do with men and sex had frightened her into closing down that side of her nature. Now she wondered if she should warn him that she was a virgin, but wasn't there a strong chance that her inexperience would turn him off? Or, at least, make him pause to consider whether they should be having sex in the first place? She didn't want Raj to stop and ESP warned her that if cautious, logical Raj got in charge again, her desire to have sex for the first time could be thwarted.

Raj, however, chased away all her apprehensive thoughts simply by taking his shirt off. As he leant back over her to toss it away, his abdominal muscles flexed like steel girders and she gazed up at his superb bronzed torso with helpless appreciation. Heat flowered low in her pelvis, making her press her thighs together on the resulting ache. Exhilaration flooded her at the knowledge that she was finally feeling what other women felt when they desired intimacy with a man.

'I thought you didn't like sex,' Raj breathed in a driven undertone.

And then I met you.

But she wasn't going to frighten him off by telling him *that*, was she?

'It's time I tried again,' she muttered obliquely.

'I will endeavour not to disappoint you,' Raj growled, his lips ghosting in a whisper of a caress across her collarbone that made her shiver, lean brown hands tugging up the nightdress inch by inch, fingertips lightly glossing over her slender thighs and finally her narrow ribcage. The butterflies fluttering in her belly took flight.

The nightdress fell away and Zoe sat up to embark on his jeans. It might be her first time but she wasn't about to lie there like some petrified Victorian virgin and let him do everything, she told herself squarely. Her hands were shaking so much though that she could hardly get the zip down and he closed a steadying hand over hers, pressing her fingers against him before arching his hips to snake lithely out of his jeans. His boxers went with them and she stared at the evidence of his arousal and then, dry-mouthed, reached out to stroke him, her heart already racing as though she had run a marathon.

The instant she touched him, Raj tugged her up against him with a hungry groan and crushed her mouth under his again, his tongue prying apart her lips and skating across the roof of her mouth before colliding with hers. Another burst of heat shot through her, tightening her muscles, and she shifted closer still, wanting the hard heat of him plastered to every inch of her. He was so passionate and she loved that passion, could feel it surging through his lean, powerful body to meet her own.

He laid her back and shaped her breasts with sensuous hands, smoothing, massaging, moulding, before dipping his head to catch a straining pink nipple in his mouth and swirl his tongue round the throbbing peak until her spine arched and a stifled gasp was torn from her. She was much more sensitive there than she had ever realised and little tingling thrills began to dart through her, trickling down into her pelvis to create a hot liquid pool between her thighs.

Her hips arched up of their own volition, her body controlling her responses, and all the time the nagging craving at the heart of her was building to an unbearable level and she was making little impatient sounds she couldn't quell. When he finally touched her where she most needed to be touched, her body jackknifed and a wild flood of sensation seized hold of her, provoking a cry from her lips. It was her very first climax and the sheer intensity of it took her by surprise.

Raj smiled down at her and kissed her even more hungrily. 'You are so receptive,' he husked.

Lying there dazed by the experience, Zoe reached up to explore him, palms spreading across his chest, captivated by the strength and heat of him before sliding lower to encounter a restraining hand.

'Not now,' Raj grated out. 'I'm too aroused and I need to be inside you. Are you protected?'

For a split second she didn't know what he was talking about and then comprehension sank in and she shook her head in an urgent negative. With a groan, Raj sprang off the bed naked and dug into his luggage, spilling out everything on the floor in wild disarray and then leafing through the tumbled garments to retrieve a wallet and extract a foil packet.

'I only have a few. I will need to buy more. I have not been with anyone recently and we must be careful.'

Warmed by his admission that he had had no recent lovers, Zoe frowned.

'Careful?' she queried.

Surprised by the question, Raj glanced at her. 'In our situation, a pregnancy would be a disaster...not that it's very likely. Look how many years it took my father to produce a child!' he urged wryly. 'For all I know a low sperm count runs in the royal genes.'

'But contraception is pretty much foolproof these days...surely?' Zoe pressed.

'Nothing's foolproof in that line. Accidents and surprises still happen,' Raj pointed out, coming back down on the bed with a smouldering look of hungry urgency silvering his stunning eyes. 'But it will *not* happen to us.'

Zoe reddened, disconcerted to find herself in the very act of picturing a little boy or girl with his spectacular dark eyes. Some day in the future, she promised herself, and most definitely she would become a mother with someone she had yet to meet. Raj would just be an experience she recalled with warmth, she told herself; nothing more, nothing less was due to the man who had rescued her from her fears.

She stretched up, winding her arms round his neck to draw him down to her and she kissed him, enjoying that freedom and that new confidence to do as she liked, and it all came from the reassuring, delightful discovery that Raj appeared to want her every bit as much as she wanted him.

He tugged at her lower lip with the edge of his teeth, sent his mouth travelling down the elegant line of her slender neck and that fast conversation was forgotten as another cycle of arousal claimed her. Her temperature rose, a fevered energy gripping her limbs as her heartbeat quickened and her breathing fractured.

Excitement quivered up from her pelvis when she felt him surge between her thighs, sliding into her inch by inch, sending the most exquisitely unexpected sensations sizzling through her.

'You're very small and tight,' Raj ground out breathlessly.

And then with a final shift of his lean hips he forged his passage and her whole body jerked with the pain of it and she cried out.

Raj stilled. 'What's wrong?'

Mortified that she had made a fuss, Zoe grimaced. 'It hurt more than I was expecting. It's my first time.'

As shock clenched Raj's lean, darkly handsome features and he began to withdraw from her, Zoe grabbed his shoulders. 'No, don't you dare stop now!' she told him. 'I've been waiting such a long time to experience this.'

The deed was already done, Raj rationalised, but anger was roaring through his taut body and it was only with difficulty that he swallowed it back because he didn't want to risk hurting her any more…even if she had chosen to have sex with him as though he was an adventurous new experience much like a day out behind the wheel of a supercar, he reflected wrathfully.

'Raj, please…don't make a fuss,' Zoe urged, studying him with huge green eyes that pleaded.

And Raj did what every nerve ending in his body urged him to do and surged deeper into the welcome of her, a low growl of sensual pleasure wrenched from him. And from that point on, no further encouragement was required. A wondrous warmth began to rise low in her pelvis, building on the visceral ache for fulfilment, making her fingernails dig into his long smooth back as excitement seized her and held her fast. The feel of him over her, inside her, all around her sent rippling tremors of joy spiralling through her and when she hit the heights again, it was explosive.

In the aftermath she felt as though she were melting into the bed in a boneless state and the very last thing she needed then was Raj freeing himself from their entangled limbs and springing off the bed to breathe rawly, 'You've got some explaining to do. You *lied* to me!'

CHAPTER SEVEN

GRABBING THE SHEET to cover herself, Zoe hauled herself up against the tumbled pillows, watching Raj yank on his jeans. Going commando, she noticed, colour flaring in her face. It was as if her mind weren't her own any more. She couldn't take her eyes off his lithe bronzed body, couldn't concentrate.

'I didn't lie,' she reasoned stiffly.

'You *lied*,' Raj repeated wrathfully. 'You said it was time you tried sex *again* when clearly you had never had sex before—'

'Well, I may have blurred the edges of the truth a bit,' Zoe mumbled defensively.

'You lied and I detest dishonesty!' Raj shot back at her fiercely.

'So what?' Zoe fired back, her temper sparking in answer to his.' It was *my* decision to make—'

'And mine. I wouldn't have touched you had I known I would be the first!' Raj bit out curtly. 'But you chose to withhold that knowledge, which was unfair—'

'Oh, for goodness' sake…' Zoe thrust the blonde hair falling round her hot face back off her damp brow. 'It was just sex. Why are you making such a production out of it? We're consenting adults, neither of us is in another relationship.'

Raj skimmed scorching dark eyes to her. 'I don't do relationships.'

'Well, I'm afraid you're *stuck* in this one,' Zoe told him with unashamed satisfaction. 'You can't have it both ways, Raj. If you don't do relationships, then you should be quite happy to have had no-strings-attached sex.'

Dark colour scoring his superb cheekbones, Raj shot her a blistering look of derision and strode out of the room. She listened to his bare feet thumping down the wooden stairs and then the slam of the front door signifying his exit from the house. Switching out the lights, she got out of bed to walk over to the window and finally picked him out striding down onto the beach. Moonlight glimmered along the hard line of his broad shoulders and danced over his curls.

Mortification gripped Zoe, who was conscious she had said stuff she didn't actually believe to hit back at him because she had felt humiliated by his annoyance. It *had* been her decision to have him as her first lover, hadn't it? But she wasn't liberal enough to plan to have casual sex with anyone, even if she had made it sound as though she were. She had simply wanted that experience, had wanted *him*. Was that so bad? But it also felt wonderful to no longer fear the act of sex, to no longer feel that she was somehow less than other women and missing out on an experience that others enjoyed.

Uneasily aware then of the ache at the heart of her from that first experience, she went into the bathroom and ran herself a bath to soak in. She had messed up, brought sex into their platonic relationship...but, hey, hadn't Raj been the one to make the first move? Why hadn't she thrown that at him? It was *his* fault they had ended up in bed. Why, in his eyes, would it have been acceptable to become intimate if she had had more experience? How had it somehow become wrong because she had been inexperienced?

Throwing on a cotton wrap and stuffing her feet into flip-flops, Zoe left the house and trudged across the sand to where Raj was walking through the whispering surf.

Raj heard her approach. There was nothing stealthy about Zoe crossing sand. He breathed in deep and slow, rising above his angry discomfiture and the guilt she had inflicted him with.

'All right, I'm sorry I didn't tell you beforehand, but you're the one who dragged *me* into bed,' Zoe reminded him flatly, her face burning. 'Regrets now are a bit late in the day and they're not going to change anything.'

'In my culture a woman's purity is highly valued and respected. That may seem outdated to you—'

'Very much so. Why should a woman be any more restricted with what she does with her body than a man is?' Zoe slung back at him half beneath her breath.

'I feel guilty that I took that innocence from you,' Raj admitted harshly.

'Even if it's what I wanted? It's not like I'm still a teenager in need of protection,' Zoe argued vehemently, surprised herself to realise how strongly she felt about the decision she had made. 'I just wanted to be like everyone else and know what it was all about instead of feeling...feeling odd,' she framed grudgingly.

'You deserved more than I gave you. It wasn't special…it *should* have been special,' he asserted with conviction.

'Was your first time special for you?' Zoe demanded, cutting in.

Disconcerted by that unexpectedly bold question, Raj gritted his teeth and opted for honesty. 'No.'

'Well, there you are, then, once again you didn't practise what you preach.'

A reluctant laugh was torn from Raj and he turned to look at her, so tiny she barely reached the centre of his chest and yet in so many ways she was absolutely fearless in her outlook, happy to express her views even when they conflicted with his. She was also too stubborn and independent to even acknowledge his point that if she had valued herself more she would not have entertained surrendering her innocence to him. People rarely confronted Raj with his mistakes or criticised him but Zoe had no such filter. She was quite correct: *he* had dragged *her* into bed.

'And I'm sorry if you don't feel the same way,' she added stiffly, 'but what we shared *did* feel special to me.'

Disconcerted, Raj sent her a gleaming glance and then his lashes dropped low. 'I'm sorry if I upset you but I do hate lies,' he murmured grimly.

'I'm usually very honest but I didn't want you to back off,' Zoe completed unevenly.

'You were curious,' Raj commented, wondering if he had ever had such an extraordinary conversation with a woman before, a conversation in which he was painfully honest and she was as well. He didn't think so and there was something remarkably refreshing about the experience.

'Yes, sorry if that makes you feel a bit like an experiment...but I suppose you were, rather, a new experience, I mean,' she mumbled apologetically.

Exactly like having a day out behind the wheel of a supercar, Raj thought again with relish, and he burst out laughing. No, no woman had ever dared to tell him before that he was an experiment, but then none had ever used that word, special, for what they had shared with him either. 'Am I allowed to ask how I scored?'

'No. That would be bad for your ego...' Zoe gazed up at him, encountering moonlit dark eyes that shimmered, and her heart skipped a beat.

'You were amazing...and special,' Raj murmured, lifting his hands to gently comb her tousled mane of hair back from her cheekbones, the pads of his fingers brushing the petal-soft skin of her face, sending a quiver of awareness arrowing through her. 'But I shouldn't have touched you. I had no right.'

'We're married.'

'In name only,' he reminded her with scrupulous accuracy, and for some reason she wanted to kick him. 'It's not meant to be real but it's starting to feel very real, which is worrying.'

'Why worrying?' she prompted.

'It wasn't supposed to be like this. We were supposed to live separate lives and make a few public appearances together and that was to be that.'

'So, we departed from the set script. But we're not hurting anyone,' she whispered, her hands settling to his lean waist, her fingers rubbing over smooth, hot skin, feeling the ripple of the muscles of his abdomen pull taut at even that slight touch.

'I don't do relationships,' he reminded her stubbornly even as he leant down to her, drawn by the ripe pink swell of her mouth.

'You're right in the middle of a relationship with me…stop kidding yourself!' Zoe countered. 'Do you think you're about to wake up some morning and find yourself handcuffed to the bed and trapped?'

Raj scooped her slight body up into his arms as if it were the most natural thing in the world to carry her and trudged back up the beach towards the house. 'If it was you cuffing me to the bed, I wouldn't fight and I wouldn't feel trapped,' he muttered huskily.

'That's probably the nicest thing you've ever said to me, but I've got to tell you that cuffing you to the bed looms nowhere on my horizon. If you don't want to be there, you can sleep on the floor,' she told him roundly.

'You said you weren't up for that option.'

'Guess I lied again,' Zoe trilled. 'I could happily consign you to the floor now.'

'And if I *want* to share the bed?' Raj left the question hanging as her lashes opened to their fullest extent, revealing emerald-green enquiry.

'You're welcome,' she said gruffly as he set her down and she kicked off her flip-flops. 'I think sex makes me hungry… I'm starving again!'

And Raj threw back his head and laughed, stalking over to the concealed fridge, discovering it was packed with prepared food in readiness for such an occasion. Zoe stiffened, marvelling at how relaxed she now felt with Raj. Barriers had come crashing down when they had shared that bed, she acknowledged, but now that she felt closer to him and no longer separate, she was more likely to get hurt. What had happened to her defences? What had happened to her belief that she was only in Maraban to become stronger and more independent? Now she was involved with Raj on a level she had never expected to be and her emotions were all over the place and making her feel insecure.

Zoe froze, frowning as she surveyed the room. 'All the dinner dishes have been cleared away.'

'The staff have been in. Our protection team probably let them know the coast was clear. The bed's probably been changed as well,' Raj forecast.

Zoe gulped. 'It's after midnight, Raj. Don't the staff sleep?'

'They work rotation shifts. Invisible service is a matter of pride to them.'

They ate snacks and she went up to bed first, the exhaustion of the long day crashing down on her all at once. She pillowed her cheek on her hand and watched Raj strip off his jeans and go for a shower, enviably indifferent to any form of self-consciousness. But then maybe had her body been as flawlessly beautiful as his she would've been equally blasé, she thought sleepily. Instead she was blessed with short legs, tiny boobs and a bottom that was a little big for the rest of her.

'What are we doing tomorrow?' she whispered when he joined her.

'It is already tomorrow,' he pointed out. 'I'm taking you to the old palace where your grandmother grew up and afterwards there'll be an informal meet-and-greet session with the locals and official photographs. My father is making as much possible use of your time in the family as he can.'

'I suppose that was the deal,' she muttered drowsily. 'It'll be interesting seeing where Azra grew up... It was almost as interesting watching your father and my grandfather politely avoid each other at the wedding, and then I was steering clear of your uncle Hakem and he was staying well away from me as well.'

Her brow furrowed at that recollection. Prince Hakem had proved to be a rather colourless little old man and she had been astonished that such a seemingly nondescript personality could be burning underneath with thwarted royal ambitions.

A husky laugh fell from Raj, his breath warming her shoulder. 'My father made a fuss about having your grandfather at the wedding but I talked him round. Stam is, after all, the man who ran off with the Banian princess my father was supposed to marry.'

'But my grandmother, Azra, and your father hadn't even met when she met Stam and fell for him,' Zoe whispered.

'My father still felt it was an insult and it rankled. Go to sleep,' Raj urged. 'This will be another long day but, after the palace visit, we are off the official schedule for the rest of our stay.'

And Zoe thought tiredly of how anxious she had been about having to make any public appearances when she'd first arrived in Maraban and of how inexplicably Raj's presence by her side, or even in the same room, soothed her apprehensions. Somehow, he made her feel safe, protected, as if nothing bad could happen while he was around. It was so silly to endow him with that much importance, she conceded ruefully, and then she slept.

What they had *was* a relationship, Raj recognised with considerable unease. It had become one the minute he married her and intimacy had only deepened the ties and made it more complex. Truly it had been naïve of him not to foresee that development, given the level of attraction they shared Zoe had said it was 'just' sex. Could he believe that, accept that? Was she really sophisticated enough to make that distinction? And could they keep it at that casual level? And in time go their separate ways without regret? It would be like a very long one-night stand, he reasoned while even his brain told him that that was a foolish misconception. He didn't want to treat Zoe the same way he treated his occasional lovers, being distant, keeping it impersonal, always hiding his true self. He felt much more comfortable with Zoe. He wanted to make her happy. For the first time ever with a woman, he would just go with the flow...

Zoe wakened in the morning in Raj's arms. 'Hey, your only body temperature seems to be hot as the fires of hell,' she complained, striving to slide away to cool off.

Raj pulled her back to him with ease and the thrust of his arousal against her stomach made her eyes widen. She looked up at him, all bronzed and in need of a shave, with blue black curls, and he was to die for and there was no denying that she was willing. 'Oh...' she said in entirely another voice.

'If it would be uncomfortable for you...?' he husked, hitching a perfect ebony brow in enquiry.

It probably would be a little bit, she acknowledged,

but there was a hungry tingle of awareness heating up between her thighs that made her hips shift with longing. 'No, it wouldn't be,' she lied shamelessly. 'But I need to clean my teeth.'

'No, you don't…you smell like strawberries and woman,' Raj framed thickly, cupping her cheekbones and devouring her mouth as though his life depended on it.

And that was that for Zoe, her heart thumping fit to burst from her chest as her body ratcheted up the scale of arousal as though it had been doing it all her life. When he kissed her, he set her on fire, when he touched her, exploring her urgently sensitive nipples and the tender flesh between her thighs with those long skilful fingers of his, the fire began to blaze out of control and she was turning and twisting, downright writhing with tormented pleasure. By the time he hooked one of her legs over his hips and plunged into her, Zoe was surging towards a climax at an unstoppable pace and the raw, hot excitement of that passionate invasion sent her flying with a choked gasp into the horizon.

'Let's see if you can do that again,' Raj growled as she thrashed under him and he surged into her afresh in a timely change of pace, aiming for long and slow rather than fast and furious.

And she caught her breath again and barely with a quivery little inhale, blonde hair lying in a mad tangle around her head as he rose over and looked down at her, black starlit eyes intent and riveting, her body still singing and pulsing from his last onslaught. His rhythm was sensual, calculated, letting the erotic tension build again and inexorably she shifted from melting to craving. His passion compelled her, and her hands slid over his back, rejoicing in the hard, smooth strength of him as rippling waves began to clench at her pelvis. A wildness took hold of her and she wrapped her legs round him and that final thrust made her soar in an excess of pleasure to the heights again.

Afterwards, he brushed her hair off her damp face and kissed her. 'I hate to hurry you when I've made you late in the first place, but we have to be out of here in an hour if you want to see the palace before we have to face the official welcome...'

'An hour?' she gasped incredulously.

'I'll call your maid and get out of here,' Raj told her helpfully. 'Am I allowed to say that you make a great friend with benefits?'

Was *that* what she was? Zoe thought about that in the shower and pulled a face. It sounded a lot bolder and a lot more laid-back than she believed she was, but who was to say she couldn't change? Wasn't that what her stay in Maraban was aimed at? Finding out who she really was without her sisters and her grandfather wrapping her in cotton wool and watching over her all the time? She was in a brave new world, she reminded herself, and aspects of it were likely to be unfamiliar and scary. Or *sobering*, she conceded ruefully, because her gut instinct was that she didn't want to be a friend with benefits for any man...even Raj.

Her maid had apparently accompanied her from the palace and already had an outfit laid out for her when she reappeared from the bathroom. Zoe cast an eye over the pale green tailored dress and decided it would do very well. At her request her hair was braided, which was cooler in the heat, and when she descended the stairs dead on time, she was smiling, thinking that a maid with hairstyling skills was an invaluable asset and a luxury she had better not become too accustomed to having. It was *all* temporary, she reminded herself, like a winning prize ticket that took her off on an extravagant holiday. Raj was, also, simply a temporary presence in her life. Maybe that was what made the 'friends with benefits' concept meaningless and possibly a little slutty. She winced at that self-judgement.

'You can't wear those shoes trekking round an old building!' Raj exclaimed, engaged in staring at her feet in what appeared to be disbelief.

Zoe sent him a dirty look. 'I'm crazy about shoes, but I'll bring a pair of flats and change into these later,' she conceded reluctantly. 'But don't you get the idea that you have the right to tell me what I should and shouldn't wear... I'm not having that!'

An unholy grin slashed Raj's often serious features as he awaited her reappearance.

The one-time home of the former Banian royal family was huge and sprawling and, although the building had been carefully conserved, it was not used for any purpose other than to house a small museum on the history of Bania and provide the public with the chance to tour Princess Azra's former apartments.

'I wish she hadn't died before I was born.' Zoe sighed, studying old black and white photos of a youthful blonde in local dress. 'Grandad showed me pictures of her. He totally adored her, you know,' she told Raj cheerfully. 'He cast off my father for refusing to do a degree in business and come and work for him. My grandmother told him he was doing the wrong thing and that he should let my dad make his own path but Grandad was too proud and stubborn to listen.'

'It is a challenge for one generation to understand what drives the next. It was years before I could appreciate that in demanding that I marry a woman he chose my father was only asking me to do what he had done himself.'

'But you were in love with someone else,' Zoe reminded him. 'You couldn't possibly have married another woman and made a success of it. You would've been full of bitterness and resentment.'

'My father believes that in our privileged position emotions cannot be allowed to make our decisions for us. I learned the hard way that he was correct,' Raj completed with a harsh edge to his voice.

'You still have to tell me about you and Nabila,' Zoe told him.

'I thought women didn't like a man to talk about previous affairs,' Raj countered in surprise, shooting her a disconcerted glance.

'I'd have to be in love with you to mind that sort of thing and all jealous and possessive and I'm *not*,' Zoe pointed out calmly. 'I'm just being nosy.'

Raj nodded, although the concept shook him because he was unconsciously accustomed to women wanting more from him than he was willing to give, which was why his sensual past consisted of more fleeting encounters than anything else. 'I studied business at one of the Gulf state universities. That's where I met her. Have you ever been in love?' he heard himself ask with astonishing abruptness, but he was, without warning, equally curious.

'No, not even close,' Zoe admitted tightly. 'What happened to me at twelve put me off trying to have a relationship with a man, and then I watched my sisters fall in love and didn't fancy it for myself. There seems to be a lot of angst and drama involved and I'm not into either. So you met Nabila at uni?'

'We were together for two years. I fell hard for her,' Raj bit out grudgingly, while wondering what superhuman qualities it would take to make Zoe fall in love with a man, and then his thoughts became even more tangled because he questioned why he was even thinking along that line. Was it exposure to Zoe? His cousin, Omar, had confided that following his marriage he'd found himself thinking weird thoughts, more like a woman, and that constant female company had that effect on the average man. Raj had to shake his head to clear it and he couldn't grasp how such random ruminations were arising in his usually logical brain.

'Obviously,' Zoe conceded. 'I mean, you weren't likely to defy your father's command for anything less...so you lived together for two years?'

'No, such intimacy was out of the question. If I expected my father to take my wish to marry Nabila seriously, it had to be non-sexual,' Raj proffered curtly. 'He would not have respected anything else.'

Zoe stopped dead and gazed up at him in wonderment. 'Are you saying you didn't sleep with her?'

'Of course, I didn't. My bride had to have an unsullied reputation. It would've been disrespectful to ask my father to countenance any other kind of relationship. He is from a different generation. He does not understand female liberation. In his day a woman's main claim to fame was her purity and a decent woman didn't give it up for anything less than a wedding ring.'

'Gosh, I was cheap,' his bride chipped in, her face suddenly on fire. 'Because as you pointed out, we're not really married in the truest sense of the word.'

'You weren't cheap,' Raj breathed as the museum custodian nervously watched their progress round the exhibits from the other side of the room. Long fingers stroked down her face and lingered below her chin to lift it. 'You were totally incredible and I was unworthy of the gift.'

'That's just flannel,' Zoe informed him, her face warming even more as she connected with brilliant dark eyes that sent butterflies fluttering in her tummy. 'We did what we did because we wanted to.'

'And every time I look at you,' Raj confided thickly, 'I want to do it again.'

'You were telling me about Nabila,' Zoe reminded him doggedly, tiny tingles of arousal coursing through her slight taut length while she fought to suppress those untimely urges. 'Not trying to turn me into a sex maniac.'

'*Could I?*' Raj asked in a roughened undertone, those gorgeous eyes pinned to her with a feverish intensity that scorched.

'It's possible,' she downplayed in haste. 'Nabila?'

'She told me she was a virgin because she probably assumed that that was what I wanted to hear. But it wasn't, I wouldn't have cared,' Raj admitted ruefully. 'So naturally I respected what she told me and I was prepared to wait until we were man and wife, but she got bored.'

'Hard to be set on a pedestal and to pretend to be something you're not,' Zoe put in thoughtfully.

'Yes, I did have her on a pedestal.' Raj grimaced. 'I was very idealistic at the age of twenty.'

'You were too young for that size of a commitment,' Zoe commented. 'What happened?'

'I refused to give her up and my father exiled me. It was my final visit and I left Maraban in a hurry. Nabila had given me a key to her apartment and my sudden return was unexpected. That was when I found her in bed with one of her so-called friends. It was clearly a long standing arrangement and what an idiot I felt!' Raj relived, his superb cheekbones rigid. 'I had surrendered everything for her and there she was, the absolute antithesis of the woman I believed her to be—a shameless cheat and a liar, who only wanted me for my status!'

'And your body, probably,' Zoe told him abstractedly, winning a startled sidewise scrutiny. 'You must've been devastated. I'm lucky. I've never been hurt like that, don't want to be either.'

Raj stared down into her beautiful expressive face and wondered why it was so very easy to talk to her about Nabila, whom he had never discussed with anyone before. It was because she didn't have a personal stake in their marriage, at least not one that he understood, because from what he had observed her new royal status and the awe it inspired meant precious little to her. 'The meet and greet downstairs starts in thirty minutes. You can put on the skyscraper heels if you must.'

'If I *must*?' Zoe queried, slinging him a look of annoyance.

'You struggle to walk in very high heels,' Raj pointed out bluntly.

'Because I never went out anywhere until I came to Maraban. I had this fabulous collection of gorgeous shoes and my sisters borrowed them and I never got to wear them until now,' Zoe told him hotly. 'I'll *learn* to walk in them!'

'Obviously,' Raj countered, realising that he had been tactless in the extreme. 'But why didn't you go out anywhere?'

'I panicked if men came onto me, couldn't handle it,' she confided reluctantly. 'But you don't do that to me for some reason.'

'Maybe because you're not falling for me,' Raj suggested glibly, while cherishing the obvious fact that she felt safer and more protected in his company.

'Yes, that could well be it,' Zoe responded cheerfully as she slid her feet into her high heels while leaning on both his arm and a door handle to balance. 'You wouldn't believe how much more confident I feel standing a few inches taller.'

Watching her sip coffee and smilingly chat by his side only minutes later, Raj decided it had nothing to do with the stupid shoes. He remembered their first meeting and her panic attack and marvelled at how much she had already changed. He had merely met her at a bad moment in a scenario that would have frightened any woman, he recognised. His fingers splayed across her spine and he concealed a grin, thinking about the scratches on his back, badges of pride for a man who knew he had satisfied his woman. Not *his* woman, he immediately corrected himself. Well, she sort of *was* his for the present, an acceptance that somehow lightened the cloud threatening his mood.

It seemed no time at all to Zoe before they were being posed in the palace's grand reception room for the photographs and then they were done, and it was a relief to not be on show any more and know that they had only a holiday ahead of them, she reflected sunnily. They were walking back to the car when a photographer popped out from behind some trees and shouted at them. Half of Raj's security team took off in pursuit of him. At the same time Raj's phone started shrilling and one of the diplomats she had met at the reception emerged with a grim face and moved in their direction with something clutched in his hand.

'What the hell?' Raj groused only half under his breath, pulling out his phone while ensuring that Zoe was safely tucked into the car awaiting them.

She watched as the diplomat proffered the magazine to Raj, saw him glance at it with patent incredulity and then compress his lips so flat they went bloodless. After that he strode back and forth in front of the car talking on his phone, his lean brown hands making angry gestures, his whole stance telegraphing his tense, dissatisfied mood.

'What's happened?' Zoe asked anxiously when he finally came off the phone and climbed in beside her.

CHAPTER EIGHT

'A STORM IN a teacup but it's put my father in a real rage.' Raj expelled a stark breath, impatience and exasperation lacing his intonation. 'Last year my father drove Maraban's only gossip magazine out of the country. Now they're based in Dubai and what they publish about us has steadily become more shocking. He should've left them alone. He has to accept that these days everything we do is watched and reported on and our family cannot hope to keep secrets the way we did when he was a boy.'

'I guess he's a bit behind the times. The press are more disrespectful of institutions nowadays. So, what's in that magazine?' she prompted, thoroughly puzzled. 'Some forgotten scandal?'

'Not even a scandal, merely an intrusion.' He had crushed the magazine between his hands and now he smoothed it out with difficulty and handed it to her. 'Of course, you can't read it but the photos are self-explanatory and this article coming out the same week as our wedding, suggesting that I wasn't allowed to marry the woman I loved because she was a commoner, may be embarrassing for my father but it is also an absurd allegation.'

Dry-mouthed now, Zoe stared down at the splash of photographs, depicting Raj with Nabila. *Old* photos, of course. She could see that they were younger but what she had not been prepared to see was the look of adoration in Raj's face as he gazed down at the other woman. He was studying Nabila as if she'd hung the moon for him and for some reason, Zoe registered, seeing those youthful carefree photos of them holding hands, larking about beside a fountain and smiling at each other *hurt*. She couldn't explain why those photos hurt but the instant she scrutinised them in detail she felt as though someone had punched her hard in the stomach because the pain was almost physical in its intensity.

What the heck was wrong with her? Was she starting to care for Raj? Was she suffering from jealousy, despite her earlier reassurance to him that she felt no such emotion concerning him? Those questions made her feel as shaky as if the ground had suddenly disappeared from under her feet. Yes, she was starting to care in the way you did begin to care more for someone when you got closer to them, she reasoned frantically and, yes, she had been jealous when she saw those photos. But none of that meant that she was necessarily falling for him.

'She was my first love and that was all,' Raj continued, wonderfully impervious to his bride's pallor and her silence. 'Very few people marry their first love and what does it matter anyway what I was doing *eight* years ago? It's a really stupid article but it *is* revealing a relationship that only our families knew about to the public. What I can't understand is how they got a hold of such private photos. I had copies but I destroyed them

after we parted and the friend who took the photos—
Omar—would never have shared them with anyone.'

'You said it was an absurd allegation,' Zoe recalled
dully. 'How so when it's true? Your father wouldn't
agree to you marrying her.'

'Not because of her parentage but because I suspect
he had had her checked out and knew a great deal more
about her than I knew at the time,' Raj admitted wryly.
'At least he had the consideration not to throw what he
had found out in my face.'

'As you said...a storm in a teacup,' Zoe remarked
rather stiffly, because all of a sudden she was tired of
hearing about anything that related to Nabila and she
could only marvel at her previous curiosity. Just then
she thought she would be happier if she never heard
the wretched woman's name spoken out loud again. As
for seeing those stupid photos of her with Raj regarding her as if he had been poleaxed, well, that had been
anything but a pleasure for a woman already labelled
as a friend with benefits. No doubt that was why she
had felt envious of the other woman.

No doubt, right at this very moment Raj was thinking
about Nabila, remembering how much he had loved and
wanted her, positively *wallowing* in sentimental memories! And on that note, Zoe decided that she would be
very, very tired that night, in fact throughout the day, so
that Raj would not dare to think she was in the mood to
provide any of those benefits he had mentioned!

'You still haven't told me how it happened,' Raj reminded Zoe stubbornly.

Raj was like a dog with a bone when he wanted in-

formation, he just kept on landing back on that same
avoidance spot of hers, an area of memory where she
never ever travelled if she could help it. She breathed
in deep, a little bit of a challenge when he was still flat-
tening her to the wall of the shower. Shower sex? Yes,
she had gained a lot of experience she had never expected to have over the past two weeks. Resolving to
keep her paws off Raj hadn't worked when he was behaving like lover of the year. It was the only analogy
she could make when she refused to let herself think
of him as a husband.

But there it was: her watch broke, so a new one studded with diamonds arrived within the hour; phone kept
on running out of charge, and a new phone was there
by bedtime so that she could talk to her sisters as usual.
She preferred flowers growing in the ground to those
cut off in their prime and stuffed for a short shelf life
into vases, and so he took her into the hills of Bania
to stage a luxury picnic beside a glorious field of wild
flowers. That had been only one of the blinders Raj
had played over the past fortnight. He hated her high
heels, seemed to be convinced she was going to plunge
down steps and, at the very least, break her neck, *but*
he had still bought her shoes, the dreamiest, absolutely
over-the-top jewel-studded sandals with soaring heels.
She had worn them out to dinner last night in a little
mountainside inn, where everyone around them had
pretended—not very well—not to know who they were
to give them their privacy.

The only problem for Zoe, who was blossoming in
receipt of such treatment, was that it was a constant
battle not to start caring too much about Raj. She kept

on reminding herself that none of this was real. Yes, he was her husband, but this was a convenient arrangement that they'd both agreed to. At best, he was just a friend, an intimate friend certainly, but beyond that she knew she dared not go. She was terrified of falling for him and if she made that mistake, she would be rejected and her heart would be broken.

'Zoe...' Raj growled, nipping a teasing trail across the soft skin of her nape to her shoulder with his lips and his teeth, sending a shudder of response through her that even very recent fulfilment could not suppress. 'I want to know how it happened.'

'And I don't want to revisit it.'

'It would be healthier for you to talk about it,' Raj told her doggedly.

'Like you talk about being bullied at military school!' Zoe flung even as she wriggled back into his lean, powerful body, registering that he was ready to go again while conceding that there was nothing new about that because Raj appeared to be insatiable. 'I practically had to cut the story out of you with a knife at your throat,' she reminded him with spirit. 'And by the way, Raj, it wasn't bullying. What you and Omar went through was abuse of the worst kind!'

'If I talked you can talk too,' Raj traded, running a long-fingered hand down over her spine, setting her alight without hesitation.

'This is sexual torture,' she told him shakily.

'All you have to do is say no,' Raj whispered, nipping at the soft lobe of her ear, flipping her long hair over his shoulder as he had learned to do, lost in the magic of her and her response for, as he had learned, it was enthralling to have that much power over a woman, as long as he never ever looked at the other side of the coin and acknowledged the reality that it was mutual.

Zoe straightened her shoulders and breathed, 'Right... I'm saying no...but you're not allowed to look at me like that!'

'Like what?' Raj prompted.

Those stunning dark silvered eyes of his shimmered with hunger and a tiny hint of hurt, and even a hint of hurt on show grabbed Zoe's heart hard and squeezed the breath out of her. She wanted him; every time she looked at him she wanted him.

But that was fine, absolutely fine, she told herself soothingly. It was just sex. She'd had a friend at university who went on a girls' holiday once purely to have sex with a lot of different men. That had been Claire's idea of fun: Raj was Zoe's idea of fun. And the world of sensual freedom she had learned to explore with Raj was the best reward of all. After the shocking attack she had survived as an adolescent, she had never dreamt that she could aspire to such freedom in her own body. Now she could only look back with a sigh when she recalled the frightened, broken young woman she had still been when she'd first met Raj.

'OK... I'll tell you,' she conceded, stepping out of the shower, surrendering to his demand but unable to do so when he was still touching her, something in her shying away in revulsion at any association between making love with Raj and what had happened to traumatise her when she was still a complete innocent.

Zoe settled down on the side of the vast bed, still

wet and dripping and not noticing. But Raj noticed, pale beneath his bronzed skin, his sculpted bone structure rigid because he was worried that he had pushed too hard for her confidences. Lifting her up, he carefully wound her like a doll into a giant fleecy towel, but when he tried to keep a soothing hold on her body, she broke away from him and dropped down into a bedside chair instead.

'There was an older boy, well, not much older, he was fourteen and I was twelve,' she trotted out shakily. 'In the same foster home. We used to play video games together… I thought he was a friend. There was a film I wanted to see, a stupid romantic comedy, and my foster mum said he could go with me, look out for me…but he didn't take me to the cinema.'

'You don't have to tell me if you don't want to,' Raj incised in a hoarse undertone.

'No, my sisters used to say I needed to talk about it, which is why I went to therapy. He didn't take me to the cinema. He took me what he said was a shortcut across wasteland and there was this old hut…and I was complaining because there was a storm and I was getting soaked.'

Her breathing was sawing noisily in and out of her struggling lungs.

'In the hut all these boys were waiting. They were a gang and the price of his entry into the gang was to bring a virgin, any virgin. They beat me up when I tried to get away and I was so badly hurt I couldn't move. They cut off my clothes with a kn-knife…and I had nothing even for them to see b-because I was a l-late developer,' she muttered brokenly, almost back there, reliving the terror, the pain and the shame of that public exposure.

Raj grasped both her trembling hands to pull her back into the present. 'It's in the past, and it can't hurt you now unless you let it… And, as you've already told me, you were lucky—you're a survivor.'

'Yes…' Her voice was stronger when she encountered shimmering dark-as-night eyes that seemed full of all the strength and calm she herself so often lacked. 'Yes, you're right. You have to be wondering how I escaped being raped. The police forced their way in to arrest one of the gang and I was rescued. But now you know why I suffer the panic attacks and why I eventually had the nervous breakdown at university—because I hadn't really dealt with what had happened to me. That was when I went for therapy and it helped enormously.'

Raj lifted her fingers to his mouth and kissed them. His hands were unsteady. All his emotions were swimming dangerously close to the surface and he was fighting to suppress them with every breath in his body. Hers was a distressing story and he now more than understood her fear of men, but there was no need for the rage inside him at those who had been ready to prey on a child for a few moments of vicious entertainment. She had been saved and they had been punished by the law. Only it wasn't enough, he thought fiercely, nowhere nearly enough punishment for the damage that had been inflicted on Zoe. In Maraban, the punishment would have been the death penalty.

As they travelled back to the palace, their honeymoon, as such, at an end, Zoe could see that telling Raj what had happened to her had made him settle back in behind his former reserve. Her small face tightened and her hands gripped together hard. She was questioning why she had shared all her secrets with him and anxious about why she was allowing herself to feel so close to him. Wasn't she acting foolishly? Wasn't it unwise in the circumstances to let every barrier between them drop?

'A surprise awaits you on your return to the palace,' Raj announced, trying to sound upbeat about what he was about to reveal, but failing miserably because he was no idiot and Vivi's cold reaction to him at the wedding had told him all he needed to know about how *he* was viewed by Zoe's family.

'A surprise?' Zoe queried.

He would have to hope that his own surprise went unnoticed while her sister was present. Dark blood highlighted Raj's exotic cheekbones as he thought about the fainting couch he had succumbed to buying and he had to wonder how he had drifted so far from his original intentions. Logic, good judgement and self-control had gone out of the proverbial window the minute he'd laid eyes on Zoe. It was that simple, that *basic*, he acknowledged grimly.

'Raffaele, Vivi's husband, is apparently attending a business meeting in Tasit and your sister accompanied him to visit you.'

To his surprise, Zoe's mouth down-curved and her chin came up, scarcely the display of uninhibited delight he had expected to see in receipt of such news. After all, she was in daily contact with her siblings, revealing a very close bond with them.

* * *

Zoe's rarely stirred temper was humming at the prospect of seeing Vivi. Vivi was only coming to visit to check up on her.

'This is a lovely surprise,' Zoe said, smiling and lying through her teeth as she hugged her older sister, wondering when her redheaded sibling would finally accept that she was a grown woman but, by nature, Vivi, a forceful personality, was very protective of those she considered weaker. It stung Zoe's pride to see herself as weak and breakable in Vivi's eyes.

'I wanted to see how you were managing.'

'My phone calls should've reassured you on that score,' Zoe pointed out as a maid brought in coffee and tiny cakes.

Vivi winced. 'Well, to be frank, they had the opposite effect because you sound so gosh-darned happy all the time.'

'My goodness, when did being happy become a sign that there was something to worry about?'

'It's a sign because I've never really heard you this happy before,' Vivi admitted ruefully. 'You can smile and laugh and seem happy on the surface but it's usually very brief and *now*, all of a sudden, when nobody's expecting it...'

'Have you noticed all the changes I've made around here?' Zoe interrupted abruptly, setting down her cup and springing up to indicate all the additional furniture in the room. 'The staff took photos of the unused rooms and sent them while we were away and I made selections. It's a big improvement, don't you think?'

'If medieval makes you hot to trot,' Vivi remarked with a sniff, strolling across the room to flick a heavily carved piece that in her opinion would have looked fabulous in a horror movie of some creepy old house.

'Let me show you around,' Zoe urged, willing to do anything to evade Vivi's curiosity, because in truth she *was* happy and she didn't really want to think too deeply about why.

Vivi glanced into the bedroom, her attention locking straight onto the male and female apparel currently being unpacked by staff. 'So, what happened to the—?'

In haste, Zoe thrust open the bathroom door, although she hadn't yet added anything to its décor, and then froze at the sight of the very opulent tasselled purple fainting couch in the centre.

'Oh, I like *that*…it's sort of sexy and decadent!' Vivi carolled, walking over to smooth a hand across the rich buttoned upholstery and flick a braided gold tassel.

Zoe was recalling her conversation with Raj and her face was burning hot as hellfire even while a little flicker of heat at her core flamed at the gesture… the *challenge*. Would she or wouldn't she? He would be wondering all day about that, she knew he would be, and a dreamy smile at the knowledge of that erotic prospect removed the tension that Vivi's arrival and awkward questions had induced.

'You know, I don't even need to ask you any more.' Vivi sighed as she returned to her coffee. 'Obviously, the separate bedroom deal crashed very quickly and you're sleeping with him. Whose idea was that? I hardly think it was yours! If you get too involved with Raj, Zoe…there will be consequences, because what you have together isn't supposed to last…and where will you be when the marriage ends?'

'It doesn't matter whose idea it was,' Zoe argued quietly. 'All that matters is that there isn't a problem of any kind with Raj and I, and our present arrangements are our private business.'

Vivi groaned out loud. 'You're besotted with him. It's written all over you,' she condemned, her concern palpable. 'That smooth bastard took advantage of you just as I feared he would!'

'Vivi!' Zoe blistered across the room in a furious voice her sister had never heard from her before. 'You do *not* talk about Raj like that!'

'I'm not saying anything I wouldn't say to his face!' Vivi shot back at her defensively. 'I'm trying to protect you but it looks like I got here a little too late for that. Damn Grandad, this is all his fault, his wretched snobbery pushing you into this marriage, and now you're going to get *hurt*.'

Zoe drew herself up to her full unimpressive height. 'There is no reason why I should get hurt.'

'I know what I saw in your face…you're in love with this guy, who only married you to please his father and use our fancy-schmancy grandmother's ancestry to enhance his standing.'

'I'm *not* in love with him,' Zoe argued fiercely. 'It sounds slutty but we're just having sex for the sake of it!'

Vivi unleashed a pained and unimpressed sigh. 'And what would you know about a relationship like that?'

Zoe lifted her head high. 'I'm learning as I go along, just like every other woman has to. I need that freedom, even if I make mistakes… It's part of growing up,' she reasoned.

'You're definitely growing up,' Vivi conceded ruefully. 'I never thought there would come a day when *you* would fight with *me*.'

'Even Winnie fights with you!' Zoe laughed and gave her much taller sister a hug, relieved the unnervingly intimate dispute was over.

After Vivi had been picked up an hour later, Zoe walked thoughtfully back to her suite with Raj. *Not. In. Love. With. Him.* She was simply happy and there was nothing wrong with being happy, was there? Zoe hadn't enjoyed much happiness in her life and she was determined to make the most of every moment.

She studied the fainting couch set out like a statement, an invitation, and she smiled before she wandered down the steps to the private courtyard around which their rooms ranged, which allowed them complete privacy.

And all around her she could see the proof of Raj's desire to please her and make her happy, for the once dark courtyard had been replanted during their absence into a spectacular jungle of greenery amongst which exotic flowers bloomed. Even the fountain she had admired, which had long since fallen out of use, was now working again, clean water sparkling down into the brightly tiled basin below. He hadn't mentioned a word about his intentions, but then he never did. He never looked for thanks either. Gifts simply appeared without fanfare, gifts like the wonderful transformation of an outdated, neglected courtyard garden.

She didn't need him to love her as he had loved

Nabila, she only needed the proof that he *cared*, Zoe reflected fiercely. And care he did with amazing efficiency and resolve. How could she expect any more than that in a pretend marriage? After all, he was already giving her much more than she had expected to receive. It wasn't going to last, she knew that, *accepted* that and that was her choice, her choice to live for today and worry about tomorrow only when it arrived...

CHAPTER NINE

ZOE SAT UP in bed and her head swam and her tummy rolled.

Worry gripped her. She had believed she had caught a virus when the symptoms first started but weeks had passed since then and the unwell feeling was lingering, despite the careful diet she had observed. Raj had wanted to get the palace doctor in but she had stalled him once a greater concern began to nag at her nerves.

Zoe grimaced at her pallid reflection in the bathroom mirror. She had lost weight and her eyes looked too big for her face. As soon as the dizziness had evaporated, she went for a shower, striving not to agonise *again* over the reality that she had not had a period since she'd arrived in Maraban. After all, she couldn't possibly be pregnant even if the light head, the nausea and her tender breasts reminded her of what her sisters had experienced during pregnancy. How could she be pregnant when Raj had not once run the risk of getting her pregnant? But, she did recall once, weeks ago in the shower when he had overlooked the necessity and she had meant to mention it but hadn't been worried enough to do so.Now she wished she had pointed out that oversight.

Of course no method of birth control was infallible, another little voice nagged at the back of her head. And how on earth was she to put her worries to rest when the acquisition of a pregnancy test in secret had so far proved beyond her capabilities. She never got the opportunity to leave the palace alone. She was surrounded by security and all too many helpful people when she went out. Let's face it, Zoe, she thought forlornly, the Crown Princess of Maraban cannot be seen buying a pregnancy test without causing a furore. It was ironic that what would have thrilled the population filled Zoe with sick apprehension because she couldn't forget Raj saying that such a development would be a disaster in their situation.

Of course, it would be when it was only a pretend marriage and if she had a boy, he would be next in line to the throne. If she was pregnant and it was a boy, she would have to live in Maraban for at least the next twenty years as Raj's ex-wife and she certainly didn't fancy that option as a future. She would have to sit on the outskirts of his life, watching him marry another woman and have a family with her. Naturally, Raj would move on after their marriage ended but she certainly didn't want to sit around nearby to actually *watch* him doing it.

When she emerged from her bedroom, dressed in a pastel-blue dress with her hair in a braid and her make-up immaculate, Bahar, her PA—or social secretary, as Zoe preferred to think of the young attractive brunette—awaited her with a list of her appointments. It pleased her tremendously that after three months away from home she had now acquired the confidence to handle visiting schools and such places without having to drag Raj everywhere with her for support. Coming to Maraban and marrying Raj had been the best decision she had ever made when it came to getting stronger and moving forward with her life.

As her breakfast was brought to the table, Zoe's stomach lurched even as she looked at it and she pushed the plate away and settled for a cup of tea. After all, she couldn't afford to eat if she was going out to an official engagement where her succumbing to a bout of sickness in public would be a serious embarrassment, she reflected with an inner shudder at the prospect. She would catch a snack later, by which time hopefully the nausea would have subsided.

Walking down the last flight of stairs, she was wondering whether or not to call in on Raj in his office when she broke out in a cold sweat. Her legs wobbled under her and she snatched at the stone balustrade to stay upright but the sick dizziness engulfing her was unstoppable and as she lurched to one side, dimly conscious that someone was seizing hold of her from behind, she passed out.

When Zoe came around slowly, she winced at the sensation of a needle in her arm and gripped the hand that was holding hers in dismay. Her eyes fluttered open as Raj leant down to her saying, 'Don't try to get up in case you faint again. Dr Fadel decided a blood test would be a good idea…sorry about that.'

The very quietness of his voice made her scan the room behind him, which seemed to be filled to the brim with anxious-looking people. Mortification made her close her eyes again and do as she was told because she had a clear recollection of almost tumbling down that last flight of stairs.

'I'll be late for my appointment,' she protested.

'You will not be leaving the palace today.'

'But...'

'Not until the doctor has diagnosed what is wrong with you,' Raj spelt out more harshly, in a tone she wasn't accustomed to hearing from him.

In shock at that attitude, she glanced up at him, but he had already moved away to speak to the older man closing a doctor's bag on the desk. She registered that she was in Raj's office on the sofa he had slept on when they were first married, and very slowly and carefully she began to inch up into a sitting position.

Raj stalked back to her. 'Stay flat and lie still,' he told her wrathfully.

He was furious with her, Zoe realised in consternation, wondering why. Possibly the uproar her faint had caused, she reflected unhappily, because the room was still crammed with staff all trying to speak to Raj at once in his own language, so she could only follow one word in three that she was hearing and those were the simple ones. Her ambition to learn Arabic was advancing only slowly. Finally, the room cleared and they were alone again.

'May I sit up now or are you going to get angry again?' Zoe murmured.

Raj gazed across the office at her and then moved forward before hovering several feet from her as though an invisible wall had suddenly come down between them. 'I apologise. I was not angry with you, I was angry with myself for neglecting your health,' he admitted tautly. 'I knew you were unwell but I listened to you when you refused to let me call the doctor in. I *shouldn't* have listened!'

'Raj, that was *my* fault, this stupid virus, and I'm not awfully fond of medics.'

'You will want to express thanks to your bodyguard, Carim. He saved your life when he prevented you from falling down the stairs. At the very least you would have been badly hurt with broken limbs,' Raj framed jaggedly, his hands clenching into fists by his side. 'But such a fall could definitely also have killed you and nothing is worth that risk.'

'Of course, it isn't,' Zoe agreed soothingly because she was shaken as well by the accident that she had so narrowly escaped. 'OK, you were right and I was wrong.'

'I swore to look after you and I have failed in my duty,' Raj informed her hoarsely.

Zoe paled. 'It's not your duty, Raj. I'm a fully grown adult and I made an unwise decision when I chose not to consult a doctor. Please don't blame yourself for my mistake.'

'How can I do anything else?' Raj shot back to her with seeming incredulity. 'You are my wife and you are in a country foreign to you. Who else should stand responsible for your well-being?'

I'm not your *real* wife. The declaration sprang to her lips but she didn't voice it, belatedly recognising that whether Raj viewed her as his real wife or otherwise he would still feel that it was his duty to ensure

her well-being. Three months ago she would happily
have flung that declaration of independence at him but
now she knew him a little better, knew the crushing
weight of responsibility he took on without complaint.
As his father, the King, suffered increasing ill health
and days he was unable to leave his quarters, more of
his obligations were falling on Raj's shoulders. Unsurprisingly, Raj didn't have an irresponsible bone in his
lean, beautiful body and he was infuriatingly good at
blaming himself for any mishap or oversight.

'I'm sorry if I seemed to speak rudely and angrily,'
Raj breathed tautly, silvered dark eyes locked to her
lovely face. 'But I was very concerned.'

'I understand that and I'm fine. In fact I think I'm
recovered enough now to make that appointment.'

'No, they will have to settle for me doing it in your
place,' Raj sliced in forcefully. 'You're not going out
anywhere until we have heard from the doctor—'

'Raj, for goodness' sake, I'm fine,' she told him
again, swinging her feet down onto the floor to punc-
tuate the statement.

'We'll see,' Raj asserted with tact as he reached for
her hand to help her upright, tugging her close to him,
his stunning dark deep-set eyes below his straight black
brows roaming over her delicate face. 'But we will not
see today…however, I am free this evening, and if you
were to feel strong enough to welcome me home on that
couch, I would be extraordinarily pleased.'

Zoe gurgled with laughter and stretched up on tiptoe
to taste his wide sensual mouth with her own. And that
was that, he was magically distracted from his over-
whelming anxiety about her welfare. Her heart ham-

mered and her fingers closed into his shirtfront because she wanted to rip it off him. Against her, she could feel him hard and ready and hunger coursed through her, turning her wanton with need.

With an enormous effort, Raj set her back from him. 'We *can't*. People are waiting for my arrival,' he reminded her raggedly. 'But it is one of those occasions when I wish I had the freedom to tell everyone but you to go to hell!'

Zoe flushed, censuring herself for tempting him merely to distract him because it had been a selfish move and he was never selfish, which made her feel bad. On the other hand, the couch invitation was welcome, she acknowledged with a tiny shiver of anticipation, wondering what had happened to the genuinely shy young woman she had been mere months earlier. She wasn't shy with Raj. In fact, she was doing stuff with Raj she had never dreamt she would ever do with any man, once alien things like purchasing very fancy lingerie and posing in it, revelling in the rush of powerful femininity his fierce desire for her and his equally audacious appreciation gave her every time. She had discovered a whole new self to explore and secretly it thrilled her.

Outside the office door, she thanked the guard who had saved her from falling and he grinned at her, telling her in broken English that he would have died sooner than let anything happen to her on his watch. His undeniable sincerity shook her and she climbed the stairs, thinking that until now she hadn't quite grasped how the people around her and those she met during engagements viewed her as Raj's wife, certainly hadn't taken that level of care and concern as seriously as they did. It struck her that many of those same people would be disappointed when she and Raj split up. But then there was nothing she could do about that, was there? She was a sham wife but *they* didn't know that, didn't know that she was nothing more than a glossy convenient lie foisted on the public, she ruminated unhappily.

She was having lunch when the middle-aged doctor she had glimpsed in Raj's office called to see her. Dr Fadel was King Tahir's doctor and resident in the palace and, fortunately for her, he had qualified in London and spoke excellent English.

After the usual polite pleasantries, he asked if he could dismiss the hovering staff and she nodded acquiescence with a slight frown, her tension rising. Of course, he was about to tell her that her hormones were all out of kilter, which was the most likely diagnosis, and she didn't want to discuss her absent menstrual cycle with an audience either.

'I am blessed to be the doctor to break such momentous news,' he then informed her with a beaming smile. 'You have conceived, Your Royal Highness...'

'Conceived...?' Zoe repeated as if she had never heard the word before, and she tottered back down into the seat she had vacated to greet him, so great was the shock of that announcement. That her deepest fear had been confirmed rocked her world to its foundations.

'The blood test was positive. Of course, it is impossible for me to tell you anything more without a further examination.' He looked at her enquiringly. 'Would that be in order? Or would you prefer another doctor, perhaps a specialist, to give you further information? I'm not inexperienced. I do have many female patients in the royal household.'

Zoe was in a daze. She pushed her hands down on the table to rise again. *Pregnant?* she was screaming inside her head, still wondering if it could be a mistake and willing to subject herself to any check-up that could possibly reveal his diagnosis *was* a mistake, she reasoned fearfully as she followed him from the room and he lamented the lack of lifts in the palace. A lift would have to be installed immediately, the doctor began telling her, particularly when her near accident earlier was taken into consideration. A pregnant woman couldn't be expected to run up and down flights and flights of stairs, particularly not a woman carrying a child he described as 'so precious a child for Maraban'.

It wouldn't be precious to Raj, Zoe thought miserably, not to a man who had frankly referred to such an unlikely event as a *disaster*. Suddenly she was in total conflict with herself and split into two opposing halves. On the one hand she adored children and she very much wanted her baby if she did prove to be pregnant, but on the other, she was sort of guiltily hoping that the doctor's verdict was wrong because of the way Raj would feel about it and that felt even more wrong.

A glimpse of the trim and determined little nurse who had jabbed her with a syringe the night she was kidnapped was not a vote winner in the troubled mood she was in, but Zoe refused to react, deeming her potential pregnancy more important as she lay down on an examination couch and an ultrasound machine was wheeled in. An instant later she heard the whirring sound of her baby's fast heartbeat and she paled, feeling foolish for thinking that the doctor could have been in error. It was an even greater surprise to discover that she was already three months along and almost into the second trimester, which meant that she had conceived very early in their marriage.

The doctor happily dispensed vitamin tablets and congratulated her on her fertility, studying her literally as if she were a walking miracle. She supposed in comparison to the last generation of the royal family, she did strike him that way because it had taken over thirty years and three wives to produce Raj.

'The King will be overjoyed,' he told her cheerfully.

'Oh, but...' Zoe hesitated, questioning if it was even possible to keep a lid on such a revelation within the palace.

'The King needs this good news, with his health as precarious as it has been,' his doctor assured her with gravity.

'Then my husband can tell him after I have *first* told *him*,' Zoe countered firmly.

But on one level she thought she was probably wasting her breath because the cat was out of the bag and there was nothing she could do about that: the doctor, the nurse and whoever had done the blood test already knew of her condition. Just how fast the news had spread was borne out only minutes later when she returned to her room and was ushered into the bedroom where tea, a ginger biscuit and the book she had been reading awaited her by the bed like a heartfelt invitation to rest as pregnant women were so often advised to do. Smothering a groan, she lay down, ironically worn out by the day she had had. Off came her shoes and then her dress and she lay back, confronted by the daunting evening lying ahead of her because she had no choice other than to tell Raj immediately. Would it sound better if she did the couch thing first? Or would that look manipulative?

In the event, she didn't get to make that decision because she slept through most of the afternoon, only wakening when the sound of a door closing jolted her awake. She opened her eyes on Raj striding towards the bed and the slumberous expression in his shimmering dark scrutiny as he looked at her lying there in her flimsy underwear. He sank down on the edge of the bed. 'How are you feeling now?'

'OK—hungry now that the sickness has taken a break. Dr Fadel said that with a little luck that should start fading soon,' she told him tightly. 'You see, I'm *not* ill as such. I'm pregnant…'

As she hesitated, her nerves getting the better of her for a moment, she studied Raj; his lean, darkly handsome features had locked tight, his jaw line clenching hard.

'I think it must've been that time in the shower just after the wedding. You forgot to use anything. I should've said something then but I really didn't think anything would come of it,' she acknowledged uncomfortably, wishing he would say something.

Raj blinked because for an instant his surroundings had vanished; what she had told him had to be the very last development he had expected, but it also led to a revelation that hit him even harder. He turned pale, in the matter of a moment recognising the situation he was in.

'We've barely got out of bed to eat for three months,'
Raj breathed in a rueful undertone. 'What can I say? I
was in charge of contraception and I forgot. So, we are
going to become parents…forgive me, I am stunned by
the concept of something so surprising.'

'You said it would be a disaster if I became pregnant,'
Zoe reminded him uncertainly, still unable to read his
mood, particularly when he sprang upright again and
started pacing across the floor, clearly too restless to
stay seated.

'A disaster more from your point of view than from
mine,' Raj qualified with level clarity. 'We agreed to
part but I cannot agree to let you leave me carrying our
child and I do not want our child raised without either
one of us. Surely we are doing well enough together for
you to stay in our marriage for some time to come?'
A straight ebony brow lifted enquiringly, intense dark
eyes scanning her triangular face for an answer. 'Could
you accept that? If we remain married, we can raise our
child together.'

A quivery little breath ran up through Zoe, allowing her lungs to function again. The backs of her eyes
prickled and stung. Until Raj had asked her to *stay* married to him, she had not realised how horribly tense she
had become and the painful tension slowly ebbed out
of her stiff muscles.

'So, we just go on as normal?' Zoe checked.

'Why not? Are we not both content as we are?' Raj
prompted tautly.

Zoe nodded but couldn't help wishing he could be
a little more emotional about staying married to her.
There she went again, wanting what she couldn't have,

she scolded herself, because she knew herself better now. She could look back and recognise the raging jealousy that had assailed her after seeing those photos of Raj with Nabila that had so clearly depicted his love for the beautiful brunette. There was nothing she could do about such feelings except keep them under control and hidden. And considering the circumstances in which they had married, each for their own very practical reasons, it was illogical and pathetic to long for Raj to fall in love with her as well.

'You said…"stay in our marriage for *some time to come*",' Zoe recited tightly. 'What sort of time frame were you considering?'

At that question for further clarification, Raj stiffened and raked long brown fingers through his tousled black curls. 'Must we be so precise?'

Zoe swallowed hard at the edge of reproof in his tone. 'Well, it would be easier for me to know how *you* see the future.'

'With you and our child together. I would impose no limits. I would like to throw away *all* the boundaries we agreed and make this a normal marriage,' Raj spelt out without hesitation. 'I still can't believe that you're pregnant.'

'Neither can I,' Zoe revealed, scrambling off the bed only to be immediately caught up into his strong arms.

'I didn't think it could happen that easily…it is a brilliant accident,' Raj murmured with husky conviction as he came down on the bed with her. 'Are we still allowed to share this bed?'

'Of course, we are. I've been fully checked out.' A kind of sick relief combined with dizzy happiness was filtering through Zoe as she dimly acknowledged that he was giving her what she most wanted. She wasn't going to have to give him up like the salted caramel ice cream she had recently become addicted to, she was going to get to *keep* him. Of course, it wasn't perfect, she conceded reluctantly, not when he only wanted her to stay married to him because she was pregnant. Even so, being accepted as a normal wife was a huge upgrade on being labelled a friend with benefits.

'What are you thinking about?' Raj chided, lying back on the bed with his gorgeous dark eyes fiercely welded to her reflective face.

'Nothing remotely important,' she told him, and she meant it when she said it even if she dimly understood even then that sooner or later she would once again fall into the trap of craving more than he had to give her.

He toyed with her mouth, soft and gentle, and then nipped wickedly at her bottom lip with the edge of his teeth. Her hands lifted and her fingers speared into his black curls, liquid heat pooling in her pelvis as he deliberately snaked his lean hips into the junction of her thighs, the thrust of his arousal unmistakeable. He was always so hot for her. It was enough, it was more than enough to be desired, cared for, appreciated. Even if she felt as though she was keeping him by default? She crushed the thought, burying it deep. She already had more with him than she had ever thought she would have, so craving anything else would be greedy.

'I want you so much,' Raj confided rawly, sitting up over her to wrench off his shirt, yank roughly at his tie. 'Knowing my baby is inside you is so sexy...'

Zoe blinked. It *was*? He was lifting her to deftly undo

her bra, groaning with satisfaction when her small pouting breasts came free to hungrily claim an engorged nipple with his mouth. A gasp was wrenched from her as he teased the other with his fingers. 'You're more sensitive there than ever,' he husked. 'I love your body.'

She knew he did: he never left it alone. He couldn't walk past her without touching her in some way and if they were alone, it almost always concluded in their bed, although they had succumbed to christening his office sofa a time or two and they had once had sex in a limousine on a long drive. He had an astonishingly strong sexual appetite. Anyone watching him could have been forgiven for thinking he hadn't had the freedom to enjoy her for a couple of days at least but that was not the case.

He tugged off her panties and yanked down the zip in his trousers, shedding his clothing with an impatience that never failed to add to her excitement. There he was, all sleek and golden and beautiful, and he was finally hers to keep like a precious possession she had been fighting for without even appreciating what she was doing or even what was happening inside her own head. She had wanted love but then what woman didn't? If *he* could settle for less, she could settle, she reasoned as he snaked down her body with darting little kisses and caresses that set her on fire, ultimately settling between her spread thighs to pleasure her in the way he enjoyed the most.

As a rippling spasm of pleasure gathered low in her body, she clutched at his hair, writhed, squirmed, begged until at last she climaxed in an explosive surge that certainly didn't feel in any way as though she were settling for less. Raj shifted over her then, hungrily kissing her, and the excitement began to rocket again as he sank into her with delicious force, pushing her legs back to deepen his penetration. Definitely not less, she told herself as she rose breathlessly to meet his every thrust, every move instinctive and raw with the excitement she could barely contain. There was more and then even more of that insanely thrilling pleasure before he sent her flying into a wild breathless climax that shattered her senses and her control, leaving her slumped in a wreck of heavy, satiated limbs in the aftermath.

She hadn't heard a phone ring, had been too far gone, but she surfaced when she realised that Raj wasn't holding her close as he usually did. She turned over, saw him talking urgently on his phone while he strode about, naked and bronzed and muscular, and she propped her chin on the heel of her hand, enjoying watching him. That enjoyment gradually faded when he went on to make several other quick calls in succession, alerting her to the knowledge that something must have happened, and because his expression changed from smiling to grim she couldn't tell whether what had happened was a good or bad thing.

'I'm afraid I'm going to have to leave you for the night,' Raj told her with a frown. 'The construction workers have stumbled on archaeological remains at the Josias site.'

'The hospital project in the capital of Maraban?'

'It's potentially a very exciting discovery but it means that the site has to close until we can get an official inspection done tomorrow, and that throws the whole project and the work crews into limbo. I'm flying out there now to meet with the managers and look at contingency plans. It is possible that we won't be able to build there at all,' he concluded gravely. 'And the hospital is very much needed in that area.'

Recalling that Nabila was the CEO of the construction firm involved, Zoe sat up, her pale hair falling round her flushed face, because she knew he was undoubtedly about to meet the other woman again for the first time in eight years and she very much wanted to be in the vicinity. 'I could come with you!' she said in sudden interruption.

'No, not this time. What would be the point? I'm likely to be in meetings most of the night and certainly all of tomorrow, sorting this out,' he told her dismissively as he strode into the bathroom.

'I would still like to have gone,' Zoe confided in a small voice to an empty room.

But did she really need to cling to him like glue? she reproved herself. There were few things more distasteful to a man than a clingy, needy and jealous woman and Raj would quickly get tired of her if she started acting paranoid and suspicious purely because he was mixing with his ex-girlfriend in a business environment. She had to grow up, she told herself urgently, not react to her stabbing insecurity with adolescent immaturity. After all, nothing was likely to change in the short term. She was pregnant and *really* married now.

And how did Raj truly feel about that development? It shocked Zoe to accept that she had not the smallest idea of how *he* felt, and the instant she registered that worrying truth, another little brick of security tumbled down from her inner wall of defences. Sadly, there was no ignoring the truth that the closest Raj had actually come to expressing his personal feelings was the assurance that he regarded her being pregnant with his child as…sexy. Although he had labelled her conception a brilliant accident, which did suggest he was pleased.

Zoe grimaced. Why couldn't he simply have said so, openly? In reality, now that she was recalling that conversation, she realised that Raj had not expressed a single emotion, which for an emotionally intense man of his ilk was not reassuring, she reflected worriedly.

Were duty and a sense of responsibility for his child all that had driven Raj's request that she stay married to him?

And if that *was* the case, what could she possibly do about it?

CHAPTER TEN

RAJ'S PHONE RANG constantly right up until he left the palace. He was feeling guilty because Zoe had been very quiet when he left. But there was no way he would have considered dragging her across country late at night, especially now that she was pregnant and he had no idea where he would be staying. Zoe looked frail for all her lack of complaint. She had lost her appetite, dropped in weight. Yet even though he had noticed he had said and done nothing because it had not even occurred to him that she could be pregnant. What kind of husband was he? Not a very good one, he decided grimly.

And now he was to become a father. A dazzling smile flashed across his lean dark features. That was a marvellous development, a near miracle in their circumstances.

His phone rang again as he awaited his limo in the forecourt of the palace and he dug it out, only to freeze in surprise as the caller identified himself for, although he had met the man, his royal status ensured that he wasn't especially friendly with anyone in that profession, and the warning the journalist gave Raj astonished him. He immediately called Omar and passed it on to him and Omar announced that he would be travelling to the hospital site as well.

In the early hours of the following morning, having dealt with a torch-lit visit to the site and with wildly excited archaeologists, who were hopeful that the legendary lost city built by Alexander the Great had been discovered on Marabanian soil, Raj was more than ready for his bed. He walked into the comparatively small hotel closest to the site. He was relieved that he hadn't succumbed to the temptation of bringing Zoe because he did not think the level of comfort on offer sufficient for a pregnant woman. As his father had remarked in wonderment when he had phoned him earlier to break their news, Zoe would have to be treated from now on like the Queen she would one day be.

Raj was smiling at the memory and sharing it with his cousin, Omar, who was beside him as he pushed open the door of his room. And then quite forcibly the warning he had received, and begun to discount because he had yet to even *see* Nabila, was revived because Nabila sat up in the bed that should've been his, the sheet tumbling to reveal her bare breasts. Filled with angry distaste at her brazen display, Raj averted his eyes, unimpressed by the expression of seemingly embarrassed innocence she had put on when she glimpsed Omar by his side.

'For goodness' sake, tell Omar to *leave*,' Nabila urged Raj.

'I'm staying,' Omar delivered with satisfaction, never having liked the brunette even when Raj had been in love with her. 'But it is gratifying to discover that you can sink even lower than I expected.'

Raj strode to the foot of the bed. 'What the hell are you playing at?' he demanded.

Deciding to ignore Omar, Nabila focused her eyes on Raj with blatant hunger. 'I want you and I really don't care what I have to do to get you this time around. Isn't that enough?' She treated him to a look of languorous enticement. 'Don't tell me you're not still curious about what it would be like between us.'

Raj's mouth curled with disgust and he swung round to stalk back to the door and address his protection team in the corridor. 'Get her out of here…and find me another room,' he ordered impatiently.

'I'm not asking for marriage this time around,' Nabila crooned behind him. 'I would be your mistress…your every secret fantasy.'

'My *wife* is my every secret fantasy,' Raj countered drily as he strode out.

At dawn, Raj was enjoying a working breakfast on the terrace at his hotel with Omar and the management team of Major Holdings, including the CEO, Nabila, who had contrived to take a seat opposite him. He ignored her to the best of his ability, barely even turning his head when she spoke.

'*Raj!*' she exclaimed, startling him while simultaneously reaching for his hand.

For a split second, he was so disconcerted by that unanticipated over-familiarity and the pleading expression she wore on her face that he did nothing and then he freed his fingers with a sudden jerk and leant back in his chair, cursing himself for not having reacted more immediately to the threat. For Nabila *was* a threat, he acknowledged in a sudden black fury, a threat to his marriage. At that moment, he had not the slightest doubt that a photographer was hiding somewhere in the vicinity, most probably one with a telephoto lens, and had captured that image of them holding hands and that that stolen photo was intended for publication with the presence of their companions eradicated.

A couple of hours later, because she was sleeping in, Zoe turned over in bed, drowsily wondering what had wakened her and failing to notice that her mobile phone was flashing on the cabinet to one side of her. She stole her hand across to the other side of the bed and then remembered that Raj was gone for the night. With a dissatisfied sigh, she dragged her fingers back from that emptiness and reminded herself that it was mortifyingly clingy to want him there *every* night. She could be perfectly happy without him, of course she could be! With no suspicion of just how soon that assumption was to be tested, Zoe went back to sleep.

Zoe wakened in astonishment to find her sisters beside her bed and blinked in disbelief. 'What are you two doing here at this hour of the day?' she demanded.

'We were shopping in Dubai so we didn't have far to come,' Winnie explained stiffly. 'We want you to come home with us. Grandad agrees.'

Zoe sat up. 'Why on earth would you want me to come home with you?'

'*Because*,' Vivi said bluntly, 'Raj is playing away behind your back and you're in love with the rat!'

Zoe frowned. 'No. Raj wouldn't do that to me,' she

said with perfect assurance because, in that line, she trusted him absolutely.

Winnie shoved a mobile phone in front of her gaze. Her lashes fluttered in bewilderment and then she focused and saw Raj with the *one* woman in the world she wouldn't trust him with. Raj in a photo holding hands with Nabila, his lean, darkly handsome features very serious, her face beseeching. Beseeching *what* from him? Zoe broke out in a sudden sweat and then just as quickly, as familiar queasiness assailed her, was forced to leap out of bed and push past her sisters to make it to the bathroom in time to be sick.

'Where did you see that photo? Raj only left last night,' she reasoned when she was able to respond, wondering exactly *when* that photo had been taken and then questioning whether the timing even mattered.

'That photo was offered to Grandad for sale first thing this morning,' Winnie told her in disgust. 'I imagine it was taken by some greedy paparazzo, who worked out what that picture would be worth on the open market.'

As Zoe drooped over the vanity unit brushing her teeth, still weak with nausea and dizziness, Vivi tugged her gently away and settled her down on the fainting couch. 'Take a deep breath and keep your head down. What's the matter with you? Are you ill?'

'Pregnant,' Zoe whispered, still in shock at that photo, fighting to withstand the great tide of pain threatening to engulf her. Raj had refused to take her with him the night before...*no wonder*! Had he known even then that he wanted the freedom to be with his ex-girlfriend?

'Pregnant?' Vivi gasped and her sisters engaged in a lively argument above her head, which Zoe was content to ignore because infinitely more important decisions loomed ahead of her, she grasped dully.

How could she remain married to a man in love with another woman and already seeing her behind her back? Holding hands with her? Although that was the least that had probably gone on between them, she recognised sickly, for it was unlikely that Raj and Nabila would not finally have taken the opportunity to have sex. Particularly not when, in that photo, they were staring at each other like long-lost lovers reunited.

'I'll be frank,' Vivi murmured with surprising quietness. 'You're in love with Raj and he's hurting you and we love you enough that we can't just stand back and allow that.'

'I'm *not* in love with him,' Zoe lied, her eyes watering in a last-ditch effort to save face with her sisters.

But there it was: the truth she had suppressed and refused to face except in the secret depths of her heart. She had fallen madly in love with her fake husband and for all the wrong reasons. Reasons like his smile and the sound of his voice and the raw power of his body over hers in bed. Reasons like the English breakfast tea he had ordered on her behalf and the glorious shoes he'd bought her and had put in the dressing room without even mentioning the purchases. Reasons that encompassed a hundred and one different things and many that she would have found hard to put into words.

Winnie's eyes were also brimming with tears. 'Come back with us to Athens…*please*!'

And Zoe's first reaction was to say no, until she considered the alternatives. She could confront Raj and he would probably admit the truth, which would not be a comfort to her. She could pretend she hadn't seen the photograph and silently agonise over it and that prospect had even less appeal. Or she could take advantage of a breathing space in which to decide what she would do next, she reasoned bravely. It wouldn't be running away, she ruminated, it would be giving herself the time to control her emotional reaction and behave like an adult and deal with the situation. If she stayed, she might cry and let him see that she had been hurt, and what was the point of that?

But what if Raj had not actually cheated on her? Raj was not by nature a cheat, she reasoned, wondering if she was clutching at straws when she thought along such lines. Naturally she didn't want to think he could've been unfaithful, but Nabila was different, Nabila was in a class of her own because once Raj had *loved* her. Could he have resisted the chance to finally be with the woman he had once loved? And wasn't hoping he might have resisted only proof that Zoe was weakly willing to make excuses for him? Shame drenched her pale cheeks with hot pink and she decided to listen to her sisters, who had much more experience than she did with men. If Winnie and Vivi both believed that Raj had succumbed to Nabila's wiles, they were probably right. She trusted their judgement more than she trusted her own because she was all too well aware that her feelings for Raj coloured her every conviction and that she wasn't capable of standing back and making an independent call.

Zoe had her maid pack only one suitcase, because

there was no advantage in advertising the fact that she was leaving and would probably never return to the royal palace. She would send for the rest of her stuff later but when she thought about that, thought about the wardrobe Raj had bought her, thought about his favourite outfits, she as quickly decided that she wanted nothing that would only serve to keep unfortunate memories alive.

Her protection team accompanied her to the airport and flatly refused to leave her there. Suppressing a sigh, she let them board her grandfather's private jet with her, knowing that Raj would recall them later after he had read her note and had seen the photo she had sent to his phone. He wouldn't require any other explanation for her departure because he was definitely not stupid.

When that photo came up on his phone, forwarded by Zoe, Raj succumbed to a rage that almost burned him alive and it took Omar stepping in to prevent him from telling Nabila in front of an audience what he thought of her filthy tactics. Omar's intervention ensured that he did what he had to do at the site, which was his duty, and went home as soon as he possibly could to talk to his wife. A single-line note informing him that she would never 'share' a man greeted his return.

The discovery that she had been removed by her siblings and flown to her grandfather's home in Greece came as a complete shock. It was closely followed by a terse phone call from Stamboulas Fotakis, who accused him of disrespecting his grandchild in a grossly offensive public disregard of his marital status. And as if those punishments were not sufficient, he was summoned by his father, who in his ineffable highly efficient way knew exactly what was happening in his son's marriage and pointed out that his son only had himself to thank for allowing a harpy like Nabila within a hundred yards of him.

'When you bring your wife home again, I will have Nabila thrown out of the country,' the King pronounced with satisfaction.

'Let us hope I can bring Zoe home,' Raj breathed with difficulty, mastering his temper but only just in the face of that provocation, for throwing Nabila out of Maraban would only create a scandal that Nabila would relish.

His arrival in Greece late that night was punctuated by further unwelcome attacks. Zoe was in bed and not to be disturbed, according to Stam Fotakis. 'She's fragile,' he told Raj in condemnation. 'She needs protection from those who would use her soft heart against her.'

'I would not use…'

Her sister, Vivi, walked into her grandfather's office and proceeded to try and tear strips off Raj but Raj wasn't taking that from anyone, least of all Zoe's fiery sibling, and an almighty row broke out before Stam ran out of patience and demanded that both of them go to bed. 'If you must, you may speak to Zoe in the morning,' he informed Raj in a ringing tone of finality.

But Raj wasn't about to be steered in a direction he didn't want to go. He let himself be shown to a guest room without any intention of *waiting* until he could see *his* wife. As soon as he was alone, he learned where her room was by the simple measure of contacting her protection team.

Zoe was curled up on a lounger on the balcony beyond her room, watching the sea silver and darken in the moonlight. Misery felt like a shroud tightly wrapped round her, denying her the air she needed to breathe. She had still to accept the concept of a life empty of Raj. Every time she contemplated that terrifying prospect, she felt as though someone were flaying the skin from her bones, only the pain was internalised. How had one man become so important to her survival that her entire world had begun to revolve around him? It both shocked and incensed her that she could have been weak and foolish enough to fall in love with a man she had known from the outset would never be hers on any permanent basis.

When the patio doors behind her slid open, she flinched, expecting it to be one of her sisters, come yet again to offer depressing advice. She didn't want the assurance that she would get over Raj. She didn't want to be told that there would eventually be another man worthier of her love in her future when just then, and against all reason and logic, all her body and her brain cried out for *was* Raj.

'Zoe...?'

In astonished recognition of that dark deep accented intonation, Zoe was startled and she leapt off the lounger and spun round. *'Raj?'* she gasped incredulously.

'Hush...' Raj put a finger to his lips in warning. 'I wouldn't put it past your family to try and drag me out physically and I don't want a fight breaking out between my protection team and your grandfather's. But I will allow no man on earth to tell me *when* I can see my wife.'

'But I'm not your wife—not really your wife,' Zoe protested. 'And I *never* was.'

Raj studied the pale triangle of her face in the moonlight and guilt cut through him because it was *his* fault that she had been hurt and upset. 'I have to explain what happened with Nabila.'

'No, you don't owe me any explanations!' Zoe cut in hastily. 'But you can't expect me to live with you and turn a blind eye to an affair either!'

'Why would I have an affair with Nabila? Have you asked yourself that?' Raj demanded, moving forward to scoop her gently up into his arms and return her with care to the lounger before stepping back to lean back lithely against the balcony wall.

'Because you still love her...' Zoe muttered ruefully.

'Why would I still love a woman who slept with another man behind my back?' Raj asked gently. 'Do you honestly believe I am so stupid that I would still blindly love a woman who was unworthy of my love and respect?'

Zoe reddened and her eyes evaded his. 'I'm not saying you're stupid, just that sometimes people can't control their feelings even when they *know* they should,' she framed uncomfortably.

'But that is not the case with Nabila. My love died the instant I realised how poorly I had judged her character. She was my first love,' Raj admitted grittily. 'At the age of twenty I also believed she would be my last love but I was very young and I was wrong. I couldn't continue to love a woman who lied and cheated once I saw her for what she was. I couldn't love a woman who only wanted me because I am wealthy and one day I will be King.'

'Well, if that's all true what were you doing holding hands with her?' Zoe demanded baldly, influenced against her will by the obvious sincerity of his self-defence.

'Before I left the palace yesterday, I received a phone call from a journalist and it was most illuminating… yes, I *know* you are impatient for an explanation but please bear with me to enable me to tell you the whole story,' Raj urged when she made a frustrated gesture with one tiny expressive hand. 'I learned from that call that Nabila had personally contacted him and given him the photos that proved the existence of our youthful romance.'

'*She* was behind the release of those photos to the gossip magazine?' Zoe exclaimed in surprise.

'Yes. I assume she wanted that information publicised as a first move in her desire to come back into my life. Evidently she assumed there would still be a place for her in my heart.' Raj's wide sensual mouth compressed. 'The journalist involved called to warn me yesterday that she was planning to wreck my marriage and had a photographer lined up in readiness.'

'Journalists love scandal. Why would he have warned you?' Zoe pressed suspiciously.

'Zoe…' Raj murmured softly. 'The gossip magazine was quite happy to publish old photos of a romance few people knew about but the owner, the journalist I mentioned, is a loyal Marabanian and he refused to get involved in framing me with Nabila in a seedy scheme likely to damage my marriage. That was a step too far for him and, instead of playing along, he warned me of her ambition to cause trouble.'

'Well, it doesn't look like the warning did you much good,' Zoe said drily.

'It put me on my guard and I took Omar with me on the trip. When I went to my hotel room that night, she was waiting for me in the bed and I had her removed. We didn't have a conversation either because I have nothing to say to Nabila,' Raj told her doggedly.

'Nothing?' Again, Zoe looked unimpressed by his claim but she was already thinking of the stunning brunette waiting in his bed for him. 'Was she undressed?'

Raj nodded.

'And you weren't even tempted?' Zoe prompted helplessly.

'No, but I think my protection team were,' he remarked wryly. 'Omar can confirm that nothing happened. He was also present at the table when she grabbed my hand.'

'Grabbed?' Zoe queried with a frown. 'But how could Omar have been there when you were alone with her?'

'I wasn't alone with her. The photo is deceptive. Three of Nabila's colleagues were also at that table with us.' Raj dug out his phone and brought up the photo for her appraisal. 'And if you look…*there*…you can just about see the sleeve of the man sitting beside me.'

Her heart thumping hard at getting that close to him again, Zoe stared down at the photo and squinted until she too registered that there was indeed a tiny glimpse of what could only have been another arm at the very edge of the picture.

'Nabila arranged for her photographer to take that photo to suggest an intimacy that does not exist between us. When she grabbed my hand, I was so disconcerted I didn't react fast enough to evade the photographer. I was too *polite* to say what I wanted to say in front of other people,' he derided with sudden visible annoyance. 'I believed I had dealt with her in the hotel room the night before and that she would leave me alone, resenting the fact that I had rejected her invitation... I was wrong, for which I am heartily sorry. But I have *nothing else* to apologise for.'

'So you say...' Zoe muttered, fixedly studying his lean, darkly beautiful face while her brain sped over everything that he had explained, seeking a crack or a hole in his account of events. 'And how do you feel about her now?'

'What would I feel but heartfelt relief that she showed me what she was before I made the mistake of marrying her?' Raj countered wryly. 'Omar is downstairs waiting to act as my witness.'

Zoe swallowed hard on that assurance before an involuntary giggle was wrenched from her. 'Raj, if you killed someone, Omar would bury the body for you! You two are *that* close. Omar in the guise of a reliable witness is a joke!'

Raj dropped fluidly down on his knees beside the lounger and studied her with raw frustration. 'Then I will produce the other people at that table for your examination,' he swore with fierce determination.

Zoe adored him in that moment because she believed him, believed that he would go to any embarrassing length to prove his innocence. He had been warned about Nabila's plans and had assumed that he had taken sufficient precautions to protect himself but the devious brunette had still contrived to catch him out. He simply wasn't sly enough to deal with a woman that shameless, he was too honourable, too loyal, too honest, and that Nabila had attempted to use his very decency against him infuriated Zoe.

'No, that won't be necessary,' Zoe told him tenderly. 'You don't need to embarrass yourself that way.'

'It wouldn't embarrass me if it gave *you* peace of mind,' Raj argued. 'That is all that matters here—'

'No, what really matters,' Zoe murmured with a new strength in her quiet voice, 'is that I *believe* you.'

'But you said Omar is no good as a witness,' he reminded her in bewilderment.

'I was sort of joking,' Zoe muttered in rueful apology. 'I *do* believe that you have told me the truth.'

'Allah be praised,' Raj breathed in his own language.

'How long did it take you to get over Nabila?' Zoe asked then with helpless curiosity.

'Not very long once what I realised what an idiot I had been!' Raj confessed in a driven undertone. 'But the whole experience damaged me, and even before I met her I was already damaged by my mother's suicide. That made it difficult for me to trust *any* woman.'

Zoe ran soothing fingertips down from a high masculine cheekbone to the hard angle of his taut jaw. 'Of course, it did,' she whispered sympathetically. 'You were badly hurt when you were still a child and then hurt and humiliated by what happened with Nabila. I can understand that.'

'But you will probably *not* understand that I never

had another relationship with a woman until I met you,' Raj admitted harshly. 'All I allowed myself was a succession of grubby one-night stands.'

'Grubby?' She questioned his wording.

'It *was* grubby when I compare those encounters to what I have found with you,' Raj confessed.

'And what have you found with me?' she whispered, her gaze held fast by the silvered darkness of his, heart pounding with anticipation, because in those eloquent eyes of his she saw what she had long dreamt of seeing but barely credited could be real.

'Love,' he said simply. 'Love like I never felt for anyone, certainly not for Nabila. That was a boy's love, this is a man's and you mean the whole world to me. I don't know how else to describe how very important you are to me...'

'You're doing great,' she mumbled encouragingly when he hesitated.

'I hate being away from you. I missed you when I went to bed last night and when I woke up this morning. Wherever you are feels like home. Whenever you smile, my heart lifts. At the beginning,' he breathed hoarsely, 'I believed it was only sexual attraction and I tried incredibly hard to resist you...but I couldn't. What I've learned since is that you are the very best thing that has ever happened to me and you make me amazingly happy.'

Zoe breathed in slow and deep and it was a challenge when her lungs were struggling for oxygen. He had just made all her dreams come true. He had just blown her every insecurity out of the water but she still had some questions. 'So why, when I told you that I was pregnant, didn't you tell me then how you felt?'

'Because I didn't know how you felt about me,' Raj responded as though that were an obvious explanation. 'And I had messed everything up with you from the start. I was worrying about you wanting to leave me and going back to the UK to get the divorce I had stupidly promised you, and wondering how I could possibly prevent that from happening. I have never been more relieved than when our unexpected but very much welcome baby gave us the excuse to stay together.'

'I didn't need an excuse,' she told him then. 'I didn't want to leave you…well, probably since the honeymoon, maybe even sooner, I'm ashamed to admit. I fell in love with you weeks and weeks ago and knew it but I wasn't going to tell you that *ever*.'

Raj sprang gracefully upright and lifted her up into his arms to sit back down on the lounger holding her tight, as if he feared she might make a sudden leap for freedom. 'I denied my feelings for a long time and tried to hold back but you give me so much joy it is hard to hide it from you,' he confided huskily. 'That you return my love is almost more than I could ever have hoped for because I love you so much it burns in me like a fire…'

A knock sounded on the patio doors. Raj rose with her in his arms as the door opened.

'What the hell—?' Vivi began in shock when she saw them.

'Bad timing, Vivi,' Zoe interrupted sharply. 'My husband loves me and I'll see you at breakfast.'

Behind her Winnie laughed and tugged Vivi back. 'Yes, breakfast promises to be fun, Raj…with Grandad grouching and Vivi giving you suspicious looks, but if Zoe trusts you, you have my trust too.'

'You turncoat!' Vivi gasped but Winnie was inexorably dragging her out of the room.

'So, where were we?' Zoe prompted as Raj deposited her on the bed and went straight across the room to lock the bedroom door in a sensible move that delighted her. 'Ah, yes, you were saying that your love is like a fire.'

'More of an eternal flame,' Raj assured her poetically. 'You've got me for life.'

'Thank goodness for that. You see, I'm not a changeable woman,' she murmured softly, eyes gliding possessively over his lean, powerful length. 'I expect and demand for ever and ever, like in all the best fairy tales.'

'Perfect,' Raj murmured hoarsely, framing her flushed face with reverent hands as he stared down at her with unashamed adoration before claiming her pink pouting lips with passionate hunger.

And it was perfect for both of them as they left behind their doubts and fears and rejoiced in their newly discovered closeness and trust. Passion united them as much as love, every sense heightened for them both by the fear that they could have lost each other.

'I love you so much,' he breathed in a hoarse groan in the aftermath.

'I love you too,' she whispered, both arms wrapped possessively round him, a glorious sense of peaceful happiness powering her with a new surge of confidence.

EPILOGUE

EIGHTEEN MONTHS LATER Zoe laughed as she watched her year-old son lurch like a tiny drunk across the floor to greet his father, because he had only begun walking for the first time the day before. Raj had been really disappointed to miss those very first steps because he had been in Moscow on business and the video Zoe had sent had only partially consoled him. Now, he swept the toddler up into his arms with noisy sounds of admiration so that Karim's little face literally shone with his sense of achievement and his delight in his father's appreciation.

Raj was a great father, keen that his son would grow up with few of the royal restrictions and traditions that had held him back during his often lonely childhood. Karim was encouraged to play with other children and he was fortunate that his many cousins on both sides of the family were regular visitors. Even King Tahir unbent in Karim's energetic and sunny presence, but then the whole of Maraban was still reacting to Karim's birth as though he were an absolute miracle. That level of interest was a big weight for one little boy to carry on his shoulders and Zoe did everything she could to ensure that his upbringing was as normal and as un-starry as she could make it, even though they lived in a royal palace. Karim also had a pair of grandfathers, who sought to outdo each other with the very lavish-ness of their gifts.

Zoe was blissfully happy in her marriage. Raj made every day they were together worth celebrating. He loved her as she had never dreamt she would ever be loved and he gave her amazing support with everything she did. He had even made an effort to strengthen his relationships with her occasionally challenging family and was now her grandfather's favourite grandson-in-law, while Vivi had apologised for her initial doubts about Raj's suitability as a husband and fully accepted him, so that Zoe could relax and mix freely with her sisters and their husbands.

Zoe's fingers slid down to press gently against the very slight swelling beneath her sundress that signified that in a few months Karim would have company in the royal nursery. She had had an easy pregnancy and an easy birth with her son and was keen to have her chil-dren close together and complete their family while she was still in her twenties. Raj had wanted her to wait a little longer but she had persuaded him because Zoe adored babies and she hadn't wanted to wait when there was no good medical reason to do so.

'You look like a splash of sunlight when you wear yellow,' Raj murmured huskily as Karim was borne off by his nanny for his bath and he intercepted his wife before she could follow them. 'Our little Prince will manage without his parents for one bathtime.'

'But—' Zoe began.

'My son has to *share* you with me,' Raj pointed out, appraising her beautiful smiling face with all-male hunger. 'And this evening when your sisters arrive to celebrate your birthday with you, it'll be giggles and girl talk and I won't get a look-in.'

'Well, if you would just wait until bedtime that wouldn't be the case,' Zoe teased.

'I waited for bedtime the last time!' Raj groaned as he bent her back over one strong arm to engage in kissing a trail across her delicate collarbone that sent a highly responsive quiver through her slight body and flushed her cheeks. 'And you didn't come to bed until *three* in the morning!'

Zoe grinned. 'That'll teach you patience!'

'I'm no good at waiting for you,' Raj confessed, bundling her up into his arms with ease and heading for their bedroom. 'I'm not any better at not missing you when I'm away and I'm even worse at getting by without you in my bed.'

'You've only been away two days, but I missed you too,' Zoe confided with a helpless sigh of contentment as he brought her down on the bed. A little ripple of positively wanton anticipation gripped her as he began to remove his business suit, revealing that long bronzed, lithe and powerful physique she adored.

'I wonder if it's normal to have sex as often as we do,' she muttered abstractedly.

'It's a great healthy workout,' Raj assured her with unholy amusement. 'And wonderfully rewarding if done right.'

'No wonder I love you,' Zoe teased him back with dancing eyes. 'You always do it right!'

'But only with you.' Raj groaned with pleasure as she skimmed her hands over him, and kissed her with a raw, passionate love that made further discussion impossible.

* * * * *

COMING SOON!

We really hope you enjoyed reading this book. If you're looking for more romance, be sure to head to the shops when new books are available on

Thursday 13th June

To see which titles are coming soon, please visit

millsandboon.co.uk/nextmonth

MILLS & BOON

Coming next month

BOUGHT BRIDE FOR THE ARGENTINIAN
Sharon Kendrick

'You need a wife, Alej. And before you look at me that way, why not? Would-be politicians have been making judicious marriages since the beginning of time. It would be an instant badge of commitment and respectability which would only help your career.'

'But I don't want to get married,' he observed caustically. 'I never did. Not with Colette. Not with anyone.'

She shrugged. 'And that's your dilemma.'

Yes.

His dilemma.

Or maybe not.

From his vantage point on top of the rumpled bedclothes, Alej studied the woman with whom he'd just had the best sex he could remember, and yet here she was calmly discussing his marriage to someone else. A wave of something like bitterness ran through him. Was she so hard-hearted that she could coolly advocate he go and find himself a wife and not really *care*? Did he mean so little to her? *Of course he did. Nothing new there, either.* Yet the irony of the situation didn't escape him because deep down he knew that if she'd displayed sadness and resentment at the thought of him marrying someone else, she wouldn't have seen him for dust.

But maybe *Emily* was exactly what he needed. For now, at least. He'd thought she'd cared for him all those years ago but he'd been wrong, just as he'd been wrong about so many things. But back then she had been barely eighteen with the world at her feet. She must have believed anything was possible and had since discovered that it was not. Because surely it hadn't been her life's ambition to end up running some crummy little business and living in a tiny London apartment. Didn't she miss the riches she had grown up with while she lived in Argentina and the kind of lifestyle which came as part of the whole package?

Even more pertinently, wouldn't she have learnt by now that no other man came close to him when it came to giving her physical pleasure? Her gushing and instant response whenever he touched her would seem to indicate so. Wouldn't marriage add a deliciously dark element to the revenge he was determined to extract from her? Wouldn't it ensure she would never really forget him, because what woman ever forgot the man who slid a golden ring onto her finger?

'I think you could be right, Emily,' he said, easing himself up on the bank of squashed pillows and slanting her a slow smile. 'I need a temporary bride—and you are the obvious candidate.'

Continue reading
BOUGHT BRIDE FOR THE ARGENTINIAN
Sharon Kendrick

Available next month
www.millsandboon.co.uk

LET'S TALK
Romance

For exclusive extracts, competitions
and special offers, find us online:

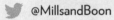 facebook.com/millsandboon

@MillsandBoon

@MillsandBoonUK

Get in touch on 01413 063232

For all the latest titles coming soon, visit
millsandboon.co.uk/nextmonth

JOIN THE
MILLS & BOON
BOOKCLUB

* **FREE** delivery direct to your door

* **EXCLUSIVE** offers every month

* **EXCITING** rewards programme

50% OFF
YOUR FIRST
PARCEL

Join today at
Millsandboon.co.uk/Bookclub